Introduction

Selma Ottilia Lovisa Lagerlöf was born on November 20, 1858, at Mårbacka, her parents' small estate in the Swedish province of Värmland. She was the third child of Erik Gustaf Lagerlöf, a sometime lieutenant in the Royal Värmland Regiment, and Louise Lagerlöf, née Wallroth, whose father was a well-to-do merchant and *brukspatron* or "foundry owner." The paternal side of the family had many pastors over the generations, including the poet and churchman Esaias Tegnér, of whose verse epic, *Frithiofs saga* (1825), about a Viking with Byronic overtones, Erik Gustaf was inordinately fond. Erik Gustaf's widowed mother lived with the family, and was the teller of the Värmland tales Selma heard in the nursery; the lieutenant's spinster sister, Lovisa, occupied the spacious pantry of the main house. Selma's older and younger sisters, Anna and Gerda, were both prettier than she, and would readily find husbands, as did Erik Gustaf's sister Anna, who wed the dashing, improvident noncommissioned officer Carl von Wachenfeldt, and died after seventeen years of marital misery. Lagerlöf described von Wachenfeldt—he sounds not a little like Gösta Berling—in her first memoir volume (*Mårbacka*, 1922), where he is called, punningly, Vackerfeldt, "Pretty-field." Graying and wrinkled, he became a hanger-on at the estate. Two brothers, Daniel, the eldest sibling, who became a physician, and Johan, who immigrated to America, completed the family roster.

Selma was plain and slightly lame. The cross-country wanderings of the majoress and Elisabet in *The Saga of Gösta Berling* may be the author's compensatory fantasies. As for dancing—a main entertainment of the Värmland gentry—she recalled, in *Ett barns memoarer* (*Memories of My Childhood*, 1930), how

Erik Gustaf forced her to attend a ball at nearby Sunne, and no one invited her to the floor. Yet, for all one knows, she did not resent this apparently cruel (or encouraging) gesture on her father's part; receiving the Nobel Prize in Literature in 1909, the first woman and the first Swede to do so, she directed her acceptance speech to his memory: "I have never met anyone who cherished such love and respect for poetry and poets."

Like her sisters, Selma was homeschooled, and her sedentary childhood was happy. She began writing stories and verse, borrowing figures from her books, "the sultans of the Arabian Nights, the knights of Walter Scott, the saga-kings of Snorri Sturluson," Iceland's medieval historian and poet. Nonetheless, in *Ett barns memoarer*, she revealed that she was not always placid. She thought she caught Uncle Wachenfeldt cheating at cards, and fell into a fit of rage. Taken off to the children's room by her mother, she believed she saw a large, dark cave, with a swampy bottom, where a dragon rested, like the monster battled by Saint Göran in Stockholm's Great Church. "The cave was in myself."

At fifteen Selma was allowed to enroll in the Advanced Female Teachers' Seminary in Stockholm; there, according to her stylized account in *En saga om en saga* (*A Tale About a Tale*, 1908), she had the illumination that would lead to *The Saga of Gösta Berling*. Trudging along a drab street with a pack of books after a lesson, she thought of two enormously popular masterpieces that she knew from home. The one was *Fredmans epistlar* (*Fredman's Epistles*, 1790) by Carl Michael Bellman, songs to be sung, as it were, by the denizens of Stockholm's taverns.[1] (Lagerlöf devoted a chapter in *Mårbacka* to the Bellman songs performed in her home; "love for them stayed in the hearts of the Mårbacka children their whole life through.") The other work she remembered was *Fänrik Ståls sägner* (*The Tales of Ensign Stål*, 1848, 1860) by the Swedish-speaking Finn Johan Ludvig Runeberg (1804–77); the Ensign is a veteran of the War of 1808–9, in which Sweden had lost Finland to Russia. The "Tales" are portraits, in verse, of the variously hardbitten or youthful officers and men of the defeated Swedish-Finnish Army. Selma told herself: "The world in which you have lived down there in Värmland is no less remarkable than Fredman's or Ensign Stål's. If you can only learn how to treat it, you'll actually have material just as rewarding." During a visit at home, Selma heard from her father about a friend from his youth, exceptionally gifted but given to drink, eking out an existence as a tutor and pastoral adjunct. "One fine day," Selma went on, writing in the third person, "the hero even got a name, and was called Gösta Berling. Where she got the name from, she never knew." Legions of Lagerlöf specialists have tried to ferret out the model or models for Gösta, just as they have for the majoress—the once beautiful Margareta Celsing, before her forced marriage to the loathsome bear-fancier Major Samzelius and her long affair with her true love, Altringer.

Having finished the teachers' seminary, Selma found a job at the Elementary School for Girls in Landskrona, across the Öresund from Copenhagen. She held the post for ten years (1885–95), taking a leave in 1891 to finish *Gösta*. She was a well-liked teacher; her subjects were church history, Swedish history, a bit of natural science, and arithmetic. She did not detest foggy south Sweden—Skåne—as Strindberg would during his "exile" (1896–97) in Lund.[2] She thrived in Landskrona's "Sewing Union" (a hotbed of incipient feminism) and burst into print with theater reviews for the local newspaper. Branching out, she published sonnets as well as play and opera reviews in *Dagny*, the new woman's magazine in Stockholm. In 1890 she won first prize in a contest announced by *Idun*, a woman's weekly, submitting five chapters that would shortly find their way into *Gösta*, among them "Ghost Stories." The judges announced that her entry was "one of the most remarkable belletristic works to have seen the light of day in our country during the most recent decades."

Yet Selma Lagerlöf also had plenty of familial burdens to bear. Her father, long in failing health (he tried to cure himself with drink), died in the summer before she reported for duty in Landskrona. Mårbacka's economy had gone from bad to worse in the course of his illness; it passed, catastrophically enough, to brother Johan before the father's death, and then briefly to sister Gerda and her husband. By 1888 the home was put up for sale at public auction; Selma attended, wanting to see Mårbacka one last time "before strangers take possession of it." In Landskrona she lived in the loft of her school. But she was not alone as she plugged away at her manuscript. Aunt Lovisa, who "could not realize that she was seventy" and gobbled bonbons, moved in with her, and her widowed mother came to stay from time to time. The Berling project went through stages. First it was a set of verse "romances," in the fashion of her father's favorite *Frithiof* and Runeberg's *Tales of Ensign Stål*, next a drama (one act of which has survived). Finally Lagerlöf settled on short prose narratives, fitted into the frame of twelve months, from Christmas to Christmas, the year the cavaliers ruled the roost at Ekeby, the estate that is the center of action in the novel.

Plenty of ingredients went into *Gösta*. For example, the uncanny "Wandering Willie's Tale" in Walter Scott's *Redgauntlet* rubbed off on "Ghost Stories." Selma, of course, had known the tales of Hans Christian Andersen from her earliest years. The sobriquet "The Traveling Companion" that she gave Sophie Elkan—the beautiful, highstrung widow and novelist she met in 1894—was borrowed from Andersen's story about the "strange fellow" who leads innocent Johannes to happiness through marvelous or frightening lands. Elkan accompanied Selma to Italy and Sicily, a journey that provided the background for Selma's second novel, *Antikrists mirakler* (*The Miracles of Antichrist*, 1897), and to the Holy Land for *Jerusalem I–II* (1901–2). Zachris Topelius, another teller of so-called fairytales from Finland, loomed so large for Lagerlöf that she devoted her only biography to him (1920); "his name was surrounded by an aura of beloved and pleasant memories." Topelius was also famous, in Runeberg's wake, for *Fältskärns berättelser* (*The Stories of a Field Surgeon*, 1857–64), novellas told by still another veteran of the War of 1808–9, about events in Sweden's and Finland's history from the death of Gustav II Adolf, the "Swedish Lion" in the Thirty Years' War, to the start of the reign of Gustav III, Bellman's art-loving patron. The field surgeon is particularly proud of the fact that he has been a "reader of many books," altogether like Selma, and that he was born the same day as Napoleon: two striking characters in *Gösta*—vain, superficial Countess Märta Dohna and brave cousin Kristoffer—are leftovers from the Napoleonic Age.

Living when and where she did, Lagerlöf of course knew her Ibsen. Peer Gynt's sudden condemnation of his drunken and extremely inventive dreaming, "lies and damned poetry," in the second act of that great verse play (1864), is quoted in *Gösta* in one of Lagerlöf's numerous authorial interruptions, at the end of chapter 11: "Oh, latter-day children! I do not ask anyone to give credence to these old stories. They may be nothing more than lies and poetry." Gregers Werle, whose persuasive tales cause the suicide of young Hedvig in Ibsen's *The Wild Duck* (1884), is called by Ibsen "the thirteenth man at table," like *Gösta*'s Sintram, the would-be devil at the Christmas Eve feast, whose suborning of the cavaliers leads to the expulsion of the majoress, and the year of their misrule. Sintram roams the roads around the lake called Löven (Fryken in geographic fact), "seeking the ruin of souls," like Satan in the prayer to Saint Michael at the end of the Tridentine Mass. His relations with the evil one are left murky in *The Saga of Gösta Berling*: Is he truly in league with the devil or rather a destructive and deranged meddler?

Kierkegaard's *Enten-Eller* (*Either-Or*, 1843) was among Lagerlöf's many books in the Landskrona loft, even though abstruse texts were not customarily her cup of tea. She made her way as far as the chapter titled "The Direct Erotic Stages of the Musical Erotic," Kierkegaard's interpretation of Mozart's *Don Giovanni*, helping to form her image of Gösta Berling as a seducer. Also, it is tempting to conjecture that Lagerlöf, living in the cultural ambiance of Copenhagen, read the Danish classic *Phantasterne* (*The Phantasts*, 1857) of Hans Egede Schack. Its narrator, Conrad Malcolm, eventually is able to turn his daydreaming to positive ends; his friend Christian is destroyed by dreaming; a third comrade, stolid Thomas, is no dreamer at all. At the end of chapter 10, "The Young Countess," Gösta salutes the dream in his great speech to the somnolent and grumpy cavaliers: "Of all the things that hands have built, what is there that has not fallen or will not fall? Oh, people, throw down the trowel and the clay form! Spread the mason's apron over your head and lie down to build the bright palace of dreams!"

However, Gösta's longest dream of love, his passion for the young countess, will lead to his quite unromantic marriage with her, in order to give a legal father to her as yet unborn child, by her doltish husband. (The poor infant expires straightaway.)

He will settle down with her, working at his lathe, a friend to the poor, a humble peasant fiddler in the lonely forest croft. One wonders if this forced happy ending (viewed with considerable skepticism by Lagerlöf's first Swedish biographer, Elin Wägner) draws on the plan of Goethe's *Faust* (in part two) to drain swamps and serve mankind thereby. Otherwise, the echoes of *Faust* in *Gösta* are detectible enough, or, for that matter, all too obvious— for example, the pact with the devil (Sintram as a provincial Mephistopheles). In the final lines of *Faust*, "Das Ewig-Weibliche / Zieht uns hinan" (The Eternal Womanly / draws us onward and upward); in Lagerlöf's finale, Gösta is saved by Elisabet and by the majoress who expires to the sound of the foundry's hammer. The cavaliers have at last undertaken honest work.

Elisabet—who shares a name with Wagner's redemptress in *Tannhäuser*—has delivered her lecture, "heroic gestures, heroic ostentation," to Gösta, who is lying bound on the floor. As is Gösta's wont, he offers an excuse: "We cavaliers are not free men. . . . We have promised one another to live for happiness and only for happiness." Elisabet rejoins, "Woe to you . . . that you should be the most cowardly among the cavaliers and last in improvement of any of them!" Lagerlöf came to love the pattern of the man gone astray, redeemed by the savior woman; in *En herrgårdssägen* (*From a Swedish Homestead*, 1899), the mad peddler-and-peasant-fiddler, "Billy Goat," is restored to his former handsome and cultured self, the estate owner and violinist Gunnar Hede, by the psychoanalytical skills of Ingrid, the frail girl whom Billy Goat, despite his madness, has saved from being buried alive. In Lagerlöf's last completed novel, *Anna Svärd* (1928), the ex-pastor Karl-Artur Ekenstedt—formerly silly, self-righteous, destructive—returns to Värmland after seven years of rehabilitation as a missionary in Africa, and approaches the cottage of his long-neglected wife, the eponymous Anna Svärd. The reader never finds out what happens: does she continue her interrupted labor of his salvation?

Lagerlöf frankly revealed the impact Thomas Carlyle's *French Revolution* had made on her as she wrote *Gösta*. The "people from the woods" march on the cavaliers in chapter 32, "The

Girl from Nygård"—"dark, embittered men jostle down toward
Ekeby's great estate; hungry women with crying children on their
arms." Moreover, Carlyle's urgent rhetoric, engaging and stirring
his audience, informs Lagerlöf's own apostrophic style. Simi-
larly, the powerful and often abusive language of the prophets
in the Old Testament crops up whenever the theme of "God's
storm" appears. Like other Swedish children of her time, Lagerlöf had been spoon-fed on the cadences of the Charles XII Bible, an equivalent to the King James version. As the chapters
"Drought" and "The Girl from Nygård" richly prove, Lagerlöf
possessed a particular genius for panoramas of disaster, and
there are several such passages in her work: the slow death of a
herd of two hundred goats, freezing in the forest, which touches
off the madness of Gunnar Hede; the sinking of the passenger
liner *L'Univers* in *Jerusalem I*, an uncanny foreshadowing of
the *Titanic*'s collision with the iceberg; the drowned sailors after the Battle of Jutland, floating in their lifejackets, their eyes
picked out by gulls, in *Bannlyst* (*The Outcast*, 1918). Sometimes her biblical allusions are quietly hilarious. Congratulating
Squire Julius on his retinue of happy girls, she writes, "Fortunate are they who can rejoice at the sunshine of life and do not
need a gourd to shield their head!" Here she's referring to God's
gracious effort to console Jonah in his discontent after his adventure with the whale: "And the Lord prepared a gourd and
made it to come up over Jonah, that it might be a shadow over
his head to deliver him from his grief."

Once *Gösta* had become a Swedish bestseller, marketing efforts were made to emphasize the festive, jovial existence of Gösta
Berling and his crew. The drawings by Georg Pauli in later Swedish editions often resemble nothing so much as the illustrations
by "Phiz," Hablot Knight Browne, for Dickens's *Pickwick Papers*.
Certainly there is a great deal of rollicking humor in *Gösta*, the
"special Swedish exuberance" praised by Fredrik Böök—the even-
tual kingmaker of the Swedish Academy, the man behind Thomas
Mann's Nobel Prize in 1929. Böök also fostered the belief that
"the bitter and the negative" were "completely foreign" to Lagerlöf. The connoisseur of arts and letters Hans Emil Larsson wrote

that "she can scarcely paint anything but the comfortable, the solid, the good," perceptions that propelled Lagerlöf swiftly into the status not only of a national icon, but also of a dependable provider of benevolent parables.

Undoubtedly, the strong admixture of humor, on many levels, contributed to *Gösta*'s fame. Lagerlöf does not hesitate to undercut her loudmouthed hero as he and the trusty Beerencreutz, pulled in the sleigh by the black steed Don Juan, abduct the surprised but willing Elisabet Dohna from Sheriff Scharling's birthday party at Munkerud: "Beerencreutz . . . look, this is life. Just as Don Juan races away with the young woman, so time races away with every person." Beerencreutz tells him to shut up: "Now they're coming after us!" Yet Gösta will not be silent: "I am Gösta Berling . . . lord of ten thousand kisses and thirteen thousand love letters. Cheers for Gösta Berling! Catch him, if you can!"

Gösta returns to Ekeby that night, in that wonderful epilogue to chapter 10, one of the parade pieces in the book. The old cavaliers want to sleep, but Gösta will not stop talking. "He just talks" (*Han bara pratar*, in plain Swedish). After he has held forth for a while, "a few snores began to sound behind the yellow-checked curtains," but "most of [the cavaliers] swore and complained at him and his follies." Lagerlöf's Gösta resembles another splashy hero of European fiction of the time, D'Annunzio's Andrea Sperelli in *Il Piacere* (*Pleasure*, 1889), the master of all the arts, the constant orator, the constant self-praiser. Oscar Wilde's Dorian Gray, from 1890, likewise unbelievably gifted and handsome, comes to a fall far more radical than Andrea's or Gösta's—he is perhaps fetched by the devil, as he loses his eternal youth. Gösta, maybe, is in danger of being fetched by the evil one too. Still, as Sintram points out, he is not yet ripe.

Like Andrea and, more discreetly, Dorian, Gösta is a seducer: the point is made repeatedly. However, the Danish critic Georg Brandes, himself notoriously priapic—in 1888 he drove the Scanian novelist Victoria Benedictsson, abandoned by him, to suicide—cast doubt on Gösta's ultimate success with the ladies, an omission Brandes naughtily attributed to Selma's inexperience: "throughout, one feels that the narrator is a maiden lady, for whom a large area of life . . . is a closed book." Seemingly, Gösta takes none of his loves to bed, not Anna Stjärnhök, not Marianne Sinclaire, not even Elisabet, after their hole-in-the-corner marriage. For Brandes, the embraces "are cold as snow and the night." The sparks of carnal fire ignited by Anna, Marianne, Elisabet, flicker out quickly.

In 1942 Elin Wägner said that Gösta was "a diaphanous and elusive figure," and Brandes thought that "psychology was the weak side" of the *Saga*. "The outlines of his form are given, but never more than the outlines. He stands before the reader, living, only in each separate situation, never as a whole, never as a human being." These strictures are unfair to Lagerlöf's implicative artistry. Gösta, an inordinately gifted speaker when the fit is on him, also has a gift for self-pity (he imagines his congregation rising up against him) and self-exculpation. He is vain, taking his revenge on the countess when she rejects his invitation to dance; it is "no honor," she says, to dance with the man who has refused to help free his benefactress, the majoress. He is the poet who has never written poetry (so he says), but when he does, the product is ever so slightly mawkish, far less gripping than the sincere verses of rejected Marianne Sinclaire. Cowardly on occasion, he is also brave, soft-hearted, and empathetic: confronted by an animal "poet" and "king," he cannot bring himself to shoot the charging bear at Gurlita Bluff.

He can be thoughtlessly cruel: he decks out the dead-drunk Captain Lennart—the ex-convict, come home to his wife—as a robber. The deed resembles the nasty trick played on the drunken visitor in Rudyard Kipling's "A Friend's Friend" in *Plain Tales from the Hills*; but there the victim deserves the treatment. (Lagerlöf admired Kipling's *Jungle Book*, which she read before starting out on *Nils Holgerssons underbara resa* [*The Wonderful Adventures of Nils*, 1906].) Nonetheless, Gösta may serve here as an instrument of the Almighty, moving in mysterious ways His wonders to perform: rejected by his wife, Captain Lennart becomes "God's pilgrim." The trick played on the feeble-minded, beautiful "Girl from Nygård" is more appalling: the planned wedding, at which she is left waiting "in the kitchen." Gösta departs to dam off the flash flood threatening Ekeby, and then leaves that worthwhile and essential task in order to help the runaway Countess Elisabet.

The Nygård girl, who bears a physical resemblance to Elisabet, returns to her forest home and falls to her death—accident or suicide? Anna Stjärnhök has accused Gösta, to the young Countess Elisabet, of having caused the death—a kind of suicide—of another simple soul, pious Ebba Dohna, surely a case of sour grapes on Anna's part (Gösta having renounced Anna with lightning speed amid his protestations of pain at doing so). She tells Elisabet about the "murder" of Ebba Dohna, she says, falsely moralizing, because she does not want him "to become a married woman's lover." Three chapters later, she washes (she claims) her hands of Gösta after having learned that he abandoned the necessary task of saving Ekeby from the surging waters in order to serve as the countess's "slave, her page." "So I see . . . that God does not have only one string on his bow. I will put my heart at ease and stay where I am needed. He can make a man of Gösta Berling without me."

In the case of the Nygård girl, as in Ebba's, Gösta's excuses are flimsy: "I never promised the girl from Nygård that I would marry her! 'Come here next Friday, then you'll see something funny' was all that I said to her. I can't help it if she liked me." Gösta delivers this excuse for the daft girl's death in response to Elisabet's outcry, "Oh Gösta, Gösta, how could you?" But Gösta has misapprehended the reason for Elisabet's question. She has remonstrated with him because he told the mob threatening Ekeby that she "was good and pure," not because he caused the Nygård girl's death. Gösta, in his turn, says nothing more about the dead girl, but praises Elisabet's "lovely soul." Lagerlöf is full of surprises and hints. Can it be that Elisabet, like Gösta, is self-centered? The reader, who has become fascinated by Lagerlöf's actually quite complex characters, is relieved to learn, in the next chapter, that Gösta, roaming the woods in suicidal despair, wants "to die at the place where the Nygård girl had been killed." He feels remorse, after all, for the joke and its consequences.

The engaged reader also feels some distress at the lot of refined Elisabet, marooned in the forest croft with her poet-fiddler Gösta, served and entertained by unbalanced Löwenborg and his painted piano table. The majoress says, "It will be a gloomy life for you, Gösta," and adds, "for Elisabet too." Indeed, the future for the novel's cast looks very bleak. Love, or Eros, so often apostrophized, seldom turns out well. Anna Stjärnhök enters into a "marriage" with the dead fiancé, Ferdinand Uggla, she has never loved. The late-life marriage of Ulrika Dillner to Sintram, of course, is doomed from the start, and, luckily for her, is annulled thanks to Anna Stjärnhök's valor. The miserly pastor of Broby blooms at the thought of a reunion, forty years too late, with the love of his youth. After their weekend of happiness, she departs, content at this new memory—"such a magnificent dream"—and the pastor "sat in his desolate home and wept in desperation." Marianne Sinclaire, caught kissing Gösta in the *tableau vivant*, carried off by him, subjected to harrowing adventures (including the dreadful scene when, in the icy night, she is shut out of her father's house), has her beauty ruined by smallpox, and is abandoned by Gösta, who puts the blame on her: "He didn't want to be her plaything any longer." In chapter 27, "Old Ballads," Marianne is wooed and won by Knight Sunshine, Adrian [Löwensköld]. "It was not happiness, not unhappiness, but she would try to live with that man."[3]

As for the cavaliers,[4] they have to leave Ekeby, despite their belated turn to honest work. Bound for his forest croft, Gösta will not accept the gift of Ekeby (already partly burned by the cavalier Kevenhüller's final invention) from the dying majoress. Gösta delivers his farewell oration to them, but his words will do them no good, deprived of their refuge, as they are, by his decision. "The pains of old age awaited them." He gives them cold comfort by wanting, he says, to believe that they have learned the answer to the questions of how "a man could be both happy and good." Whether Gösta, eloquent to the end, realizes it or not, he paraphrases the Hávamál of the *Elder Edda* about the existential choice between selflessness and selfishness. The "dear old men," the cavaliers, also get a handsome sendoff from the narrator, even more verbally gifted than Gösta himself.

Selma Lagerlöf was scarcely the naïve or artless teller of tales as she was perceived by some observers, for example, the refined poet and judge of literature Oscar Levertin, to whom Georg Brandes had assigned the task of presenting Lagerlöf to Germany (1904) in a handsome series, Die Literatur. Thomas Mann, that master of irony, knew better. Introducing the *Gesammelte Werke*, the ten-volume set of her works issued in Munich (1924), Mann described the portrait of her included in it: her "bright, energetic face" looked toward the observer "in its pinched asymmetry, kindly and almost sly," and sly she was. The chapter "Lady Musica" quite unbelievably requires the twelve cavaliers to perform Haydn's Ninety-Second Symphony. Its mostly merry melodies are intended to lift Gösta's gloom after Elisabet's escape into an unknown fate. Löwenborg plays his soundless Beethoven on his piano table; is the reader supposed to think of deaf Beethoven? In the chapter's last line, the "melancholy" of Gösta is dispelled; the Swedish word is *mjältsjukan*. Did Lagerlöf want her Swedish audience to think of "Mjältsjukan," the famous confessional lyric of Esaias Tegnér, the son of Värmland, the erotically tormented Bishop of Växjö?

Lagerlöf plays many little jokes on her readers. Sintram gets his name from a tale by Friedrich de la Motte-Fouqué, *Sintram und seine Gefährten* (1815), about a splendid young knight from Drontheim (Trondhjem in Norway); in a reenactment of Albrecht Dürer's *Ritter, Tod und Teufel* (Knight, Death, and Devil), this Sintram thrusts the cruciform hilt of his sword at the evil one and sends "the terrible stranger" flying. The prim British novelist Charlotte Yonge translated it as *Sintram and His Companions*, and the book became a children's classic in late Victorian England. In chapter 4, "Gösta Berling, the Poet," Gösta throws the three volumes, bound in red leather, of Madame de Staël's *Corinne, ou L'Italie* (1814–15) to the wolves, pursuing him and Anna Stjärnhök through the winter night, as he sets forth in his sleigh to save Anna from marriage to ugly, old Dahlberg. Does this mean that *The Saga of Gösta Berling* will triumph over de Staël's protracted tale of the fiery Corinne's passion for the considerably less passionate Lord Oswald Nelvil? That Lagerlöf's

Värmland, in the North, is just as exciting as Corinne's Italy, with its art treasures so minutely described?

Lagerlöf was a patriot of her native province, tucked up against the Norwegian border, and the birthplace of great men—Tegnér; the historian Anders Fryxell (a very old man Selma knew in her childhood and celebrated in *Mårbacka*); the poet Erik Gustaf Geijer, Tegnér's contemporary. One of Geijer's often anthologized poems describes the independent peasant (one likes to think, from Värmland), another the charcoal burners who provided the fuel for the rural iron foundries attached to the Värmland estates. Geijer devoted a picturesque segment of his memoirs to this grand form of cottage industry; his father owned a foundry at Ransäter, not far from *Gösta Berling* country. The foundries were on the brink of their decline in the 1820s, when the novel is set; they would fall victim to the railroads and city factories. Water transportation from Ekeby, on the route taken by the cavaliers in chapter 17, "Iron from Ekeby," was no longer necessary, nor were the countryside foundries. A nostalgia for the Värmland of the past emerged decades before Lagerlöf conceived *Gösta*—in *Wermlänningarne*, "tragic-comic speech, song, and dance play" (1846), by Fredrik August Dahlgren with music by Andreas Randel. (*Oklahoma!* might be a rough American equivalent.) *Gösta*'s success was prepared, in some measure, by Dahlgren and Randel's beloved quasi-operetta.

Sven Stolpe has made the alluring proposal that *Gösta* is, in fact, a series of "little operas," with verbal arias, melodramatic situations, and, above all, the outsized emotions to be found in the nineteenth-century repertoire. And, as every operagoer knows, the characters in Donizetti, Bellini, Verdi, are controlled by a God often appealed to or railed against. Just so in *Gösta*; in its "Prologue" or overture, the majoress says, when Gösta wants to lay himself down and die: "Oh, you may fly boldly, you wild birds, but our Lord knows the net that will catch you." Never missing the chance for self-dramatization, Gösta agrees: "He is a great and strange God. . . . He has eluded me and rejected me, but he will not let me die. His will be done!"

The full manuscript of *Gösta* was accepted by Fritiof Hellberg's "humbug-house" in Stockholm, the derogatory term coined by the novelist Bo Bergman, who had seen the samples in *Idun* and looked forward to the book's publication in a worthier venue. Some reviews were favorable: the young poet Gustaf Fröding, from Värmland, destined to become one of Sweden's greatest poets, liked the way his compatriot conjured up the glories of their common home. Major critics were far less enthusiastic. The dean of the critical corps, Karl Warburg, thought *Gösta* was a "mightily strange narration" and was irritated by "the *unnaturalness of the style*" (his italics). He recommended that the authoress undertake "retellings of folk-tales . . . which she ought to be able to reproduce with a poetic mood." A crueler blow was delivered by Carl David af Wirsén, the powerful secretary of the Swedish Academy; he compared *Gösta* to antiquated, sentimental novels aimed at a female audience. Composing the "modern" part of a monumental history of Sweden's literature (1911), Warburg made torturous amends: "The faults of the book, which at first caught the eyes of professional critics and which, in several quarters, caused an undervaluing of its merits, were partly its jumpy, rather loose structure . . . and partly its uncontestedly, albeit not uncontested, mannered style." Wirsén opposed Lagerlöf's selection for the Nobel Prize, trying instead to advance the candidacy of Algernon Charles Swinburne, of all people.

A sea change in *The Saga of Gösta Berling*'s fortunes came shortly; the above-mentioned Georg Brandes wrote his glowing review of the Danish translation for the tone-setting newspaper *Politiken*. Just returned from a Christmas vacation in Copenhagen, Selma sent her mother a clipping, "nice to read after Warburg and Wirsén, for Brandes is the most distinguished man in the North." He made no bones about his enthusiasm for "the material's surprising singularity and the originality of the presentation," going on to the "narrative's rhythmically fluid, often quite simply lyric style. Privately, the authoress must have written a great deal of verse in order to achieve this prose." *Gösta*'s variety was wonderful: "[Lagerlöf] wanted to paint not a picture but a whole picture-gallery." Yet Brandes, too, unmindful of the consequences, gave his authority to the notion of Lagerlöf as a "naïve" artist: "her warm, living imagination is like a child's. Exactly like a child's." The child is full of surprises: "We are led along detours until, without being prepared, we suddenly stand face to face with what the author wants to show us." Immediately, Selma Lagerlöf was recruited by the ambitious publisher Karl Otto Bonnier and became a luminary of his stable, to the financial advantage of them both. The story collection *Osynliga länkar* (*Invisible Links*) appeared at Bonniers in 1894, followed by a new edition of *Gösta*, acquired from Hellberg, in 1895, the year Selma resigned from her teaching post. In 1897 she moved to Falun, the old mining town in Dalecarlia, a neighboring province to Värmland, and just as rich in local lore; it had a distinctive literary (and supernatural) nimbus because of E. T. A. Hoffmann's tale "The Mines at Falun." Lagerlöf's younger sister Gerda lived there with her husband, as did a sturdy friend from Landskrona days, Valborg Olander, of whom Sophie Elkan, the traveling companion, was not a little jealous. The year of Lagerlöf's honorary doctorate at Uppsala, 1907, her aunt Lovisa died, and, for the funeral, Selma returned to Värmland and to look in on Mårbacka, purchasing it in 1910. She transformed it into a profitable farm, run by herself, supported by a large staff. A keen businesswoman, she produced super-healthy oatmeal, labeled "Mårbacka Oats-Power." Mårbacka attracted so many sightseers and wellwishers that she had trouble finding the peace to write. Greta Garbo tried to drop in on her in the summer of 1935, but she was in the hospital at Karlstad. They met the next year in Stockholm; Lagerlöf's theatrical adaptation of *The Saga of Gösta Berling* had had its premiere there in March 1935, to mixed reviews. Only nineteen, Garbo had played the role of Elisabet in Mauritz Stiller's silent film of 1924, called, in English, *The Atonement of Gösta Berling*.

Lagerlöf fell afoul of the Nazi propaganda machine after 1933 for bringing Jewish intellectuals, such as her biographer Walter Berendsohn and the poet Nelly Sachs, to safety in Sweden. When the Soviet Union attacked Finland on November 30, 1939, she hesitated to think of her country going to its neighbor's aid, lest the Russians retaliate, "a hard fate for old Sweden." Nevertheless, she gave to the beleaguered Finns all the gold medals she had received over the long course of her career. She died at Mårbacka on March 16, 1940, her sister Gerda at her side. In a last letter to a friend, she told her not to brood so much: "You know that we human beings haven't been vouchsafed the gift of looking into God's council chamber."

The success and example of *The Saga of Gösta Berling* may have encouraged Verner von Heidenstam—a future Nobel Prize winner (1916)—to complete *Karolinerna* (*The Charles Men*, 1897–98), a double series of carefully wrought novellas centered on Charles XII, the "warrior king" whose extravagant military adventures started the destruction of the Swedish Empire. The ten interconnected novellas of the Norwegian Tryggve Andersen's *I Cancelliraadens Dage* (*In the Days of the Councillor*, 1897), take place in a backwater of the Napoleonic Wars.[5] Sigrid Undset's novels from medieval Norway, collectively called after their heroine, Kristin Lavransdatter, appeared from 1920 on, expanding on a world Lagerlöf had briefly entered in the novellas of *Drottningar i Kungahälla* (*Queens of Kungahälla*, 1899). It has been suggested that the sudden fame of Undset, younger by a quarter of a century (and a Nobel Prize winner, 1928), prompted the aging Lagerlöf to embark on *her* set of novels that move from the age of Charles XII to, principally, the 1830s in Värmland: *Löwensköldska ringen* (*The Ring of the Löwenskölds*, 1925); *Charlotte Löwensköld* (1925); and *Anna Svärd* (1928). Was envy a creative stimulus here? Long ago, Lagerlöf herself had been the target of envy: Strindberg planned to do a caricature of her as "Tekla Lagerlök" (Laurel-Onion) in his hateful *Svarta fanor* (*Black Banners*, 1907), and, never a recipient of the Nobel Prize, he harrumphed that "some people value my dramatic production (forty plays) more highly than the Great Selma's Novels." (Did he remember that, in 1887, he had written a very popular novel, *Hemsöborna* [*The People of Hemsö*], whose hero, the Värmlander Carlsson, plays a trick on the drunken Pastor Nordström even more drastic than the one Gösta and his fellows play on Captain Lennart?) During Isak Dinesen's (Karen Blixen's) years in Africa, authorial envy may again have been at work. Blixen refused to agree that, as the manageress of a coffee farm, she in any

way resembled the pipe-smoking majoress. Grabbing an opening provided by an American correspondent, she allowed that
great writers, such as "Ibsen, Shaw, Tolstoy, and Lagerlöf, are
likely to lose something of their talent in later years," a thrust at
the Löwensköld cycle. Surely, the author of *Seven Gothic Tales*
and *Winter's Tales* had learned from Lagerlöf, whose books were
on the library shelves at Blixen's Mbogani House.

The Saga of Gösta Berling came out in German in 1896, the
first of what would be six translations. Marie Herzfeld, the lit-
erarily acute friend of Hugo von Hofmannsthal, touted it in the
climactic essay of *Die skandinavische Literatur und ihre Tenden-
zen* (*Scandinavian Literature and its Tendencies*, 1898): "a mix-
ture of adventure novel, educational novel [bildungsroman,
high praise in the German critical vocabulary], and psychologi-
cal novel." Thomas Mann quickly became a faithful reader of the
author of "the old tale" of Gösta Berling (calling it a *Mär*, a
word suggestive of the *Nibelungenlied*!). For Rainer Maria Rilke
Gösta was "incomparable" and, like Mann, he closely followed
Lagerlöf's production (even trying to read *Nils Holgersson* in
the original Swedish). But he gave up on her in the midst of reading *Bannlyst* (*The Outcast*, 1918, strangely called *Das Heilige
Leben*, "The Holy Life," in German), not grasping that the murderer Lamprecht was still another of Lagerlöf's arrogant and ego-
tistical specimens of evil, a theme first broached in Sintram and
then in the Scots mercenaries' home invasion and mass-murder
of *Herr Arnes penningar* (*Sir Arne's Hoard*, 1903), which was
turned into a play, *Winterballade*, by Gerhart Hauptmann, in the
war year 1917. From his Swiss refuge in 1920, Rilke wrote, about
Das Heilige Leben: "I was quite cross with this old school-
marm" and "there's no depending on Selma Lagerlöf any longer."
Paul Géraldy, the French playwright and master of the *bon mot*,
compared Lagerlöf to Homer; Marguérite Yourcenar, the author
of *Hadrian's Memoirs*, devoted a major essay to the "conteuse
épique," concluding with praise of the "admirable tales, pure as
the unpolluted lakes of Värmland," and especially one of the
paralipomena to *Gösta*, "A Tale from Halstanäs," in *Osynliga
länkar*, on the later years of Colonel Beerencreutz. Russia welcomed *Iosta Berling* with open arms (from 1904 on); the scholar

Maria Nikolayeva proposes that Värmland's estate life seemed immediately familiar to an audience steeped in Turgenev, and Vivi Edström sees a "direct correspondence" between pious Ebba Dohna and Lisaveta Michailovna, who enters a cloister in *A Nest of Gentlefolk*. (Nikolayeva also wonders if Lagerlöf's easy switches from the real to the fantastic, as in "Ghost Stories," rubbed off on Mikhail Bulgakov's *The Master and Margarita*.) The music historian Alan Mallach has recently claimed that Riccardo Zandonai's opera *I cavalieri di Ekebù* (1925), with a libretto by Arturo Rossato, is not an oddity but rather a gem in the "autumn" of Italian *verismo*. Zandonai-Rossato emphasize the dark side of Lagerlöf's vision: the villains, Samzelius and Sintram, have much dirty work to do; the majoress, "la Comandante," is allotted a telling mezzo-soprano part; and the loves of a tormented "Giosta" are reduced to one, a frightened Anna. The orchestration—plenty of bass clarinet, bassoon, and tuba—is heavy, the incessant percussion effects eerie.

In the Anglophone world, *Gösta* got several translations from 1898 on, by Pauline Bancroft Flach, Lillie Tudeer, and Robert Bly (a revision of Flach), but has never found a critical champion, or been taken quite seriously. Peter Graves has tracked down Lagerlöf's reputation in England. Not very apt comparisons have been made with Thomas Hardy and George Eliot, among others. D. H. Lawrence, translating Giovanni Verga's *Mastro Don Gesualdo* in Sicily, decided that Verga's text was "one of the genuine emotional extremes of European literature: just as Selma Lagerlöf or Knut Hamsun may be the other extreme, northwards." Yet Verga seems "more real than these." Voices that could have carried weight (Graves names Shaw, H. G. Wells, Arnold Bennett, Rebecca West, Virginia Woolf) stayed silent. In the United States, Henry Goddard Leach, for years the head of the American-Scandinavian Foundation, wrote an introduction (1918) to a reprint of Lillie Tudeer's translation (1898), and told how, on a walking tour of Värmland, he discovered that Värmland people were "as blithe today but not so romantic" as their forebears in Gösta Berling's time. It is profoundly to be hoped that Paul Norlen's translation will win Selma Lagerlöf's novel the serious critical attention it deserves.

GEORGE C. SCHOOLFIELD

NOTES

1. Fredman ("Peace-man," a pun on Latin *bellum*, "war"), the prosti-
   tute Ulla Winblad, the bass-player Father Berg, the wigmaker Mow-
   itz, Corporal Mollberg, and more.
2. Strindberg used this university-and-cathedral town as the threatening backdrop of his play *Påsk* (*Easter*, 1901).
3. In *Anna Svärd*, written some thirty-five years after *Gösta*, Marianne
   has died after a year of marriage to Adrian. The sometime Knight
   Sunshine bullies his second wife—who plays to his moods—and
   five plain daughters. He is drowned trying to save his ne'er-do-well
   brother's perky child (from a union with a gypsy woman), and the
   little girl, a tow-headed charmer, also dies under the ice. (She has been
   kidnapped by the wrong-headed zealot Karl-Artur Ekenstedt.) Gustava Sinclaire's affection for her vile-tempered husband, Melchior,
   can bloom only after he has been felled by a stroke.
4. Historically, the military men among the cavaliers, Beerencreutz,
   Fuchs, Kristian, Kristoffer, Örneclou, Ruster, are already discards,
   leftovers from Sweden's last continental adventures, in Pomerania
   and at the Battle of Leipzig (1813), the "Battle of Nations," where
   Swedish artillery played a small part in Napoleon's defeat. Captain
   Lennart has been involved, like shady Sintram, in the futile little war
   with Norway of 1814. (That former half of the "Twin Kingdoms
   of Denmark-Norway" had been bestowed on Sweden by the Treaty
   of Kiel, and the belligerent Norwegians wanted to be rid of their
   new "personal union" with the Swedish crown.) Rather ungratefully,
   Lagerlöf adduces no veterans from the war with Russia of 1808–9,
   celebrated by Johan Ludvig Runeberg.
5. Danish rule in Norway, incorporated by the councillor himself, was
   decaying, as was the Danish-Norwegian official class, amid gaming,
   drinking, and adultery.

Suggestions for Further Reading

The Northland Edition of Selma Lagerlöf's works (through 1914) appeared in 1917 (Garden City, NY: Doubleday, Page). Single translations of later works, including the three volumes of memoirs, were published by Doubleday from 1924 to 1937. Most monographs on Lagerlöf in English are antiquated: Harry E. Maule's worshipful *Selma Lagerlöf: The Woman, Her Work, Her Message* (Doubleday, 1917, 1926); Walter A. Berendsohn's *Selma Lagerlöf, Her Life and Work* (Doubleday, 1932), adapted from the German original edition of 1927; Hanna Astrup Larsen's *Selma Lagerlöf* (Doubleday, 1936); a chapter on Lagerlöf in Alrik Gustafson's *Six Scandinavian Novelists* (Princeton: Princeton University Press, 1940; New York: American Scandinavian Foundation, 1940). Vivi Edström's *Selma Lagerlöf* (Boston: Twayne, 1984) is compact and dependable. "The Scandalous Selma Lagerlöf" by Nils Afzelius, *Scandinavica* 5 (1966), a reduction and translation of the title essay in his *Selma Lagerlöf, den förargelseväckande* (Lund: Glerrup, 1969), is strongly to be recommended, as are the helpful articles by Erland Lagerroth, "The Narrative Art of Selma Lagerlöf: Two Problems," *Scandinavian Studies* 31 (1961) and "Selma Lagerlöf Research 1900–1964, A Survey and an Orientation," *Scandinavian Studies* 37 (1965). For Lars G. Warme's *History of Swedish Literature* (Lincoln: University of Nebraska Press, 1996), Susan Brantly spoke of the "importance of history and tradition" in *Gösta*, and Selma Lagerlöf's "acute sense of divine providence." A full life-and-works volume on Selma Lagerlöf in English, taking her copious correspondence and recent scholarship into account, is a desideratum.

The secondary literature in Swedish is enormous: Vivi Edström's Gothenburg dissertation of 1960, *Livets stigar: Tiden, handlingen och livskänslan i Gösta Berlings saga* (The Paths of Life: Time, Action, and Life-Feeling in *Gösta Berling's Saga*, with English summary; Stockholm: Norstedt, 1960) is basic, as is her *Selma Lagerlöf: Livets vågspel* (Life's Daring Game; Stockholm: Natur och kultur, 2002). Henrik Wivel's *Snödrottningen: En bok om Selma Lagerlöf och kärleken* (The Snow Queen: A Book about Selma Lagerlöf and Love; Copenhagen: Gad, 1988; Stockholm: Bonniers, 1990), is fascinating because of its effort to uncover "the hidden Selma Lagerlöf." Two recent and important studies concern themselves with the Swedish reception of Selma Lagerlöf: Lisbeth Stenberg's *En genialisk lek: Kritik och överskridande i Selma Lagerlöfs tidiga författarskap* (Genius at Play: Criticism and Transcendence in Selma Lagerlöf's Early Texts; Gothenburg: Göteborgs universitet, 2001), and Anna Nordlund's *Selma Lagerlöfs underbara resa genom den svenska litteraturhistorien 1891–1996* (The Wonderful Adventures of Selma Lagerlöf Through Swedish Literary History 1891–1996; Stockholm: Östling, 2005), both with English summary.

Peter Graves's "The Reception of Selma Lagerlöf in Britain" appeared in *Selma Lagerlöf Seen from Abroad / Selma Lagerlöf i utlandsperspektiv*, edited by Louise Vinge (Stockholm: Royal Academy of Letters, 1998). Unfortunately, the symposium's papers included neither a survey of Selma Lagerlöf's reception in America, nor a thorough exploration of Selma Lagerlöf's overwhelming popularity in German-speaking countries. (Sibylle Schweitzer's *Selma Lagerlöf: Eine Bibliographie* [Marburg: Schriften der Universitätsbibliothek Marburg, 1900], provided a necessary tool for such an investigation.)

GEORGE C. SCHOOLFIELD

A Note on the Translation

Not one but two English translations of *The Saga of Gösta Berling* appeared soon after it was first published in Sweden in 1891: a British version by Lillie Tudeer (1898) and an American version by Pauline Bancroft Flach (1898). Both versions have been criticized for omissions large and small, while Tudeer occasionally adds material not found in the original. The eight chapters omitted in Tudeer's version were reinstated (translated by Velma Swanston Howard) in a 1918 edition of the Tudeer translation published by the American Scandinavian Foundation. Since then, however, no one has attempted a complete, new translation into English. (In 1962 the American poet Robert Bly published an edited version of Flach's translation.) Among the many challenges in translating Lagerlöf is capturing the various registers in her narrative voice (from deceptively simple to passionately lyrical, with more than an occasional touch of unabashed melodrama). The present translator has tried to convey the author's distinctive voice in English and produce a narrative that is a pleasure to read—as it is in Swedish.

I wish to thank Tracey Sands and Sonia Wichmann for reading and commenting on draft versions of the translation; Linnea Donnen for help with weaving terminology; and Tiina Nunnally, Lori Ann Reinhall, and Linda Schenck for helpful suggestions.

This translation is dedicated to the memory of Göran Tunström (1937–2000), a fine novelist and a stalwart champion of the works of Selma Lagerlöf.

PAUL NORLEN

The Saga of Gösta Berling

PROLOGUE

I. THE MINISTER

At long last the minister stood in the pulpit.

The congregation raised their heads. So, there he was after all. The service would not be canceled this Sunday, as it had been the previous Sunday and many Sundays before that.

The minister was young, tall, slender, and radiantly handsome. If you had set a helmet on his head and hung a sword and breastplate on him, you could have chiseled him in marble and named the image after the most beautiful of the Athenians.

The minister had the deep eyes of a poet and the firm, rounded chin of a general; everything about him was lovely, fine, expressive, glowing through and through with genius and spiritual life.

The people in the church felt strangely subdued seeing him like that. They were more accustomed to seeing him stagger out of the inn in the company of merry companions, such as Beerencreutz, the colonel with the ample white mustaches, and the strong Captain Kristian Bergh.

He had been drinking so excessively that he had not been able to perform his duties for several weeks, and the congregation had been compelled to complain about him, first to his dean and then to the bishop and the consistory. Now the bishop had come to the parish to conduct an inquiry. He was sitting in the chancel with a gold cross on his chest, with clergymen from Karlstad and ministers from the neighboring parishes seated around him.

There was no doubt that the minister's conduct had exceeded the bounds of what was permitted. At that time, in the 1820s, there was a certain degree of indulgence in matters of drinking, but this man had neglected his office for the sake of drinking, and now he would lose it.

He stood in the pulpit, waiting, while the last verse of the pulpit hymn was being sung.

A sense of certainty came over him, as he was standing there, that he had nothing but enemies in the church, enemies in every pew. Among the gentry in the balcony, among the farmers down in the church, enemies among the confirmands in the chancel, nothing but enemies. An enemy was pumping the organ, an enemy played it. He had enemies in the church wardens' pew. Everyone hated him, everyone—from the little children who were carried into the church, up to the church sexton, a formal and arthritic soldier who had been at the battle of Leipzig.

The minister would have liked to fall down on his knees and beg them for mercy.

But the very next moment a dull anger came over him. He remembered well what he had been like a year ago, when he ascended this pulpit for the first time. He was an irreproachable man at that time, and now he was standing there, looking down at the man with the gold cross around his neck who had come there to judge him.

While he read the introduction, wave after wave of blood rushed up to his face; this was anger.

Yes, it was true that he'd been drunk, but who had the right to accuse him on that account? Had anyone seen the parsonage where he had to live? The spruce forest was dark and gloomy and grew right up to the windows. Water dripped down through the black ceiling, along the damp, moldy walls. Wasn't liquor a necessity to keep your courage up, when rain or drifting snow swept in through cracked windowpanes, when the poorly tended earth wouldn't yield bread enough to keep hunger at bay?

His next thought was that he was precisely the kind of minister they deserved. They drank, all of them. Why should he alone restrain himself? The man who buried his wife got drunk at the funeral reception; the father who had christened his child had a drinking bout afterward. The churchgoers drank on the way home from church; most of them were drunk by the time they arrived home. It served them right to have a drunken minister.

It was while making his official rounds, when dressed in his

thin vestments he'd driven for miles across frozen lakes, where all
the cold winds seemed to meet; it was as he was tossed around on
these same lakes in a boat in storm and pouring rain; it was when
he had to get out of the sleigh in a blizzard and clear a path for the
horse through drifts as high as a house, or as he waded through
the forest marsh, it was then that he'd learned to love liquor.

The days of that year had plodded along in heavy gloom.
Farmers and gentry kept all their thoughts fixed on matters of
the soil, but in the evening their spirits cast off their chains, liber-
ated by liquor. Inspiration came, hearts were warmed, life became
radiant, song resounded, there was a scent of roses. Then the
serving room at the inn had become a Mediterranean flower
garden to him: grapes and olives hung down above his head,
marble pillars glistened in the dark foliage, wise men and poets
strolled under palms and plantains.

No, he, the minister up there in the pulpit, knew that without liquor, life couldn't go on in this part of the country; all of
his listeners knew that, yet now they wanted to condemn him.

They wanted to tear the minister's gown off of him, because
he had entered the house of their God drunk. Oh, all of these
people, did they themselves have, could they believe that they
had, any other God than liquor!

He had read the introduction, and he lowered his head to re-
cite the Lord's Prayer.

There was dead silence in the church during the prayer. But
suddenly with both hands the minister took firm hold of the cords
that fastened his vestments. It seemed to him as though the whole
congregation, with the bishop in the lead, was stealing up the
stairs of the pulpit to tear the vestments off of him. He got down
on his knees without turning his head, but he could just feel them
tugging, and he saw them so clearly, the bishop and the other clergymen, the deans, the church wardens, the organist and the whole
congregation in a long line, tearing and pulling to get his vestments loose. And he imagined to himself vividly how all of these
people who were tugging so eagerly would fall over one another
on the steps when his vestments came loose, and the whole line
down there, who hadn't been able to actually pull on this cloth-

ing, but rather just on the coattails of those standing in front of them, would also fall down.

He saw this so clearly that he had to smile, there on his knees, but at the same time a cold sweat broke out on his brow. The whole thing was simply too dreadful.

So, he was now to be a condemned man because of liquor. He would be a defrocked minister. Was there anything more wretched on this earth?

He would become one of the beggars on the road, lying intoxicated by the edge of the ditch, go dressed in rags, associate with vagabonds.

The prayer was over. He should start reading his sermon. Then a thought occurred to him and halted the words on his lips. He realized that this was the last time he would get to stand up there in the pulpit and proclaim the glory of God.

For the last time—this touched the minister. He forgot all about liquor and the bishop. He thought that he must use this opportunity to bear witness to the glory of God.

He imagined that the church floor, with all the listeners, sank deep, deep down, and that the roof was lifted off the church, so that he was looking into heaven. He stood alone, completely alone in his pulpit; his spirit took flight toward the open skies above him, his voice became strong and powerful, and he proclaimed the glory of God.

He was a man of inspiration. He abandoned what he'd written; thoughts came down upon him like a flock of tame doves. He felt as though it wasn't he who was speaking, but he also realized that this was the greatest thing on earth, and that no one could reach higher in radiance and majesty than he, who was standing there proclaiming the glory of God.

As long as inspiration's tongue of flame burned over him, he spoke, but when it died out and the roof lowered back down onto the church, and the floor came up again from far, far below, then he bowed his head and wept, at the thought that life had given him his best hour, and now it was over.

After the service came the inquiry and congregational meeting. The bishop asked if the congregation had any complaints against their minister.

The minister was no longer angry and defiant like before the sermon. Now he felt ashamed and lowered his head. Oh, all those miserable drinking stories that would now be told!

But there were none. It was completely silent around the large table in the parish hall.

The minister looked up, first at the organist, no, he was silent; then at the church wardens, then at the wealthy farmers and the owners of the ironworks; they all kept silent. They kept their lips pressed tightly together and looked with some embarrassment down at the table.

"They're waiting for someone to go first," thought the minister.

One of the church wardens cleared his throat.

"I think that we have an exceptional minister," he said.

"Reverend, you've heard for yourself how he preaches," the organist put in.

The bishop said something about the numerous cancellations of services.

"The minister has the right to be sick, just like anybody else," the farmers declared.

The bishop alluded to their dissatisfaction with the minister's way of living.

They defended him with a single voice. He was so young, their minister, there was nothing wrong with him. No, if he would always just preach the way he had today, they wouldn't exchange him for the bishop himself.

There were no accusers, nor could there be a judge.

The minister felt how his heart expanded and how easily the blood was flowing through his veins. No, that he no longer walked among enemies, that he had won them over, when he thought it least likely that he would be allowed to continue to be a minister!

After the inquiry, the bishop and the other clergymen and the deans and the most distinguished men of the parish had dinner at the parsonage.

One of the neighbor ladies had taken over the arrangements for the meal, for the minister was a bachelor. She had arranged everything in the best manner, and it opened his eyes to the fact that the parsonage was really not so bad. The long dinner table was set out under the spruce trees, and looked very attractive with a white tablecloth, with blue and white china, with glistening glasses and folded napkins. Two birches arched over the entrance, juniper boughs were strewn across the floor of the vestibule, a wreath of flowers was hanging from the ridge of the roof, flowers were placed in all the rooms, the smell of mold was driven out, and the green windowpanes glistened jauntily in the sunshine.

The minister was thoroughly delighted. He thought that he would never drink again.

There was no one who was not pleased at the dinner table. Those who had been broad-minded and forgiving were pleased with themselves, and the distinguished ministers were pleased, because they had avoided a scandal.

The good bishop raised his glass and said that he had set out on this journey with a heavy heart, for he had heard some bad rumors. He had gone out to meet a Saul; but see, Saul was already transformed into a Paul, who would work harder than all the rest. And the pious man spoke further of the rich gifts that their young brother possessed, and praised them. Not so that he might feel proud, but rather so that he would exert all his energies to keep close watch on himself, as one who bears an excessively heavy and valuable burden on his shoulders must do.

The minister did not get drunk that afternoon, but he was intoxicated. All this great, unexpected happiness was a heady experience. Heaven had allowed the fiery tongue of inspiration to flame over him, and the people had given him their love. The blood still continued to flow feverishly and at a furious pace through his veins when evening came and the guests had gone. Far into the night he sat awake in his room, letting the night air stream in through the open window so as to cool this fever of happiness, this sweet unrest, which wouldn't allow him to sleep.

Then a voice was heard.

"Are you awake, minister?"

A man came walking across the grass up to the window. The minister looked out and recognized Captain Kristian Bergh, one of his faithful drinking companions. He was a wayfaring man without house or farm, this Captain Kristian, and a giant in body and strength; he was as large as Gurlita Bluff and as stupid as a mountain troll.

"Of course I'm up, Captain Kristian," the minister replied. "Do you think this is a night for sleeping?"

And hear now what this Captain Kristian tells him! The giant has had his suspicions, he has realized that now the minister is going to be afraid to drink. He would never have any peace again, thought Captain Kristian, for these clergymen from Karlstad, who had been there once, could come again and take the vestments from him at any time, if he drank.

But now Captain Kristian has set his heavy hand to the good work, now he has fixed it so that those clergymen will never come again, not them and not the bishop either. After this the minister and his friends will be able to drink as much as they want there in the parsonage.

Hear what a great deed he has carried out, he, Captain Kristian, the strong captain!

When the bishop and the two other clergymen had climbed into the covered cart and the doors had been securely closed behind them, then he had climbed up onto the driver's seat and driven them a good ten miles in the light summer night.

And then Kristian Bergh let the reverends feel how precariously life is seated in the human body. He let the horses run at a frenzied pace. That would serve them right, for not allowing an honorable man to have a drink.

Do you think he drove them along the road, do you think he avoided bumps? He drove across ditches and fields of stubble, he drove at a dizzying gallop along hillsides, he drove along the lakeshore, the water whirling around the wheels, he came close to getting stuck in the marsh, and took off across bare rock, so that the horses stood sliding on stiffened legs. And all the while the bishop and the clergymen sat behind the leather curtains, faces wan, mumbling prayers. They had never had a worse journey.

And imagine how they must have looked, when they arrived at the inn at Rissäter, alive, but shaking like buckshot in a leather pouch.

"What's this supposed to mean, Captain Kristian?" says the bishop, as he opens the carriage door for them.

"It means that the bishop should think twice before he comes here on another inquiry about Gösta Berling," says Captain Kristian, and he has thought that sentence out beforehand so as not to forget what he wanted to say.

"Then tell Gösta Berling," says the bishop, "that neither I nor any other bishop will be coming to see him again."

See, the strong Captain Kristian tells about this deed, standing by the open window in the summer night. For Captain Kristian had only just left the horses at the inn, and then he came down to the minister with the news.

"Now you can be calm, minister and dear friend," he says.

Ah, Captain Kristian! The clergymen sat with wan faces behind the leather curtains, but the minister in the window looks a great deal paler in the light summer night. Ah, Captain Kristian!

The minister even raised his arm and aimed a dreadful blow against the giant's rough, stupid face, but he restrained himself. He pulled down the window with a crash and stood in the middle of the room, shaking his clenched fist toward the sky.

He, who had felt the fiery tongue of inspiration, he, who had been able to proclaim the glory of God, stood there thinking that God had played a terrible joke on him.

Wouldn't the bishop believe that Captain Kristian had been sent by the minister? Wouldn't he believe that he had been a hypocrite and a liar all day? Now he would pursue the inquiry against him in earnest; now he would have him suspended and defrocked.

When morning came, the minister had left the parsonage. He did not stay to defend himself. God had mocked him. God was not willing to help him. He knew that he would be defrocked. It was God's will. So he might as well leave at once.

This happened in the early 1820s in a far-off parish in western Värmland.

This was the first misfortune that befell Gösta Berling; it would not be the last.

For such foals, as cannot bear the spur or the lash, find life difficult. With every pain that befalls them, they bolt away on wild paths toward gaping abysses. As soon as the path is stony and the journey troublesome, they know no other recourse than to upset their load and run off in madness.

II. THE BEGGAR

One cold day in December a beggar came wandering up the hills of Broby. He was dressed in the shabbiest rags, and his shoes were so worn that his feet were wet from the cold snow.

Löven is a long, narrow lake in the province of Värmland, laced up in a few places by long, narrow straits. To the north it extends up toward the forests of Finnmark, to the south down toward Vänern. Several parishes spread out along its shores, but Bro parish is the largest and wealthiest. It occupies a good part of the shores of the lake on both the east and west side, but the largest farmsteads are on the west side—manor houses such as Ekeby and Björne, widely known for wealth and beauty, and the large village of Broby with its inn, courthouse, sheriff's residence, parsonage, and marketplace.

Broby sits on a steep incline. The beggar had gone past the inn, which sits at the foot of the hill, and was plodding up toward the parsonage, which sits farthest up.

Walking ahead of him on the hill was a little girl, who was pulling a sled loaded with a sack of flour. The beggar caught up with the girl and started talking with her.

"Such a little horse for such a big load," he said.

The child turned around and looked at him. She was a little thing, twelve years old with piercing, sharp eyes and a pinched mouth.

"God grant that the horse were smaller and the load larger, then it would last that much longer," the girl replied.

"Is this your own fodder you're dragging home then?"

"God help me but I have to get my food myself, little as I am."

The beggar took hold of the sled handle to push it.

The girl turned around and looked at him.

"You mustn't think you'll get anything for it," she said.

The beggar started to laugh.

"You must be the daughter of the minister at Broby."

"Yes, yes, so I am. Many a girl has a poorer father; no one has a worse one. That's the plain truth, though it's a shame that his own child should have to say it."

"He sounds stingy and mean, this father of yours."

"He is stingy, and he is mean, but his daughter will likely be even worse, if she lives, people say."

"I think people are right. I would just like to know where you came across that sack of flour."

"Well, there won't be any harm in telling you about it. I took grain from Father's grain bin this morning, and now I've been to the mill."

"Won't he see you when you come dragging it home with you?"

"You must have left your master too soon. Father is away visiting a sick person, don't you see?"

"Someone is driving up the hill behind us. I hear the creaking from under the runners. What if it's him who's coming!"

The girl listened, peering, then she started to wail.

"It's Father," she sobbed. "He's going to kill me. He's going to kill me."

"Well, now, good counsel is hard to find and quick thinking better than silver and gold," said the beggar.

"Look," said the child, "you can help me. Take the rope and pull the sled, then Father will think it's yours."

"Then what shall I do with it?" asked the beggar, putting the rope across his shoulders.

"Pull it wherever you want to for now, but come up to the parsonage with it when it gets dark. You can be sure I'll be watching you. You must come with the sack and the sled, do you understand?"

"I'll have to try."

"God have mercy on you, if you don't come," called the girl, as she ran away from him, hurrying home before her father.

The beggar turned the sled with a heavy heart and pushed it down to the inn.

The poor wretch had had a dream, as he walked in the snow with half-naked feet. He had been thinking about the great forests north of Löven, about the great Finnmark forests.

Down here in Bro parish, where he was now traveling along the strait that connects upper and lower Löven, in these parts renowned for wealth and joyfulness, with estate next to estate, ironworks by ironworks: here every road was too heavy for him, every room too narrow, every bed too hard. Here he must bitterly long for the peace of the great, endless forests.

Here he could hear flails pounding at every barn, as if the grain would never be completely threshed. Loads of timber and charcoal wagons came unceasingly down from the inexhaustible forests. Endless ore carts traversed the roads in deep tracks, which hundreds of predecessors had carved out. Here he saw sledges, filled with passengers, hurry between the farms, and it seemed to him as though joy were holding the reins, and beauty and love were standing on the runners. Oh, how the poor wretch longed to be up in the peace of the great, endless forests!

Over there, where the trees stand up straight like pillars from the even ground, where the snow rests in heavy layers on the motionless branches, where the wind is powerless, only playing quietly in the topmost needles, there he wished to wander farther and farther in, until one day his strength would fail him, and he would fall down under the great trees, dying of hunger and cold.

He longed for the great, murmuring grave above Löven, where he would be overpowered by the forces of disintegration, where hunger, cold, weariness, and liquor would finally succeed in killing this poor body, which could endure anything.

He had arrived at the inn; there he would wait for evening. He went into the serving room and sat in dull repose on the bench by the door, dreaming of the endless forests.

The proprietress took pity on him and gave him a dram of liquor. She even gave him two, because he asked so eagerly.

But more than that she would not give him, and the beggar fell into drunken despair. He must drink more of this strong, sweet liquor. He must once again feel his heart dance in his body and his thoughts flare in intoxication. Oh, this sweet grain wine! Summer sun, summer birdsong, summer scent and beauty were floating around in its white wake. One more time, before he vanishes in night and darkness, he wants to drink sun and happiness.

So first he traded away the flour, then the flour sack, and finally the sled for liquor. From this he got good and drunk, and slept away a good part of the afternoon on a bench at the inn.

When he awoke, he realized that there was only one thing left for him to do. Because this wretched body had taken all dominion over his soul, because he could drink up what a child had entrusted to him, because he was a disgrace to the earth, he must free it from the burden of so much wretchedness. He must give freedom back to his soul, let it go to God.

Lying on the bench in the inn, he judged himself: "Gösta Berling, defrocked minister, accused of having drunk up the flour of a hungry child, sentenced to death. Death by what means? Death in the snowdrifts."

He seized his cap and stumbled out. He was neither completely awake nor completely sober. He wept in pity for himself, for his pitiful, soiled soul, which he must set free.

He did not go far and he did not stray from the road. By the roadside itself there was a high snowdrift. There he threw himself down to die. He closed his eyes and tried to sleep.

No one knows how long he lay like that, but there was still life in him when the daughter of the Broby minister came running along the road with a lantern in her hand and found him in the drift by the roadside. She had stood for hours, waiting for him; now she had run up the hills of Broby trying to find him.

She recognized him at once, and then she started shaking him and shouting with all her might to get him to wake up.

She had to know what he had done with her sack of flour.

She had to call him back to life at least long enough so that he could tell her what had become of her sled and her flour sack. Dear Father would kill her if she had frittered away his sled. She bit the beggar on the finger and clawed him in the face, all the while shrieking in despair.

Then someone came driving up the road.

"Who the hell is it who's shrieking?" came a gruff voice.

"I want to know what this fellow has done with my flour sack and my sled," sobbed the child, pounding with clenched fists on the beggar's chest.

"Are you clawing a frozen person like that? Up with you, wildcat!"

The rider was a tall, heavyset woman. She got out of the sledge and walked over to the drift. She took the child by the neck and tossed her up on the road. After that she leaned over, stuck her arms under the beggar's body, and lifted him up. Then she carried him to the sledge and laid him in it.

"Come along into the inn, wildcat," she called to the minister's daughter, "so we can hear what you know about this business."

An hour later the beggar was sitting on a chair by the door in the best room of the inn, and the commanding woman who had rescued him from the snowdrift was standing in front of him.

The way Gösta Berling saw her now, on the way home from a charcoal run in the forest, with sooty hands and a chalk pipe in her mouth, dressed in a short, unlined sheepskin and striped, handwoven wool skirt, with brogues on her feet and a knife sheath across her chest, the way he saw her with gray hair brushed straight back over an aged, beautiful face, this was the way he had heard her described a thousand times, and he realized that he had met up with the renowned majoress of Ekeby.

She was the most powerful woman in Värmland, the sovereign of seven ironworks, accustomed to giving orders and being obeyed; and he was only a wretched man under a death sentence, bereft of everything, knowing that every road was too heavy for him, every room too confined. His body shivered with terror, while her gaze rested upon him.

She stood silently, looking at the human wretchedness before her: the swollen red hands, the emaciated countenance, and the splendid head, which even in decline and negligence radiated a wild beauty.

"So this is Gösta Berling, the mad minister," she said inquiringly.

The beggar sat motionless.

"I am the majoress at Ekeby."

A shiver passed through the beggar's body. He clasped his hands, raising his eyes in a longing gaze. What would she do with him? Would she force him to live? He shuddered before her strength. And yet he had been so close to reaching the peace of the endless forests.

She began the struggle by telling him that the daughter of the Broby minister had got back her sled and flour sack, and that she, the majoress, had a refuge for him, as for many another homeless wretch, in the cavaliers' wing at Ekeby. She offered him a life of play and pleasure, but he replied that he must die.

Then she struck the table with her fist and let him hear her unvarnished thoughts.

"So then, he wants to die, so that's what he wants. I wouldn't wonder much about that, if only he were alive. Look, such an emaciated body and such powerless limbs and such dull eyes, and he thinks he has something left to kill. Do you think you have to be lying stiff and cold, nailed under a coffin lid, to be dead? Don't you think I can see how dead you are, Gösta Berling?

"I see that you have a skull for a head, and I can picture the worms creeping out of your eye sockets. Don't you feel that your mouth is full of dirt? Don't you hear how your bones rattle, when you move?

"You have drowned yourself in liquor, Gösta Berling, and dead you are.

"The only life left in you is in your skeleton, and you won't begrudge those bones the chance to live, if you call that living. It's as if you would begrudge the dead a dance over the grave mounds in the starlight.

"Are you ashamed of having been defrocked, since you now want to die? I will tell you, there would be more honor in using your gifts and becoming something useful on God's green earth. Why didn't you come to me at once—then I would have put everything right again for you. Yes, I suppose you must be expecting great honor from being shrouded and laid out on sawdust and called a beautiful corpse?"

The beggar sat calm, almost smiling, while she thundered out her angry words. No danger, he rejoiced, no danger. The endless forests are waiting, and she has no power to turn my soul away from there.

But the majoress fell silent and paced a few times back and forth in the room; then she took a seat by the stove, put her feet up on the hearth, and rested her elbows on her knees.

"Hell's bells," she said, chuckling to herself. "What I'm saying is truer than I realize myself. Don't you think, Gösta Berling, that most people in this world are dead, or half dead? Do you think I'm living? Oh my, no! Oh my, no!

"Yes, look at me, you! I am the majoress at Ekeby, and I am no doubt the most powerful woman in Värmland. If I wave my finger, the governor comes running, if I wave two fingers, the bishop comes running, and if I wave three, then consistory and aldermen and all the mill owners in Värmland dance a *polska* on the square in Karlstad. Hell's bells, lad, I'm telling you that I am nothing more than a dressed-up corpse. God knows how little life there is in me."

The beggar leaned forward on the chair and listened with senses alert. The old majoress sat rocking before the fire. She did not look at him as she spoke.

"Don't you think," she continued, "that if I were a living person, who saw you sitting there, worthless and wretched, contemplating suicide, don't you think I could take those thoughts from you in a breath? Then I would have tears for you, and prayers going up one side and down the other, and I would save your soul—but I am dead.

"Have you heard that I was once the beautiful Margareta Celsing? That wasn't yesterday, but I can still cry my old eyes out over her. Why should Margareta Celsing be dead, and Margareta Samzelius live; why should the majoress at Ekeby live, tell me, Gösta Berling?

"Do you know what Margareta Celsing was like? She was slim and slender and shy and innocent, Gösta Berling. She was the sort on whose grave the angels weep.

"She knew nothing of evil, no one had done her sorrow, she was good to everyone. And she was beautiful, truly beautiful.

"There was a stately man, his name was Altringer. God knows how he happened to be traveling up there in the wilds of Älvdalen, where her parents had their ironworks. Margareta Celsing saw him; he was a handsome, stately man, and he loved her.

"But he was poor, and they agreed to wait for each other for five years, as the ballad says.

"When three years had passed, she had another suitor. He was ugly and mean, but her parents thought he was rich, and they forced Margareta Celsing, by hook and by crook, with blows and harsh words, to take him as her husband. You see, on that day Margareta Celsing died.

"Since then there has been no Margareta Celsing, only Majoress Samzelius, and she was not good, not shy, she believed in much that was evil and gave no heed to what was good.

"I'm sure you know what happened next. We were living at Sjö by Löven here, the major and I. But he was not rich, like people said. I often had difficult days.

"Then Altringer came back, and now he was rich. He became the master at Ekeby, which borders on Sjö; he made himself master over six other ironworks on Löven. He was capable, enterprising; he was a wonderful man.

"He helped us in our poverty: we rode in his wagons, he sent food to our kitchen, wine to our cellar. He filled my life with banquets and amusements. The major went off to war, but what did we care about that! Oh, it was like a long dance of amusements around the shores of Löven.

"But there was evil talk about Altringer and me. If Margareta Celsing had been alive then, this would have caused her great sorrow, but it was nothing to me. I did not yet understand, however, that it was because I was dead that I had no feelings.

"Then the talk about us came up to my father and mother, where they lived among the charcoal stacks in the forests of Älvdal. The old woman did not hesitate long; she came down here to talk with me.

"One day, when the major was away and I was sitting at table with Altringer and several others, she came traveling. I saw her enter the dining room, but I could not feel that she was my mother, Gösta Berling. I greeted her as if she were a stranger and invited her to sit down at my table and take part in the meal.

"She wanted to talk to me, as if I had been her daughter, but I said to her that she was mistaken: my parents were dead, they had both died on my wedding day.

"Then she went along with the game. She was seventy years old, and she had ridden more than a hundred and twenty miles in three days. Now she sat down at the dining table without further ado and helped herself to some food; she was a very strong person.

"She said that it was unfortunate that I had suffered such a loss on just that day.

"'The most unfortunate thing,' I said, 'was that my parents hadn't died the day before; then the wedding would not have taken place.'

"'Are you not content with your marriage, gracious majoress?' she then asked.

"'Yes,' I said, 'now I am content. I will always be content and obey the will of my dear parents!'

"She asked if it had been my parents' will that I should heap shame upon myself, and them, and betray my husband. I showed little honor to my parents by letting myself be talked about by one and all.

"'They made their bed, now let them lie in it,' I answered her. 'And besides, you, strange woman, should understand that I do not intend to allow anyone to defame my parents' daughter.'

"We ate, the two of us. The men around us sat silently and did not dare raise knife and fork.

"The old woman stayed a day to rest; then she left.

"But as long as I saw her, I could not understand that she was my mother. I knew only that my mother was dead.

"As she was about to leave, Gösta Berling, and I was standing beside her on the stair, and the wagon had pulled up, she said to me: 'I have been here a whole day, without you greeting me as your mother. On desolate roads I traveled here, more than a hundred and twenty miles in three days. And my body trembles with shame for your sake, as if it were being whipped with branches. May you be denied, as I have been denied; disowned, as I have been disowned! May the highway be your home, the haystack your bed, the charcoal pile your stove! Shame and disgrace be your wage, may others strike you, as I strike you!'

"And she gave me a hard slap on the cheek.

"But I lifted her up, carried her down the stairs, and set her in the wagon.

"'Who are you to curse me?' I asked, 'who are you to strike me? I won't tolerate that from anyone.'

"And I gave her a slap in return.

"The wagon left at once, but then, at that moment, Gösta Berling, I knew that Margareta Celsing was dead.

"She was good, and innocent; she knew nothing of evil. The angels had wept on her grave. If she had lived, she would not have struck her mother."

The beggar over by the door had listened, and for a moment the words had deadened the sound of the enticing murmur of the endless forests. Look, look at this powerful woman; she made herself his equal in sin, his sister in perdition, to give him courage to live. Thus would he learn that there was sorrow and guilt on other heads than his. He got up and went over to the majoress.

"Now will you live, Gösta Berling?" she asked with a voice that broke into tears. "What should you die for? A good minister might well have been made out of you, but never was the Gösta Berling that you drowned in liquor so gleamingly innocent-white as the Margareta Celsing I smothered in hatred. Will you live?"

Gösta fell down on one knee before the majoress.

"Forgive me," he said, "I cannot."

"I am an old woman, tempered by much sorrow," answered the majoress, "and I am sitting here, laying bare my soul to a beggar, whom I found half frozen in a snowdrift by the side of the road. It serves me right. If you go and become a suicide, then at least you cannot tell anyone about my craziness."

"Majoress, I am no suicide, I am a doomed man. Don't make the fight too hard for me! I must not live. My body has taken dominion over my soul, so I must let him go free, let him go to God."

"I see. Do you think that's where you're going?"

"Farewell, majoress, and thanks!"

"Farewell, Gösta Berling."

The beggar got up and went toward the door with hanging head and dragging steps. This woman made the road up to the great forests heavy for him.

When he came to the door, he had to look back. Then he met the gaze of the majoress, where she sat quietly looking at him. He had never seen such a transformation in a face, and he remained standing and stared at her. She, who had just been enraged and threatening, sat in quiet transfiguration, and her eyes shone with merciful, compassionate love. There was something within him, in his own uncivilized heart, which burst at that gaze; he leaned his head against the doorpost, extended his arms over his head, and wept until his heart would have burst.

The majoress tossed her chalk pipe into the stove and came over to Gösta. Her movements were suddenly as tender as a mother's.

"There, there, my boy!"

And she pulled him down alongside her on the bench by the door, so that he wept with his head against her lap.

"Are you still going to die?"

Then he wanted to leap to his feet. She had to hold him back by force.

"Now I say to you that you may do as you wish. But I promise you that if you want to live, then I will take the Broby minister's daughter to me and make a person out of her, so that she can thank her God that you stole her flour. So, will you?"

He lifted his head and looked her right in the eyes.

"Do you mean it?"

"Yes I do, Gösta Berling."

Then he wrung his hands in anguish. He saw before him those piercing eyes, the pinched lips, and emaciated little hands. So the young creature would get protection and care, and the marks of degradation would be erased from her body, the evil from her soul. Now the road up to the endless forests was closed to him.

"I will not kill myself as long she is under the majoress's care," he said. "I knew well enough that the majoress would force me to live. I knew right away that the majoress was too much for me."

"Gösta Berling," she said solemnly, "I have fought for you as though for myself. I said to God: 'If there is anything of Margareta Celsing alive in me, then allow her to come forth and show herself, so that this man may not go and kill himself.' And he allowed it, and you saw her, and therefore you could not go. And she whispered to me that at least for the sake of the poor child, you ought to give up your intent to die. Oh, you may fly boldly, you wild birds, but our Lord knows the net that will catch you."

"He is a great and strange God," said Gösta Berling. "He has eluded me and rejected me, but he will not let me die. His will be done!"

From that day on Gösta Berling became a cavalier at Ekeby. Twice he tried to get away from there and make his own way, to live off his own labor. The first time the majoress granted him a cottage near Ekeby; he moved there, intending to live as a laborer. He succeeded for a time, but soon tired of the loneliness and the daily toil, and again became a cavalier. The second time was when he became a tutor at Borg for Count Henrik Dohna. During that time he fell in love with the young Ebba Dohna, the count's sister, but when she died, just as he thought he was close to winning her, he gave up every thought of being anything other than a cavalier at Ekeby. It seemed to him that for a defrocked minister all roads to rehabilitation were closed.

CHAPTER I

THE LANDSCAPE

Now I must describe the long lake, the fertile plain, and the blue hills, because this was the setting where Gösta Berling and the cavaliers of Ekeby lived out their eccentric existence.

The lake has its sources rather far up in the north, which is a splendid country for a lake. The forest and the hills never cease in gathering water for it; streams and brooks tumble down into it year-round. It has fine, white sand on which to extend itself, promontories and small islands to reflect and observe, water sprite and sea witch have free rein there, and the lake quickly grows large and lovely. Up there in the north the lake is happy and amiable: you need only see it on a summer morning, lying there drowsily under a veil of mist, to feel how merry it is. First it teases for a while, creeping slowly, slowly along out of its light covering, so bewitchingly beautiful that you hardly recognize it, but then with a jerk it throws off the covers and lies there exposed and bare and rosy, glistening in the morning light.

But the lake is not content with this playful life; he laces himself up into a narrow sound, bursting forth through some sand dunes to the south, seeking a new realm for himself. And he finds such a domain: he grows larger and mightier, with bottomless deeps to fill and an industrious landscape to adorn. But now the water gets darker too, the shore less varied, the winds harsher, its entire character sterner. A stately, grand lake it is. Many are the vessels and log rafts that pass there, only late does he have time to go into hibernation, seldom until after Christmas. He is often in a surly mood: the lake can churn white with wrath and wreck sailboats, but he can also lie in dreamy calm, reflecting the sky.

But the lake wishes to travel even farther out into the world, although the hills appear more and more rugged and his scope more cramped the farther down he comes, so that once again he must creep along between the sand shores as a narrow sound. Then he broadens out again for the third time, but no longer with the same beauty and majesty.

The shorelines sink and become uniform, gentler winds blow, the lake goes into an early hibernation. He is still lovely, but he has lost the frenzy of youth and the strength of his prime—he is a lake like any other. With two arms he fumbles for the way to Lake Vänern, and when that is found, he plunges into the weakness of old age along steep precipices and goes with a final, booming exploit into rest.

The plain is just as long as the lake, but you might think that it has difficulty emerging between lakes and hills, all the way from the basin at the northern end of the lake, where it first dares to spread out, and then onward, until victoriously it lies down in indolent repose by the shore of Vänern. It can only be that the plain would prefer to follow the lakeshore, long as it is, but the hills grant it no peace. The hills are mighty granite walls, covered by forest, full of gorges difficult to move in, rich in moss and lichen, in ancient days home to a multitude of wild animals. One often encounters a marshy bog or a tarn with dark water up among the extensive ridges. Here and there is also a charcoal stack or an open place, where timber and wood have been removed, or a burned clearing; these testify that the hills can also endure work. But normally they lie in carefree repose, content to let shadows and daylight play their eternal game across their slopes.

And the plain, which is pious and rich and loves work, carries on a constant war with these hills, all, by the way, in a spirit of friendliness.

"It is really quite enough," says the plain to the hills, "if you place your walls round about me, that is security enough for me."

But the hills will not listen to such talk. They send out long rows of hillocks and bare plateaus all the way down to the lake. They raise grand lookout towers on every promontory and actually leave the lakeshore so seldom that the plain can roll in the soft sand of the lake bed in only a few places. But it does no good if the plain tries to complain.

"Be glad that we are standing here," say the hills. "Think of the time before Christmas, when, day after day, the deathly cold mists roll across Löven. We do good service, where we stand."

The plain laments that it has little room and a poor view.

"You are stupid," the hills reply, "you should just feel how the wind blows down here by the lake. At the very least a granite back and a coat of spruce is needed to endure it. And furthermore, you can be content looking at us."

Yes, look at the hills, that is just what the plain does. It must sense all the marvelous nuances of light and shadow that traverse across them. It knows how in the illumination of midday they sink down below the horizon, low and pale light blue, and in morning and evening light rise to venerable heights, clear blue like the sky at the zenith. At times the light can fall so sharply across them that they turn green or blue-black, and every single pine, every road and gorge is visible from miles away. It does happen in certain places that the hills move aside and let the plain come up and look at the lake. But once it sees the lake in its fury, as it hisses and spits like a wildcat, or sees it covered by the cold smoke that arises when the sea witch is busy with brewing and washing, then it quickly acknowledges that the hills are right and withdraws into its cramped prison again.

From ancient times people have cultivated the magnificent plain, and it has become a large district. Anywhere a river with its white-foaming rapids throws itself down the lakeshore slope, ironworks and mills appeared. On the light, open places where the plain comes up to the lake, churches and parsonages were built, but at the edges of the valleys, halfway up the hillside, on stone-covered ground where seeds do not thrive, are the farmyards and officers' quarters and an occasional manor house.

However, it must be noted that in the 1820s the area was far from as developed as it is now. There was much forest and lake and bog then that can now be cultivated. The people were not as numerous either and made their living partly through transports and day labor at the many ironworks, partly by working in other places; agriculture could not feed them. At that time the residents of the plain dressed in homespun clothing, ate oat bread, and were content with a daily wage of twelve shillings. There was great need among many of them, but that was often relieved by an easy, happy temperament and an inborn handiness and capability.

But these three—the long lake, the fertile plain, and the blue hills—formed one of the loveliest landscapes, and still do, just as today the people are still vigorous, courageous, and talented. Now they have also made great progress both in well-being and in education.

May all go well for those who live up there by the long lake and the blue hills! And now I wish to relate a few of their memories.

CHAPTER 2

CHRISTMAS NIGHT

Sintram is the name of the malevolent mill owner at Fors, a man with long arms and clumsy, apelike body, with bald head and ugly, sneering face, he whose pleasure is in inciting mischief.

Sintram is his name, who takes on only vagabonds and rowdies as hired hands and has only quarrelsome, mendacious maids in his service, he who inflames dogs to fury by sticking needles in their muzzles and lives happily in the midst of spiteful people and savage animals.

Sintram is his name, whose greatest joy is to dress up in the form of the foul fiend, with horns and tail and horse's hooves and hairy body and, suddenly emerging from dark corners, from baking oven or woodshed, to frighten timid children and superstitious women.

Sintram is his name, who enjoys turning old friendship into new hatred and poisoning hearts with lies.

Sintram is his name—and one day he came to Ekeby.

Pull the big wood sledge into the smithy, let it stand in the middle of the floor, and lay a cart bed over the stakes! Now we have a table. Cheers for the table, the table is ready!

Bring out chairs, anything that can be used to sit on! Over here with three-legged shoemaker's stools and empty barrels! Over here with worn-out old armchairs without backs, and out with the runnerless racing sleigh and the old coach! Ha, ha, ha, out with the old coach, it can be a platform!

Just look at it, one wheel has been driven to bits, no, the whole wagon body! Only the driver's seat remains; the cushion is wrecked, moss spreading over it, the leather is red with age.

The ramshackle old thing is tall as a house. Prop it up, prop it up, otherwise it will fall!

Hurrah! Hurrah! It is Christmas night at the Ekeby ironworks.

Behind the silk curtains of the double bed the major and majoress are sleeping, sleeping in the belief that the cavaliers' wing is sleeping. Hired hands and maids may sleep, heavy with porridge and bitter Christmas beer, but not the gentlemen in the cavaliers' wing. How can anyone think that the cavaliers' wing is sleeping!

No bare-legged smiths are turning the molten pieces of iron, no soot-covered boys are pushing coal barrows; the great hammer hangs from the ceiling like an arm with a clenched fist, the anvil stands empty, the furnaces do not have their red maws open to devour coal, the bellows are not creaking. It is Christmas. The smithy is sleeping.

Sleep, sleep! Oh, you human children, sleep while the cavaliers are awake. The long tongs stand upright on the floor with tallow in their claws. From the shining copper ten-pot kettle, the blue flames of the *brulot* flare high up against the darkness of the ceiling. Beerencreutz's horn lantern is hanging up on the tilt hammer. The yellow *punsch* glistens in the bowl like a bright sun. There are tables, there are benches. The cavaliers are celebrating Christmas night in the smithy.

There is merriment and clamor, music and song. But the din of the midnight feast awakens no one. All the noise from the smithy dies away in the powerful roar of the rapids just outside.

There is merriment and clamor. Imagine, if the majoress were to see them!

What of it? She would certainly seat herself among them and empty a goblet. A capable woman she is; she does not turn away from a thunderous drinking song or a game of *kille*. The richest woman in Värmland, plucky as a man, proud as a queen. She loves song and sounding fiddles and hunting horns. Wine and card playing she likes, and tables, wreathed with happy guests, are her joy. She likes to see the storehouses being used, dancing and merriment in chamber and hall, and the cavaliers' wing filled with cavaliers.

Look at them round the bowl, cavalier by cavalier! There are twelve of them, twelve men. No mayflies, no dandies, but men whose reputation will long live on in Värmland, courageous men, strong men.

No dried-up parchments, no tied-up money pouches, poor men. Carefree men, cavaliers all day long.

No mama's boys, no sleepy gentlemen on their own estate. Wayfaring men, merry men, knights of a hundred adventures.

For many years now the cavaliers' wing has stood empty. Ekeby is no longer the chosen refuge of homeless cavaliers. Retired officers and poor nobles no longer drift around Värmland in rickety one-horse carriages. But let the dead live, let them rise again, those happy, carefree, eternally young ones!

All of these celebrated men can play one or more instruments. All of them are as full of peculiarities and proverbs and flashes of wit and songs as an anthill is full of ants, but each one, however, has his particular great singularity, his highly treasured cavalier virtue, which separates him from the rest.

Foremost of all of them who are sitting round the bowl, I will mention Beerencreutz, the colonel with the great white mustaches, *kille* player, singer of Bellman songs, and along with him his friend and war comrade, the taciturn major, the great bear hunter Anders Fuchs, and as the third in the company little Ruster, the drummer, who had long been the colonel's servant, but won the rank of cavalier by skillfulness in *punsch* feats and singing bass. Then old second-lieutenant Rutger von Örneclou, ladies' man, dressed in cravat and wig, decked out in ruffles and made up like a woman, must be mentioned. He was one of the finest cavaliers, and likewise Kristian Bergh, the strong captain, who was a comical hero, but as easy to fool as a giant in a fairy tale. Short, pear-shaped Squire Julius, witty, amusing, and well talented, was often in the company of these two: orator, painter, singer of songs, and teller of anecdotes. He would gladly practice his wit on the gouty second-lieutenant and the stupid giant.

There was also the big German, Kevenhüller, inventor of the self-propelled wagon and the flying machine, whose name still resounds in these murmuring forests. A knight he was by birth and in appearance as well, with great, twirling mustaches, pointed full beard, aquiline nose, and narrow, slanting eyes in a net of crisscrossed wrinkles. There sat the great warrior, cousin Kristoffer, who never went outside the walls of the cavaliers' wing except when a bear hunt or a daring adventure was waiting, and next to him uncle Eberhard, the philosopher, who had not drifted to Ekeby for pleasure and games but rather to be able, undisturbed by the worries of making a living, to fulfill his great work in the science of sciences.

Last of all I will now mention the best of the group, modest Lövenborg, that pious man, who was too good for this world and understood little of its ways, and Lilliecrona, the great musician, who had a good home and always longed for it, but nonetheless must remain at Ekeby, for his spirit required richness and variety to be able to endure life.

These eleven had all left youth behind them, and several had entered old age, but in the midst of them there was one who was no more than thirty years old and still possessed all the powers of soul and body unbroken. This was Gösta Berling, the cavalier of cavaliers, who all by himself was a greater orator, singer, musician, hunter, drinking champion, and player than all the others. He possessed all the cavalier virtues. What a man the majoress had made of him!

Look at him now, standing up on the rostrum. The darkness settles down over him from the black ceiling in heavy festoons. His fair head glistens out of that darkness like one of the young gods, the young bearers of light, who organized chaos. There he stands, slender, beautiful, adventurous.

But he speaks with deep gravity.

"Cavaliers and brothers, it is almost midnight, the feast is far advanced, it is time to drink a toast to the thirteenth at the table!"

"Dear brother Gösta," calls out Squire Julius, "there is no thirteenth here, there are only twelve of us."

"At Ekeby a man dies every year," Gösta continues in an ever gloomier voice. "One of the guests of the cavaliers' wing dies, one of the happy, the carefree, the eternally young dies. What of it? Cavaliers must not grow old. If our trembling hands cannot lift the glass, our dimming eyes not discern the cards, what then is life to us, and what are we to life? Of the thirteen who celebrate Christmas night in the smithy at Ekeby, one must die, but every year a new one comes to complete our number. A man skilled in the handiwork of joy, a man who can handle fiddle and cards, must come and make our group complete in number. Old butterflies should have the sense to die while the summer sun is shining. Cheers to the thirteenth!"

"But, Gösta, there are only twelve of us," the cavaliers object, not touching their glasses.

Gösta Berling, whom they called the poet, although he never wrote verse, continues with unperturbed calm.

"Cavaliers and brethren! Have you forgotten who you are? You are the ones who uphold pleasure in Värmland. You are the ones who put the strings in motion, keep the dance going, let song and play resound through the land. You know to keep your hearts away from gold, your hands from work. If you did not exist, then the dance would die out, summer would die out, the roses die out, card playing die out, song die out, and in all of this blessed land there would be nothing but iron and mill owners. Pleasure will live as long as you do. For six years now I have celebrated Christmas night in the smithy at Ekeby, and never before has anyone refused to drink to the thirteenth."

"But, Gösta," they then shout, "since there are only twelve of us, how can we drink to the thirteenth?"

Deep concern shows itself on Gösta's face.

"Are there only twelve of us?" he says. "Why is that, shall we die out from the earth? Shall there be only eleven of us next year, and the following year only ten? Shall our name become legend, our group annihilated? I call him, the thirteenth, for I have stood up to drink his health. From the depths of the sea, from the inner domains of the earth, from the heavens, from hell I call him who shall complete the cavaliers' company."

Then there is a rattling in the chimney, then the cover of the smelting furnace is thrown open, then the thirteenth arrives.

Hairy he comes, with tail and horse's hoof, with horn and pointed Vandyke beard, and at the sight of him the cavaliers spring up with a shout.

But with unbridled merriment Gösta Berling cries out, "The thirteenth has arrived—*skoal* to the thirteenth!"

So he has arrived, the ancient enemy of mankind, come to the bold ones who disturb the peace of the holy night. Friend of broom-riding witches, who signs his contracts in blood on coal-black paper, he who danced with the countess at Ivarsnäs for seven days and could not be driven away by seven ministers, he has arrived.

Thoughts are flying at frantic speed through the heads of the old adventurers at the sight of him. They wonder for whose sake he is out this night.

Many of them were ready to hurry off in terror, but they soon realized that the horned one had not come to fetch them down to his dark realm, but rather that the clinking of beakers and drinking songs had enticed him. He wanted to delight in the joys of men during the sacred Christmas night and throw off the burden of rule during this time of joy.

Oh, cavaliers, cavaliers, who among you recalls anymore that this is Christmas night! It is now that angels sing for the shepherds of the field. It is now that children worry about sleeping so soundly that they will not wake up in time for the glorious early morning service. Soon it will be time to light the candles in Bro church, and far off in the forest homes during the evening the boy has made ready a resinous torch, with which he will light the way to church for his girl. In all homes the housewife has set candelabras in the windows, ready to be lit as the churchgoers file past. The organist goes over the Christmas hymns in his sleep, and the old dean lies in bed, testing whether he has voice enough to sing: "Glory to God in the highest, and on earth peace, goodwill toward men!"

Oh, cavaliers, it would have been better for you to lie quietly in your beds on this night of peace than to keep company with the prince of evil!

But they greet him with shouts of welcome, just as Gösta had done. They place a goblet, filled with flaming *brulot*, in his hand. They make room for him at the table at the place of honor, and they see him there with joy, as though his foul satyr face bore the sweet features that belonged to the love of their youth.

Beerencreutz invites him to a game of *kille*, Squire Julius sings his best songs for him, and Örneclou talks to him about beautiful women, those glorious beings who make life sweet.

He is quite comfortable, the horned one, as he leans back with princely posture on the driver's seat of the old carriage and with claw-equipped hand brings the filled goblet to his smiling mouth.

But Gösta Berling, naturally, makes a speech for him.

"Your grace," he says, "we have long awaited you here at Ekeby, for you must have difficulty gaining access to any other paradise. Here we live without sowing or spinning, as your grace perhaps already knows. Here the grilled sparrows fly into your mouth, here bitter beer and sweet liquor flow in brooks and streams. This is a good place, make note of that, your grace!

"We cavaliers have surely also waited for you, for our number has scarcely been complete before. Look, it is the case that we are somewhat more than we pretend to be; we are the poem's ancient band of twelve that proceeds through the ages. There were twelve of us, when we ruled the world on the cloud-covered top of Olympus, and twelve when we lived as birds in Ygdrasil's green crown. Wherever poetry went forth, there we followed. Did we not sit, twelve men strong, at King Arthur's round table, and did twelve paladins not go in Charles the Twelfth's great army? One of us has been Thor, another Jupiter, as any man should be able to see in us yet today. The divine splendor can be sensed under the rags, the lion's mane under the donkey hide. Time has treated us badly, but when we are there, the smithy becomes a Mount Olympus and the cavaliers' wing a Valhalla.

"But, your grace, our number has not been complete. It is well known that in the poem's band of twelve there must always be a Loki, a Prometheus. Him we have lacked.

"Your grace, we bid you welcome!"

"Look, look, look," says the evil one. "Such fine words, fine words. And I, who don't have time to reply. Business, lads, business, must be off in a moment, otherwise I would so gladly be at your service, in any capacity whatsoever. Thanks for this evening, old chatterboxes. We'll meet again."

Then the cavaliers ask where he intends to go, and he replies that the noble majoress, the mistress of Ekeby, awaits him to get her contract renewed.

Then great astonishment takes hold of the cavaliers.

A stern, capable woman she is, the majoress at Ekeby. She lifts a bushel of rye onto her broad shoulders. She follows the transport of ore, gathered from the mining fields of Bergslagen, on the long road to Ekeby. She sleeps like a peasant driver on the floor of the barn with a sack as a pillow. In winter she may keep watch over a charcoal stack, in summer follow a raft of logs down Löven. She is a commanding woman. She swears like a street urchin and governs her seven ironworks and her neighbors' farms like a king, governs her own parish and the neighboring parishes, yes, the whole of beautiful Värmland. But for homeless cavaliers she has been like a mother, and therefore they have kept their ears closed when slander whispered to them that she was in league with the devil.

Thus they ask him with great astonishment what kind of contract she has made with him.

And he, the black one, answers them that he has granted the majoress her seven ironworks against the promise that every year she would send him a soul.

Oh, what terror now constricts the hearts of the cavaliers!

Of course they knew it, but they had not realized it before.

At Ekeby a man dies every year, one of the guests of the cavaliers' wing dies; one of the happy, the carefree, the eternally young, dies. What does it matter, cavaliers must not grow old! If their trembling hands are not able to lift the glass, their dimming eyes not able to discern the cards, what then is life to them, and what are they to life? Butterflies should have the sense to die while the sun is shining.

But now, only now do they grasp the proper meaning of things.

Curse that woman! That is why she has given them many a good meal, that is why she lets them drink her bitter beer and her sweet liquor, so that they might stagger from the drinking halls and card tables of Ekeby down to the king of damnation, one each year, one for each passing year.

Curse that woman, that witch! Strong, splendid men had come to this Ekeby, come there to fade away. For there she ruined them. Their brains were mushrooms, dry ash their lungs, and darkness their spirit, as they sank down on the deathbed and were ready for the long journey, without hope, without a soul, without virtue.

Curse that woman! Better men than them have died like that, and so would they.

But the cavaliers do not long remain paralyzed by the weight of terror.

"You king of damnation," they shout, "you shall never again make a contract written in blood with that witch; she shall die!" Kristian Bergh, the strong captain, has thrown the smithy's heaviest sledgehammer across his shoulders. He wants to bury it to the shaft in the head of that sorceress. No more souls will be sacrificed by her.

"And you yourself, horned one, we should set you on the anvil and let the tilt hammer loose. We should hold you still with tongs under the hammer blows and teach you to go hunting for cavalier souls."

He is cowardly, the black gentleman, that has long been known, and talk of the tilt hammer does not please him. He calls Kristian Bergh back and starts to negotiate with the cavaliers.

"Take the seven ironworks this year, take them yourselves, cavaliers, and give me the majoress!"

"Do you think we are as low-down as she is?" Squire Julius cries out. "We want to have Ekeby and all the ironworks, but you have to take care of the majoress yourself!"

"What does Gösta say, what does Gösta say?" asks the gentle Lövenborg. "Gösta Berling must speak. His opinion on such an important decision must be heard."

"All of this is madness!" says Gösta Berling. "Cavaliers, don't let yourselves be fooled by him! What are we against the majoress? Things must go as they will for our souls, but of my own free will we should not become a bunch of ungrateful wretches and behave like scoundrels and traitors. I have eaten the majoress's food for too many years to betray her now."

"Yes, go to hell, Gösta, if that's what you want! We would rather run Ekeby ourselves."

"But are you out of your mind, or have you drunk yourselves out of your senses? Do you think this is the truth? Do you believe that he over there is the evil one? Don't you see that the whole thing is a damned lie?"

"Now, now, now," says the black gentleman, "that man doesn't notice that he is well on his way to being ready, and yet he has been at Ekeby for seven years. He doesn't see how far he has come."

"For pity's sake, man! I helped put you in the furnace myself."

"As if that would make any difference, as if I wouldn't be as good a devil as anyone else. Well, well now, Gösta Berling, aren't you the steady one. You've really turned out nice under the majoress's care."

"She is the one who rescued me," says Gösta. "What would I be without her?"

"See, see, as if she hasn't had her own reasons for keeping you here at Ekeby. You can lure many into the trap; you have great talents. One time you tried to get away from her, you let her give you a cottage, and you became a worker; you wanted to eat your own bread. Every day she came past the cottage, and she had beautiful girls in her company. One time Marianne Sinclaire was along; then you threw away your spade and leather apron, Gösta Berling, and became a cavalier again."

"The road went that way, you beast."

"Yes, yes, of course, the road went that way. Then you came to Borg, became a tutor there for Henrik Dohna and just about became Countess Märta's son-in-law. Who was it who caused young Ebba Dohna to hear that you were only a defrocked minister, so that she turned you down? It was the majoress, Gösta Berling. She wanted you back."

"What of it!" says Gösta. "Ebba Dohna died shortly thereafter. I never would have had her anyway."

Now the black gentleman came up close to him and hissed right in his face: "Died, yes of course she died. Killed herself for your sake, she did, but they haven't told you that yet."

"You're not a bad devil," says Gösta.

"It was the majoress who controlled everything, I'm telling you. She wanted to have you back in the cavaliers' wing."

Gösta burst out laughing.

"You're not a bad devil," he cries out wildly. "Why shouldn't we make a contract with you? You can probably get us the seven ironworks, if you so please."

"Nice to see that you are no longer against good fortune."

The cavaliers let out a sigh of relief. They were so far gone that they were not capable of anything without Gösta. If he had not wanted to go along with the deal, then it could not have been made. And yet it was a great thing for destitute cavaliers to get seven ironworks to rule over.

"Now make note of this," says Gösta, "that we are taking the seven ironworks to save our souls, but not to become the kind of mill owner who counts money and weighs iron. We will not become dried-up parchments nor tied-up money pouches, but rather we will be and remain cavaliers."

"Wisdom's own words," mumbles the black gentleman.

"Therefore, if you want to give us the seven ironworks for one year, then we will accept them, but note that if during that time we do anything that is not like a cavalier, then you may take all twelve of us when the year is out, and give the ironworks to whomever you wish."

The evil one rubbed his hands together with delight.

"But if we always behave like true cavaliers," continued Gösta, "then you may never again make a contract on Ekeby, and you will receive no payment for this year either from us or the majoress."

"That is hard," says the evil one. "Oh, dear Gösta, I really ought to get one soul, one single poor little soul. Couldn't I get the majoress then; why are you saving the majoress?"

"I do not trade in such wares," roars Gösta, "but if you want to have anyone, then you can take old Sintram at Fors, he's ready, I can answer for that."

"There, there, there, that sounds all right," says the black gentleman without blinking. "The cavaliers or Sintram, they can balance each other out. It will be a good year."

And then the contract was written with blood from Gösta

Berling's little finger on the evil one's black paper and with his quill pen.

But when it is done, the cavaliers rejoice. Now all the world's glory shall belong to them for one year, and then there is always some way out.

They move the chairs aside, form a circle around the kettle of *brulot* standing in the middle of the sooty floor, and swing around in a wild dance. At the center of the circle the evil one dances with high leaps, and at last he falls down flat next to the kettle, tips it over, and drinks.

Then Beerencreutz throws himself down beside him and likewise Gösta Berling, and after them all the others lie in a circle around the kettle, which is rolled from mouth to mouth. At last a shove tips it over, and the hot, sticky liquid washes over the prostrate men.

When the confederates get up, the evil one is gone, but his golden promises hover like glistening crowns over the heads of the cavaliers.

CHAPTER 3

CHRISTMAS DINNER

On Christmas Day Majoress Samzelius gives a great dinner at Ekeby.

She presides as hostess at a table set for fifty guests. She sits there in brilliance and splendor; the short sheepskin, striped woolen stockings, and chalk pipe are nowhere to be seen. She rustles in silk, gold weighs down her bare arms, pearls cool her white neck.

Where then are the cavaliers, where are they who drank a toast to the new masters of Ekeby on the sooty floor of the smithy from a scoured copper kettle?

The cavaliers are sitting at a separate table in a corner by the tiled stove; on this day there is no room for them at the great table. To their table the food arrives late, the wine sparingly; the glances of the beautiful women are not sent in that direction, no one there listens to Gösta's jokes.

But the cavaliers are like tamed foals, like satisfied beasts. The night only gave them an hour's sleep, then they went to the early morning Christmas service, illuminated by torches and stars. They saw the Christmas candles, they heard the Christmas hymns, their faces were like those of smiling children. They forgot Christmas night in the smithy, the way you forget a bad dream.

The majoress at Ekeby is great and powerful. Who dares lift an arm to strike her, who dares move his tongue to bear witness against her? Certainly not the poor cavaliers, who for many years have eaten her bread and slept under her roof. She puts them where she wants, she can close her door to them when she wants, and they are not even able to escape her power. God have mercy on their souls! They could not survive far from Ekeby.

The guests are enjoying themselves at the great table; there Marianne Sinclaire's beautiful eyes are shining, there the low laughter of the happy Countess Dohna resounds.

But among the cavaliers the mood is gloomy. What would it cost, for those who were to be thrown into the abyss for the majoress to be allowed to sit at the same table as her other guests? What kind of mean business is this with the table in the corner by the tile stove! As if the cavaliers were not worthy of being in the company of respectable people!

The majoress prides herself on sitting between the count at Borg and the dean in Bro. The cavaliers hang their heads like disowned children. And as time passes, the night's thoughts awaken in them.

The merry flashes of wit, the lusty exaggerations, arrive at the table in the corner by the tiled stove like timid guests. There the wrath of the night and its promises make their way into their brains. Squire Julius leads the strong captain, Kristian Bergh, to believe that there will not be enough of the grilled grouse now being passed around the large table for all the dinner guests, but this provokes no delight.

"There won't be enough," he says. "I know how many they have. But they haven't been at a loss about what to do, Captain Kristian; they've grilled crows for us here at the little table."

But Colonel Beerencreutz's lips curl only into a faint smile under the forbidding mustaches, and Gösta looks as though he were thinking about murdering someone the whole time.

"Why shouldn't all the food be good enough for the cavaliers?" he asks.

Finally a plate heaped with splendid grouse arrives down at the little table.

But Captain Kristian is angry. Hasn't he devoted a lifetime of hatred for crows, for those ugly, cawing, flying insects?

He hated them so bitterly that he would put on a woman's long garment in the autumn and tie a kerchief around his head, and make himself ridiculous to every man just to get within shooting range of them, where they were eating grain on the fields.

He sought them out at the courting dance on the bare fields in the spring and killed them. He sought out their nests in summer and evicted the shrieking, featherless chicks or crushed the unhatched eggs.

Now he snatches the plate of grouse.

"Don't you think I recognize them?" he roars at the servant. "Do I have to hear them cawing to recognize them? Damnation, serving Kristian Bergh crow! Damnation!"

And with that he takes the grouse one by and one and heaves them against the wall.

"Damnation," he shouts as he does so, so that the room rocks, "serving Kristian Bergh crow! Damnation!"

And in the same way that he used to hurl helpless crow chicks against the rocks, now he lets grouse after grouse swish toward the wall.

Gravy and fat are flying around him; the crushed birds bounce to the floor.

And the cavaliers' wing rejoices.

Then the majoress's angry voice penetrates to the cavaliers' ears.

"Throw him out!" she calls to the servants.

But they don't dare approach him. He is Kristian Bergh, after all, the strong captain.

"Throw him out!"

He hears the shout, and terrible in his wrath he now turns toward the majoress, the way a bear turns from one fallen enemy to a new attacker. He goes up to the horseshoe-shaped table. The huge man's steps thunder heavily against the floor. He stops across from her with the tabletop between them.

"Throw him out!" the majoress roars yet again.

But he is furious; his furrowed brow, his large, clenched fists inspire fear. He is a giant in stature, a giant in strength. Guests and servants shudder and dare not touch him. Who would dare touch him now, when rage has taken his senses?

He stands right in front of the majoress and shakes his fist at her.

"I took the crow and threw it against the wall. Do you think I did the right thing?"

"Get out, captain!"

"Watch it, hag! Serve Kristian Bergh crow! Would I be doing the right thing, if I were to take you with your seven damned—"

"Hell's bells, Kristian Bergh, don't swear. No one swears here but me."

"Do you think I'm afraid of you, troll hag? Do you think I don't know how you got your seven ironworks?"

"Silence, captain!"

"When Altringer died, he gave them to your husband because you had been his lover."

"Won't you be quiet!"

"Because you had been such a faithful wife, Margareta Samzelius. And the major accepted the seven ironworks and let you run them and pretended to know nothing. And Satan has been responsible for the whole business; but now it will be over for you."

The majoress sits down; she is pale and trembling. Then she confirms in a soft, peculiar voice, "Yes, now it's over for me, and this is your doing, Kristian Bergh."

At that tone Kristian Bergh begins to tremble, his facial features are contorted, and tears of dread come to his eyes.

"I am drunk," he shouts, "I don't know what I'm saying, I haven't said a thing. A dog and a thrall, a dog and a thrall, I've been nothing more to her for forty years. She is Margareta Celsing, whom I have served all my life. I say nothing bad about her. Could I say anything bad about the beautiful Margareta Celsing? I am the dog who guards her door, the thrall who carries her loads. She may kick me, she may beat me! Now you see that I endure in silence. I have loved her for forty years. How could I say anything bad about her?"

And a strange sight it is to see how he gets down on his knees and begs for forgiveness. And as she is sitting on the other side of the table, he goes on his knees around the table, until he approaches her, when he bows down and kisses the hem of her skirt, and the floor is wet with his tears.

But not far from the majoress sits a small, strong man. He has curly hair, small, slanted eyes, and a protruding jaw. He resembles a bear. He is a man of few words, who prefers to go his own, silent way and let the world take care of itself. He is Major Samzelius.

He gets up, when he hears Captain Kristian's accusatory words, and the majoress gets up, as do all fifty of the guests. The women weep with alarm for what is now to come; the men stand timidly, and at the majoress's feet is Captain Kristian, kissing the hem of her skirt, wetting the floor with tears.

The major's broad, hairy hands clench slowly; his arm is raised.

But the woman speaks first. She has a muted tone in her voice, which is not her usual.

"You stole me," she burst out. "You came like a robber and took me. They forced me at home with blows, with hunger and harsh words, to become your wife. I have acted toward you as you have deserved."

The major's broad fist is clenched. The majoress retreats a few steps. Then she speaks again.

"Live eels wriggle under the knife; a forced wife takes a lover. Are you going to strike me now for what happened twenty years ago? Why didn't you strike me then? Don't you recall how he was living at Ekeby, while we were at Sjö? Don't you recall how he supported us in our poverty? We rode in his carriages, we drank his wine. Did we hide anything from you? Weren't his servants your servants? Didn't his gold weigh down your pocket? Didn't you accept the seven ironworks? You kept silent then and accepted them, when you should have struck, Berndt Samzelius, when you should have struck."

The man turns away from her and looks at all those present. He reads in their faces that they agree with her, that they all thought he had taken property and gifts for his silence.

"I didn't know it," he says, stomping the floor.

"It is good that you know it now," she interjects with a shrilly resounding voice. "I used to be afraid that you would die without having found it out. It is good that you know it now, so that I can speak freely with you who have been my lord and jailer. Know it now, that in any case I was his, from whom you stole me. May they who have slandered me all know it now!"

It is her old love that exults in her voice and shines from her eyes. Her husband stands before her with raised fist. She discerns horror and contempt on the fifty faces before her. She senses that it is the final hour of her power. But she cannot keep from rejoicing, as she speaks openly of her life's sweetest memory.

"He was a man, a splendid man. Who are you, that you could put yourself between us? Never have I seen the like of him. He gave me happiness, he gave me property. Blessed be his memory!"

Then the major lowers his raised arm without striking—now he knows how he should punish her.

"Out," he roars, "out of my house!"

She stands still.

But the cavaliers stand, faces pale, staring at each other. Now everything was about to be fulfilled as the black one had foretold. Now they saw the consequences of the majoress's contract not having been renewed. If this is true now, then it must also be true that for more than twenty years she had sent cavaliers to hell and that journey had been prescribed for them too. Oh, that witch!

"Out with you!" continued the major. "Beg for your bread on the highway! You shall not have any happiness from his money, you shall not be allowed to live on his estates. It is over for the majoress at Ekeby. The day you set foot in my house, I am going to kill you."

"Are you driving me away from my home?"

"You have no home. Ekeby is mine."

A spirit of timidity comes over the majoress. She retreats all the way to the door, and he follows closely after her.

"You, who have been the misfortune of my life," she complains, "shall you also have the power to do this to me now?"

"Out, out!"

She leans against the doorpost, clasping her hands together and holding them to her face. She thinks of her mother and mumbles to herself, "May you be denied, as I have been denied, may the highway be your home, a haystack your bed! So it has come to that after all. It has come to that."

It was the good, old dean at Bro and the sheriff from Munkerud who now came up to Major Samzelius and tried to calm him. They told him that he would do best in letting all these old stories rest, let everything be as it was, forget and forgive.

He shakes away the gentle hands from his shoulder. He was terrible to come near, just as Kristian Bergh had been.

"This is not an old story," he shouts. "I have not known a thing before today. Until now I have not been able to punish the adulteress."

With that word the majoress raises her head and regains her former courage.

"Sooner you should leave than I. Do you think I'll give in to you?" she says. And she steps away from the door.

The major does not reply, but he watches her every movement, ready to strike, if he cannot be rid of her in any other way.

"Help me, good gentlemen," she cries, "to get this man bound and carried out, until he regains the use of his mind. Remember who I am and who you are! Think about that, before I have to give in to him! I run all the activities of Ekeby, and he sits all day long, feeding the bears in their cave. Help me, good friends and neighbors! There will be misery without limit here, if I am no longer here. The farmer has his livelihood from cutting my forest and driving my pig iron. The charcoal burner lives off of providing my charcoal, the log floater from transporting my timber. I am the one who doles out the work that brings in riches. Smiths, carpenters, and loggers live by serving me. Do you think that he over there can keep up my work? I am telling you, if you drive me out, you are letting famine in."

Once again a number of hands are raised to help the majoress; once again gentle hands are placed persuasively on the major's shoulder.

"No," he says, "away with you! Who wants to defend the adulteress? I am telling you, I am, that if she does not go willingly, then I will pick her up in my arms and carry her down to my bears."

With these words the raised hands were lowered.

Then, in her utmost distress, the majoress turns to the cavaliers.

"Would you also allow me to be driven from my home, cavaliers? Have I let you freeze outside in the snow in winter, have I denied you bitter beer and sweet liquor? Did I expect reward or work from you, because I gave you food and clothing? Have you not played at my feet, secure as children at their mother's side?

Hasn't there been dancing in my halls? Haven't amusements and laughter been your daily bread? Let not this man, who has been my life's misfortune, drive me away from my home, cavaliers! Do not let me become a beggar on the highway!" With these words Gösta Berling had stolen his way over to a lovely, dark-haired girl, who was sitting at the great table.

"You were at Borg quite a bit five years ago," he says. "Do you know whether it was the majoress who told Ebba Dohna that I was a defrocked minister?"

"Help the majoress, Gösta!" is all the girl can answer.

"You may know that first I want to find out if she made me into a murderer."

"Ah, Gösta, what kind of thoughts are those? Help her, Gösta!"

"You don't want to answer, I see. So Sintram has probably told the truth." And Gösta goes back down among the cavaliers. He does not lift a finger to help the majoress.

Oh, if only the majoress had not sat the cavaliers at a separate table over in the corner by the tiled stove! Now the night's thoughts have wakened in their brains; now wrath is flaring on their faces, not less than the major's own.

In unmerciful hardness they stand silent at her entreaties.

Must everything they see attest to the visions of the night?

"It shows that she hasn't got her contract renewed," murmurs one.

"Go to hell, troll hag!" shrieks another. "By rights it should have been us who chased you to the door."

"Blockheads," old, feeble uncle Eberhard calls to the cavaliers, "don't you realize that it was Sintram?"

"Of course we understand, of course we know," answers Julius, "but what of it! Can't it be true anyway? Doesn't Sintram do the devil's business? Haven't they made an agreement?"

"Go then, Eberhard, you go and help her!" they mock. "You don't believe in hell. Go then!"

And Gösta Berling stands quietly, without a word, without a movement.

No, from this threatening, murmuring, combative cavaliers' wing the majoress will get no help.

Now she again backs up to the door and raises her clasped hands to her eyes.

"May you be denied, as I have been denied!" she calls out to herself in her bitter sorrow. "May the highway be your home, a haystack your bed!"

Then she places one hand on the door handle, but the other she raises toward the sky.

"Mark this, you, who now let me fall! Mark this, that your hour will soon come! Now you will be scattered, and your place will stand empty. How will you stand, when I do not support you? You, Melchior Sinclaire, who has a heavy hand and lets his wife feel it, watch out! You, minister of Broby, now comes the punishment! Mrs. Captain Uggla, see to your house, poverty is coming! You young, beautiful women, Elisabet Dohna, Marianne Sinclaire, Anna Stjärnhök, do not believe that I am the only one who must flee from my home. And watch you, you cavaliers, now a storm is coming across the land. Now you will be wiped away from the earth, now your day is past, now it is truly past! I do not complain for myself, but for you, for the storm will pass over your heads, and who will stand when I have fallen? And my heart laments for the poor people. Who will give them work when I am gone?"

Now the majoress opens the door, but then Captain Kristian raises his head and says: "How long must I lie here at your feet, Margareta Celsing? Will you not forgive me, so that I may stand up and fight for you?"

Then the majoress fights a hard battle with herself, but she sees that if she forgives him, then he will rise up and fight with her husband, and the man who has faithfully loved her for forty years will become a murderer.

"Shall I forgive now too?" she says. "Are you not the cause of all my misfortune, Kristian Bergh? Go to the cavaliers, and be pleased with your work!"

Then the majoress left. She left calmly, leaving dismay behind her. She fell, but she was not without greatness even in her degradation. She did not lower herself to effeminate sorrow, but still in old age she rejoiced over the love of her youth. She did not lower herself to complaint and piteous weeping, as she left every-thing; she did not tremble at the thought of wandering around the countryside with walking stick and beggar's pouch. She only felt sorry for the poor farmers and the happy, carefree people on the shore of Löven, for the poor cavaliers, for all of those whom she had protected and maintained.

She was abandoned by everyone, and yet she had power to reject her last friend so as not to make him a murderer.

She was a remarkable woman, great in vigor and desire for action. We will not soon see her like.

The next day Major Samzelius departed from Ekeby and moved to his own farm, Sjö, which is very close to the main ironworks.

In Altringer's will, through which the major got the iron-works, it was clearly arranged that none of the works could be sold or given away, but rather after the major's death they would all go in inheritance to his wife or her heirs. As the major thus could not embezzle the hated inheritance, he put the cavaliers to rule over it, that he might thereby do Ekeby and the other six ironworks the greatest damage.

As no one in the province doubted that the malevolent Sintram did the devil's business, and as everything he had promised them was so brilliantly fulfilled, the cavaliers were quite certain that the contract would be fulfilled to the letter, and they were com-pletely decided not to do anything wise or useful or womanish during the year, completely convinced as they were that the ma-joress was an evil witch, who wanted their ruin.

Old uncle Eberhard, the philosopher, ridiculed their faith, but who asked the opinion of such a person, who was so stubborn in his disbelief that if he was lying in the midst of the flames of the abyss and saw all the devils standing and sneering at him, he would still have maintained that they did not exist, because they could not exist, for uncle Eberhard was a great philosopher.

Gösta Berling did not tell anyone what he believed. It is cer-tain that he scarcely felt a debt of gratitude to the majoress for having made him a cavalier at Ekeby; it seemed better to him now to be dead than to continue on with the awareness that he had been guilty of Ebba Dohna's suicide. He did not raise his hand to take revenge on the majoress, but not to help her either. He was not capable of it. But the cavaliers had come to great power and glory. Christmas was at hand with parties and amusements, the hearts of the cavaliers were filled with rejoicing, and whatever sorrow may have weighed on Gösta Berling, he did not show it on his face or on his lips.

CHAPTER 4

GÖSTA BERLING, THE POET

It was Christmas, and there was to be a ball at Borg.

At that time—and soon it will be sixty years ago—a young Count Dohna was living at Borg; he was newly married, and he had a young, beautiful countess. It would no doubt be merry at the old count's estate.

An invitation had also come to Ekeby, but it turned out that of all those who were celebrating Christmas there that year, Gösta Berling, whom they called "the poet," was the only one who had any desire to go.

Borg and Ekeby are both on Löven's long lake, but on opposite shores. Borg is in Svartsjö parish, Ekeby in Bro. When the lake cannot be crossed, it is a six- or seven-mile journey from Ekeby to Borg.

The impoverished Gösta Berling was outfitted for the party by the older gentlemen as if he had been a king's son and had to bear up the honor of a kingdom.

The tailcoat with its gleaming buttons was new; the ruffles were starched and the leather shoes shined. He wore a fur of the finest beaver skin and a sable cap over his light, curly hair. They spread out a bear hide with silver claws across his sleigh and gave him the black Don Juan, pride of the stable, to drive.

He whistled to his white dog Tancred and grasped the braided reins. Rejoicing he drove, surrounded by the shimmer of wealth and pomp, he who shone enough already with the beauty of his body and the playful genius of his spirit.

He left early in the morning. It was Sunday, and as he drove past he heard hymn singing from Bro church. Then he followed the desolate forest road that leads to Berga, where Captain Uggla was then living. There he intended to stop for dinner.

Berga was not a rich man's home. Hunger knew the way to the turf-covered captain's residence, but Gösta was received with humor, enjoyed songs and games like other guests, and left as unwillingly as they.

Old Miss Ulrika Dillner, who managed chores and weaving at Berga farm, stood on the steps and welcomed Gösta Berling. She curtsied to him, and the loose curls that hung down over her brown face with its thousand wrinkles were dancing with joy. She led him into the hall, and then she started to tell about the people at the farm and their varied fates.

Distress was at the door, she said, grim times prevailed at the Berga farm. They did not even have any horseradish for dinner with their salted meat; Ferdinand and the girls had set Disa to a sleigh and driven down to Munkerud to borrow some.

The captain was off in the woods again and would no doubt come home with a tough rabbit, which would cost more in butter to prepare than it was worth itself. That's the sort of thing he called getting food for the household. Somehow it would all work out, if he didn't come back with a wretched fox, the worst animal our Lord created, useless both dead and alive.

And the captain's wife, well, she was not up yet. She lies there reading novels, just as she does every day. She was not created to work, that angel of God.

No, someone who was old and gray like Ulrika Dillner would have to do that. It was tramp, tramp night and day to hold the misery together. And it wasn't always so easy, for the truth was that one whole winter they had not had any meat there in the house other than bear ham. And she expected no great reward, nor had she seen any, but she expected they would not throw her out on the road either, when she no longer could do her share for her food. They regard even a housemaid as a person in this household, and one day they would no doubt give old Ulrika an honorable burial, if they had anything to buy a casket with.

"For who can know how it will work out?" she exclaims, drying her eyes, which were always so quick to tear up. "We have debts with the malevolent mill owner Sintram, and he can take all of it away from us. To be sure, Ferdinand is now engaged to the wealthy Anna Stjärnhök, but she is getting tired, she is getting tired of him. And what will become of us then with our three cows and our nine horses, with our cheerful young girls, who want to go from ball to ball, with our dry fields, where nothing grows, with our kind Ferdinand, who will never become a rich man! What will become of this entire blessed house, where everything thrives, except the work?"

But it was dinnertime, and the household gathered. Kind Ferdinand, the gentle son of the house, and the merry daughters came home with the borrowed horseradish. The captain came, energized by a swim in a hole in the ice in the marsh and a hunt in the forest. He threw open the window to get some air and shook Gösta's hand with manly force. And the captain's wife came, dressed in silk, with broad lace falling down over her white hands, which Gösta was allowed to kiss.

Everyone greeted Gösta with joy, the jokes came flying into the circle, and merrily they asked him, "How are you all doing at Ekeby, how are you doing in the promised land?"

"Milk and honey are flowing there," he answered then. "We empty the hills of iron and fill our cellars with wine. The fields wear gold, from which we gild the misery of life, and we cut down our forests to build ninepin alleys and summerhouses."

But the captain's wife sighed and smiled at the reply, and a single word forced its way across her lips: "Poet!"

"I have many sins on my conscience," answered Gösta, "but I have never written a line of poetry."

"You are still a poet, Gösta; you will have to bear that nickname. You have lived more poems than our poets have written."

Then the captain's wife spoke, gentle as a mother, about his squandered life. "I will live in order to see you become a man," she said. And he felt it sweet to be egged on by this gentle woman, who was such a faithful friend, and whose strong, romantic heart was burning with love for great actions.

But when they finished their cheerful meal and enjoyed the horseradish meat and cabbage and fritters and yule beer and

Gösta had got them to smile and cry by telling about the major
and the majoress and the Broby minister, sleigh bells were heard
in the farmyard, and immediately thereafter the malevolent
Sintram entered the room.

He radiated satisfaction, all the way from his bald head down
to his big, flat feet. His long arms were swinging, and his face was
contorted. It was easy to see that he was bringing bad news.

"Have you heard," asked the malevolent man, "have you
heard that today the banns were read in Svartsjö church for the
first time for Anna Stjärnhök and rich Dahlberg? She must have
forgotten that she was engaged to Ferdinand."

They had not heard a word about it. They were astonished,
and sorrowful.

They were already imagining their home pillaged in order to
pay the debt to the malevolent man: the beloved horses sold, and
likewise the worn furniture, which had been inherited from the
captain's wife's home. They saw the end of the merry life with
parties and journeys from ball to ball. Bear ham would be back
on the table, and the young ones would have to go away and
serve among strangers.

The captain's wife caressed her son and let him feel the consolation of a never-failing love.

And yet—there sat Gösta Berling in the midst of them, and the
unconquerable one was hatching a thousand plans in his head.

"Listen," he cried out, "it is not yet time to think about lamentation. It is the minister's wife down in Svartsjö who has arranged this. She has power over Anna now, since she's living
with her at the parsonage. It is she who has induced her to
abandon Ferdinand and take old Dahlberg, but they are not yet
wed and they aren't going to be either. Now I'm going to Borg
and will see Anna there. I will talk to her, I will tear her away
from the minister, from her fiancé. I will bring her here tonight.
Then old Dahlberg will not get any more good out of her."

So it was. Gösta drove alone to Borg without getting to drive
any of the cheerful girls, but with warm wishes they followed
his journey from home. And Sintram, who rejoiced over the fact
that old Dahlberg would be tricked, decided to stay at Berga in

order to see Gösta return with the unfaithful girl. In an outburst of goodwill, Sintram even draped his green travel sash around him, a gift from Miss Ulrika herself.

But the captain's wife came out on the steps with three small books, bound in red leather, in her hand.

"Take them," she said to Gösta, who was already seated in the sleigh, "take them, if you don't succeed! It is *Corinne*, Madame de Staël's *Corinne*. I do not want them to go to auction."

"I will not fail."

"Oh, Gösta, Gösta," she said, passing her hand across his bare head, "strongest and weakest of people! How long will you remember that the happiness of a few poor people is in your hands!"

Once again Gösta flew along the highway, pulled by the black Don Juan, followed by the white Tancred, and the exultation of adventure filled his soul. He felt like a young conqueror; the spirit was upon him.

His way led him to the parsonage in Svartsjö. He pulled in there and asked if he might not be allowed to drive Anna Stjärnhök to the ball. And indeed he was allowed to. He had a beautiful, willful girl with him in the sleigh. Who wouldn't want to ride behind the black Don Juan!

The young people were silent at first, but then she began the conversation, defiant as rashness itself.

"Have you heard, Gösta, what the minister read out in the church today?"

"Did he say that you are the most beautiful girl between Löven and the Klara River?"

"You are stupid, Gösta; people know that well enough. He read the banns for me and old Dahlberg."

"Verily I would have let you sit in the sleigh and sat myself here in the back, if I had known that. Verily I would not have wanted to drive for you at all."

And the proud heiress replied, "I'm sure I would have made it there without you, Gösta Berling."

"It's a shame, though, Anna," said Gösta meditatively, "that your father and mother are not still alive. Now you are the way you are, and no one can be sure about you."

"It's an even bigger pity that you haven't said that before, then someone else would have gotten to drive me."

"The minister's wife thinks like I do, that you need someone to be in your father's place, otherwise I suppose she wouldn't have put you in harness together with such an old nag."

"It isn't the minister's wife who decided it."

"Oh, dear me, have you picked out such a fine fellow yourself?"

"He isn't taking me for the money."

"No, the old men, they only chase after blue eyes and red cheeks, and dreadfully sweet they are, when they do it."

"Oh, Gösta, have you no shame!"

"But do keep in mind that you are not playing with the young fellows anymore. It's over with dancing and games. Your place is in the corner sofa—or perhaps you intend to play cards with old Dahlberg?"

Then they were silent, until they were driving up the steep hills at Borg.

"Thanks for the ride! It will be some time before I ride with Gösta Berling again."

"Thanks for the promise! I know many a one who has rued the day he rode with you to a banquet."

Hardly timid, the village's defiant beauty entered the ballroom and surveyed the assembled guests.

First of all she saw little bald-headed Dahlberg by the side of the tall, slender, light-haired Gösta Berling. She had a good desire to drive the both of them out of the room.

Her fiancé came up to invite her to a dance, but she met him with heartbreaking surprise.

"Are you going to dance? You don't usually do that!"

And girls came up to congratulate her.

"Don't show off, girls! You shouldn't think that anyone has fallen in love with old Dahlberg. But he is rich, and I am rich, therefore we suit each other well."

The old women came up to her, pressed her white hand, and spoke of life's greatest happiness.

"Congratulate the minister's wife," she said then. "She's happier about it than I am."

But there stood Gösta Berling, the merry cavalier, greeted with enthusiasm for his healthy smile and for his beautiful words, which showered gold dust over the gray fabric of life. Never before had she seen him the way he was this evening. He was not a reject, an outcast, a homeless jester, no, he was a king among men, a born king.

He and the other young men conspired against her. She would have to think about how badly she behaved when she gave herself away, with her beautiful face and her great wealth, to an old man. And they let her sit for ten dances.

She was seething with fury.

On the eleventh dance a man came, the lowliest among the lowly, a wretch that no one else wanted to dance with, and asked her to dance.

"The bread is gone, the hash can come to the table," she said.

They played a game of forfeits. Light-haired girls put their heads together and sentenced her to kiss the one she liked the most. And with smiling lips they expected to see the proud beauty kiss old Dahlberg.

But she arose, stately in her fury, and said, "May I not just as well slap the face of the one I like the least?"

The following moment Gösta's cheek burned under her steady hand. He turned flaming red, but he kept his composure, grasped her hand, holding it fast for a second, and whispered, "Meet me in half an hour in the red drawing room on the ground floor!"

His blue eyes sparkled down on her and surrounded her with chains of enchantment. She felt that she must obey.

She met him there with pride and harsh words.

"What concern is it of Gösta Berling whom I marry?"

He did not yet have tender words on his lips, nor did it seem advisable to speak of Ferdinand at once.

"To me it does not seem too severe a punishment that you had to sit for ten dances. But you want permission to break vows and promises unpunished. If a better man than I had taken the punishment in his hands, he might have made it harder."

"What have I done to all of you that I can't be left in peace? You are persecuting me because of the money. I will throw it into Löven, then whoever wants it can fish it out."

She put her hands to her face and wept bitterly.

This touched the poet's heart. He was ashamed of his severity. He spoke in a soothing tone of voice.

"Oh, child, child, forgive me! Forgive poor Gösta Berling! No one cares what a wretch like him says or does, you know that. No one cries over his wrath; you might just as well cry over a mosquito bite. It was madness, but I wanted to prevent our most beautiful and richest girl from marrying that old man. And now I have only distressed you."

He sat down on the sofa beside her. Slowly he placed his arm around her waist in order to support and hold her up with caressing tenderness.

She did not withdraw. She pressed herself against him, threw her arms around his neck, and wept with her lovely head leaning against his shoulder.

Oh, poet, strongest and weakest among people, it was not around your neck those white arms should rest.

"If I had known this," she whispered, "never would I have taken the old man. I have been watching you this evening; no one is like you."

But between pale lips Gösta forced out, "Ferdinand."

She silenced him with a kiss.

"He is nothing, no one is anything more than you. To you I will be faithful."

"I am Gösta Berling," he said gloomily, "you cannot marry me."

"You are the one I love, you are the finest of men. You don't need to do anything, be anything. You were born a king."

Then the poet's blood was seething. She was lovely and sweet in her love. He enclosed her in his arms.

"If you want to be mine, you cannot stay in the parsonage. Let me drive you up to Ekeby this night; there I will know how to defend you until we celebrate our wedding."

A turbulent ride in the night ensued. Obeying the call of love, they let Don Juan carry them away. It was as if the creaking under the runners were the complaint of the betrayed. What did they care about that? She was hanging on to his neck, and he leaned forward and whispered in her ear, "Can any bliss compare in sweetness to stolen joy?"

What did reading the banns mean? They had love. And people's wrath? Gösta Berling believed in fate, fate had compelled them: no one can fight against fate.

If the stars had been wedding candles, which had been lit for her wedding, if Don Juan's bells had been church bells, calling people to witness her marriage to old Dahlberg, then she still would have had to flee with Gösta Berling. Fate is that powerful.

They had come safely past the parsonage and Munkerud. They had about a mile and a half left to Berga and then three miles over to Ekeby. The road passed along the forest edge; to the right of them were dark hills, to the left a long, white valley.

Then Tancred came rushing up. He ran so that he seemed to be above the ground. Howling with terror, he jumped up into the sleigh and cowered next to Anna's feet.

Don Juan started and set off, out of control.

"Wolves!" said Gösta Berling.

They saw a long, gray line stretching out along the stone fence. There were at least a dozen of them.

Anna was not afraid. The day had been well blessed with adventures, and the night promised to be its like. This was life—rushing along over sparkling snow, defying wild animals and people.

Gösta swore, leaned forward, and gave Don Juan a powerful rap with the whip.

"Are you afraid?" he asked.

"They intend to intercept us up there, where the road curves."

Don Juan ran, running a race with the wild animals of the forest, and Tancred howled in fury and fear. They reached the curve in the road at the same time as the wolves, and Gösta drove off the foremost one with the whip.

"Oh, Don Juan, my boy, how easily you would escape from twelve wolves, if you didn't have us people to drag along."

They tied the green travel sash behind them. The wolves were afraid of it and for a time kept at a distance. But when they overcame their fear, one of them ran, panting, with tongue hanging and jaws open, up to the sleigh. Then Gösta took Madame de Staël's *Corinne* and threw it into his jaws.

Again they gained a moment's breathing room, while the animals tore apart this booty, and then again they felt the tugging, as the wolves tore at the green travel sash, and heard their panting breath. They knew that they would not encounter any human dwellings before Berga, but it seemed worse than death to Gösta to see those whom he had betrayed. He also understood that the horse would tire, and what would become of them then?

Then they saw Berga farm at the forest edge. Lights were burning in the windows. Gösta knew well enough for whose sake.

Yet—now the wolves were fleeing, fearful of the nearness of humans, and Gösta drove past Berga. Nevertheless he came no farther than to the place where the road plunges into the forest anew, where he saw a dark group ahead of him—the wolves were awaiting him.

"Let's turn around to the parsonage and say that we've been having a pleasure ride in the starlight. This won't do."

They turned, but at the next moment the sleigh was surrounded by wolves. Gray forms could be seen flashing past them, white teeth shining in wide-open jaws, and the glowing eyes shining. They were howling with hunger and blood-thirst. Their gleaming teeth were ready to cut into tender human flesh. The wolves were jumping up onto Don Juan and hung fast onto the harness. Anna sat, wondering whether they would eat her up completely, or if something would be left so that the next morning people would find torn-apart limbs on the trampled, bloody snow.

"Now it's a matter of life and death," she said, bowing down and gripping Tancred by the neck.

"Let him be, it won't help! It's not for the dog's sake that the wolves are out tonight!"

With that Gösta drove into Berga farm, but the wolves pursued him all the way up to the steps. He had to defend himself against them with the whip.

"Anna," he said, as they stopped at the steps, "God did not want this. Keep a good face now, if you are the woman I take you for, keep a good face!"

Inside they heard the clang of bells and came out.

"He has her," they called, "he has her! Long live Gösta Berling!" And the new arrivals were torn from embrace to embrace.

Not many questions were asked. The night was far advanced, the travelers were shaken by their dangerous journey and needed to rest. It was enough that Anna had come.

All was well. Only *Corinne* and the green travel sash, Miss Ulrika's esteemed gift, were destroyed.

The whole house was sleeping. Then Gösta got up, dressed, and slipped out. Completely unnoticed he took Don Juan out of the stall, set him before the sleigh, and intended to take off. Then Anna Stjärnhök came out of the house.

"I heard you go out," she said. "Then I got up too. I am ready to leave with you."

He went up to her and took her hand.

"Don't you understand yet? This cannot happen. God does not want it to. Listen now and try to understand. I was here at dinner and saw their laments over your faithlessness. Then I went to Borg to bring you back to Ferdinand. But I have always been a wretch and will never be otherwise. I betrayed him and kept you for my own account. Here is an old woman who believes I will become a man. I betrayed her. And another poor old thing will freeze and starve here simply to be able to die among friends, but I was ready to let the malevolent Sintram take her home. You were lovely, and sin was sweet. Gösta Berling is so easy to entice. Oh, what a wretch I am!—I know how much they love their home, the people inside, but still only just now I was ready to leave it to be pillaged. I forgot everything for your sake, you were so sweet in your love. But now, Anna, now since I have seen their joy, I do not want to keep you, no, I don't want to. You are the one who would have made a human being out of me, but I may not keep you. Oh, you my beloved! He up there is playing with our will. Now it is time that we bow ourselves under his chastising hand. Say that from this day on you will take your burden upon yourself! Inside there all of them are counting on you. Say that you want to stay with them and become their support and help! If you love me, if you will ease my deep sorrow, then promise me this! My beloved, is your heart so big that it can conquer itself and smile at it?"

She received the message of privation with enthusiasm.

"I will do what you want—sacrifice myself and smile at it."

"And not hate my poor friends?"

She smiled mournfully. "As long as I love you, I will love them."

"Now for the first time I know what kind of woman you are. It is heavy to leave you."

"Farewell, Gösta! Go now with God! My love shall not lure you into sin!"

She turned to go inside. He followed her.

"Will you soon forget me?"

"Go now, Gösta! We are only human."

He threw himself down on the sleigh, but then she came back.

"Aren't you thinking about the wolves?"

"I am thinking about just them, but they have done their work. They have nothing more to do with me tonight."

Once again he extended his arms to her, but Don Juan became impatient and set off. He did not pick up the reins. He sat, turned around, and looked back. Then he leaned against the frame and cried in despair.

"I have possessed happiness and driven it away from me. I myself drove her away from me. Why didn't I keep her?"

Oh, Gösta Berling, strongest and weakest among people!

CHAPTER 5

LA CACHUCHA

Warhorse, warhorse! Old one, now standing tethered on the field, do you recall your youth?

Do you recall the day of battle, courageous one? You sprang forth as if you were borne by wings, your man floated above you like flickering flames, on your black brisket splashes of blood glistened among frothy foam. In a harness of gold you sprang forth, the ground thundering beneath you. You shivered with pleasure, courageous one. Oh, how lovely you were!

It is a gray, twilight hour up in the cavaliers' wing. In the large room the cavaliers' red-painted cases stand along the walls, and their feast-day clothes hang on hooks in the corner. The firelight from the fireplace plays on white-plastered walls and on gold-checked curtains that conceal the box beds on the walls. The cavaliers' wing is not a royal state room, not a seraglio with upholstered divans and soft pillows.

But from within, Lilliecrona's fiddle is heard. He is playing "La Cachucha" in the twilight. Over and over again he plays it.

Cut off the strings, break apart the bow! Why is he playing this confounded dance? Why is he playing it just when Örneclou, the lieutenant, is lying ill with gout pains so severe that he can't move in his bed? No, tear the fiddle from him and throw it against the wall, if he won't stop!

La cachucha, is that for us, maestro? Will it be danced across the tottering floorboards of the cavaliers' wing, between cramped walls, blackened with smoke and greasy with grime, under its low ceiling? Curse you, the way you play!

La cachucha, is that for us, for us cavaliers? Outside the snowstorm howls. Do you mean to teach the snowflakes to dance in rhythm, are you playing for the light-footed children of the blizzard?

Female bodies, which tremble under the pulse beat of hot blood, small sooty hands, which have thrown aside the cooking pot to grasp the castanets, naked feet under tucked-up skirts, yard coated with flakes of marble, crouching gypsies with bagpipe and tambourine, Moorish arcades, moonlight and black eyes, do you have those, maestro? If not, let the fiddle rest!

Cavaliers are drying their wet clothes by the fire. Should they swirl around in their tall boots with iron-shod heels and thumb-thick soles? They have waded through the ell-deep snow the whole day to reach the bear's winter lair. Do you think they should dance in their wet, steaming homespun clothes, with the shaggy bruin as a partner?

Evening sky, glittering with stars, red roses in dark female hair, tormenting sweetness in the evening air, untaught grace in the movements, love rising out of the earth, raining from the sky, hovering in the air, do you have this, maestro? If not, why force us to long for such things?

Cruelest of men, are you sounding the attack for a tethered warhorse? Rutger von Örneclou is lying in his bed, imprisoned by gout pains. Spare him the torment of sweet memories, maestro! He too has worn a sombrero and a gaudy hairnet, he too has owned a velvet jacket and a sash with a dagger tucked in it. Spare old Örneclou, maestro!

But Lilliecrona plays *la cachucha*, always *la cachucha*, and Örneclou is tormented like the lover who sees the swallow make its way to his beloved's distant dwelling; like the stag who is chased past the refreshing spring by the hastening drive.

Lilliecrona takes the fiddle from his chin for a moment.

"Lieutenant, do you remember Rosalie von Berger?"

Örneclou swears a terrible oath.

"She was light as a candle flame. She glistened and danced like the diamond at the tip of the bow. I'm sure you remember her from the theater in Karlstad. We saw her when we were young, do you remember, lieutenant?"

And the lieutenant remembered! She was small and breathless. She was sparklingly fiery. She could dance *la cachucha*. She taught all the bachelors in Karlstad to dance *la cachucha* and snap the castanets. At the governor's ball a *pas de deux* was danced by the lieutenant and Miss von Berger, costumed as Spaniards.

And he had danced the way you dance under the fig trees and plane trees, like a Spaniard, a real Spaniard.

No one in all of Värmland could dance *la cachucha* like him. No one could dance it, so that it was worth mentioning, better than he.

What a cavalier Värmland lost, when the gout stiffened his legs and large bumps grew over his joints! What a cavalier he had been, so slender, so beautiful, so knightly! Handsome Örneclou he was called by those young girls who could have fallen into mortal feud over a dance with him.

Then Lilliecrona again starts *la cachucha*, always *la cachucha*, and Örneclou is carried back to old times.

There he stands, and there she stands, Rosalie von Berger. They had just been alone together in the changing room. She was a Spaniard, he a Spaniard. He was allowed to kiss her, but carefully, for she was afraid of his blackened mustaches. Now they are dancing. Ah, the way you dance under fig trees and plane trees: she gives way, he follows, he becomes bold, she proud, he wounded, she conciliatory. When at last he falls to his knees and receives her in his outstretched arms, a sigh passes through the ballroom, a sigh of rapture.

He had been like a Spaniard, a real Spaniard.

Just at that bow stroke he had bowed like that, stretched his arms like that, and set forth his foot in order to float forward on tiptoe. What grace! He could have been chiseled in marble.

He does not know how it happened, but he has got his foot over the edge of the bed, he is standing upright, he is bowing, he raises his arms, snaps his fingers, and wants to float forward across the floor in the same way as before, when he used such tight shiny leather shoes that the stocking foot had to be cut away.

"Bravo, Örneclou! Bravo, Lilliecrona, play some life into him!"

His foot betrays him; he cannot get up on tiptoe. He kicks with one leg a few times, but no more than that; he again falls down on the bed.

Handsome *señor*, you have grown old.

Perhaps the *señorita* has as well?

It is only under the plane trees of Granada that *la cachucha* is danced by eternally young gypsies. Eternally young, like the roses are, because every spring there are new ones.

So the time has come to cut off the fiddle strings.

No, play, Lilliecrona, play *la cachucha*, always *la cachucha*!

Teach us that although we in the cavaliers' wing now have sluggish bodies and stiff limbs, yet in our feelings we are always the same, always Spaniards.

Warhorse, warhorse!

Say that you love the sounding trumpet, which lures you away at a gallop, even if you tug your foot bloody on the iron links of the tether!

CHAPTER 6

THE BALL AT EKEBY

Oh, women of bygone ages!

To speak of you is like speaking of heaven: you were pure beauty, pure light. Eternally youthful, eternally lovely and tender as a mother's eyes, when she looks down at her child. Soft as young squirrels you curled around a man's neck. Never did your voices quiver with rage, never did your brows furrow, never did your gentle hands become rough and hard. Sweet vestals, you stood like jeweled images in the temple of the home. Incense and prayers were offered to you, through you love performed its miracles, and poetry affixed a gold-gleaming halo around your head.

Oh, women of bygone ages, this is the story of how yet another one of you gave Gösta Berling her love.

A fortnight after the ball at Borg there was a party at Ekeby.

What a party it was! Old men and women would turn young again, smiling and happy, if they as much as spoke of it.

But no wonder, for at that time the cavaliers were sole masters of Ekeby. The majoress was wandering around the countryside with a beggar's purse and cane, and the major was living at Sjö. He could not even be present at the party, for smallpox had broken out at Sjö, and he was afraid of spreading the contagion further.

What a wealth of enjoyment was packed into those twelve sweet hours, starting with the popping of the cork of the first wine bottle at the dinner table up to the final stroke of the fiddle, when midnight had long since passed. Down they sank into the abyss of time, those spangled hours, enchanted by fiery wine, by the most luscious food, by the grandest music, by the cleverest plays, by the loveliest tableaux. Down they sank, dizzy from the most delirious dance. Where else could be found such smooth floors, such courtly cavaliers, such beautiful women!

Oh, women of bygone ages, well you understood how to brighten up a ball. Currents of fire, of genius and youthful energy, coursed through anyone who approached you. It was worth the effort to squander your gold on the wax candles that would light up your fairness, on the wine that fostered the merriment in your hearts; for your sake it was worth the effort to dance the soles of your shoes to dust and wear out the arm that wielded the fiddle bow.

Oh, women of bygone ages, it was you who held the key to the gate of paradise.

The halls of Ekeby are swarming with the sweetest of your sweet company. There is the young Countess Dohna, sparklingly happy and desirous of play and dance, as befits her twenty years; and there are the beautiful daughters of the judge at Munkerud and the happy misses of Berga; there is Anna Stjärnhök, a thousand times more beautiful than before in the tender melancholy that has come over her ever since that night when she was pursued by the wolves; there are many more as well, who are not yet forgotten, I suppose, but soon will be; and there is also the beautiful Marianne Sinclaire.

She—the celebrated one, who had shone at the king's court, glistened in the castles of counts, the queen of beauty, who has traveled around the countryside and received homage everywhere; she, who struck the spark of love wherever she appeared, had condescended to come to the cavaliers' ball.

At that time the honor of the province of Värmland was held high, borne by many proud names. The happy children of that beautiful land had much to be proud of, but when they mentioned their glorious ones, they never neglected to mention Marianne Sinclaire.

The saga of her conquests filled the land.

There was talk of the crowns of counts that had hovered over her head, of the millions that had been laid at her feet, of the warriors' swords and poets' wreaths, whose brilliance enticed her.

And not only was she beautiful. She was brilliant and erudite. The best men of the day were happy to converse with her.

She herself was not an author, but many of her ideas, the seeds of which she planted in the souls of her poetic friends, came alive in verse.

She seldom remained for long in Värmland, in bear country. Her life was spent in constant travels. Her father, the wealthy Melchior Sinclaire, sat at home at Björne with his wife, allowing Marianne to travel to her distinguished friends in the great cities or at the grand estates. His enjoyment was in telling about all the money she went through, and both of the old people lived happily in the sheen from Marianne's radiant existence.

Her life was a life of amusements and applause. The air around her was love, love was her light and lantern, love her daily bread.

She herself had often loved—often, often—but never had such a fire of desire lasted long enough so that the shackles that bind for life could be forged.

"I'm waiting for him, the strong one who will take me by storm," she used to say about love. "Until now he hasn't climbed over any walls or swum across any moats. He has come tamely, without wildness in his gaze and madness in his heart. I await the mighty one, who will carry me out of myself. I want to know love so strong within me, that I tremble at the thought of him; now I only feel the kind of love at which my prudence smiles."

Her presence gave fire to the conversation, life to the wine. Her glowing soul raised the tempo in the fiddle bows, and the dance floated in sweeter delirium than before across the boards she touched with her dainty foot. She was radiant in the tableaux, she brought genius to the comedies, her lovely lips . . .

Oh, hush, it wasn't her fault, it was never her intention! It was the balcony, it was the moonlight, the lace veil, the knight's attire, the song, that were to blame. These poor young people were innocent.

All this that led to so much misfortune was done, however, with the best of intentions. Squire Julius, who was knowledgeable about everything, had arranged a tableau, solely so that Marianne could shine in all her brilliance.

In the theater that was set up in the large salon at Ekeby, the hundred guests sat watching the yellow moon of Spain wander across a dark night sky on the stage. A Don Juan came stealthily along the street in Seville and stopped under an ivy-clad balcony. He was disguised as a monk, though an embroidered cuff could be seen sticking out under his sleeve and the point of a shining rapier under the hem of his robe.

The disguised one raised his voice in song:

> The mouth of no girl do I kiss
> nor raise my lips to goblet's rim
> a foaming glass of wine.
> A cheek whose skin a pale caress
> a glance from me has set on fire
> such looks do not my heart inspire,
> a gaze in search of mine.

> Come not to the grated window,
> *señora*, with your beauty fair!
> Away from you I shrink.
> A rosary and cowl to show
> my heart is in the Virgin's care,
> and water, should the fever flare,
> my one consoling drink.

When he fell silent, Marianne came out onto the balcony, dressed in black velvet and a lace veil. She leaned out over the railing and sang, slowly and ironically:

> Why do you tarry, pious man,
> at midnight at my balcony?
> Do you pray for my soul?

But then suddenly warmly and lively:

> No, quickly flee! Someone may come.
> Your rapier will be seen 'ere long.
> They hear, despite all sacred song,
> spurs jingling at your heels.

At these words the monk cast off his disguise, and Gösta Berling stood under the balcony in a silk and gold knight's costume. He did not heed the beauty's warning, but on the contrary he climbed up one of the balcony posts, swung himself over the balustrade, and just as Squire Julius had arranged it, fell to his knees at the feet of the lovely Marianne.

She smiled fetchingly at him, as she extended her hand for him to kiss, and while the two young people were looking at each other, absorbed in love, the curtain fell.

And before her was Gösta Berling, his face pliant as a poet's and bold as a commander's, with deep eyes, glistening with roguishness and genius, that begged and coaxed. He was lithe and powerful, fiery and captivating.

While the curtain went up and down, the two young people remained standing in the same position. Gösta's eyes held fast the beautiful Marianne, they begged, they coaxed.

The applause died out, the curtain remained still; no one could see them.

Then the beautiful Marianne leaned down and kissed Gösta Berling. She didn't know why; she had to. He extended his arms around her head and held her tight. She kissed him again and again.

But it was the balcony, it was the moonlight, it was the lace veil, the knight's costume, the song, the applause, that were all to blame; these poor young people were innocent. They hadn't wished for this. Nor had she turned down noble crowns, which had hovered over her head, and left behind the millions that had lain at her feet, out of longing for Gösta Berling; nor had he already forgotten Anna Stjärnhök. No, they were without guilt; neither of them had wished for this.

It was gentle Lövenborg, with a tear in his eye and a smile on his lips, who was the curtain puller that day. Distracted by many sorrowful memories, he took scarce notice of the things of this world and had never learned to manage them properly. When he saw that Gösta and Marianne had taken a new position, he believed that this too was part of the tableau, and so he began to pull on the curtain rope.

The young people on the balcony noticed nothing, until the storm of applause again came thundering toward them.

Marianne gave a start and tried to flee, but Gösta held her fast, whispering:

"Be still now, they think this is part of the tableau."

He felt how her body shuddered and how the fervor of the kisses died out on her lips.

"Don't be afraid," he whispered, "lovely lips have the right to kiss."

They had to remain standing, while the curtain went up and down, and each time the hundred pairs of eyes saw them, just as many hands thundered forth a storm of applause.

For it is lovely to see two beautiful, young people portraying the happiness of love. No one could believe that these kisses were anything other than theatrical illusion; no one suspected that the *señora* was trembling with shame and the knight from worry. No one could believe that the whole thing wasn't part of the tableau.

Finally Marianne and Gösta were standing behind the stage.

She drew her hand across her forehead toward the hairline.

"I don't understand myself," she said.

"For shame, Miss Marianne," he said, grimacing and throwing out his hands. "Kissing Gösta Berling, for shame!"

Marianne had to laugh.

"Everyone knows that Gösta Berling is irresistible. My mistake is no greater than others'."

And they agreed in perfect accord to put on a good face, so that no one would suspect the truth.

"Can I be sure that the truth will never come out, Gösta?" she asked, as they were about to join the audience.

"That you can, Miss Marianne. The cavaliers can keep quiet, I can speak for them."

She closed her eyes. A peculiar smile crossed her lips.

"If the truth comes out anyway, what would people think about me, Gösta?"

"They wouldn't think anything, they would know that this means nothing. They would think that we were in character and kept on acting."

Yet another question came stealthily out from under the low-ered eyelids, under the assumed smile.

"But you yourself, Gösta? What do you think about this?"

"I think that Miss Marianne is in love with me," he joked.

"Don't believe such a thing"—she smiled—"or I will have to stab you with this Spanish dagger of mine to show that you are wrong, sir."

"Women's kisses are costly," said Gösta. "Is my life the price for kissing Miss Marianne?"

Then from Marianne's eyes came a glance flashing at him, so sharp that it felt like a slap.

"I want to see you dead, Gösta Berling, dead, dead!"

These words ignited an old longing in the poet's blood.

"Alas," he said, "would that these words were more than words, that they were arrows that came whirring from a dark thicket, that they were a dagger or poison and had the power to destroy this wretched body as well as grant my soul free-dom!"

She was again calm and smiling.

"Childishness," she said, taking his arm to make their way out among the guests.

They kept their costumes on, and their triumphs were re-newed when they showed themselves outside the stage. Every-one praised them. No one suspected anything.

The ball began again, but Gösta fled from the ballroom.

His heart smarted after Marianne's glance, as if it had been wounded by sharp steel. He understood the meaning of her words well enough.

It was shameful to love him, it was shameful to be loved by him, a shame worse than death.

He would never dance again, he never wanted to see them again, those beautiful women.

He knew it well enough. Those lovely eyes, those red cheeks did not blaze for him. Not for him did these light feet hover, subdued laughter ring. Yes, dance with him, feel passionate about him, that they could do; but none of them would have seriously wanted to become his.

The poet made his way into the smoking room with the older

gentlemen and took a seat at one of the gaming tables. He happened to sit down at the same table where the mighty master of Björne was playing *knack*, alternating with Russian bank, and gathering a tall pile of coins in front of him.

The stakes were already high. Now Gösta's arrival made them even more so. Green banknotes were brought out, and the pile of money in front of mighty Melchior Sinclaire steadily kept on growing.

But the coins and banknotes were accumulating in front of Gösta as well, and soon he was the only one holding out in the battle against the great iron magnate at Björne. Soon even that large pile of money made its way from Melchior Sinclaire over to Gösta Berling.

"Gösta, my boy," the mill owner shouted with laughter, as he gambled away everything that was in his wallet and purse. "What should we do now? I'm broke, and I never gamble with borrowed money; I promised my mother that."

He found a way, however. He gambled away his watch and beaver-fur coat, and was just about to wager his horse and sleigh, when Sintram stopped him.

"Wager something to win on," the evil master of Fors advised him. "Wager something that can change your bad luck!"

"Heaven knows what I will come up with then!"

"Play for what's dearest to your heart, Melchior, play for your daughter!"

"You can safely venture that, squire," said Gösta with a laugh. "I'll never bring home those winnings."

The mighty Melchior could do nothing but laugh himself. He was averse to having Marianne's name brought up at the gaming table, but this was so utterly insane that he couldn't get angry. Gamble away Marianne to Gösta, sure, he could gladly venture that.

"That is to say," he explained, "that if you can win her consent, Gösta, then I'll wager my blessing on the marriage on this card here."

Gösta wagered all of his winnings and the play began. He won, and iron magnate Sinclaire stopped playing. He realized that he couldn't fight with bad luck.

The night proceeded onward; midnight had passed. The cheeks of the lovely women started to turn pale, their curls unwind, their flounces wrinkle. The old ladies rose from their sofas and said that since the ball had now lasted for twelve hours, it might be time for them to head home.

And the lovely party should be over, but then Lilliecrona himself took hold of the fiddle and started playing the final *polska*. The horses were waiting by the gate, the old wives were putting on their furs and bonnets, the old gentlemen wound their travel sashes and buttoned their overshoes.

But the young people could not tear themselves away from the dance. They were dancing in their coats, they were dancing every kind of *polska*; the dancing was frantic. As soon as a lady was abandoned by a cavalier, another came and carried her off with him.

And even the melancholy Gösta Berling was pulled into the whirl. He would dance away the sorrow and humiliation, he wanted to have a delirious lust for life in his blood again. He wanted to be happy, he like all the others. And he danced so that the walls of the room were spinning and his mind was whirling.

So, what sort of lady was it he'd carried off with him in the midst of the flock? She was light and lithe, and he knew that currents of fire were passing between him and her. Oh, Marianne!

While Gösta was dancing with Marianne, Sintram was already in his sleigh down in the yard, and next to him stood Melchior Sinclaire.

The great mill owner was impatient at being forced to wait for Marianne. He stamped in the snow in his large overshoes, patting his arms against the bitter cold.

"Perhaps you shouldn't have gambled away Marianne to Gösta, Sinclaire," said Sintram.

"What did you say?"

Sintram put the reins in order and lifted his whip before he replied.

"That kissing wasn't part of the tableau."

The mighty iron magnate raised his arm for a deathblow, but Sintram was already gone. He drove, whipping the horse to a furious speed without daring to look back, for Melchior Sinclaire had a heavy hand and little patience.

The mill owner at Björne went into the ballroom to look for his daughter and saw then how Gösta and Marianne were dancing.

The final *polska* appeared wild and delirious. Some couples were pale, others fiery red; the dust was like smoke in the hall, the wax candles glowing, burned down to the holders, and in the midst of this ghostly destruction Gösta and Marianne were flying along, royal in their inexhaustible strength, their beauty flawless, happy to abandon themselves to glorious motion.

Melchior Sinclaire watched them awhile; but then he left and let Marianne dance. He slammed the door hard, stamped dreadfully in the stairway, and without further ado sat down in the sleigh, where his wife was already waiting, and drove home.

When Marianne finished dancing and asked about her parents, they were gone.

When she knew this for certain, she however showed no surprise. She got dressed silently and went out onto the yard. The women in the dressing room thought she was driving in her own sleigh.

But she hurried in her thin silk shoes along the road without speaking to anyone about her distress. In the darkness no one recognized her as she walked along the side of the road; no one could believe that this late-night wanderer, who was driven up onto the high snowdrifts by sleighs hurrying past, was the beautiful Marianne.

When she could safely be in the middle of the road she began to run. She ran as long as she was able, then she walked, and then she ran again. An appalling, tormenting anxiety was driving her.

From Ekeby to Björne it can't be farther than at the most about a mile and a half. Marianne was soon home, but she almost believed she'd gone the wrong way. As she was approaching the yard, all the doors were closed, all the lights extinguished— perhaps her parents hadn't arrived.

She went up and knocked a few times heavily on the entry door. She took hold of the door handle and shook it, so that it reverberated throughout the house. No one came and opened,

but as she was going to release the iron, which she had taken hold
of with her bare hands, the frozen skin was torn from her hand.

The great iron magnate Melchior Sinclaire had gone home to
close the gates of Björne to his only child.

He was intoxicated from much drinking, wild with rage. He
hated his daughter because she liked Gösta Berling. Now he
locked the servants in the kitchen and his wife in the bedroom.
With solemn oaths he promised them that he would beat sense-
less anyone who tried to let Marianne in. They knew well enough
that he would keep his word.

No one had ever seen him so angry. No greater sorrow had
ever befallen him. If his daughter had appeared before him, perhaps he would have killed her.

He had given her gold jewelry and silk clothes; he had had a
fine sensibility and book learning inculcated in her. She had
been his pride, his honor. He had been as proud of her as if she
wore a crown. Oh, his queen, his goddess, his celebrated, lovely,
proud Marianne! Had he spared anything for her? Had he not
considered himself purely too simple to be her father? Oh,
Marianne, Marianne!

Should he not hate her, when she is in love with Gösta Berling
and kisses him? Should he not reject her, close his door to her,
when she wants to disgrace her loftiness by loving such a man!
Let her stay at Ekeby, let her run to the neighbors to find lodging
for the night, let her sleep in the snowdrifts, it's all the same,
she is already dragged in the filth, the lovely Marianne. Her sheen
is gone. The sheen of her life is gone.

He is lying in his bed in there and hears how she is pounding
on the outside door. What is that to him? He is sleeping. Out
there stands the one who wants to marry a defrocked minister;
he has no home for such a one. If he had loved her less, if he had
been less proud of her, then he might have let her in.

Well, he couldn't deny them his blessing. He'd gambled that
away. But open his door to her, that he wouldn't do. Oh,
Marianne!

The beautiful young woman was still standing outside the door
of her home. By turns she shook the lock in impotent rage, by

turns she fell to her knees, folding her wounded hands and praying for forgiveness.

But no one heard her, no one answered, no one opened.

Oh, wasn't this dreadful! I am seized with alarm, when I tell it. She returned from a ball, where she had been the queen. She had been proud, rich, happy, and within a moment she was cast into such bottomless misery. Locked out of her home, abandoned to the cold, not scorned, not beaten, not cursed, simply locked out with cold, implacable lack of feeling.

I think about the cold, starry night that arched over and around her; the great, expansive night with the empty, deserted fields of snow, with the silent forests. All was sleeping, all was sunk into painless sleep, there was only one living point in all of this slumbering whiteness. All the sorrow and anxiety and terror, which is otherwise doled out across the world, was creeping along toward this lonely point. Oh, God, to suffer alone in the midst of this sleeping, iced-over world!

For the first time in her life she encountered mercilessness and hardness. Her mother didn't care to leave her bed to save her. Old servants, who had guided her first steps, heard her and didn't move a muscle for her sake. For what crime was she being punished? Where could she expect compassion, if not here at this door? If she had murdered, she would still have knocked on it, believing that those inside would forgive her. If she had degenerated into the most wretched of creatures, come devastated and in rags, she would still have gone confidently up to this door and expected a loving welcome. This door was the entrance to her home; behind it she could encounter only love.

Had her father not tested her enough now? Wouldn't they soon open the door?

"Father, Father!" she cried, "let me come in! I'm freezing, I'm shaking! It's terrible out here!"

"Mother, Mother, you who have taken so many steps to serve me. You, who have watched over me so many nights, why are you sleeping just now? Mother, Mother, watch again this one night, and I will never more cause you sorrow!"

She cries out and then sinks into breathless silence to listen for a reply. But no one heard her, no one obeyed her, no one answered.

Then she wrings her hands in anguish, but her eyes have no tears.

The long, dark house with its locked doors and unlit windows is eerily unmoving in the night. What would become of her now that she was homeless? She was branded and disgraced, as long as the sky arched over her. And her father himself was pressing the red-hot iron down into her shoulder.

"Father," she calls yet again, "what will become of me? People will believe everything bad about me."

She wept in agony, her body was stiff with cold.

Woe, that such misery could descend on one who recently stood so high! That it is so easy to be transported into the deepest misery! Why shouldn't we be anxious about life? Who is sailing in a secure vessel? Round about us sorrow swells like a churning sea; see the waves hungrily licking the sides of the ships, see them rush up to board. Oh, no safe redoubt, no solid ground, no secure vessel, as far as the eye can see, only an unknown sky over an ocean of sorrow!

But hush! Finally, finally! Quiet steps are coming through the entry hall.

"Is it you, Mother?" asked Marianne.

"Yes, my child."

"May I come in now?"

"Father doesn't want to let you come in."

"I've run through the snowdrifts in my thin shoes from Ekeby. I've been standing here an hour, pounding and calling. I'm freezing to death out here. Why did you leave without me?"

"My child, my child, why did you kiss Gösta Berling?"

"But tell Father then, it doesn't mean I like him. It was a game. Does he think I want Gösta to be mine?"

"Go to the foreman's quarters, Marianne, and ask if you can stay there tonight. Father is drunk. Father won't listen to reason. He's held me prisoner up there. I slipped out when I thought he was sleeping. He'll kill you, if you come in."

"Mother, Mother, should I go to strangers, when I have a home? Are you as hard-hearted as Father? How can you let this happen, that I'm locked out? I'll lie down in the snowdrift out-side here, if you don't let me in, Mother."

Then Marianne's mother placed her hand on the door handle to open it, but at the same moment heavy steps were heard in the attic stairwell, and a harsh voice was calling her.

Marianne listened: her mother hurried away, the harsh voice cursed her, and then . . .

Marianne heard something dreadful—she could hear every sound from the silent house.

She heard the thud of a blow, of the rap of a cane or a box on the ears, then she detected a faint racket and then once again a blow.

He was beating her mother! The terrifying, the gigantic Mel-chior Sinclaire was beating his wife!

And in wan dismay Marianne, writhing with anxiety, threw herself down on the doorway. Now she was crying, and her tears froze to ice on the threshold of her home.

Mercy, pity! Open, open, so that her own back might bend un-der the blows! Oh, how could he beat Mother, beat her because she didn't want to see her daughter dead in the snowdrift the next day, because she wanted to console her child!

That night a great humiliation fell onto Marianne. She had dreamed she was a queen, and there she lay, hardly better than a whipped thrall.

But she got up in cold rage. Once again she struck her bloody hand against the door and called, "Hear what I'm telling you, you who are beating Mother. You will weep, Melchior Sin-claire, weep!"

Thereupon the lovely Marianne went and laid herself to rest in the snowdrift. She threw off her fur and lay in her black vel-vet dress, easily discernible against the white snow. She lay there and thought about how her father would come out the next day on his early morning walk and find her there. She wished only this, that he himself might find her.

Oh Death, pale friend, is it not as true as it is consoling, that I can never avoid meeting you? Even to me, the dullest of the world's workers, you will come, loosen the worn leather shoe from my foot, tug the whisk and the milk pail from my hand, remove the work clothes from my body. With gentle force you stretch me out on a lace-adorned bed, you adorn me with draping full-length linens. My feet no longer need shoes, but my hands are covered with snow-white gloves that no tasks will soil. Sanctified by you to the sweetness of rest, I sleep a thousand-year sleep. Oh redeemer! The dullest of the world's workers am I, and I dream with a shiver of pleasure of that moment when I will be taken up into your kingdom.

Pale friend, you may freely exercise your force against me, but I will tell you this: your struggle was harder with the women of bygone ages. The power of life was strong in their slender bodies; no cold could cool their hot blood.

You had lain the lovely Marianne on your bed, oh Death, and you sat by her side, as an old nurse sits by the cradle to rock the baby to sleep. You faithful old nurse, who knows what is good for human children, how it must annoy you, when playmates come who waken your sleeping child with noise and commotion. How angry you must have been, when the cavaliers lifted the lovely Marianne from the bed, when a man placed her against his chest, and warm tears fell from his eyes down onto her face.

At Ekeby all the lights were out and all the guests had gone. The cavaliers stood alone in the cavaliers' wing around the final, half-emptied bowl.

Then Gösta tapped on the edge of the bowl and gave a speech for you, women of bygone ages: To speak of you, he said, would be like speaking of heaven; you were pure fairness, pure light. Eternally youthful, eternally lovely and tender as a mother's eyes, when she looks down at her child. Soft as young squirrels you curled around a man's neck. Never was your voice heard quivering with rage, never did your brow furrow, never did your gentle hand become rough and hard. Sweet vestals, you stood like jeweled images in the temple of the home. Incense and prayers were offered to you, through you love performed its miracles, and poetry affixed a gold-gleaming halo around your head.

And the cavaliers leaped up, dizzy with wine, dizzy from his words, their blood rushing in festive joy. Old uncle Eberhard and lazy cousin Kristoffer did not stay out of the game. With blazing speed the cavaliers harnessed the horses to sledge and sleigh and hurried out into the cold night to give homage once again to those who are never honored enough, to sing a serenade to each one of them with the rosy cheeks and the clear eyes that so recently shone in the broad halls of Ekeby.

Oh, women of bygone ages, how it must have pleased you as you journeyed into the sweet heaven of dreams, to be wakened by a serenade from the most faithful of your knights. Well must it please you, as it well pleases a departed soul to be wakened by the sweet music of the heavens.

But the cavaliers did not get far on this pious crusade, for as soon as they had come to Björne, they found the beautiful Marianne lying in the drift, just by the gateway to her home.

They shook with wrath upon seeing her there. It was like finding a venerated saint lying mutilated and plundered outside the gate of the church.

Gösta shook his clenched fist toward the dark house. "You children of hatred," he shouted, "you hailstorms, you northern storms, you devastators of God's paradise!"

Beerencreutz lit his horn lantern and shone it down into the pale-blue face. Then the cavaliers saw Marianne's wounded hands and the tears that had frozen to ice in her eyelashes, and they wailed like women, for she was not only a sacred icon but a beautiful woman, who had been a source of joy for old hearts.

Gösta Berling fell down on his knees beside her.

"Now here she lies, my bride," he said. "She gave me the bridal kiss a few hours ago, and her father has promised me his blessing. She lies waiting for me to come and share her white bed."

And Gösta lifted the lifeless one up in his strong arms.

"Let us take her home to Ekeby!" he cried. "Now she's mine. I've found her in the snowdrift, now no one shall take her from me. We won't waken those people inside there. What would she do there within those doors, against which she has struck her hand bloody?"

He was allowed to do as he wished. He set Marianne down into the first sleigh and sat down by her side. Beerencreutz positioned himself behind and took the reins.

"Rub her with snow, Gösta!" he ordered.

The cold had paralyzed her limbs, but no more than that. Her wildly agitated heart was still beating. She had not even lost consciousness; she was aware of everything about the cavaliers, and how they had found her, but she could not move. So she was lying stiff and rigid in the sleigh, while Gösta Berling rubbed her with snow and alternately wept and kissed her, and she felt an overwhelming desire to be able simply to raise her hand enough that she could return a caress.

She remembered everything. Lying there stiff and unmoving, she thought clearly like never before. Was she in love with Gösta Berling? Yes, she was. Was that simply a fancy for an evening? No, it had existed a long time, for many years.

She compared herself to him and the other people in Värmland. They were all as spontaneous as children. Whatever desire moved them, they followed. They lived only the outer life, had never investigated the depths of their souls. But she had become the sort of person one becomes by traveling out among people; she could never abandon herself completely to anything. When she loved—or whatever she did—it was as though half of her self stood and looked on with a cold sneer. She had longed for a passion to come and pull her along with it in wild recklessness. And now he had arrived, the mighty one. As she kissed Gösta Berling on the balcony, then for the first time she had forgotten herself.

And now the passion again came over her; her heart was beating so that she could hear it. Would she not soon be master of her limbs? She felt a wild joy at being shut out of her home. Now she could be Gösta's without hesitation. How silly she'd been, having suppressed her love for so many years. Oh, it's grand, it's grand to yield to love. But would she ever be free of these chains of ice? She had been ice on the inside and fire on the surface, now it was the other way around, a soul of fire in a body of ice.

Then Gösta feels how two arms slowly rise up around his neck in a weak, powerless embrace.

He barely felt it, but Marianne thought that in her suffocating embrace she had given expression to the bound-up passion inside her.

And when Beerencreutz saw this, he let the horse run as it liked along the familiar road. He raised his gaze and peered stubbornly and unceasingly at the Seven Sisters.

CHAPTER 7

THE OLD CONVEYANCES

Friends, children of humankind! If you should find yourselves reading this at night, whether sitting or lying down, just as I am writing this during the silent hours, then you must not heave a sigh of relief here and think that the good gentlemen cavaliers of Ekeby were allowed an undisturbed sleep, after they had come home with Marianne and found her a good bed in the best guest room next to the large parlor.

They did go to bed, and they did fall asleep, but it was not their lot to sleep in peace and quiet until midday, as it might perhaps have been mine and yours, dear readers, if we had been awake until four and our limbs were aching with fatigue.

After all, it must not be forgotten that at this time the old majoress was wandering around the countryside with her beggar's pouch and walking stick, and that it was never her way, when she had any important business, to show any regard for the comfort of a tired-out sinner. Now she was even less inclined to do so, as she had decided to drive the cavaliers from Ekeby that very night.

Gone was the time when she sat in splendor at Ekeby, sowing joy across the earth, the way God sows stars across the heavens. And while she was wandering homeless around the countryside, the great estate's power and honor was left to be tended by the cavaliers, like the wind tends the ashes, like the spring sun tends the snowdrift.

It sometimes happened that six or eight of the cavaliers would drive out on a long sleigh with a team and sleigh bells and braided reins. If they then encountered the majoress as she wandered like a beggar, they did not lower their eyes.

The boisterous group would raise clenched fists toward her. With a sudden turn of the sleigh she would be forced up into the roadside drifts, and Major Fuchs, the bear killer, always took the opportunity to spit three times to remove any evil effects of this encounter with the hag.

They had no compassion for her. To them she was as ugly as a witch as she walked along the road. If an accident had befallen her, they would not have grieved any more than someone who, firing a loaded shotgun on Easter Eve, grieves over striking a troll hag flying past.

Persecuting the majoress was a matter of salvation to them, the poor cavaliers. People have often been cruel and tormented one another with great severity when they have feared for their souls.

When, far into the night, the cavaliers staggered from the drinking tables over to the windows to see if the night was calm and starlit, they often noticed a dark shadow gliding across the yard, and they understood that the majoress had come to see her beloved home. Then the cavaliers' wing was shaken by the old sinners' scornful laughter, and jeers flew down to her through the open windows.

In truth, lack of feeling and arrogance began to encroach upon the hearts of the cavaliers. Sintram had implanted hatred in them. Their souls would not have been in greater danger if the majoress had remained at Ekeby. More die in flight than during battle.

The majoress did not feel overly angry with these cavaliers.

If the power had been hers, she would have punished them with a birch rod like naughty boys, and afterward given them back her kindliness and favor.

But now she feared for the beloved estate, which was left to be cared for by the cavaliers, the way the wolves watch the sheep, the way the cranes watch the spring grain.

There must be many who have suffered the same sorrow. She is not the only one who has seen destruction ravage a beloved home and knows what it feels like when well-tended farms decline. They have seen their childhood home gaze at them like a wounded animal. Many feel like miscreants, when they see the trees there wither away under mosses and the sanded pathways covered by tufts of grass. They want to throw themselves on their knees on these fields, which in times past gloried in rich harvests, and beg them not to blame them for the shame that has befallen them. And they turn away from the poor old horses; let someone bolder look them in the eye! And they dare not stand at the gate and see the cattle coming home from pasture. No spot on the earth is as odious to enter as a dilapidated home.

Oh, I beg you, all of you who tend fields and meadows and parks and beloved, joy-bringing flower gardens, tend them well! Tend them in love, in labor! It is not good that nature grieves for people.

As I think about what this proud Ekeby must suffer under the governance of the cavaliers, then I wish that the majoress's attack had achieved its goal and that Ekeby had been taken from the cavaliers.

It was not her intention to come back to power herself.

She had but one goal: to free her home from these lunatics, these grasshoppers, these wild robbers, after whose rampaging no grass would grow.

While she went begging around the countryside, living off alms, she constantly had to think of her mother, and the thought took firm hold in her heart, that there would be no respite for her until her mother lifted the curse from her shoulders.

No one had yet reported the old woman's death, so she must still be alive up there at the ironworks in the Älvdal forests. Ninety years of age, she still lived a life of unremitting labor, watching over milk pans in summer, over charcoal stacks in winter, working until her death, longing for the day when she would have completed her life's calling.

And the majoress thought that the old woman must have had to live so long in order to be able to lift the curse from her existence. A mother who had called down such misery on her child would not be allowed to die.

The majoress wanted to go to the old woman so that they both might find peace. She wanted to wander up through the dark forests beside the long river to her childhood home. Until then she would find no peace. There were many who in those days offered her warm homes and gifts of faithful friendship, but she remained nowhere. Bitter and angry she went from farm to farm, for she was oppressed by this curse.

She wanted to wander up to her mother, but first she wanted to care for her beloved estate. She did not want to go and leave it in the hands of irresponsible spendthrifts, of useless drinking champions, of negligent embezzlers of God's gifts.

Should she leave only to return and find her inheritance ravaged, her hammers silent, her horses emaciated, her servants stolen away?

Oh no, once again she would rise up in her power and drive away the cavaliers.

She well understood that her husband gleefully saw that her inheritance was being embezzled. But she knew him well enough to know that if only she were to drive away his grasshoppers, he would be too sluggish to acquire new ones. If the cavaliers were removed, then her old foreman and inspector could manage the activities of Ekeby in the accustomed ways.

And so for many nights her dark shadow had glided along the dark paths of the ironworks. She had sneaked in and out of the crofters' cottages, she had whispered with the miller and the mill hands in the lower floor of the large mill, she had conferred with the smiths in the dark coal shed.

And they had all sworn to help her. The honor and power of the great ironworks would no longer be left to be tended by negligent cavaliers, the way the wind tends the ashes, the way the wolf tends the herd of sheep.

And on this night, when the merry gentlemen had danced, played, and drunk until they had sunk down into their beds in dead-tired slumber, on this night they had to leave. She has let them exult, the carefree ones. She has been sitting in the smithy in bitter expectation, biding her time for the end of the ball. She has waited even longer for the cavaliers to come back again from their nocturnal journey. She has been sitting in silent expectancy, until she was told that the last candle flame was extinguished in the windows of the cavaliers' wing and the great estate was sleeping. Then she got up and went out.

The majoress ordered all the people of the estate to gather by the cavaliers' wing; she herself went ahead up to the courtyard.

There she went up to the main building, knocked, and was admitted. The Broby minister's young daughter, whom she had brought up to be a capable servant, met her.

"My lady is so warmly welcome," the servant said, kissing her hand.

"Blow out the candle!" said the majoress. "Do you think I can't find my way here without a light?"

And then she began her circuit through the silent house. She went from the cellar to the attic and said farewell. With stealthy steps she passed from room to room.

The majoress was conversing with her memories. The servant neither sighed nor sobbed, but tear upon tear flowed unchecked from her eyes as she followed her mistress. The majoress had her open the linen cabinet and the silver cabinet and stroked the fine damask tablecloths and stout silver tankards with her hand. She caressed the massive pile of down bolsters up in the linen closet. All the implements, looms, spinning wheels, and spindles, she had to feel them all. She stuck her hand probingly down into the spice barrel and felt the rows of tallow candles hanging from rods in the ceiling.

"The candles are dry now," she said. "They can be taken down and put away."

She was in the cellar, carefully lifting the beverage barrels and feeling the rows of wine bottles.

She was in the pantry and the kitchen, touching everything, examining everything. She reached out her hand and said farewell to everything in her house.

Finally she went into the living quarters. In the dining hall she felt the top of the large drop-leaf table.

"Many have eaten their fill at this table," she said.

And she proceeded through all the rooms. She found the long, broad sofas in their places; she laid her hand on the cool surfaces of the marble tables, which, borne up by gilded griffins, supported mirrors with a frieze of dancing goddesses.

"This is a wealthy house," she said. "A splendid man he was, who gave me all this to preside over."

In the parlor where the dance had just whirled, the stiff-backed armchairs were already standing rigidly ordered along the walls.

She went over to the clavier and very slowly struck a note.

"Nor have joy and merriment been lacking here in my time either," she said.

The majoress also went into the guest room next to the parlor.

It was coal-black in there. The majoress fumbled around with her hand, ending up right in her servant's face.

"Are you crying?" she said, for she felt her hand wet from tears.

Then the young girl burst into sobs.

"My lady," she cried, "my lady, they will destroy everything. Why does my lady leave us and let the cavaliers devastate her house?"

Then the majoress pulled on the curtain tie and pointed out at the yard.

"Am I the one who taught you to cry and complain?" she exclaimed. "Look outside, the yard is full of people; tomorrow there will no longer be a single cavalier at Ekeby."

"Then will my lady come back again?" asked the servant.

"My time is not yet come," said the majoress. "The highway is my home and the haystack my bed. But you will tend Ekeby for me, girl, while I am away."

And they went on. Neither of them knew or realized that Marianne was sleeping in this very room.

Nor was she asleep. She was wide awake, heard everything, and understood everything.

She had been lying there on the bed, composing a hymn to love.

"You splendid man, who has raised me above myself," she said, "I was in bottomless misery, and you have transformed it into a paradise. On the iron handle of the closed doorway my hands were caught and torn, on the doorstep of my home my tears were frozen into pearls of ice. The chill of anger turned my heart to ice, when I heard the blows on my mother's back. I wanted to sleep away my anger in the cold drift, but you have come. Oh love, you child of fire, you have come to someone frozen through from much cold. If I compare my misery to the splendor I have thereby won, it seems to me nothing. I am freed from all bonds, I have no father, no mother, no home. People will believe everything bad about me and turn away from me. Well, so has it pleased you, oh love, for why should I stand higher than my beloved? Hand in hand we will travel out into the world. Gösta Berling's bride is poor. He found her in the snowdrift. So let us make a nest together, not in high halls, but in a crofter's cottage at the forest edge. I will help him to watch the charcoal pile, I will help him set snares for grouse and hares, I will cook his food and mend his clothes. Oh, my beloved, I will miss you and grieve while I sit alone at the forest edge and await you, do you believe it? I will, I will, but not for days of riches, simply for you, simply for you will I peer and long, for your footsteps on the forest path, for your happy song, as you come with your ax on your back. Oh, my beloved, my beloved! As long as my life continues, I could sit and wait for you."

Thus she had been lying there, composing hymns to the heart's all-governing god, and had not shut her eyes in sleep at all when the majoress came in.

When she was gone, Marianne got up and put on her clothes. Once again she must clothe herself in the black velvet dress and the thin ball shoes. She wrapped the bedcover around her like a shawl and once again hurried out into the dreadful night.

Calm, starlit, and biting cold, the February night still rested over the earth; it was as if it would never come to an end. And the darkness and the cold it spread this long night lasted for a long time on the earth, long after the sun had come up, long after the drifts through which the lovely Marianne had walked had turned to water.

Marianne hurried away from Ekeby to get help. She could not let the men who had lifted her out of the drift and opened their hearts and home to her be driven away. She would go down to Sjö, to Major Samzelius. She was in a hurry. She could not be back for at least an hour.

When the majoress had said farewell to her home, she went out onto the yard, where the people awaited her, and the battle for the cavaliers' wing began.

The majoress positions the people round about the high, narrow building, whose upper story is the cavaliers' renowned home. In the large room up there with the lime-plastered walls, the red-painted chests, and the large drop-leaf table where the *kille* cards swim in spilled liquor, where the broad beds are covered by yellow-checked bed curtains, there the cavaliers are sleeping. Ah, those carefree men!

And in the stable, before a full stall, the cavaliers' horses are sleeping and dream of the journeys of their youth. Sweet it is in the days of rest to dream of youth's wild deeds; of trips to market, when for nights and days they must stay outside under the open sky; of races home from the Christmas morning service; of test-driving before a horse trade, when drunken gentlemen brandishing the reins stretched out of the carriage across their backs and bellowed swear words in their ears. Sweet it is to dream, knowing they will never again leave the filled mangers, the warm stalls of Ekeby. Oh, those carefree ones!

In a shabby old wagon shed, to which broken-down coaches and superannuated sleighs are brought, there is a marvelous collection of old conveyances. There are rack wagons painted green and spindle-sided wagons of red and yellow. There stands the first carriole seen in Värmland, won by Beerencreutz as war booty in the year 1814. There are all imaginable types of one-horse carriages, chaises with rocking springs, and peculiar instruments of torture with the seat resting on wooden springs. There is everything, the murderous "coffee burners" and *halvanningar* and gigs celebrated in song in the days of the highways. And there was the long sleigh that holds twelve cavaliers, and cold cousin Kristoffer's covered sleigh and Örneclou's old family sleigh with the moth-eaten bear hide and a worn coat of arms on the cover as well as the racing sleighs, an infinity of racing sleighs.

Many are the cavaliers who have lived and died at Ekeby. Their names are forgotten on earth, and they no longer have a place in people's hearts, but the majoress has stored away the vehicles in which they came to the estate. She has assembled them all in the old wagon shed.

And in there they stand and slumber and let the dust fall thick, thick upon them.

Nails and spikes loosen their hold in the rotting timber, the paint falls off in long flakes, the stuffing in the cushions and pads pokes out of holes that moths have produced.

"Let us rest, let us fall apart!" say the old conveyances. "We have shaken long enough on the roads, we have drawn quite enough moisture into us during rain showers. Let us rest! It was long ago that we drove off with the young gentlemen to their first ball, it was long ago that we drove out, newly painted and shining, on the sleighing party's sweet adventures, long ago we brought the merry heroes down to the fields of Trossnäs on muddy spring roads. Most of them are sleeping; the last and the best of them never intend to leave Ekeby, never again."

And so the leather in the carriage apron is cracking, the wheel rings loosen, spokes and hubs rot. The old vehicles do not care to live; they want to die.

The dust already lies over them like a funeral pall, and under its cover they let old age have its way with them. In irrepressible idleness they stand there and decay. No one touches them, and still they fall to pieces. Once a year the wagon shed is opened, in the event a new comrade has arrived who wants to settle down in earnest at Ekeby, and as soon as the doors are closed, tiredness, sleep, decay, the weakness of old age settle over this one as well. Rats and rodents and moths and deathwatch beetles and you name it, the predators, throw themselves upon it, and it rusts and rots in dreamless, delightful disquiet.

But now in the February night the majoress orders the door opened to the wagon shed.

And with lanterns and torches she has the vehicles picked out that belong to Ekeby's current cavaliers: Beerencreutz's old carriole and Örneclou's coat of arms–adorned carriage and the narrow covered sleigh that has protected cousin Kristoffer.

She doesn't care whether these are vehicles for summer or winter, she simply sees to it that each of them will get his own.

And in the stable they are now being wakened, all the old cavalier horses, who were just dreaming before full mangers.

Dream will become reality, you carefree ones.

Once again you will endure the steep hills and the musty hay in the sheds of the inns and the spiked whips of intoxicated horse traders and furious races on glassy ice so slippery you tremble to set foot on it.

Now they are in their proper form, those old vehicles, when the small, gray fjord horses are set in front of a tall, ghostlike chaise or when the high-legged, bony riding horses are harnessed to low racing sleighs. The old animals whinny and snort, as the bit is set in their toothless mouths; the old conveyances creak and squeak. Pitiful brittleness, which ought to have been allowed to sleep in peace until the end of time, is now dragged out for inspection: stiff hock joints, limping forelegs, spavin and strangles come to light.

The stable hands, however, manage to get the draft animals harnessed to the vehicles, then they go over and ask the majoress in which vehicle Gösta Berling should ride, for as everyone knows, he came to Ekeby riding in the majoress's coal cart.

"Harness Don Juan to our best racing sleigh," says the majoress, "and spread out the bearskin with the silver claws across it!" And when the stable hand grumbles, she continues, "There is not a horse in my stable I would not give to be rid of that fellow, don't forget that!"

So now the vehicles are awake and the horses likewise, but the cavaliers are still sleeping.

Now it is their turn to be ushered out into the winter night, but it is a more dangerous deed to attack them in their beds than to usher out the stiff-legged horses and rickety old conveyances. They are bold, strong, dreadful men, hardened by a hundred adventures. They are ready to defend themselves to the death; it is no easy matter to usher them out of their beds against their will and down to the vehicles that are to carry them away.

So the majoress sets fire to a haystack standing so close to the yard that the flames must shine in to the cavaliers where they are sleeping.

"The haystack is mine, all of Ekeby is mine," she says.

And when the stack is all ablaze, she calls out, "Wake them now!"

But the cavaliers are sleeping within well-closed doors. The entire crowd of people outside starts shouting the dreadful, frightening words, "A fire has broken out! Fire!" But the cavaliers sleep.

The master smith's heavy sledge thunders against the entryway, but the cavaliers sleep.

A hard-packed snowball breaks the window and flies into the room, bouncing against the bed curtain, but the cavaliers sleep.

They are dreaming that a beautiful girl is throwing a handker-chief toward them, they dream about applause behind a low-ered curtain, they dream of merry laughter and the deafening din of midnight banquets.

It would take a cannon shot at their ear, a sea of ice-cold water to wake them.

They have bowed, danced, played music, acted, and sung. They are heavy with wine, emptied of energy, and are sleeping a sleep as deep as death.

This blessed sleep is about to save them.

The people start to think that this calm conceals a danger. What if this means that the cavaliers are already out getting help? What if this means that they stand ready, with fingers on the trigger, on guard behind the window or the door, ready to fall on the first one who intrudes?

These men are shrewd, aggressive, their silence must mean something. Who can believe that they would let themselves be surprised in their hibernation like a bear?

The people howl out their "Fire has broken out!" over and over, but nothing helps.

Then, when all hesitate, the majoress herself takes an ax and breaks open the outer door.

Then she rushes in alone up the stairs, throws open the door to the cavaliers' wing, and roars into the room, "Fire has bro-ken out!"

This is a voice that finds better resonance in the cavaliers' ears than the people's bellowing. Accustomed to obeying that voice, twelve men fall out of bed at once, see the firelight, pull on their clothes, and rush down the steps out into the yard.

But in the entryway stands the large master smith and two sturdy mill hands, and great shame overtakes the cavaliers. All of them are seized as they come down, thrown down on the ground, and have their feet bound, whereupon they are carried with no further ado over to the conveyance that has been deter-mined for each one of them.

No one escaped; they were all captured. Beerencreutz, the stern colonel, was bound and carried away, likewise Kristian Bergh, the strong captain, and uncle Eberhard, the philosopher.

Even the unconquerable, the terrible Gösta Berling, was captured. The majoress had succeeded. She was still greater than all the cavaliers.

They are deplorable to look at, as they sit with bound limbs in the shabby old vehicles. There are hanging heads and angry looks, and the yard quakes with oaths and wild outbursts of impotent wrath.

But the majoress goes from one to the other.

"You must swear," she says, "never to come back to Ekeby."

"Watch it, troll hag!"

"You must swear," she says, "otherwise it is I who will throw you into the cavaliers' wing again, tied up as you are, and then you will burn up in there, for tonight I will burn down the cavaliers' wing, just so you know that."

"You wouldn't dare, majoress!"

"Wouldn't dare! Isn't Ekeby mine? Oh, you rogue! Don't you think I remember how you spit after me on the road? Do you think I didn't have a desire just now to set this on fire and let all of you burn up inside? Did you lift a finger to defend me when I was driven from my home? No, so swear!"

And the majoress stands there so dreadful, although perhaps she is pretending to be angrier than she is, and so many men, armed with axes, stand around her, that they must swear to prevent a greater misfortune from occurring.

Then the majoress has their clothes and cases fetched from the cavaliers' wing and loosens their bonds. Then the reins are put into their hands.

But during all this much time has passed, and Marianne has made her way down to Sjö.

The major was not a late-sleeping gentleman; he was dressed when she arrived. She met him in the yard; he had been out taking breakfast to his bears.

He did not say much in reply to her talk. He simply went in to the bears, set a muzzle on them, led them out, and hurried away to Ekeby.

Marianne followed him at a distance. She was about to collapse from fatigue, but then she saw a bright firelight in the sky and was nearly frightened to death.

What kind of night was this? A man beats his wife and lets his child freeze almost to death outside his door. Did a woman now intend to burn her enemies alive, did the old major intend to let his bears loose on his people?

Overcoming her fatigue, she hurried past the major and rushed up toward Ekeby at a wild pace.

She arrived well ahead of him. Once in the yard, she made her way through the crowd. When she stood in the middle of the circle, face-to-face with the majoress, she cried out as loud as she could, "The major, the major is coming with the bears!"

There was dismay among the people; all of their glances sought out the majoress.

"You've fetched him," she said to Marianne.

"Flee!" she cried out with increasing urgency. "Away, for God's sake! I don't know what the major is thinking of, but he has the bears with him."

All stood quietly with eyes directed at the majoress.

"I thank you for your help, children," she said calmly to the people. "All that has happened tonight has been arranged so that none of you can be taken to court or thereby come to grief. Go home now! I will not see any of my people murder or be murdered. Go now!"

The people, however, stood still.

The majoress turned to Marianne.

"I know that you are in love," she said. "You are acting in the madness of love. May the day never come when you must helplessly watch the devastation of your home! May you always be master of your tongue and your hand, when anger fills your soul!

"Dear children, come now, come!" she continued, turning toward the people. "May God now protect Ekeby; I must go to my mother. Oh, Marianne, when you regain your senses, when Ekeby is pillaged and the countryside sighs in distress, then think about what you have done tonight, and take care of the people!"

With that she left, followed by all the people.

When the major came up to the yard, he found no living thing there except Marianne and a long row of horses with vehicles and riders, a long, deplorable row, where the horses were no worse off than the vehicle, the vehicle no worse than the owner. They were all much the worse for wear in the battle of life.

Marianne went over and released those who were tied up.

She noticed how they bit their lips and looked away. They were ashamed like never before. Greater disgrace had never befallen them.

"I wasn't any better off when I was on my knees on the stairway at Björne a few hours ago," said Marianne.

And so, dear reader, what happened further that night, how the old conveyances got into the shed, the horses into the stable, and the cavaliers into the cavaliers' wing, I will not try to relate. Dawn began to appear over the eastern hills, and day came with clarity and calm. How much calmer are bright, sunlit days than dark nights, under whose sheltering wings the predator hunts and the owls hoot!

This alone will I say, that when the cavaliers had again come in and found a few drops in the last bowl to fill their glasses, a sudden enthusiasm came over them.

"*Skoal* to the majoress!" they cried out.

She is a matchless woman! What more could they desire than to be allowed to serve her, to worship her?

Isn't it awful that the devil took control of her, and that the point of all her strivings is to send the cavaliers' souls to hell?

CHAPTER 8

THE GREAT BEAR IN
GURLITA BLUFF

In the darkness of the forests live unholy animals, whose jaws are armed with gruesomely glistening teeth or sharp beaks, whose feet bear sharp claws that long to cling tightly to a blood-filled throat, and whose eyes gleam with a desire to kill.

There live the wolves that come forth at night and chase the farm folk's sleigh, until finally the wife must take the little child who is sitting on her lap and throw it out to them, in order to save her own life and her husband's.

There lives the lynx, which the people call *göpa,* for in the forest at least it is dangerous to say its right name. Anyone who has mentioned it during the day must see carefully to the doors and openings of the sheep barn toward evening, for otherwise it will come. It climbs right up the sheep barn wall, for its claws are strong as steel nails, glides in through the narrowest opening, and throws itself on the sheep. And the *göpa* hangs at their throats and drinks their blood and murders and scratches, until every single sheep is dead. It does not stop its wild dance of death among the terrified animals as long as any of them show a sign of life.

And in the morning the farmer finds all the sheep lying dead with throats torn apart, for *göpa* leaves nothing living behind where she ravages.

There lives the owl that hoots in the twilight. If you imitate him then, he will come swooping down over you on broad wings and tear out your eyes, for he is not a real bird; he is a ghost.

And there lives the most terrible of them all, the bear, who has the strength of twelve men and who, when he has become a killer bear, can only be felled with a silver bullet. Can anything give an animal a greater aura of terror than this, that he can only be felled with a silver bullet? What kind of hidden, terrible powers are there that dwell within him and make him impervious to common lead? A child may lie awake for many hours, shuddering at this wicked animal, whom the evil powers protect.

And if someone were to meet him in the forest, large and tall as a walking cliff, then that person should not run, not defend himself either, but instead throw himself to the ground and pretend to be dead. Many small children have lain on the ground, in their minds, with the bear upon them. He has rolled them around with his paw, and they have felt his hot, panting breath in their face, but they lie quietly until he has gone off to dig a hole to hide them in. Then they slowly get up and steal away, leisurely at first, but then with increasing haste.

But think, think if the bear had not found them to be really dead, but rather kept on biting awhile, or if he had been very hungry and wanted to eat them right away, or if he had seen them as they moved and run after them! Oh, God!

Terror is a witch. She sits in the forest twilight, composing troll songs for human ears and filling their hearts with gruesome thoughts. The result is paralyzing fear, which stifles life and blocks out the beauty of smiling places. Nature is spiteful, treacherous as a sleeping snake, not to be believed. There is Löven lake in magnificent beauty, but don't trust him, he is waiting for prey: every year he must collect his tax of drownings. There is the forest, peaceful and enticing, but don't trust him! The forest is full of unholy animals, possessed by the souls of evil trolls and bloodthirsty scoundrels.

Don't trust the brook with its smooth water! Wading in it after sundown brings sudden illness and death. Trust not the cuckoo who called so merrily in spring! Toward autumn he becomes a hawk with forbidding eyes and gruesome claws! Trust not the moss, not the heather, not the rock; nature is evil, possessed by invisible forces who hate humankind. There is no place where you can safely set your foot. It is strange that your weak race can avoid so much persecution.

Terror is a witch. Is she still sitting in the dark of the Värmland forests, singing troll songs? Does she still darken the beauty of smiling places, does she still paralyze the joy of being alive? Her dominion has been great, that I know, I who have had steel in my crib and charcoal in the bathwater, that I know, I who have felt her iron hand around my heart.

But no one should think that I am now going to tell of something gruesome and terrible. This is only an old story about the great bear in Gurlita Bluff that I must relate, and it is completely up to anyone to believe it or not, just as it should be with all real hunting stories.

The great bear has his home on the splendid hilltop known as Gurlita Bluff, which rises, sheer and inaccessible, on the shore of upper Löven.

The roots of an overturned pine, between which the peat moss still hangs, form walls and roof around his dwelling, branches and twigs shield it, the snow insulates it. He can lie inside there and sleep a good, calm sleep from summer to summer.

Is he a poet then, a delicate dreamer, this hirsute forest king, this slant-eyed robber? Does he want to sleep away the bleak nights and colorless days of the cold winter, to be wakened by purling brooks and birdsong? Does he want to lie there, dreaming of ripening lingonberry slopes and of anthills filled with brown, tasty beings, and of the white lambs who pasture on the green slopes? Does he, the fortunate one, want to avoid the winter of life?

Outside the driving snow blows hissing in between the pines, outside the wolf and fox prowl around, crazy with hunger. Why should the bear alone get to sleep? May he rise up and feel how the cold bites, how heavy it is to wade in deep snow. May he rise up!

He has bedded down so well. He is like the sleeping princess in the fairy tale; just as she is awakened by love, so he wants to be wakened by spring. By a sunbeam that filters in through the twigs and warms his muzzle, by a few drops from the melting snowdrift that moisten his fur, he wants to be wakened. Woe to anyone who disturbs him at the wrong time.

If only someone were to ask how the forest king wants to arrange his existence! Not that a swarm of buckshot were suddenly to come whistling between the twigs and work its way into his hide like angry mosquitoes!

Suddenly he hears shouts, clamor and shots. He shakes sleep out of his limbs and pushes aside the twigs to see what it is. There is work to be done for the old combatant. It is not spring that rumbles and clamors outside his winter lair, nor is it the wind that throws down spruce trees and tears up the drift snow, but it is the cavaliers, the cavaliers from Ekeby.

Old acquaintances of the forest king. He no doubt recalls the night when Fuchs and Beerencreutz sat in ambush in the barn of a Nygård farmer, where a visit by him was expected. They had just fallen asleep over their flask of liquor when he swung in through the turf roof, but they woke up as he was about to lift the dead cow from the stable, and fell upon him with rifle and knife. They took the cow from him and his one eye, but he salvaged his life.

Yes, the cavaliers and he are indeed old acquaintances. The forest king no doubt recalls how they came upon him another time, when he and his high consort had just lain down for a winter's sleep in the old royal fortress here on Gurlita Bluff and had cubs in the den. He no doubt recalls how they came upon them unsuspecting. He did get away, tossing aside everything in his way, but he had to limp the rest of his life from a shot that he took in his thigh, and when at night he returned to the royal fortress, the snow was red-colored from the blood of his high consort, and the royal children were carried off to the plain to grow up there and be the servants and friends of man.

Yes, now the ground is trembling, now the drift that covers the winter lair is shaking, now he bursts out, the great bear, the old enemy of the cavaliers. Attention now, Fuchs, old bearkiller, attention, Beerencreutz, colonel and *kille* player, attention, Gösta Berling, hero of a hundred adventures!

Curses on all poets, all dreamers, all love-heroes! There stands Gösta Berling now with his finger on the trigger, and the bear is coming right toward him. Why doesn't he shoot, what is he thinking about?

Why doesn't he send a bullet in the broad brisket at once; he is standing in the right place to do it. The others will not have a chance to shoot at just the right moment. Does he think he is on parade for the forest monarch?

Gösta is of course dreaming of the lovely Marianne, who is now lying seriously ill at Ekeby, taken sick after that night when she slept in the snowdrift.

He is thinking about her, who is also a victim of the curse of hatred that is on the earth, and he shudders at himself, who has gone out to pursue and kill.

And there comes the great bear right toward him, blind in one eye from a cut by a cavalier's knife, limping on one leg from a bullet from a cavalier's rifle, surly and shaggy, alone ever since they killed his wife and carried off his children. And Gösta sees him as he is: a poor, hunted animal, whose life he will not take from him, the last thing he has left, since humans have taken everything else away from him.

"May he kill me," thinks Gösta, "but I won't shoot."

And while the bear charges toward him, he stands completely still as if on parade, and as the forest king stands right in front of him, he shoulders the rifle and takes a step to one side.

Then the bear continues his way, well knowing that he has no time to lose, charges into the forest, clears a path through man-high drifts, trundles along steep slopes, and flees irretrievably, while all those who had stood with triggers cocked waiting for Gösta's shot fire their rifles after him.

But it is in vain; the circle is broken and the bear is gone. Fuchs grumbles and Beerencreutz swears, but Gösta only laughs.

How could they expect that a person as fortunate as he should do harm to one of God's created beings?

Thus the great bear in Gurlita Bluff came out of that business alive, and he is wakened from his winter sleep; the farmers find that out. No bear can more readily tear apart the roofs of their low, cellarlike sheep pens than he, none can better slip out of a trap.

The people at upper Löven were soon at a loss with him. Message after message was sent down for the cavaliers, that they should come up and kill the bear.

Day after day, night after night during all of February the cavaliers now wander up to upper Löven to find the bear, but he

avoids them. Has he learned shrewdness from the fox and quick-
ness from the wolf? If they lie in wait at one farm, then he ravages at the neighboring farm; if they search for him in the forest,
then he pursues the farmer who comes driving across the ice.
He has become the boldest of robbers; he creeps into the loft and
empties Mother's honey jar, he kills the horse hitched to Father's sleigh.

But gradually they begin to understand what kind of bear this
is and why Gösta was not able to shoot at him. Terrible to say,
dreadful to believe, but this is no ordinary bear. No one can imagine felling him, as long as he does not have a silver bullet in his
rifle. A bullet of silver and bell metal, cast on a Thursday evening
at the new moon in the church tower, without the minister or
organist or any person knowing of it, would quite certainly kill
him, but such a bullet is perhaps not so easy to secure.

At Ekeby there is a man who, more than anyone else, must be
mortified by all this. This is, as can well be understood, Anders
Fuchs, the bear killer. He is losing both appetite and sleep in the
indignation over not being able to fell the great bear in Gurlita
Bluff. Finally he too understands that the bear can only be felled
with a silver bullet.

The forbidding major, Anders Fuchs, was not a handsome
man. He had a heavy, clumsy body and a wide, red face with
hanging pouches under his cheeks and multiple chins. The
small, black mustaches sat stiff as brushes above his thick lips,
and his black hair stood rough and thick straight out from his
head. Besides that he was a man of few words and a glutton. He
was not the sort that women meet with sunny smiles and open
arms, nor did he look at them with approval in return. No one
thought he would ever see a woman he could put up with, and
everything in the realm of love and romance was far removed
from him.

Then comes a Thursday evening, when the moon is just two
fingers wide and lingers over the horizon a few hours after the
sun has set, when Major Fuchs heads away from Ekeby without
mentioning where he intends to go. He has flint and steel and a
bullet mold in his hunting vest and the rifle on his back and goes

up to Bro church to see what fortune may be willing to do for an honorable man.

The church is on the eastern shore of the narrow sound between upper and lower Löven, and Major Fuchs has to cross the sound bridge to get there. Thus he is walking down toward the bridge deep in thought without looking up toward the Broby hills, where the houses are sharply outlined against the evening sky, or toward Gurlita Bluff, which raises its round crown in the evening radiance; he is only looking toward the ground, brooding about how he will get hold of the church key, without anyone knowing about it.

As he comes down onto the bridge, he hears someone shouting so desperately that he has to raise his eyes.

At that time Faber, the little German, was the organist in Bro. He was a delicate fellow, meager both in weight and in merit. And the parish clerk was Jan Larsson, a capable farmer but poor, for the Broby minister had tricked him out of his paternal inheritance, a whole five hundred *riksdaler*.

The parish clerk wanted to marry the organist's sister, fine little Miss Faber, but the organist would not let him have her, and therefore the two were not friends. This evening the parish clerk has met the organist down at the bridge and rushed right at him. He grasps him by the chest and lifts him right out over the bridge railing and swears that he will throw him down into the sound if he does not give him the fine little miss. The little German will not yield, however; he struggles and shouts, saying "no" all the while, although below him he sees the black furrow of open water rushing along between white borders.

"No, no," he shouts. "No, no!"

And it is uncertain whether or not the parish clerk in his fury would have let him dance down into the cold, black water, in the event Major Fuchs had not come down to the bridge just then. Now the parish clerk becomes afraid, sets Faber down on solid ground, and runs away as fast as he can.

Little Faber now falls on the major's neck to thank him for his life, but the major shoves him aside and says that is nothing to be thankful for. The major has no love for Germans, ever since he was billeted in Putbus at Rügen during the Pomeranian War.

He had never in his life been so close to starving to death as during that time.

Then little Faber wants to run up to Sheriff Scharling and accuse the parish clerk of attempted murder, but the major lets him know that that sort of thing does not pay in this country, for there is no penalty for killing a German.

Then little Faber calms down and invites the major to his home to eat pork sausage and drink *mumma.*

The major goes with him, for he thinks that the organist must surely have a church key there at home, and so they walk up the hill where Bro church is, with parsonage, parish clerk's home, and organist's residence round about it.

"Excuse me, excuse me," says little Faber, as he and the major step into his home. "It's not exactly tidy inside here today. We've been busy, my sister and I. We have butchered a rooster."

"I'll be damned!" exclaims the major.

The fine little Miss Faber comes right in after that with *mumma* in large clay mugs. Now everyone knows that the major did not look at women with approval, yet he had to observe little Miss Faber with pleasure, as she showed up so pretty in a lace cap. Her light hair was so smoothly brushed around her forehead, her home-woven dress was so natty and so blindingly clean, her small hands were so helpful and eager, and her little face so rosy and round, that he could not help thinking that if he had seen such a little woman twenty-five years ago, he surely would have gone ahead and courted her.

As pretty and rosy-red and nimble as she is, her eyes are completely cried out. This is exactly what infuses him with such tender thoughts about her.

While the men eat and drink, she passes in and out of the room. One time she goes over to her brother, curtsies, and says, "How do you command, my brother, that we should place the cows in the shed?"

"Place twelve to the left and eleven to the right, then they won't butt each other," says little Faber.

"What in blazes, do you have that many cows, Faber?" exclaims the major.

But the way it was with that business was that the organist only had two cows, but he called one of them "Eleven" and the other one "Twelve," so that it would sound important when he talked about them.

And then the major was informed that Faber's barn was being rebuilt, so the cows go out during the day and at night stand in the woodshed.

Little Miss Faber passes out of and into the room; again she comes up to her brother, curtsies to him, and says that the carpenter had asked how high the barn ought to be made.

"Look at the cow," organist Faber says then, "look at the cow!"

Major Fuchs thinks that was well answered.

All at once the major starts to ask the organist why his sister's eyes are so red, and then he is informed that she cries because he will not allow her to marry the poor parish clerk, indebted and without inheritance as he is.

From all this Major Fuchs starts to sink into deeper and deeper thought. He empties mug after mug and eats sausage after sausage, without noticing it. Such appetite and thirst make little Faber dizzy, but the more the major eats and drinks, the clearer his mind becomes and the more decisive his heart.

His decision to do something for little Miss Faber also grows firmer.

In the meantime he has been keeping his eyes on the large key with the curled bit that is hanging on a knob by the door, and no sooner does little Faber, who has to keep the major company at the drinking mug, lay his head on the table and start snoring, than Major Fuchs takes hold of the key, puts his cap on, and hurries away.

One minute later he is feeling his way up the tower stairs, lit by his small horn lantern, and finally comes up to the bell room, where the bells open their wide chasm above him. Up there he first scrapes off a little bell metal with a file and is just about to take out the bullet mold and brazier from his hunting vest when he notices that he is lacking the most important thing: he has not brought any silver with him. If there is to be any power in the bullet, of course it must be cast there in the tower. Now every-thing is in order: it is Thursday evening and a new moon, and no one knows he is there, and now he can do nothing. He sends up an oath in the silence of the night with such vigor in it that it resonates in the bells.

Immediately thereafter he hears a faint noise from down in the church and thinks he can hear steps on the stairs. Yes, verily, so it is, heavy footsteps are coming up the stairs.

Major Fuchs, up there swearing so that the bells quiver, be-comes a trifle thoughtful at this. He may well wonder who it is who is coming to help him with the bullet molding. The steps come nearer and nearer. Whoever is coming intends to go all the way up to the bell tower.

The major sneaks away, far in among beams and rafters, and extinguishes the horn lantern. He is not exactly afraid, but the whole business would be ruined if someone were to see him standing up there. No sooner has he hidden himself than the new arrival sticks his head up over the floor.

The major knows him well: it is the stingy Broby minister. He, who is well nigh mad with greed, has the habit of hiding his treasures in the most peculiar places. Now he is coming with a bundle of banknotes that he wants to stash away in the tower room. He does not know that someone is watching him. He lifts up a plank in the floor and sets down the money, and then he makes his way out again.

But the major does not delay, he lifts up the same plank. Oh, so much money! Bundle upon bundle of banknotes, and among them brown leather bags full of silver coins. The major takes just as much silver as is needed for a bullet; the rest he lets be.

As he is coming down to the ground again, he has the silver bullet in his rifle. He is wondering about what else fortune has in store for him this night. Thursday nights are peculiar, as everyone knows. First he makes a turn up to the organist's residence. Imagine now if that rogue of a bear knew that Faber's cows were in a miserable shed, as good as under the open sky.

Well, in truth does he not see something black and big com-ing across the fields over toward the woodshed; it must be the bear.

He sets the rifle to his cheek and is just about to fire, but then he changes his mind.

Miss Faber's cried-out eyes appear before him in the darkness; he thinks that he wants to help her and the parish clerk a little, but it is no doubt hard for him not to get to kill the great bear of Gurlita Bluff himself. Later he himself said that nothing in the world was so trying to him, but because the little miss was such a fine, charming little woman, he just had to do something for her.

He goes to the parish clerk's home, wakens the parish clerk, brings him out half dressed and half naked, and says that he should shoot at the bear that is sneaking around outside Faber's woodshed.

"If you shoot that bear, then he will no doubt give you his sister," he says, "for then at once you will be an honored man. This is no ordinary bear, and the best men in the country would take it as an honor to fell it."

And he sets his own rifle in his hand, loaded with a bullet of silver and bell metal, cast in a church tower on a Thursday evening at the new moon, and he cannot keep from shaking with jealousy, because someone other than he will get to shoot the great forest king, the old bear of Gurlita Bluff.

The parish clerk aims, God help us, aims as if he intended to fell the great bear otherwise known as Ursa Major, which goes in orbit around the North Star high up in the sky, and not a wandering bear on flat ground, and the shot goes off with a bang heard all the way up to Gurlita Bluff.

But however he aimed, the bear falls. That's how it is when you shoot with a silver bullet. The bear is hit in the heart, even if you've aimed at Ursa Major.

People immediately come rushing out of all the nearby farms and wonder what's going on, for never has a shot thundered louder and wakened more sleeping echoes than this one, and the parish clerk is much praised, for the bear had been a true plague upon the land.

Little Faber also comes out, but now Major Fuchs is cruelly deceived. There stands the parish clerk surrounded with honor, and he has even saved Faber's cows in the bargain, but the little organist is neither moved nor grateful. He does not open his arms to him nor does he greet him as a brother-in-law and hero.

The major stands, furrowing his eyebrows and stamping his foot in wrath over such wretchedness. He wants to speak and explain to the greedy, pinch-hearted little fellow what a deed this is, but then he starts to stammer so that he cannot get out a word. And he becomes angrier and angrier at the thought that he has forsaken the honor of felling the great bear to no avail.

Oh, this is plainly impossible for him to grasp, that someone who has done such a great deed would not be worthy of winning the proudest bride!

The parish clerk and a few fellows are going to flay the bear; they go over to the whetstone and sharpen the knives. The others go inside and go to bed; Major Fuchs remains alone with the dead bear.

Then he goes up to the church once again, once again puts the church key in the lock, climbs up narrow stairs and crooked steps, wakens the sleeping doves, and once again approaches the tower room.

Later, when the bear was being flayed under the major's supervision, a bundle of five hundred *riksdaler* in banknotes is found between his jaws. It is impossible to say how they got there, but this is after all a marvelous bear, and because the parish clerk has felled the bear, the money is his, that's clear enough.

When this becomes known, little Faber also realizes what an honorable deed the parish clerk has performed, and he explains that he would be proud to become his brother-in-law.

On Friday evening Major Fuchs returns to Ekeby after having been present at a shooting feast in the parish clerk's home and an engagement party at the organist's residence. He walks along the road with a heavy heart: he experiences no joy that his enemy has fallen, and he feels no pleasure at the splendid bear hide the parish clerk has given him.

Now many might believe that he is grieving that the fine little miss will belong to another. Oh no, he feels no sorrow about that. But this is what bothers him: that the old, one-eyed forest king is now fallen, without his having been able to shoot the silver bullet at him.

So then he comes up to the cavaliers' wing, where the cavaliers are sitting around the fireplace, and without a word throws down the bearskin in the midst of them. No one should think that he told about his mission! It was only long, long afterward that anyone could pry out of him what really happened. Nor did he reveal the Broby minister's hiding place, and perhaps the minister never noticed the theft.

The cavaliers inspected the hide.

"This is a beautiful hide," says Beerencreutz. "I can only imagine how this lad came up out of his winter sleep, or maybe you shot him in his lair?"

"He was shot in Bro."

"Yes, he wasn't as big as the Gurlita bear, was he," says Gösta, "but this was a fine animal."

"If he had been one eyed," says Kevenhüller, "then I would believe you had felled the old one yourself, but this one has no wounds or scars by the eye, so it can't have been the one."

Fuchs swears at his stupidity, but then his face lights up, so that he becomes truly handsome. So the great bear has not fallen from another man's shot after all.

"Lord God, how good you are!" he says, clasping his hands together.

CHAPTER 9

THE AUCTION AT BJÖRNE

We young ones often had to wonder at the old people's stories. "So was there a ball every day, throughout your radiant youth?" we asked them. "Was life just one long fairy tale then?"

"Were all the young ladies lovely and charming at that time, and did every banquet end with Gösta Berling running off with one of them?"

Then the old people would shake their venerable heads and go on to tell about the whirring of spinning wheels and the rustling of the loom; about kitchen utensils, about the thumping of the flail and the rhythm of the ax in the forest; but it didn't take long before they were back on the old pathways. Then sleighs drove up to the entry stairs, then horses hurried away through dark forests with merry young people, then the dance whirled and the fiddle strings snapped. With thunderous crashing the wild pursuit of adventure surged round Löven's long lake. From far away its rumble was heard. The forest shook and fell, all the forces of destruction let loose: the conflagration blazed, the rapids raged, the wild animals prowled hungrily around the farms. Under the hooves of the eight-legged horses all quiet contentment was trampled into dust. Wherever the chase surged past, there the hearts of men flared up in wildness, and the women had to flee from their homes in blanched terror.

And we young ones sat marveling, silent, ill at ease and yet blissful. "Such people," we thought. "We will never see their like."

"Didn't the people of that time ever *think* about what they were doing?" we asked.

"Of course they thought, children," the old people would answer.

"But not like we think," we persisted.

And then the old people did not understand what we meant.

But we were thinking, we, in the peculiar spirit of self-observation, which had already made its way inside us. We were thinking about him with the eyes of ice and the long, crooked fingers, he who sits in the soul's darkest corner and tears apart our being, the way old women pick apart scraps of silk and wool.

Bit by bit the long, hard, crooked fingers had plucked, until our entire self was lying there like a heap of rags, and thus our best feelings, our most original thoughts, everything we had done and said, had been examined, cross-examined, picked apart, and the eyes of ice had been watching, and the toothless mouth had smiled scornfully and whispered, "See, it's rags, only rags."

There was one of the people of that time too, who had opened her soul to the spirit with the eyes of ice. He sat by one of them, keeping watch at the source of action, smiling scornfully at evil and good, fathoming everything, judging nothing, investigating, searching, picking apart, paralyzing the movements of the heart and the force of thought by smiling scornfully without return.

The lovely Marianne carried the spirit of self-observation within her. She felt his eyes of ice and scornful smile follow every step, every word. Her life had turned into a play, where he was the only spectator. She was no longer a person: she did not suffer, she did not rejoice, she did not love, she performed the role of the lovely Marianne Sinclaire, and self-observation sat with staring eyes of ice and diligent, disassembling fingers and watched her perform.

She was divided into two halves. Pale, unsympathetic, and scornful, one half of herself sat and watched how the other half acted, and never did the peculiar spirit that picked apart her being have a word of feeling or sympathy.

But where then had he been, the pale watcher at the source of action, that night when she learned to feel the fullness of life? Where was he, when she, the sensible Marianne, kissed Gösta Berling before a hundred pairs of eyes, and when in anger she threw herself down into the snowdrift to die? Then the eyes of ice were blinded, then the scornful smile was paralyzed, for passion had stormed forth through her soul. The roar of the wild pursuit of adventure had thundered in her ears. She had been a whole person for this one, terrible night.

Oh, you god of self-mockery, when Marianne with endless effort managed to lift her rigid arms and throw them around Gösta's neck, then, like old Beerencreutz, you had to turn your eyes away from the earth and look at the stars.

During that night you had no power. You were dead, while she composed her hymns of love, dead, while she hurried down to Sjö after the major, dead, when she saw the flames coloring the sky red above the treetops.

Look, they had come, the powerful storm birds, the griffins of demonic passions. With wings of fire and claws of steel they came rushing down upon you, you spirit with the eyes of ice, they sank their claws into your neck and flung you away into the unknown. You were dead and crushed.

But now they have rushed on, those proud, those mighty birds, whose path knows no calculation and no observer has followed; and out of the depths of the unknown the strange spirit of self-observation was resurrected and had once again settled down in the soul of the lovely Marianne.

For the entire month of February Marianne lay ill at Ekeby. When she sought out the major at Sjö, she had been infected with smallpox. With all its violence this horrible disease had thrown itself upon her, who was terribly sickened and exhausted. She had been near death, but toward the end of the month she was, however, restored. She was still weak and very disfigured. She would never again be called the lovely Marianne.

This, however, was not yet known by anyone other than Marianne and her nurse. Even the cavaliers did not yet know it. The sickroom, where the smallpox raged, was not open to everyone.

But when is the power of self-observation greater than during the long hours of recovery? Then it sits and stares and stares with its eyes of ice and picks and picks with its knotted, hard fingers. And if you look carefully, behind it sits an even paler being, who

stares and paralyzes and smiles scornfully, and behind that another and another, smiling scornfully at one another and at the
whole world.

And while Marianne was looking at herself with all those staring eyes of ice, all original feelings inside her died.

She was lying there, pretending to be sick; she was lying there,
pretending to be unhappy, pretending to be in love, pretending
to be vengeful.

She was all of that, and yet it was only pretend. Everything
turned to pretense and unreality under the eyes of ice that were
watching her, while they in turn were watched by a pair behind them, who were watched by another pair in an infinite
perspective.

All of life's strong forces were slumbering. She had power for
fervent hatred and devoted love for a single night, not more.

She did not even know if she loved Gösta Berling. She longed
to see him, to test whether he could move her outside of herself.

While the reign of illness lasted, she had only one lucid
thought: she had taken care that her illness would not become
known. She did not want to see her parents, she did not want
reconciliation with her father, and she knew that he would change
his mind if he was allowed to see how sick she was. Therefore
she ordered that her parents, and everyone else besides, should
be told that the troublesome eye disease that always came over
her when she visited her home parish forced her to remain in-
doors behind drawn curtains. She forbade her nurse from saying how sick she was, forbade the cavaliers from fetching a
doctor from Karlstad. She had smallpox, to be sure, but only a
mild case; there were medicines enough in the cabinet at Ekeby
to save her life.

She never thought about dying; she was simply waiting for a
day of health to be able to go to the minister with Gösta and request to have the banns published.

But now the sickness and fever were gone. She was again cold
and sensible. To her it was as though she alone was wise in this
world of madmen. She neither hated nor loved. She understood
her father; she understood them all. Anyone who understands
does not hate.

She had found out that Melchior Sinclaire intended to have an auction at Björne and be rid of all his possessions, so that she might not inherit anything after him. It was said that he would make the devastation as thorough as possible: first he would sell furniture and household utensils, then the livestock and implements, and finally the farm itself, and he would put all the money in a sack and sink it into the depths of Löven. Her inheritance would be embezzlement, confusion, and devastation. Marianne smiled with approval when she heard this: such was his character, so must he act.

It seemed strange to her that she had composed the great hymn of love. Like others, she had dreamed of a charcoal burner's hut. Now it seemed peculiar to her that she had ever had a dream.

She sighed for nature. She was tired of this constant playacting. She never had a strong feeling. She scarcely grieved for her beauty, but she shuddered at the pity of strangers.

Oh, one moment of forgetfulness of herself! A gesture, a word, an action that was not calculated!

One day, when the contagion has been cleared from the rooms and she was dressed, lying on a sofa, she had Gösta Berling summoned. The reply came that he had gone to the auction at Björne.

It was in truth a great auction at Björne. It was an old, wealthy home. People had come a long way to attend the sale.

The great Melchior Sinclaire had thrown together all the property of the household into the large drawing room. There were thousands of objects, assembled in piles that reached from the floor to the ceiling.

He himself had gone round the house like an angel of destruction on judgment day throwing together what he wanted to sell. Things belonging to the kitchen: the black kettles, wooden chairs, pewter tankards, copper pans, all this was left in peace by him, for there was nothing about them that reminded him of Marianne; but this was also the only thing that escaped his wrath.

He broke into Marianne's room, devastating everything. Her dollhouse was there and her bookshelf, the little chair he had had made for her, her trinkets and clothes, her bench and bed, all of that must go.

And then he went from room to room. He snatched up every-thing he found displeasing and carried large loads down to the auction room. He panted under the weight of sofas and marble tops, but he persevered. And he tossed it all together in frightful confusion. He threw open the sideboards and took out the mag-nificent family silver. Away with it! Marianne had touched it. He filled his arms with snow-white damask and smooth linen tablecloths with handsbreadth hemstitching, honorably hand-crafted work, the fruits of many years of labor, and threw it all down on the piles. Away with it! Marianne was not worthy of owning it. He stormed through the rooms with piles of porce-lain, hardly being careful not to break plates by the dozen; he seized the genuine cups on which the family coat of arms was branded. Away with them! May whoever wants to, use them! He threw down mountains of bed linens from the attic: bolsters and pillows so soft that you sank down into them as if into a wave. Away with them! Marianne had slept on them.

He threw indignant glances at the old, familiar furniture. Was there a chair that she hadn't sat on once, or a sofa that she hadn't used, or a picture that she hadn't looked at, a chandelier that had not illuminated her, a mirror that had not reproduced her features? Gloomily he clenched his fists against this world of memories. He would have gladly rushed at them swinging a club and crushed them into tiny bits and pieces.

Yet it seemed to be an even more brilliant revenge to have an auction of all this. It would all go to strangers! Off to be soiled in crofters' cottages, to decay under the care of indifferent strangers. Did he not know the chipped auction furniture in farm cottages, fallen into disrepute like his lovely daughter? Away with them! May they stand with torn-open stuffing and worn-off gilding, with broken legs and stained surfaces, and long for their former home! Away with them to all the corners of the sky, so that no eye may find them, no hand collect them!

When the auction began, he had filled half the room with an unbelievable muddle of piled-up household utensils.

On the other side of the room he had set up a long counter. Behind it stood the auctioneer making outcries, the scriveners sat there making notes, and Melchior Sinclaire had a cask of liquor standing there. In the other half of the room, in the entryway, and in the yard were the buyers. There were lots of people, much noise and merriment. Purchases were steady, and the auction lively. But at the cask of liquor, with all his property in enormous confusion behind him, sat Melchior Sinclaire, half drunk and half crazy. His hair rose in wiry tufts over his red face, his eyes were rolling, bitter and bloodshot. He shouted and laughed as if he had been in the best of spirits, and he called anyone who made a good offer over to him and offered him a drink.

Also among those who saw him there was Gösta Berling, who had slipped in among the crowd of buyers, but avoided coming before the eyes of Melchior Sinclaire. He became thoughtful at that sight, and his heart felt a premonition of misfortune.

He wondered where Marianne's mother might be during all this. And now he went, intractable in his will, but driven forward by fate, to seek out Mrs. Gustava Sinclaire.

He had to pass through many doors before he found her. The great iron magnate had a short temper and little patience for lamentation and women's complaining. He had tired of seeing her tears flow at the fate that had befallen the treasures of her home. He became furious that she could weep for linen and bedsheets, when what was more important was that his lovely daughter herself was lost, and so with clenched fists he had chased her ahead of him through the house out into the kitchen all the way into the pantry.

Farther than that she could not escape, and he had been content to see her there, crouched down behind the stairs, awaiting hard blows, perhaps death. He let her remain there, but he locked the door and put the key in his pocket. She could sit there then, while the auction was going on. She didn't have to starve, and his ear was in peace from her lamentation.

There she sat, still imprisoned in her own pantry, when Gösta came walking through the corridor between the kitchen and the drawing room. There he saw Mrs. Gustava's face in a small window that sat high up on the wall. She had climbed up on the stair step and was looking out of her prison.

"What are you doing up there, aunt Gustava?" asked Gösta.

"He's shut me in," she whispered.

"The mill owner?"

"Yes, I thought he was going to kill me. But listen, Gösta, take the key to the drawing room door and go into the kitchen and unlock the pantry door with it, then I'll come out. That key goes here."

Gösta obeyed, and in a few minutes the small woman was standing out in the kitchen, which was completely empty.

"You should have let one of the maids open up with the drawing room key," said Gösta.

"Do you think I want to teach them that trick? Then I would never again have anything left alone in the pantry. And besides, I took the opportunity to clean on the topmost shelves. They needed it, you know. I don't understand how I could have let them get so full of rubbish."

"You have a lot to take care of, aunt," said Gösta apologetically.

"Yes, you can say that. If I'm not everywhere, then neither spinning wheel nor loom is going at the right speed. And if . . ."

Here she stopped and dried a corner of her eyes.

"God help me, the way I'm talking," she said, "I likely won't have anything to look after anymore, not me. He's selling off all that we have."

"Yes, that is a misery," said Gösta.

"You know that big mirror in the drawing room, Gösta. It was so remarkable, for the glass in it was whole, and there was nothing wrong with the gilding. I got it from my mother, and now he wants to sell it."

"He's crazy."

"You can say that. I guess he's no better than that. He won't stop before we have to go and beg on the highway, like the majoress."

"It won't go that far anyway," answered Gösta.

"Yes, Gösta. When the majoress went away from Ekeby, she prophesied misfortune for us, and now it's coming. She would not have let it happen, that he would sell Björne. And just think, his own porcelain, the genuine cups from his own home, are to be sold. The majoress would never have allowed it."

"But what is going on with him?" asked Gösta.

"Oh, it's just that Marianne hasn't come back. He has been waiting and waiting here. He has walked up and down the lane for days on end, waiting for her. He is longing himself crazy; but I don't dare say anything, not me."

"Marianne believes that he is angry with her."

"Listen, you, she doesn't believe that. She knows him well enough, but she is proud and won't take the first step. They're rigid and hard the both of them, and they have nothing to complain about. I'm the one who is stuck in the middle."

"You do know, don't you, that Marianne is going to marry me?"

"Oh, Gösta, she'll never do that. She says that just to annoy him. She is too spoiled to marry a poor man, and too proud as well. Go on home and tell her that if she doesn't come soon, all of her inheritance will go to waste. Oh, he's probably throwing away everything without getting anything for it."

Gösta became downright angry with her. There she sat at a large kitchen table and did not have the heart for anything other than her mirrors and her porcelain.

"You ought to be ashamed, aunt!" he burst out. "There you throw your daughter out into the snowdrift, and then you think that it is only spitefulness on her part not to come back. And you think she is no better than that she would abandon the one she cares for, just because she would otherwise lose her inheritance."

"Dear Gösta, don't be angry, not you too. I don't even know what I'm saying. I tried everything to open the door for Marianne, but he took me and dragged me away. They're always saying here at home that I don't understand anything. I won't begrudge you Marianne, Gösta, if you can make her happy. It isn't so easy to make a woman happy, Gösta."

Gösta looked at her. How could he have just raised his voice in wrath against a person such as her! She was frightened and persecuted, but with such a good heart.

"You haven't asked how Marianne is doing," he said slowly.

She burst into tears.

"Won't you get angry if I ask you?" she said. "I've been longing to ask the whole time. Think, I don't know any more about her, other than that she's alive. Not a greeting have I had from her the whole time, not even when I sent clothes to her, and then I thought that you and her didn't want me to know anything about her."

Gösta could not stand it anymore. He was wild, he was dizzy—at times God must send his wolves after him to force him into obedience—but the tears of the old woman, the old woman's complaints were harder for him to endure than the howling of wolves. He let her know the truth.

"Marianne has been sick the whole time," he said. "She has had smallpox. She was supposed to get up today and lie on the sofa. I haven't seen her since that first night."

Mrs. Gustava rose to the floor with a leap. She let Gösta stand there, rushing without a word in to her husband.

The people in the auction room saw her coming up to him and excitedly whisper something in his ear. They saw how his face became even redder, and his hand, resting on the tap, twisted it around so that the liquor streamed out onto the floor.

It struck all of them that if Mrs. Gustava had come with such important news, the auction would immediately end. The auctioneer's gavel did not strike, the scriveners' pens halted, no new offers were heard.

Melchior Sinclaire emerged from his thoughts.

"Well," he shouted, "what about it?"

And the auction was in full swing again.

Gösta remained sitting in the kitchen, and Mrs. Gustava came weeping out to him.

"It didn't help," she said. "I thought he would stop if he heard that Marianne had been sick, but he's letting it go on. I know he wants to, but now he's ashamed."

Gösta shrugged his shoulders and said farewell to her without further ado.

In the entryway he encountered Sintram.

"Such damn fun entertainment!" exclaimed Sintram, rubbing his hands together. "You're a master, Gösta, you are. Heavens, what a mess you've been able to make!"

"It will get more fun in a while," whispered Gösta. "The Broby minister is here with a sleigh full of money. They're saying that he wants to buy all of Björne and pay cash. Then I'll be want-ing to see the great mill owner, uncle Sintram."

Sintram drew his head down between his shoulders and laughed to himself for a long time. But then he was off to the auction room and all the way over to Melchior Sinclaire.

"If you want a drink, Sintram, then you've got to God help me make a bid first."

Sintram came all the way up to him.

"You're lucky now as always, brother," he said. "There's a big man come to the farm with a sleigh full of money. He's buy-ing Björne and all the inside and outside inventory. He's talked to a good many to buy up things for him. It seems he doesn't want to be seen here too long."

"You can surely say who he is, brother, then I'll surely offer you a drink for your trouble."

Sintram took the drink and two steps back, before he replied: "It seems to be the Broby minister, brother Melchior."

Melchior Sinclaire had many better friends than the Broby minister. There had been a feud going on between them for years. There were stories going around about how the great mill owner would lie in wait on dark nights on roads where the minister might pass, and how he had given him many an honorable thrash-ing, that fawner and tormentor of farmers.

It was well that Sintram had taken a few steps backward; how-ever, he did not completely escape the great man's wrath. He got a liquor glass between the eyes and the whole cask of liquor at his feet. But then came a scene that gave his heart joy for a long time.

"Does the Broby minister want my farm?" roared Squire Sinclaire. "Are you here buying my things for the Broby minis-ter? Oh, you ought to be ashamed. You ought to learn some manners!"

He got hold of a candlestick and an inkhorn and threw them out among the throng of people.

It was all the bitterness of his poor heart that could finally be vented. Roaring like a wild animal, he clenched his fists at those standing around and threw whatever missiles he had at them.

Liquor glasses and bottles flew across the room. He was beside himself in his wrath.

"This is the end of the auction," he roared. "Out with you! Never in my day shall the Broby minister have Björne. Out with you! I'll teach you, I will, to buy for the Broby minister!"

He let loose on the auctioneer and the scriveners. They rushed away. In their confusion they turned over the counter, and the mill owner broke into the throng of peaceful people with indescribable fury.

There was flight and wild confusion. A few hundred people crowded toward the door, fleeing from a single man. And he stood still, roaring his "Out with you!" He sent curses after them, now and then sweeping at the piles with a chair that he swung like a club.

He pursued them out into the entryway, but no farther. When the last outsider had left the stairs, he went back into the drawing room, locking the door behind him. Then he pulled together a mattress and a few pillows, lay down on them, fell asleep in the midst of all the destruction, and did not awaken again until the next day.

When Gösta got home, he found out that Marianne wanted to speak with him. That was a good coincidence. He had just been wondering how he would talk things over with her.

As he came into the murky room where she was lying, he had to stop a moment by the door. He did not see where she was.

"Stay where you are, Gösta!" Marianne then said to him. "It may be dangerous to come close to me."

But Gösta had come, taking the stairs two steps at a time, quivering with eagerness and longing. What did he care about contagion! He wanted to enjoy the blessedness of seeing her.

For she was beautiful, his beloved. No one had such soft hair, such a clear, radiant forehead. Her entire face was a play of beautifully contoured lines.

He thought of her eyebrows, clearly and sharply outlined like the honeyguide on a lily, and of the bold curve of her nose and of her lips, softly contoured like rolling waves, and of the elongated oval of her cheek and the exquisitely fine form of her chin.

And he thought of the pale rose color of her skin, of the enchanting impression of her coal-black eyebrows under the light hair and of the blue eyes, swimming in clear white, and of the glimmer of light in the corners of her eyes.

She was splendid, his beloved. He thought about what a warm heart she concealed under her proud exterior. She had energy for devotion and sacrifice, concealed under her fine skin and proud words. It was blessedness to see her.

In two leaps he had stormed up the stairs, and she thought that he would stay over by the door. He stormed through the room and fell to his knees by her pillow.

But his intention was to see her, kiss her, and bid her farewell.

He loved her. He would no doubt never stop loving her; but his heart was accustomed to being trampled.

Oh, where would he find her, this rose without support and roots, that he could take up and call his own? Not even her, whom he had found cast out and half dead by the roadside, would he be able to hold on to.

When would his love raise its song so loud and clear that no discord cut through it? When would his castle of happiness be built on a foundation that no other heart longed for in worry and loss?

He thought about how he would say farewell to her.

"There is great lamentation in your home," he would say. "My heart is torn apart at the thought of it. You must go home and give your father back his reason. Your mother lives in constant mortal danger. You must go home, my love."

See, such words of self-denial he had on his lips, but they remained unsaid.

He fell to his knees at her pillow, and he took her head between his hands and kissed her; but then he found no words. His heart started to pound violently, as if it would burst his chest.

The smallpox had ravaged her fair face. Her skin had become rough and pockmarked. Never more would the red blood shimmer forth on her cheeks, or the fine blue veins be seen on her temples. Her eyes were flat under swollen eyelids. Her eyebrows had fallen off and the enamel gleam of the whites of her eyes was broken in yellow.

All was devastated. The bold lines were changed to rough and heavy ones.

There were more than a few who later grieved for Marianne Sinclaire's past fairness. All over Värmland people complained of the loss of her light skin, her flashing eyes and blonde hair. Beauty was esteemed there like nowhere else. These happy people grieved, as if the land had lost a jewel in the crown of its honor, as if the sunlit radiance of its existence had been stained.

But the first man who saw her after she had lost her beauty did not abandon himself to sorrow.

Inexpressible feelings filled his soul. The longer he looked at her, the warmer he felt inside. Love grew and grew like a river in spring. In waves of fire it poured forth from his heart, it filled all of his being, it climbed up into his eyes as tears, sighed on his lips, trembled in his hands, in his whole body.

Oh, to love her, to defend her, to keep her from harm, free from harm!

To be her slave, her guardian spirit!

Love is strong, when it has received the fiery baptism of pain. He could not speak with Marianne about separation and self-denial. He could not leave her. He owed her his life. He could commit mortal sins for her sake.

He did not speak one reasonable word, only wept and kissed, up until the time when the old nurse found it was time to lead him out.

When he was gone, Marianne lay thinking about him and his agitation. "It is good to be so loved," she thought.

Yes, it was good to be loved, but how about herself? What did she feel? Oh, nothing, less than nothing.

Was it dead, her love, or where had it gone? Where was it hiding, child of her heart?

Was it still alive, had it crept into the darkest corner of her heart and sat there, freezing under the eyes of ice, frightened by the pale scornful laughter, half smothered under the knotty fingers?

"Oh, my love," she sighed, "child of my heart! Do you live, or are you dead, dead like my beauty?"

The next day the great mill owner went to see his wife early.

"See to it that there's order in the house again, Gustava!" he said. "I'm going to bring Marianne home."

"Yes, dear Melchior, there will surely be order here again," she replied.

With that everything was clear between them.

One hour later the great iron magnate was on his way to Ekeby.

There was no nobler, more benevolent old gentleman than the mill owner as he sat in the sleigh with its cover lowered in his best fur and his best sash. Now his hair was combed flat over his head, his face was pale, and his eyes had sunk down into their sockets.

And there was no limit to the brilliance that streamed down from the sky over the February day. The snow glistened like the eyes of young girls when the first waltz begins. The birches stretched their fine lacework of thin, brown-red twigs toward the sky, and on some of them sat a fringe of small, glittering icicles.

There was brilliance and festive shimmer over the day. The horses threw their forelegs up as if in a dance, and the coachman had to crack the whip in pure joy.

After a short journey, the great mill owner's sleigh stopped outside the large stairway at Ekeby.

The servant came out.

"Where are the masters?" asked the mill owner.

"They are hunting the great bear at Gurlita Bluff."

"All of them?"

"All of them, squire. Those who don't go along because of the bear, at least go along for the lunch basket."

The iron magnate laughed so that it echoed across the silent yard. He gave the servant a *daler* for his reply.

"Now say to that daughter of mine that I am here to get her! She doesn't need to freeze. I have a covered sleigh and a wolf skin to wrap her in."

"Would you care to step in, squire?"

"Thank you! I'm fine where I am."

The fellow disappeared, and the mill owner began his wait.

He was in such a marvelous mood that day that nothing could annoy him. He had probably thought that he would have to wait a little for Marianne; perhaps she wasn't even up yet. For the time being he had to amuse himself by looking around.

On the cornice hung a long icicle that the sunshine was having dreadful trouble with. It began on top, melting a drop loose and then wanting it to fall to the ground along the icicle. But before it got halfway, it was frozen again. And the sunshine continued making fresh attempts, still without success. But finally there was a freebooter of a sunbeam that clung tight to the tip of the icicle, a little one that shone and sparked with eagerness, and sure enough, it reached its goal: a drop fell resoundingly to the ground.

The mill owner watched and laughed. "You didn't do too bad, you," he said to the sunbeam.

The yard was silent and deserted. Not a sound was heard in the great house. But the iron magnate did not get impatient. He knew that women needed a lot of time before they were ready.

He sat and watched the dovecote. The birds had a grate in front of the opening. They were enclosed, as long as winter lasted, so that the hawk would not wipe them out. Now and then a dove came and stuck its white head out between the bars.

"She's waiting for spring," said Melchior Sinclaire. "But she has to be patient for the time being."

The dove came so regularly that he took out his watch and observed her with watch in hand. Exactly every three minutes she stuck out her head.

"No, my little friend," he said, "do you think spring will be ready in three minutes? She'll have to learn to wait."

And he himself had to wait, but he had plenty of time.

At first the horses scraped impatiently in the snow, but then they got sleepy from standing and blinking in the sunlight. They leaned their heads together and slept.

The coachman sat straight on the stand with whip and reins in hand and his face turned directly toward the sun and slept, slept so that he snored.

But the mill owner did not sleep. He had never been less inclined to sleep. He had seldom had more enjoyable hours than during this happy wait. Marianne had been sick. She had not been able to come before, but now she would come. Oh, of course she would. And everything would be fine again.

Now she really would understand that he was not angry with her. He had come personally with two horses and a covered sleigh.

Over by the entrance to the beehive sat a titmouse occupied with a really devilish trick. He would have his dinner of course, and sure enough he was knocking on the entrance to the beehive with his sharp little beak. But inside the hive the bees were hanging in a large, dark sack. Everything is in the strictest order; the stewards dole out the food rations, the cupbearer runs from mouth to mouth with nectar and ambrosia. The ones that are hanging farthest in change places with the ones outside at a steady crawl, so that heat and comfort might be evenly divided.

Then they hear the knocking of the titmouse, and the whole hive buzzes with curiosity. Is it friend or enemy? Is it a danger to the community? The queen has a bad conscience. She cannot wait in peace and quiet. Do you think it is the murdered drone's phantoms that are haunting out there? "Go out and see what it is!" she orders her sister, the doorkeeper. And this is done. With a "Long live the Queen!" she rushes out, and hi! the titmouse is over her. With neck extended and wings shaking with excitement he seizes her, crushes her, eats her, and no one carries the news of her fate in to the queen. But the titmouse starts knocking again, and the queen bee continues to send out her doorkeepers, and all of them disappear. No one comes back to tell who has knocked. Ugh, it is getting dreadful inside in the dark hive! Vengeful spirits are pursuing their game outside. If only one lacked ears! If only one could refrain from being curious! If only one could wait in peace!

The great Melchior Sinclaire laughed so that he had tears in his eyes at the stupid womenfolk inside the hive and at the clever, yellow-green rogue outside.

There's no trick to waiting when you are completely sure of your business, and when there is plenty to divert your thoughts with.

There comes the big farm dog. He sneaks up on the very tips of his paws, keeping his eyes on the ground and wagging his tail a little, as if he intended to be off on the most indifferent errand. Suddenly he starts to eagerly dig in the snow. No doubt the old scoundrel has concealed ill-gotten goods there.

But just as he is lifting his head to see whether he can now eat in peace, he becomes quite disappointed by seeing two jays in front of him.

"Thief!" say the jays, looking like conscience itself. "We are police officers. Over here with the stolen goods!"

"Oh, hush, you rascals! I'm the farm sheriff."

"Just the right one!" they mock.

The dog throws himself over them, and they flee with languid wing strokes. The dog rushes after them, jumping and barking. But while he is chasing the one, the other is already back. She flies down into the hole, tearing at the piece of meat, but doesn't manage to lift it. The dog jerks the meat to himself, holding it between his paws and biting into it. The jays sit down right in front of him and say mean things. He glares sternly at them while he eats, and when things get much too crazy, he rushes up and drives them away.

The sun started to sink down against the western hills. The great mill owner looked at his watch. It was three o'clock. And Mother, who had dinner ready at twelve!

Just then the servant came out and reported that Miss Marianne wished to speak with him.

The mill owner placed the wolf skin over his arm and went up the steps in a marvelous mood.

When Marianne heard his heavy steps coming up the stairs, she did not yet know whether she would go home with him or not. She only knew that she must have an end to this long waiting.

She had hoped that the cavaliers would come home, but they did not. So she herself had to see that all of this would come to an end. She couldn't hold out any longer.

She had thought that he would go his way in anger when he had waited for five minutes, or that he would break down the doors or try to set fire to the house.

But there he sat, calm and smiling, and only waited. She harbored neither hatred nor love for him. But there was an inner voice in her, that warned her as it were about once again placing herself in his power. And besides, she wanted to keep her word to Gösta.

If he had fallen asleep, if he had spoken, if he had been worried, if he had shown any sign of hesitation, if he had the wagon driven away in the shadows! But he was simply patience and certainty.

Certain, so contagiously certain that she would come, if only he waited.

Her head hurt. Every nerve twitched. She could not find peace as long as she knew that he was sitting there. It was as if his will carried her, bound, down the stairs.

So she would at least speak with him.

Before he came, she had the curtain drawn up, and she arranged herself so that her face came into full daylight.

In that way she no doubt intended to set him to a type of test, but Melchior Sinclaire was a remarkable man that day.

When he saw her, he did not make a gesture, he did not let out a cry. It was as if he had not seen any change in her. She knew how highly he had adored her fair appearance. But he did not show any sign of sorrow. He mastered his whole being so as not to distress her. This touched her. She began to understand why her mother still held him dear.

He showed no hesitation. He came neither with reproaches nor excuses.

"I will wrap the wolf skin around you, Marianne. It's not cold. It's been on my lap the whole time."

In any case he went over to the fire and warmed it.

Then he helped her get up from the sofa, wrapped the fur around her, hung a shawl over her head, pulled it down under her arms, and tied it on her back.

She let it happen. She was without a will of her own. It was good to be sheltered, it was sweet not to need to decide. Above all good for anyone who was as picked apart as her, for anyone who did not own a thought or a feeling that was her own.

The great mill owner lifted her up, carried her down to the sleigh, drew up the cover, tucked the blankets around her, and drove away from Ekeby.

She closed her eyes and sighed, partly in pleasure, partly in loss. She was leaving life, real life, but then that might as well be the same to her; she could not live, only pretend.

A few days later, her mother arranged it so that she happened to encounter Gösta. She sent for him while the mill owner was taking his long walk up to the log drivers, and led him in to Marianne.

Gösta came in, but he neither greeted her nor spoke. He remained standing over by the door and looked at the ground like an obstinate boy.

"But Gösta!" exclaimed Marianne. She was sitting in her armchair, and looked at him half amused.

"Yes, that's my name."

"Come here, come all the way up to me, Gösta!"

He went slowly up to her, without raising his eyes.

"Come closer! Get on your knees here!"

"Good Lord, what good will all this do?" he exclaimed, but he obeyed.

"Gösta, I want to tell you that I think it was best that I came back home."

"Let's hope they won't throw Miss Marianne out into the snowdrifts anymore."

"Oh, Gösta, don't you like me anymore? Do you think I'm too ugly?"

He pulled down her head and kissed her, but he appeared equally cold.

She was actually amused. If it pleased him to be jealous of her parents, what of it? It would soon pass. Now it amused her to try to win him back. She scarcely knew why she wanted to keep him there, but she wanted to. She was reminded that he had nonetheless succeeded in freeing her from herself, if only for once. He was probably the only man who would be able to do so yet again.

And now she began to talk, eager to win him back. She said that it had not been her intention to abandon him forever, but for the sake of appearances they must break off their connection for a while. He himself could see that her father stood on the threshold of madness, that her mother was in constant mortal danger. He must understand that she had been forced to go home.

Then his anger burst out in words. She didn't need to put on airs. He didn't want to be her plaything any longer. She had abandoned him as soon as she had been able to go home, and he could not love her anymore. When he came home from the hunt the day before yesterday and found her gone without a greeting, without a word, then his blood had frozen in his veins; he had been close to dying from sorrow. He could not love the one who had caused him so much pain. And besides, she had never loved him. She was a coquette, who wanted to have someone who kissed and caressed her here in the home parish too, that was all.

So did he think that she was accustomed to letting bachelors caress her?

Oh well, he probably believed that. Women were not as holy as they appeared. Selfishness and coquetry from beginning to end! No, if she had known how he felt, when he came home from the hunt! It was as if he had waded in ice water. He would never overcome that pain. It would follow him throughout the rest of his life. He could never again be human.

She tried to explain to him how it had all happened. She tried to remind him that she had always been faithful.

Yes, it was all the same, for now he no longer loved her. Now he had seen through her. She was selfish. She did not love him. She had gone without even saying good-bye.

Over and over again he came back to this. She was almost enjoying the scene. She could not get angry. She understood his anger so well. She did not fear any real breakup either. Finally, though, she became worried. Had there been such a change in him that he could no longer love her?

"Gösta!" she said. "Was I selfish when I went to Sjö after the major? I did remember that they had smallpox there. It isn't good to go out in thin shoes in the cold and snow either."

"Love lives from love and not from services and good deeds," said Gösta.

"So you want us to be strangers from here on, Gösta?"

"That's what I want."

"Gösta Berling is very changeable."

"I'm usually accused of that."

He was cold, impossible to thaw, and in reality she herself was even colder. Self-observation sat and smiled scornfully at her attempts to pretend to be in love.

"Gösta!" she said, as she made yet another effort. "I have never consciously wronged you, even if it might appear so. I beg you: forgive me!"

"I cannot forgive you."

She knew that if she possessed a genuine emotion, she would have won him back. And she tried to pretend to be impassioned. The eyes of ice mocked her, but still she tried. She did not want to lose him.

"Don't go, Gösta! Don't leave angry! Think of how ugly I've become! No one can love me again."

"I don't either," he said. "You'll have to get used to seeing your heart trampled on, like other people."

"Gösta, I have never been able to love anyone but you! Forgive me! Don't abandon me! You are the only man who can save me from myself."

He pushed her away from him.

"You don't speak the truth," he said with icy calm. "I don't know what you want from me, but I see that you're lying. Why do you want to hang on to me? You're so rich that you should never lack for suitors."

And with that he left.

And as soon as he had shut the door, loss and pain in all of its majesty made its entry into Marianne's heart.

It was love, child of her own heart, that came out of its corner where the eyes of ice had banished him. He came, the longed-for one, now when it was too late. Now he stepped forth, serious and almighty, and loss and pain held up his royal mantle.

When Marianne could with real certainty say to herself that Gösta Berling had abandoned her, she experienced a purely physical pain so terrible that she was almost knocked unconscious. She pressed her hands against her heart and sat for hours in the same place, struggling with tearless sorrow.

And it was she herself who suffered, not a stranger, not an actress. It was she, herself.

Why had her father come and separated them? Her love had not been dead. It was simply in her state of weakness after the illness that she had not been able to experience its power.

Oh God, oh God, that she had lost him! Oh God, that she had awakened so late!

Ah, he was the only man, he was the conqueror of her heart! She could take anything from him. Hardness and angry words from him simply inclined her to humble love. If he had struck her, she would have crept over to him like a dog and kissed his hand.

She seized pen and paper and wrote with terrible ardor. First she wrote about her love and loss. Then she pleaded, not for his love, only for his mercy. It was a kind of verse that she wrote.

She did not know what she should do to get some relief for this dull pain.

When she had finished, she thought that if he were to see this, he might still believe that she loved him. Well, why shouldn't she send what she had written to him? The next day she would send it, and she no doubt believed that it would lead him back to her.

The next day she was anxious and in conflict with herself. What she had written appeared so pitiful and stupid to her. It had neither rhyme nor meter. It was only prose. He would only laugh at such verses, wouldn't he?

Her pride also awakened. If he did not love her anymore, then it was a terrible degradation to beg for his love.

At times wisdom came to her and said that she ought to be happy that she had escaped from the connection with Gösta and all the miserable conditions that would come with it.

The torment of her heart was, however, so awful that at last her feelings had to prevail. Three days after the day when she had become aware of her love, she had the verses bound and Gösta Berling's name written on the cover. They were not sent, however. Before she had found a suitable messenger, she had heard such things about Gösta Berling that she realized it was already too late to win him back.

But it became her lifelong sorrow that she had not sent the verses in time, while she could have won him.

*

All her pain bound itself fast on this point: "If I had not hesitated so long, if I had not hesitated so many days!"

They—these written words—would have won for her the
happiness of life, or at least the reality of life. She was certain
that they would have led him back to her.

Sorrow, however, came to do her the same service as love. It
made her into a whole person, capable of devoting herself to good
as well as bad. Seething emotions coursed freely through her soul
without being blocked by the ice-cold of self-observation. Then
she was also, despite her ugliness, much loved.

It is said, however, that she never forgot Gösta Berling. She
grieved for him the way you grieve over a wasted life.

And her poor verses, which for a time were much read, are
long since forgotten. Yet they seem strangely moving, the way I
see them, written on yellowed paper, with washed-out ink and a
cramped, neat handwriting. The loss of an entire life is bound up
in these poor words, and I write of them with a certain mystic
dread, as if secret powers were dwelling in them.

I ask you to read them, and think about them. Who knows
what power they might have had if they had been sent? They are,
however, passionate enough to bear witness to a true emotion.
Perhaps they would have led him back to her.

They are touching enough, tender enough in their awkward
formlessness. No one can wish them otherwise. No one will want
to see them tied up in the chains of rhyme and meter, and yet it
is so melancholy to think that perhaps just this imperfection hin-
dered her from sending them in time.

I ask you to read them, and love them. It is a person in a state
of great distress who has written them.

> Child, you have loved, but never more
> shall you taste the delights of love.
> Storms of passion have shaken your soul.
> Be glad, you have now come to rest.
> No more are you tossed in towering delight.
> Be glad, you have now come to rest.
> No more to be lowered to painful depths,
> oh, never more!

Child, you have loved, but never more
shall your soul be set on fire.
You were like a field of dried-up grass,
consumed by fire for one brief moment.
From billowing smoke-clouds and flakes of ash
the birds of the heavens fled howling in fear.
May they return home! You will burn no more,
can no longer burn.

Child, you have loved, but never more
shall you hear the voice of love.
The force of your heart, like tired children,
who are sitting on hard school benches,
long to be out in freedom and games,
but no one calls to them now.
They sit like forgotten outposts:
no one calls to them now.

Child, the only one is gone
and with him all love and delight in loving.
He, whom you loved so, as if he had taught you
to fly on wings into air, into space.
He, whom you loved so, as if he had given you
the only certain spot in a flooded village,
he is gone, he, who alone knew how to
open the door to your heart.

*

I will ask you for a single thing, you my beloved:
Never place on me the burden of hate!
The weakest of all things weak, is not this a human heart?
How would it live under the cutting thought
that it would to another be torment?

Oh, my beloved, if you would murder me,
acquire no dagger, buy not poison or rope!
But let me simply know that you would see me vanish

from earth's verdant meadows, from the richness of life,
and I will sink into the grave.

You gave me the life of life. To me you gave love.
And now you take back your gift. Oh, I know it well,
but do not exchange it for hate!
I still love to live. Oh, remember that!
But I know I would die under hatred's burden.

CHAPTER 10

THE YOUNG COUNTESS

The young countess sleeps until ten o'clock in the morning and wants fresh bread on the breakfast table every day. The young countess does tambour stitching and reads poetry. She knows nothing about weaving and food preparation. The young countess is spoiled.

But the young countess is happy and lets her cheerfulness shine over everything and everyone. Her long morning sleep and the fresh bread are gladly forgiven, for she lavishes good deeds on the poor and is friendly to everyone.

The father of the young countess is a Swedish aristocrat who has lived in Italy his whole life, detained there by the beautiful countryside and one of that beautiful country's loveliest daughters. When Count Henrik Dohna was traveling in Italy, he had been received in the home of this nobleman, made the acquaintance of his daughters, married one of them, and brought her with him to Sweden.

She, who had always been able to speak Swedish and was brought up to love everything Swedish, feels quite at home up in the bear country. She spins around so happily in the long dance of amusements that whirl around Löven's long lake that one might believe she had always lived up there. Little does she understand, however, what it is to be a countess. There is no ostentation, no stiffness, no condescending dignity in this young, happy being.

It was the old gentlemen who liked the young countess the most. It was remarkable what success she had with old gentlemen. When they had seen her at a ball, then you could be certain that the whole lot of them—the judge in Munkerud and the dean in Bro and Melchior Sinclaire and the captain at Berga—would explain to their wives in deepest confidence, that if they had met the young countess forty or thirty years ago . . .

"Yes, then she was not even born yet," the old wives say.

And the next time they meet, they tease the young countess for taking the old gentlemen's hearts from them.

The old wives view her with a certain anxiety. They remember Countess Märta so well. She had been just as happy and good and beloved when she came to Berga the first time. And of her there had only become a vain, pleasure-seeking coquette, who nowadays could think of nothing but her diversions. "If she only had a husband who could keep her to work!" the old wives say. "If only she could set up a loom!" For setting up looms: that consoles all sorrows, that devours all interests, that has been the salvation of many women.

The young countess would gladly become a good housewife. She knows nothing better than living as a happy wife in a good home, and she often comes to the large gatherings and sits down with the old women.

"Henrik really wants me to learn to be a capable housekeeper," she says, "like his mother is. Teach me how you set up a loom!"

Then the old women let out a twofold sigh: first for Count Henrik, who believes that his mother is a capable housekeeper, and second, over the difficulty of initiating this young, ignorant being in such complicated things. You only need to talk with her about lea and heddle, about harness and pulleys, about plain weave and tabby, before her head starts spinning, much less when the talk goes to bird's-eye and goose-eye and overshot.

No one who sees the young countess can help but wonder why she married the stupid Count Henrik.

Pity the person who is stupid! You have to feel sorry for him, wherever he is. And you have to feel the sorriest for anyone who is stupid and lives in Värmland.

There were already many stories about Count Henrik's stupidity, and he is no more than a few years over the age of twenty. It might be mentioned how he entertained Anna Stjärnhök at a sleighing party a few years ago.

"You are beautiful, Anna," he said.

"You talk, Henrik."

"You are the most beautiful in all of Värmland."

"I am certainly not."

"You are the most beautiful at this sleighing party anyway."

"Oh, Henrik, I'm not either."

"Yes, but you must be the most beautiful in this sleigh. That you can't deny."

No, that she couldn't.

For Count Henrik is not beautiful. He is as ugly as he is stupid. They usually say about him that the head that sits on his thin neck has been handed down in his family for a few hundred years. That is why the brain is so used up in the most recent heir. "It is clear that he has no head of his own," it is said. "He's borrowed his father's. And he doesn't dare bow his head; he's afraid of losing it. He already has yellowed skin and a wrinkled forehead. That head has probably been in use on both the father and the grandfather. Why else would his hair be so thin and his lips so bloodless and his chin so pointed?"

He always has troublemakers around him who entice him into saying stupid things and then collect them, spread them, enable them.

It is a good thing for him that he doesn't notice anything. He is solemn and dignified in all his conduct. Can he imagine that others are not that way too? Dignity has settled into his body: he moves deliberately, he walks straight, he never twists his head without his whole body following along.

He had been in Munkerud at the judge's a few years before. He had come riding, wearing a high hat, yellow trousers, and shiny boots, and sat stiff and proud in the saddle. All went well upon his arrival. But when he was to ride away again, it happened that one of the hanging branches in the lane of birches knocked off his hat. He got off, put on the hat, and again rode forth under the same branch. Again the hat was knocked off. This was repeated four times.

Finally the sheriff went up to him and said, "What if you were to ride to one side of the branch next time?"

The fifth time he came successfully past the branch.

But it is the case, however, that the young countess likes him despite his old man's head. She didn't know of course that in his own country he was surrounded by such a martyr's crown of stupidity, when she saw him down in Rome. Abroad there had been some of the radiance of youth about him, and they had been united under such extremely romantic circumstances. You should only hear the countess tell about how Count Henrik had to abduct her. Monks and cardinals had fallen into a rage because she wanted to abandon her mother's religion, to which she had previously adhered, and become a Protestant. The hoi polloi had been in an uproar. Her father's palace had been besieged. Henrik was pursued by bandits. Mother and sister had pleaded with him to forgo the marriage. But her father was furious that the Italian mob would hinder him from giving his daughter to whomever he wanted. He ordered Count Henrik to abduct her. And so, because it was impossible for them to get married at home without it being discovered, she and Henrik sneaked away on backstreets and all kinds of dark roads to the Swedish consulate. And when she had renounced her Catholic faith there and become a Protestant, they were immediately wed and sent off northward in a rapidly driven travel carriage. "There wasn't time to read the banns, you see. There just wasn't time," the young countess would say. "And it was gloomy of course getting married at a consulate and not in one of the beautiful churches, but otherwise Henrik would have had to be without me. Down there everyone is so hot tempered, Papa and Mama and cardinals and monks, everyone is hot tempered. That was why everything had to be done so secretively, and if the people had seen us sneak away from home, they would surely have killed the both of us to save my soul. Henrik was of course already doomed to damnation."

But the young countess loves her husband, even since they have come home to Borg and are living a more settled life. She loves the radiance in him from the ancient name and his heroic forefathers. She likes to see how her presence softens the stiffness in his being and to hear how his voice becomes tender when she is talking to him. And besides, he cares for her and spoils her, and then after all she is married to him. The young countess can simply not imagine that a married woman would not love her husband.

In a certain respect he also corresponds to her ideal of manliness. He is upright and a lover of truth. He has never gone back on his given word. She considers him a true nobleman.

On the eighth of March Sheriff Scharling celebrates his birthday, and then a lot of people are traveling up the Broby hills. Then people from the east and west, familiar and unfamiliar, invited and uninvited, always come to the sheriff's farm. All are welcome. All will find plenty of food and drink, and in the ballroom there will be elbow room enough for eager dancers from seven parishes.

The young countess is coming too, just as she goes any place where dance and merriment can be expected.

But the young woman is not happy when she arrives. It is as if she had a premonition that now it was her turn to be dragged into the wild hunt of adventure.

On the way she sat, observing the sinking sun. It came down from a clear sky, leaving no gold rims on puffy clouds behind. Pale gray twilight air, shot through by cold storm winds, blanketed the area.

The young countess saw how the day and the night were fighting and how all living things were seized with terror at the struggle between the two mighty forces. The horses hastened away with the last load so as to soon come under a roof. The woodcutters hurried home from the forest, the maids from the barn. The wild animals were howling at the forest edge. The day, the favorite of humankind, had been conquered.

The light went out, colors turned pale. Cold and ugliness were all she saw. What she had hoped, what she had loved, what she had done seemed to her also to be enshrouded in the gray twilight. It was the hour of fatigue, defeat, powerlessness, for her as for all of nature.

She was thinking that her own heart, which now in its sparkling joy enveloped existence in purple and gold, she was thinking that this heart would perhaps one day lose its power to light up her world.

"Oh powerlessness, my own heart's powerlessness!" she said to herself. "Suffocating gray twilight goddess, one day you will be the mistress of my soul. Then I will see life as ugly and gray, as perhaps it really is, then my hair will whiten, my back be bent, my brain paralyzed."

Just then the sleigh turned into the sheriff's farm, and as the young countess was just then looking up, her eyes fell on a grated window in a side building and at a sternly staring face behind it.

This face belonged to the majoress at Ekeby, and the young woman knew that now her enjoyment was ruined for that evening.

It is possible to be happy when you don't see sorrow, simply hear it being talked about like a guest in a foreign land. It is harder to preserve the heart's happiness when you stand eye to eye with night-black, sternly staring distress.

The countess probably knows that Sheriff Scharling has put the majoress in jail, and that she must undergo interrogation for the acts of violence she carried out at Ekeby the same night the great ball was held there. But she has simply not imagined that she would be kept in custody there at the sheriff's farm, so close to the ballroom that from there you could see into her room, so close that she must hear the dance music and the happy clamor. And now the thought of her takes away all the countess's joy.

The young countess does dance both a waltz and a quadrille. She does take part in both the minuet and the anglaise, but between each dance she has to slip over to the window and look over at the side building. There is light in the majoress's window, and she can see how she paces back and forth in her room. She seems to never rest, but paces constantly.

The countess has no joy at all from the dance. She is only thinking about how the majoress is pacing back and forth in her prison, like a captured animal. She marvels that all the others can dance. Certainly there are many who are just as upset as she from knowing that the majoress is so near to them, and yet there is no one who lets on. A forbearing people live in Värmland.

But for every time she has looked out, her feet move more heavily in the dance, and laughter seems to catch in her throat.

The sheriff's wife notices her, as she wipes the condensation from the windowpane to see out, and comes over to her.

"Such a nuisance! Oh, such a nuisance this is!" she whispers to the countess.

"I think it's almost impossible to dance this evening," the countess whispers back.

"It's not my wish either that we have a ball here while she is imprisoned there," answers Mrs. Scharling. "She has been in Karlstad the whole time since she was arrested. Now her interrogation will soon take place, and that's why she was brought here today. We couldn't put her in the miserable jail at the courthouse, so she had to be in the weaving room in the side building. She should have been allowed to be in my drawing room, countess, if all of these people hadn't been coming just today. You hardly know her, countess, but she has been like a mother and a queen to all of us. What will she think of us, who are dancing here, while she is in such great distress? It's just as well that most of them don't know she's there."

"She ought never to have been arrested," the young countess says sternly.

"No, that is a true word, countess, but there was no other way, if even worse misfortunes weren't going to happen. No one thought she would set fire to her own haystacks and drive away the cavaliers, but the major of course was prowling around on the hunt for her. God knows what he would have done if she hadn't been locked up. Scharling has had to suffer a lot of mortification because he arrested the majoress, countess. Even in Karlstad they were dissatisfied with him, because he didn't look the other way about everything that was happening at Ekeby. But he did what he believed was best."

"But now she'll be convicted, won't she?" says the countess.

"Oh no, countess, she won't be convicted. The majoress at Ekeby will probably be set free, but that is still too much for her, all of this that she has had to bear in recent days. She'll probably go crazy. You can understand, such a proud woman, how can she stand being treated like a criminal? I think that it would have been best if she had been allowed to go free. Perhaps she would have escaped on her own."

"Let her loose!" says the countess.

"Anyone other than the sheriff or his wife can do it, of course," whispers Mrs. Scharling. "We do have to guard her. Especially tonight, when so many of her friends are here, two fellows are standing guard outside the door, so that no one can get in to her. But if someone were to take her out, countess, then we would both be happy, both Scharling and I."

"Might I be allowed to go to her?" says the young countess.

Mrs. Scharling grasps her eagerly around the wrist and leads her out. In the entryway they throw on a pair of shawls, and then they hurry across the yard.

"It's not certain that she will talk even to us," says the sheriff's wife. "But she can still see that we haven't forgotten her."

They come into the first room of the side building, where the two men are guarding the barred door, and without being obstructed they go in to the majoress. She is staying in a large room, filled with looms and other equipment. It is actually used as a weaving room, but it has bars on the windows and strong locks on the door, so that in emergencies it can be used as a jail.

Inside the majoress continues to pace without paying visible heed to them.

She has embarked on a long journey these days. She cannot recall anything other than that she is walking the hundred and twenty–some miles up to her mother, who is sitting up there in the Älvdal forests, waiting for her. She never has time to rest. She has to walk. Restless urgency has overtaken her. Her mother is over ninety. Soon she will be dead.

She has measured up the length of the floor in ells, and now she is counting the laps, adding up the ells to cords and the cords to half miles and miles.

Her way seems heavy and long, and yet she dares not rest. She wades forth through deep drifts. She hears the endless forests sighing over her as she walks. She rests in the Finn's cabin and in the charcoal burner's hut of branches. Sometimes, when there is no other person within several miles, she has to break off branches into a shelter and rest under the root of an overturned spruce.

And finally she has reached the goal, the hundred and twenty–some miles are over, the forest opens, and red buildings stand on a snow-covered yard. The Klara River rushes foaming along in a series of small rapids, and from the familiar roar she hears that she is home.

And her mother, who could see her coming, begging, just as she knew she would, comes to meet her.

When the majoress has come that far, she always looks up, glances around her, sees the closed door, and knows where she is.

Then she wonders if she is going crazy and sits down to think and rest. But after a while she is in motion again, adding up the ells and cords to half miles and miles, taking brief rests in Finn cabins and sleeping neither night nor day, before she has again covered those more than one hundred and twenty miles.

During the entire time she has been imprisoned she has almost never slept.

And both of the women who have come to see her look at her with anxiety.

The young countess would later always remember her the way she was walking there then. Later she sees her often in her dreams and then awakens from the sight with her eyes wet with tears and a lament on her lips.

The old woman is anxiously run-down; her hair looks thin, and loose strands are forcing their way out of her narrow braid. Her face is slack and sunken, her clothes untidy and torn. But despite all this she has so much of the lofty, generally inviting mistress remaining that she does not simply inspire pity, but veneration as well.

But what the countess would clearly recall were the eyes: sunken, turned in, not yet robbed of all the light of reason, but almost ready to go out and with a spark of wildness lurking in the depths, so that you had to fear that the old woman might attack you at any moment, her teeth ready to bite, fingers ready to claw.

They have now been standing there a good while, when the majoress suddenly stops before the young woman and looks at her with a stern gaze. The countess takes a step back and grasps Mrs. Scharling's arm.

The majoress's features suddenly gain life and expression, her eyes look out into the world with complete comprehension.

"Oh no, oh no!" she says and smiles, "it's not that bad yet, my dear young lady."

She invites them to sit down and also sits down herself. She takes on an air of old-fashioned stateliness, familiar from the great parties at Ekeby and the royal balls in the governor's residence in Karlstad. They forget the rags and the jail and see only the proudest and richest woman in Värmland.

"My dear countess!" she says. "What might induce you to leave the dance to come and see a lonely old woman like me? You must be very good."

Countess Elisabet cannot reply. Her voice is choked with emotion. Mrs. Scharling answers in her place, that she has not been able to dance because she has been thinking about the majoress.

"Dear Mrs. Scharling," answers the majoress, "am I so far gone that I disturb the young people in their enjoyment? You mustn't cry over me, my dear young countess," she continued. "I am a mean old woman who deserves her fate. You don't think it's right to strike your mother, do you?"

"No, but—"

The majoress interrupts her and brushes the curly, light hair off of her forehead.

"Child, child," she says, "how could you go and get married to that stupid Henrik Dohna?"

"But I love him."

"I see how it is, I see how it is," says the majoress. "A nice child and nothing more, weeps with the distressed and laughs with the happy. And forced to say 'yes' to the first one who says, 'I love you.' Yes indeed, yes. Go in and dance now, my dear young countess! Dance and be happy. There is nothing bad in you."

"But I want to do something for the majoress."

"Child," says the majoress solemnly, "an old woman lived at Ekeby who kept the winds of the heavens captive. Now she is imprisoned, and the winds are free. Is it strange that a storm is passing over the land?

"I, who am old, have seen it before, countess. I feel it. I know that the thundering storm of God is coming over us. First it sweeps forth over the large realms, then over the small, forgotten communities. God's storm forgets no one. So it passes over the great as well as the small. It is a fine thing to see God's storm coming.

"God's storm, the blessed Lord's weather, is blowing across the earth! Voices in the air, voices in the waters, they sound and terrify! Make God's storm thundering! Make God's storm terrifying! May the squalls move out across the land, rush forth against tottering walls, breaking the locks that have rusted, and the houses that lean, about to fall!

"Anxiety will spread across the land. The small birds' nests will fall from their strongholds on the branch. The hawk's nest at the top of the pine will be cut to the earth with a loud boom, and the wind will hiss with its dragon tongue all the way into the owl's nest in the crevice of the rock.

"We thought that everything was fine here with us, but it was not. God's storm is probably needed. I understand it, and I am not complaining. I simply want to be allowed to go to my mother."

She suddenly breaks down.

"Go now, young woman!" she says. "I have no more time. I have to go. Go now, and watch out for those who are riding on the storm clouds!"

With that she resumed her wandering. Her features slackened, her gaze turned inward. The countess and Mrs. Scharling had to leave her.

As soon as they were in among the dancers again, the young countess went right up to Gösta Berling.

"I bring greetings to Mr. Berling from the majoress," she says. "She is waiting for Mr. Berling to take her out of the prison."

"Then she'll just have to wait, countess."

"Oh, help her, Mr. Berling!"

Gösta gazes darkly before him. "No," he says, "why should I help her? What debt of gratitude do I have to her? Everything that she has done for me has been to my undoing."

"But, Mr. Berling—"

"If she had never existed," he says heatedly, "I would now be sleeping up there under the endless forests. Should I be obliged to risk my life for her, because she made me a cavalier at Ekeby? Do you believe, countess, that much distinction goes along with that position?"

The young countess turns away from him without answering. She is angry.

She goes to her place, thinking bitter thoughts about the cavaliers. They have come here with horns and fiddles and intend to let the bows rub against the strings until the horsehair is worn out, without thinking that the merry notes resound over to the prisoner's miserable room. They have come here to dance until the soles of their shoes turn to dust, and it doesn't occur to them that their old benefactress can see their shadows sweeping past within the steamed-up windowpanes. Oh, how gray and ugly the world became! Oh, what a shadow distress and hard-heartedness cast across the young countess's soul!

After a while Gösta comes to invite her to dance.

She refuses abruptly.

"Don't you want to dance with me, countess?" he asks, turning very red.

"Not with you nor with any other of the Ekeby cavaliers," she says.

"So we are not worthy of such an honor?"

"It's no honor, Mr. Berling. But I find no enjoyment in dancing with those who forget all the dictates of gratitude."

Gösta has already turned on his heels.

This scene is heard and seen by many. All think the countess is right. The cavaliers' ingratitude and heartlessness toward the majoress have aroused general indignation.

But in those days Gösta Berling is more dangerous than a wild animal in the forest. Ever since he came home from the hunt and found Marianne gone, his heart has been like an aching sore. He has a good mind to inflict a bloody injustice on someone and spread sorrow and torment in wide circles.

If she wants it that way, he says to himself, then it will be as she wants. But she won't get to spare her own hide either. The young countess likes abductions. She will get her fill. He has nothing against an adventure. For eight days he has been grieving for the sake of a woman. That may be long enough. He calls Beerencreutz, the colonel, and Kristian Bergh, the strong captain, and the phlegmatic cousin Kristoffer, who never hesitates at a deranged adventure, and seeks counsel with them about how the offended honor of the cavaliers should be avenged.

———

Then comes the end of the banquet. A long row of sleighs drives up to the yard. The gentlemen put on their furs. The ladies look for their coats in the hopeless disorder of the dressing room.

The young countess has been in a hurry to leave this hateful ball. She is the first one done of the ladies. She stands, smiling, in the middle of the floor and watches the confusion, as the door is thrown open and Gösta Berling appears on the threshold.

No man has the right to force his way into this room, however. Old ladies stand there in their thin hair, after they have pulled off their decorative caps. And the young women have hiked up their skirts under the furs, so that the stiff frills will not pinch during the ride home.

But without paying any heed to the cries to stop, Gösta Berling rushes over to the countess and seizes her.

And he lifts her in his arms and races out of the room to the entryway and from there out onto the stairs with her.

The shrieks of the surprised women could not stop him. As they hurry after, they see only how he throws himself into a sleigh with the countess in his arms.

They hear the driver crack the whip and see the horse set off. They know the driver—it is Beerencreutz. They know the horse—it is Don Juan. And in deep distress at the fate of the countess, they call on the men.

And they do not waste time asking many questions; instead they rush to the sleighs. And with the count in the lead, they chase after the abductor.

But he is lying in the sleigh, holding fast to the young countess. He has forgotten all sorrow, and dizzy with the intoxicating pleasure of the adventure, he is singing at full volume a ballad of love and roses.

He holds her pressed close to him, but she makes no attempt to flee. Her face, white and stony, is close to his chest.

Oh, what should a man do when he has a pale, helpless face so close to him, when he sees the light hair that otherwise shadows the white, radiant forehead pushed back, and when the eyelids have closed heavily over the roguish glitter of gray eyes?

What should a man do, when the red lips are fading away under his eyes?

Kiss then, naturally, kiss the fading lips, the closed eyes, the white forehead.

But then the young woman wakes up. She pulls away. She is like a coiled spring. And he has to struggle with all of his strength to keep her from throwing herself out of the sleigh, until he forces her, subdued and trembling, down into one corner of the sleigh.

"Look!" Gösta then says quite calmly to Beerencreutz, "the countess is the third one that Don Juan and I are carrying off this winter. But the others clung to my neck with kisses, and she will neither be kissed by me nor dance with me. Can you figure these women out, Beerencreutz?"

But as Gösta drove from the farm, as the women shouted and the men swore, as the sleigh bells jingled and the whips cracked and everything was shouting and confusion, the men who were guarding the majoress began to feel strangely uneasy.

"What's going on?" they thought. "What are they shouting about?"

Suddenly the door flew open, and a voice called to them, "She is gone. Now he's leaving with her."

They ran out, running like madmen, without looking to see whether it was the majoress or who it was who was gone. Luck was with them, so that they even got into one of the sleighs speeding away. And they drove both long and well, before they found out whom they were pursuing.

But Bergh and cousin Kristoffer went calmly up to the door, broke the lock, and opened it for the majoress.

"You are free, majoress," they said.

She came out. They stood, straight as sticks, on either side of the door and did not look at her.

"You have a horse and sleigh outside here, majoress."

Then she went out, settled into the vehicle, and drove away. No one pursued her. No one knew where she was going either.

On the Broby hills Don Juan hurries toward the ice-covered surface of Löven. The proud runner is flying forth. Bracing, ice-cold air whistles past the riders' cheeks. The sleigh bells ring. Stars and moon are shining. The snow is blue-white, shining with its own luster.

Gösta senses poetic thoughts awakening within him. "Beerencreutz," he says, "look, this is life. Just as Don Juan races away with the young woman, so time races away with every person. You are necessity, guiding the journey. I am desire, who captures free will. And so she is pulled, the powerless one, ever deeper and deeper downward."

"Don't talk!" roars Beerencreutz. "Now they're coming after us!"

And with whistling strokes of the whip he eggs Don Juan on to an ever wilder pace.

"There are the wolves, here the prey!" Gösta cries out. "Don Juan, my lad, imagine that you are a young moose! Rush forth through the thicket, wade through the marsh, take a leap from the mountain ridge down into the clear lake, swim across it with courageously uplifted head, and vanish, vanish into the saving darkness of the dense pine forest! Run, Don Juan, old abductor! Run like a young moose!"

Delight fills his wild heart at the hastening pace. The shouts of the pursuers are for him a song of rejoicing. Delight fills his wild heart as he feels the countess's body shaking with terror, as he hears her teeth rattling.

Suddenly the iron grip by which he has held her is loosened. He stands up in the sleigh and waves his cap.

"I am Gösta Berling!" he shouts, "lord of ten thousand kisses and thirteen thousand love letters. Cheers for Gösta Berling! Catch him, if you can!"

And at the next moment he is whispering in the countess's ear, "Isn't this a good pace? Isn't this a royal ride? Beyond Löven lies Vänern. Beyond Vänern lies the sea, everywhere endless expanses of clear, blue-black ice and beyond that a radiant world. Rolling thunder in the freezing ice, harsh cries behind us, shooting stars above, and clinging sleigh bells before us! Onward! Always onward! Do you have the desire to try that journey, young, lovely lady?"

He has set her free. She pushes him intensely from her.

The next moment finds him on his knees at her feet.

"I am a wretch, a wretch! The countess should not have provoked me. You stood there so proud and fine, never believing that a cavalier's fist could reach you. Heaven and earth love you. You should not increase the burden for those whom heaven and earth despise."

He pulls her hands to him and raises them to his face.

"If you only knew," he says, "what it is to know yourself to be rejected! No one asks what you are doing. No, no one asks."

At the same moment he notices that she has nothing on her hands. He pulls a pair of large leather gloves out of his pocket and puts them on her.

With that he has once again become completely calm. He adjusts himself in the sleigh, as far from the young countess as possible.

"The countess does not need to be afraid," he says. "Don't you see where we're going, countess? You can understand that we don't dare do you any harm."

She, who had been almost out of her mind with fear, now sees that they have already driven across the lake and that Don Juan is struggling up the steep hills at Borg.

They stop the horse by the stairs to the count's estate and let the young countess get out of the sleigh at the door to her own home.

But when she is surrounded by servants who come rushing out, she regains her courage and presence of mind.

"Take care of the horse, Andersson!" she says to the driver. "Would these gentlemen who have driven me home be so kind as to come in awhile? The count will be coming soon."

"As the countess wishes," says Gösta, getting out of the sleigh at once. Beerencreutz casts the reins aside without a moment's hesitation. But the young countess goes before them and shows them into the parlor with ill-concealed *schadenfreude*.

The countess probably expected that the cavaliers would hesitate at the suggestion to wait for her husband.

They didn't know then what a stern, upright man he was. They didn't fear the inquisition he would hold with them, who had violently seized her and forced her to ride with them. She wanted to hear him forbid them to set foot in her home ever again.

She wanted to see him call in the servants to point out the cavaliers as men whom they would henceforth never let past the gates of Borg. She wanted to hear him express his contempt, not only at what they had done to her, but also at their way of treating the old majoress, their benefactress.

He, who to her was pure tenderness and indulgence, he would rise up in righteous severity against her oppressors. Love would put fire in his words. He, who protected and respected her as a being of a finer type than any other, he would not allow vulgar men to swoop down on her like birds of prey on a sparrow. She was glowing with a thirst for vengeance.

Beerencreutz, the colonel with the dense, white mustaches, however, stepped undauntedly into the dining room and went over to the fire, which was always lit when the countess came home from a party.

Gösta stopped in the darkness by the door, silently observing the countess, while the servant relieved her of her outer clothes. As he watched this young woman, he became happier than he had been for many years. It became so clear to him, it was as certain to him as a revelation, although he did not understand how he had discovered it, that within her she had the loveliest soul.

For the time being it was bound and slumbering, but it would no doubt emerge. He became so happy at having discovered all the purity and piety and innocence that dwelled deep within her. He was almost ready to laugh at her because she looked so angry and stood with cheeks glowing and eyebrows knitted.

"You don't know how gentle and good you are," he thought.

That side of her being that was turned toward the material world would never do her inner self complete justice, he thought. But Gösta Berling must be her servant from this moment, the way all that is beautiful and divine must be served. Yes, there was no use regretting that he had just carried on so violently toward her. If she had not been so afraid, if she had not pushed him aside so tempestuously, if he had not perceived how all of her being was agitated by his brutality, then he would never have known what a fine and noble spirit resided within her.

He could not have believed it before. She had simply been merriment and an eagerness to dance. And then she had been able to get married to the stupid Count Henrik.

Yes, now he would be her slave until his death: dog and thrall, as Captain Kristian would say, and nothing more.

He sat down by the door, Gösta Berling, and with clasped hands held a kind of church service. Not since that day when for the first time he felt inspiration's tongue of fire upon him, had he experienced such holiness in his soul. He did not let himself be disturbed, although Count Dohna came in with a number of people, who swore and lamented at the cavaliers' behavior.

He let Beerencreutz receive the storm. In indolent calm this man, tested in many adventures, stood over by the fire. He had set his foot up on the grating, rested his elbow on his knee and his chin on his hand, and looked at those who came storming in.

"What is all this supposed to mean?" the little count roared at him.

"It means," he said, "that as long as there are womenfolk on the earth, there will also be fools who dance to their tune."

The young count became red in the face.

"I am asking what this means!" he repeated.

"I'm asking that too," mocked Beerencreutz. "I'm asking what it means that Henrik Dohna's countess doesn't want to dance with Gösta Berling."

The count turned questioningly toward his wife.

"I couldn't do it, Henrik!" she exclaimed. "I couldn't dance with him or any of them. I was thinking about the majoress, whom they let languish in jail."

The little count straightened out his stiff body and raised his old man's head.

"We cavaliers," said Beerencreutz, "allow no one to insult us. Anyone who doesn't want to dance with us must ride with us. No harm has been done to the countess, and with that the matter can be over."

"No!" said the count. "The matter cannot be over with that. I am the one who answers for my wife's actions. Now I am asking why Gösta Berling did not turn to me to get satisfaction when my wife had offended him."

Beerencreutz smiled.

"I am asking!" repeated the count.

"You don't ask the fox for permission to take his hide off," said Beerencreutz.

The count put his hand on his narrow chest.

"I have a reputation for being a just man," he burst out. "I can judge my servants. Why should I not be able to judge my wife? The cavaliers do not have the right to judge her. I void the punishment which they have applied to her. It has never happened, do you understand, gentlemen? It has never happened."

The count shouted out these words in the highest falsetto. Beerencreutz cast a quick glance out over the congregation. There was not one of those present—Sintram and Daniel Bendix and Dahlberg and all, whoever it might have been who had followed along inside—who was not enjoying how he was fooling the stupid Henrik Dohna.

The young countess understood at once. What was it that should count for nothing? Her anxiety, the cavaliers' hard grip on her tender body, the wild song, the wild words, the wild kisses, should all that not have happened? Did this evening not exist, over which the gray twilight goddess did not rule?

"But, Henrik—"

"Silence!" he said. And he straightened up to give her a lecture as punishment. "Curse you, that you who are a woman have wanted to set yourself up as a judge over men!" he says. "Curse you, that you who are my wife dares to offend someone whose hand I gladly grasp! What do you have to do with the cavaliers having put the majoress in jail? Didn't they have the right? You can never know how a man must be enraged in the depths of his soul when he hears talk of women's infidelity. Do you yourself intend to walk that evil path, since you are coming to the defense of such a woman?"

"But, Henrik—"

She complained like a child and stretched out her arms as if to ward off the angry words. She had perhaps never heard such hard words directed at her. She was so helpless among these hard men, and now her only defender turned against her. Never more would her heart have the power to light up the world.

"But, Henrik, it's you after all who should protect me!"

Gösta Berling was attentive now, when it was too late. To be sure, he didn't know what he should do. He wished her so well. But he dared not force his way in between husband and wife.

"Where is Gösta Berling?" the count inquired.

"Here!" said Gösta. And he made a pitiful attempt to laugh off the matter. "The count was just about to give a speech, and I fell asleep. What would the count say if we were to go home now and let you go to bed?"

"Gösta Berling, because my countess has refused to dance with you, I command that she kiss your hand and ask you for forgiveness."

"My dear Count Henrik," said Gösta smiling, "this is not a hand that is suitable for a young woman to kiss. Yesterday it was red with blood from a wounded moose, tonight black with soot after a fistfight with a charcoal burner. The count has pronounced a noble and high-minded sentence. That is satisfaction enough. Come, Beerencreutz!"

The count placed himself in his way.

"Don't go!" he said. "My wife must obey me. I want my countess to know where willful behavior will lead."

Gösta stopped, helpless. The countess was completely pale, but she did not move.

"Go!" said the count.

"Henrik, I cannot."

"You can," said the count sternly. "You can. But I know what you want. You want to force me to fight with this man, because you, in your capriciousness, do not like him. Well then, if you do not want to give him satisfaction, then I will. It is always dear to you women, if men are killed for your sakes. You have committed the wrong, but will not redeem it. So I have to do it. I will fight a duel, my countess. In a few hours I will be a bloody corpse."

She gave him a long look. And she saw him as he was: stupid, cowardly, inflated with arrogance and vanity, the most lamentable of people.

"Calm down!" she said. And she had become as cold as ice. "I will do it."

But now Gösta Berling was completely beside himself.

"You may not, countess! No, you may not! You are only a child, after all, a weak, innocent child, and you would kiss my hand! You have such a white, lovely soul. I will never get close to you again. Oh, never again! I bring death and destruction over everything good and guiltless. You must not touch me. I tremble before you like fire before water. You may not!"

He stuck his hands behind his back.

"That means nothing to me, Mr. Berling. Now it means nothing to me. I ask you for forgiveness. I ask you, to let me kiss your hand."

Gösta kept his hands behind his back. He considered his position. He approached the door.

"If you do not accept this satisfaction that my wife is offering, I must fight with you, Gösta Berling, and I must impose another, harder punishment on her besides."

The countess shrugged her shoulders. "He is crazy with cowardice," she whispered. "Let it happen now! It means nothing that I am humiliated. That is just what you wanted the whole time."

"Did I want that? Do you think that I wanted that? Well, if I no longer have any hands to kiss, then you must see that I haven't wanted that," he exclaimed.

He ran over to the fire and put his hands into it. The flames wrapped around them, the skin wrinkled, the nails crackled. But at the same moment Beerencreutz caught him by the neck and threw him headlong onto the floor. He stumbled against a chair and remained sitting. He was almost ashamed at such a stupid prank. Would she not think that he simply did it to show off? Doing a thing like that in a room full of people would have to look like stupid showing off. There hadn't been a hint of danger.

Before he could think about getting up, the countess was on her knees beside him. She took hold of the red, sooty hands and observed them.

"I will kiss them, kiss them," she exclaimed, "as soon as they are not too tender and sore!" And the tears were streaming from her eyes as she saw the blisters rise up under the singed skin.

Then he became like a revelation of an unknown magnificence for her. That such things could still happen on this earth, that such a thing could be done for her! No, what a man, what a man was this, ready for everything, magnificent in good as in evil, a man of great deeds, powerful words, a man of spectacular actions! A hero, a hero made from a different substance than others! Slave of a caprice, of the desire of the moment, wild and terrible, but possessor of a savage power, shrinking from nothing.

She had been so dejected the entire evening, seen nothing but sorrow and cruelty and cowardice. Now all was forgotten. The young countess was again happy at being alive. The twilight goddess was beaten. The young countess saw light and color brighten the world.

It was the same night up in the cavaliers' wing.

There they were calling down curses over Gösta Berling. The old gentlemen wanted to sleep, but it was impossible. He did not allow them any peace. It was in vain that they drew the bed curtains and blew out the candles. He simply talked.

Now he let them know what an angel the young countess was and how he worshipped her. He would serve her, adore her. He was now content that everyone had abandoned him. Now he could devote a lifetime to her service. She despised him, naturally. But he would be satisfied to lie at her feet like a dog.

Had they given any notice to the island Lagön out in Löven? Had they seen it from the south, where the rugged cliff rises precipitously out of the water? Had they seen it from the north, where it sinks toward the lake in a slow descent, and where the narrow sandbank, overgrown with large, magnificent spruce trees, meanders up to the water's edge and forms the most marvelous ponds? Up there on the steep cliff top, where remnants of an old pirate fort still remain, he would build a palace to the young countess, a palace of marble. Broad stairs, at which boats covered with streamers could land, would be carved into the rock down to the lake. There would be radiant halls and high towers with gilded pinnacles. It would be a suitable residence for the young countess. The old wooden hovel on Borg's point was not worthy for her to even set foot in.

When he had held forth like that for a while, a few snores began to sound behind the yellow-checked curtains. But most of them swore and complained at him and his follies.

"People," he then says solemnly, "I see the green earth covered by human works or by remnants of human works. The pyramids weigh down the earth, the tower of Babel has pierced the sky, lovely temples and gray castles have risen out of the gravel. But of all the things that hands have built, what is there that has not fallen or will not fall? Oh, people, throw down the trowel and the clay form! Spread the mason's apron over your head and lie down to build the bright palace of dreams! What does the spirit have to do with temples of stone and clay? Learn to build imperishable castles of dreams and visions!"

With that he went laughing to rest.

When the countess shortly afterward found out that the majoress was freed, she sent a dinner invitation to the cavaliers.

And with that began her long friendship with Gösta Berling.

CHAPTER 11

GHOST STORIES

Oh, latter-day children!

I have nothing new to tell you, only what is old and almost forgotten. Legends I have from the nursery, where the little ones sat on low stools around the storyteller with the white hair, or from the log fire in the cabin, where farmhands and crofters sat and talked, as steam rose from their wet clothes and they pulled knives from leather sheaths at their necks to spread butter onto thick, soft bread, or from the parlor, where old gentlemen sat in rocking chairs and, enlivened by a steaming toddy, talked of bygone times.

Then a child who had listened to the storyteller, to the workingmen, to the old gentlemen, stood at the window in the winter evening; then the child saw no clouds at the sky's edge, instead the clouds were cavaliers, who sped across the firmament in rickety one-horse carriages, the stars were wax candles lit in the old count's estate on Borg's point, and the spinning wheel that whirred in the next room was pedaled by old Ulrika Dillner. For the child's head was filled by the people of olden times. The child loved and lived for them.

But if such a child, whose entire soul was fed with legends, was sent across the dark attic into the pantry after linen or rusks, then those small feet hurried, then the child came flying down the stairway through the landing and into the kitchen. For up there in the darkness the child must think about all the old stories it had heard about the malevolent mill owner at Fors, who had gone in league with the devil.

The malevolent Sintram's remains have long rested at Svartsjö cemetery, but no one believes that his soul has been called to God, as it says on the gravestone.

While he lived, he was one of those to whose home a heavy coach, harnessed with black horses, might drive up on long, rainy Sunday afternoons. A dark-clad, elegant gentleman then climbs from the carriage and, with cards and refreshment, helps to pass away the sluggish hours, which in their monotony have brought the master of the house to despair. The card party continues until after midnight, and when the stranger leaves in the morning light, he always leaves a calamitous farewell gift behind.

As long as Sintram was on the earth, he was one of those whose arrival was boded by spirits. Specters go before them: their carriages roll into the yard, their whips crack, their voices sound on the stairs, the entry door opens and shuts. Dogs and people awaken from the clamor, it is so strong, and yet no one comes; it is only specters who go before them.

Ugh, these ghastly people whom the evil spirits seek out! What kind of big, black dog might it have been that showed itself at Fors in Sintram's time? He had terrible, sparkling eyes and a long, blood-dripping tongue that hung far out of his panting throat. One day, just as the farmhands had been in the kitchen and had dinner, he had scratched on the kitchen door, and all the maids had screamed in terror, but the biggest and strongest of the farmhands had taken a burning stick of wood out of the stove, thrown open the door, and thrown it into the dog's mouth.

Then he fled with a terrible howling, flames and smoke coming out of his mouth, sparks whirling around him, and his tracks on the road shining like fire.

And was it not dreadful, that every time the mill owner drove home from a journey, the team was changed for him? He rode with horses, but when he came at night, he always had black bulls before the wagon. The people who lived along the road saw the large, black horns silhouetted against the night sky as he passed by, and heard the animals' bellowing, and were horror-struck at the row of sparks that claws and wagon wheels coaxed out of the dry gravel.

Yes, no doubt those little feet needed to hurry to get across the large, dark attic. What if something terrible, if the one whose name cannot be said, had come out of a dark corner up there! Who could be certain? It was not only the bad ones he showed himself to. Hadn't Ulrika Dillner seen him? Both she and Anna Stjärnhök could tell of times that they had seen him.

Friends, children of humankind, you who dance, you who laugh! I beg you sincerely, dance carefully, laugh gently, for so much misfortune may arise, if your thin-soled silk shoes trample sensitive hearts instead of hard planks, and your lusty, silver-ringing laughter may drive a soul to despair.

It was certainly so that the feet of the young had trampled too hard on old Ulrika Dillner, and the laughter of the young had sounded too presumptuously in her ear, for an irresistible longing suddenly came over her for the title and dignity of a married woman. She finally said yes to the malevolent Sintram's long courtship, followed him to Fors as his wife, and lived apart from her old friends at Berga, the dear old chores, and the familiar worry about daily bread.

It was a match that went quickly and merrily. Sintram courted at yuletide, and the wedding was in February. That year Anna Stjärnhök was living in Captain Uggla's home. She was a good replacement for old Ulrika, who could go out and capture the title of Mrs. without pangs of conscience.

Without pangs of conscience, but not without remorse. It was not a good place she was moving to: the large, empty rooms were filled with eerie fright. As soon as it got dark, she started to shudder and feel scared. She was about to lose her mind with homesickness.

The long Sunday afternoons were harder than anything else. They never had an end, neither them nor the long line of painful thoughts that dragged along through her mind.

Then one day in March, when Sintram had not come home from church for dinner, it happened that she went into the parlor on the upper floor and sat down at the piano. It was her final consolation. The piano, with a flute player and a shepherdess painted on the white cover, was her own, inherited from her parental home. She could complain her woes to it; it understood her.

But is that not both deplorable and ridiculous? Do you know what she is playing? Only a *polska*, and she, who is so sorely distressed!

She doesn't know anything else. Before her fingers stiffened around whisk and carving knife, she learned this one *polska*. It still sits in her fingers, but she cannot play any other piece, no funeral march, no passionate sonata, not even a lamenting folk song, only that *polska*.

She plays it as often as she has something to confide to the old piano. She plays it both when she wants to cry and when she wants to smile. When she celebrated her wedding, she played it, and when she entered her home for the first time, and likewise now.

The old strings seem to understand her; she is unhappy, unhappy.

A wayfarer who passes by and hears the *polska* might believe that the malevolent mill owner is holding a ball for neighbors and relatives, so merrily it sounds. It is an exceedingly jaunty and lusty melody. In former days she has played levity in and hunger out at Borga farm with it. When it sounded, everyone got up to dance. It broke the bonds of rheumatism around joints and fooled eighty-year-old cavaliers up onto the floor. The whole world might want to dance to that *polska*, so lusty it sounds—but old Ulrika is weeping.

She has moody, peevish servants around her and bad-tempered animals. She longs for friendly faces and smiling mouths. It is this, her desperate longing, which the happy *polska* must interpret.

People have a hard time realizing that she is Mrs. Sintram. Everyone calls her Miss Dillner. See, that is the idea, that the *polska* melody should explain her remorse over the vanity that enticed her to chase after the title of wife.

Old Ulrika plays, as if she wanted to break the strings. There is so much to drown out: cries of distress from poor farmers, curses from tormented crofters, scornful laughter from defiant servants, and first and last the shame, the shame of being a wicked man's wife.

To these notes Gösta Berling has led young Countess Dohna up in the dance. Marianne Sinclaire and her many admirers have danced to it, and the majoress at Ekeby has moved to its rhythm when the handsome Altringer was still alive. She sees them pair by pair, united in youth and beauty, whirling past. A stream of merriment passed from them to her, from her to them. It was her *polska* that made their cheeks glow, their eyes radiate. She is separated from all that now. May the *polska* thunder—so many memories, so many sweet memories to drown out!

She plays to deaden her anxiety. Her heart wants to burst in terror when she sees the black dog, when she hears the servants whispering about the black bulls. She plays the *polska* over and over again to deaden her anxiety.

Then she notices that her husband has come home. She hears him come into the room and sit down on the rocking chair. She recognizes the rocking so well, as the rocker creaks against the floor plank, that she does not even turn around.

All the while as she is playing, the rocking continues. Now she no longer hears the notes, only the rocking.

Poor old Ulrika, so tormented, so lonely, so helpless, gone astray in a hostile country, without a friend to complain to, without anyone to console her other than a rattling piano, that answers her with a *polska*!

This is like loud laughter at a burial, a drinking song in church.

While the rocking chair continues to rock, she suddenly hears how the piano laughs at her lament, and she stops in the middle of a measure. She gets up and looks over at the rocking chair.

But the very next moment she is lying unconscious on the floor. It was not her husband who sat in the rocking chair, but another—the one whose name small children dare not speak, the one who would frighten them to death, if they encountered him in the desolate attic.

Can anyone, whose soul has been fed with legends, ever free herself from its control? The night wind is howling outside, a ficus and oleander are whipping the balcony pillars with their stiff leaves; the sky vaults dark over the extended hills, and I, sitting alone in the night and writing, with the lamp lit and the curtain drawn, I, who am old now and ought to be wise, I feel the same shivers creeping up my spine as when I heard this story for the first time, and I have to keep raising my eyes from my work to see whether someone hasn't come in and hidden in the corner over there; I have to look out at the balcony to be certain that a black dog does not spring up over the railing. It never leaves me, this terror that is aroused by the old stories, when the night is dark and solitude profound, and at last it becomes so overpowering to me that I have to drop the pen, creep down into my bed, and pull the blanket up over my eyes.

It was my childhood's great, secret admiration that Ulrika Dillner survived that afternoon. I would not have.

It was fortunate that Anna Stjärnhök came driving to Fors immediately thereafter, and that she found her on the parlor floor and wakened her to life again. But it would not have gone as well with me. I would already have been dead.

I wish for you, dear friends, that you might avoid seeing the tears of old eyes.

Or that you might not stand helpless when a gray head leans against your breast to get support, or when old hands are clasped around yours in silent prayer. May you avoid seeing the old drowned in sorrow that you cannot comfort!

What are the complaints of the young, then? They have strength, they have hope. But what a misery it is, when the old weep, what despair when they, who have been the support of your youthful days, sink into powerless complaint!

There sat Anna Stjärnhök listening to old Ulrika, and she saw no way out for her.

The old woman wept and trembled. Her eyes were wild. She talked and talked, sometimes so confusedly, as if she no longer knew where she was. The thousand wrinkles that crisscrossed her face were twice as deep as usual; the loose locks of hair that hung down over her eyes, straightened by tears; and her entire long, emaciated form was shaking with sobs.

Finally Anna Stjärnhök had to put an end to the moaning. She made a decision. She would take her back to Berga with her. It was true that she was Sintram's wife, but she could not remain at Fors. The mill owner would drive her crazy if she stayed with him. Anna Stjärnhök decided to take old Ulrika away.

Oh, how the poor thing was happy and terrified at this decision! But she would not dare leave her husband and her home. Perhaps he would send the big, black dog after her.

But Anna Stjärnhök overcame her resistance, partly with joking, partly with threats, and in half an hour she had her beside her in the sleigh. Anna drove herself, and old Disa pulled the sleigh. The going was miserable, for it was long into March, but it did old Ulrika good to ride in the familiar sleigh again behind the familiar horse, which had been a faithful servant at Berga at least as long as she.

As she now was in good spirits and in a fearless mood, this old household thrall, she stopped crying as they drove past Arvidstorp, by Högberg she was already laughing, and as they drove past Munkeby, she was in the process of telling about how it was in her youth, when she served with the countess at Svanaholm.

They now drove into the desolate, unpopulated areas north of Munkeby on a hilly, stony road. The road made its way to all the hills it could possibly reach, it crept up to their tops in a slow curl, but rushed as fast as it could across the level valley bottoms in order to immediately find a new precipice to climb over.

They were just about to drive down Västratorp Hill when old Ulrika suddenly fell silent and seized Anna hard by the arm. She was staring at a big, black dog by the roadside.

"Look!" she said.

The dog set off into the forest. Anna did not see much of him.

"Drive," said Ulrika, "drive as fast as you can! Now Sintram will get word that I have gone."

Anna tried to laugh away her anxiety, but she kept on.

"Soon we'll be hearing his sleigh bells, you'll see. We'll hear them before we come up to the top of the next hill."

And as Disa panted a moment at the top of Elof's Hill, the peal of sleigh bells was heard below them.

Now old Ulrika became completely crazy with anxiety. She shook, sobbed, and moaned just like a short while ago in the parlor at Fors. Anna wanted to urge Disa on, but the horse simply turned its head and gave her a look of inexpressible astonishment. Did she think that Disa had forgotten when it was time to run and when it was time to canter? Did she want to teach her how to pull a sleigh, teach her, who knew every stone, every bridge, every gate, every hill, going back more than twenty years?

During this the peal of sleigh bells was getting closer and closer.

"It's him, it's him! I know his sleigh bells," old Ulrika moans.

The peal is getting closer and closer. Sometimes it is so unnaturally loud that Anna turns around to see if the head of Sintram's horse isn't next to the sleigh; sometimes it dies away. They hear it first to the right, then to the left of the road, but they see no one driving. It is as if the peal of the sleigh bells alone was pursuing them. The way it is at night, when you go home from a dinner party, that's the way it is now. These sleigh bells peal in melodies, sing, speak, reply. The forest resounds with the din they create.

Anna Stjärnhök almost longs that the pursuers would finally get so close to them that she would see Sintram himself and his red horse. She gets a gruesome feeling from this dreadful peal of sleigh bells.

"Those sleigh bells are torturing me," she says.

And immediately the words are picked up by the bells. "Torture me," they ring. "Torture me, torture, torture, torture me," they sing in all possible melodies.

It was not so long ago she drove this same way, pursued by wolves. In the darkness she had seen the white teeth glistening in wide-open jaws, she had imagined that her body would be torn apart by the wild animals of the forest, but then she had not been afraid. She had not experienced a more magnificent night. The horse that had pulled her had been strong and beautiful, strong and beautiful was the man who shared the adventure's delight with her.

Ah, this old horse, this old, helpless, trembling travel companion! She feels so powerless that she wants to cry. She cannot escape this dreadful, arousing peal of sleigh bells.

Then she keeps quiet and gets out of the sleigh. This must have an end. Why should she run away, as if she were afraid of this malevolent, despicable wretch?

Finally she sees a horse's head come forth out of the gathering twilight and after the head a whole horse, a whole sleigh, and in the sleigh sits Sintram himself.

She notices, however, that it is not as if they had come along the highway, this sleigh and this horse and mill owner, but rather as if they had been created right there before her eyes and appeared out of the twilight when they were finished.

Anna throws the reins to Ulrika and goes up to Sintram.

He reins in the horse.

"Look, look," he says, "what good luck for a poor man! Dear Miss Stjärnhök, let me move my travel companion over into your sleigh. He's going to Berga this evening, and I am in a hurry to get home."

"Who is your travel companion, mill owner?"

Sintram rips open the carriage apron and shows Anna a fellow who is lying asleep on the floor of the sleigh. "He's a little drunk," he says, "but what does that matter? He'll keep on sleeping. It's a familiar person by the way, Miss Stjärnhök, it's Gösta Berling."

Anna shudders.

"Look, I should say," Sintram continued, "that anyone who abandons his beloved sells him to the devil. That was the way I got him in my claws. You think you are doing so well, of course. Forsake, that's a good thing, and love, that's a bad thing."

"What do you mean, mill owner? What are you talking about?" asked Anna, quite shaken up.

"I mean that you should not have let Gösta Berling leave you, Miss Anna."

"God willed it, mill owner."

"Sure, sure, that's how it is, to forsake is good, to love is bad. The good Lord does not like to see people happy. He sends wolves after them. But what if it wasn't God that did that, Miss Anna? Could it not just as well have been me, who called my little gray lambs from Dovrefjäll to pursue the young man and the young girl? Think if it was me who sent the wolves, because I didn't want to lose one of my own! Think if it wasn't God who did it!"

"You will not tempt me into doubting that matter, mill owner," says Anna in a weak voice, "then I am lost."

"Look here now," says Sintram, leaning down across the sleeping Gösta Berling, "look at his little finger! That little wound will never heal. We took blood there when he signed the contract. He is mine. Blood has a power of its own. He is mine, it is only love that can release him, but if I get to keep him, he will be delightful."

Anna Stjärnhök struggles and struggles to be free of this enchantment that has seized her. All of this is just madness, madness. No one can swear away his soul to the evil tempter. But she has no power over her thoughts, the twilight is settling so heavy over her, the forest stands so dark and silent. She cannot escape the ghastly terror of the hour.

"Perhaps you think," the mill owner continues, "that there is not much left of him to corrupt? Don't believe it! Has he tortured farmers, has he betrayed poor friends, has he cheated at cards? Has he, Miss Anna, been the lover of married women?"

"I think that you are the evil one himself!"

"Let us trade, Miss Anna! Take Gösta Berling, take him and marry him! Keep him and give them at Berga the money! I relinquish him to you, and you know that he is mine. Think about the fact that it is not God who sent the wolves after you here in the night, and let us trade!"

"What do you want in exchange, mill owner?"

Sintram sneered.

"Me, what do I want? Oh, I'll be content with a little. I will only have that old woman in your sleigh, Miss Anna."

"Satan, tempter," cries Anna, "get away from me! Should I betray an old friend who is relying on me? Should I leave her to you, so that you can torment her into madness?"

"Look, look, calm, Miss Anna! Think about it! Here is a young, splendid man and there an old, worn-out hag. I must have one of them. Which of them will you let me have?"

Anna Stjärnhök laughed in desperation.

"Do you think, mill owner, that we should stand here and trade souls, the way you trade horses at Broby market?"

"Yes, exactly. But if you wish, Miss Anna, we will arrange it in a different way. We will think about the honor of the Stjärnhök family name."

With that he begins to call and shout in a loud voice to his wife, who is sitting in Anna's sleigh, and to the girl's inexpressible horror she obeys the call at once, gets out of the sleigh, and comes shaking and shivering over to them.

"Look, look, look, such an obedient wife!" says Sintram. "It's not your fault, Miss Anna, that she comes when her husband calls. Now I'll lift Gösta out of my sleigh and leave him here. Leave him *forever*, Miss Anna. Whoever wants to can pick him up."

He bends over to pick up Gösta, but then Anna leans all the way down to his face, setting her eyes on him and hissing like a provoked animal, "In the name of God, go home with you! Don't you know who is sitting in the rocking chair in the parlor waiting for you? Do you dare let that gentleman wait?"

For Anna, it is almost the high point of the day's atrocities to see how these words affect the malevolent man. He pulls the reins to him, turns, and drives homeward, driving the horses to a wild gallop with whip strokes and wild shouts. Down the terrifying hill goes the life-threatening ride, while sparks flash in a long row under the runners and hooves in the thin March snow cover.

Anna Stjärnhök and Ulrika Dillner stand alone on the road, but they do not say a word. Ulrika shudders at Anna's wild glances, and she has nothing to say to the poor old woman, for whose sake she has sacrificed her beloved.

She wanted to cry, rage, roll around on the road and strew snow and sand on her head.

Before she had felt the sweetness of abandonment; now she felt its bitterness. What was it to sacrifice your love against sacrificing the soul of your beloved!

They drove up to Berga in the same silence, but when they were there and the parlor door was opened, Anna Stjärnhök fainted for the first and last time in her life. Inside both Sintram and Gösta Berling were sitting, conversing in calm. The toddy tray was already there. They must have been there at least an hour.

Anna Stjärnhök fainted, but old Ulrika stood calmly. She had no doubt noticed that there was something not quite right about the one who had pursued them on the highway.

Then Captain Uggla and his wife made financial arrangements with the mill owner so that old Ulrika was allowed to stay at

Berga. He yielded quite good-naturedly. "He certainly doesn't want to drive her crazy," he said.

Oh, latter-day children!

I do not ask anyone to give credence to these old stories. They may be nothing more than lies and poetry. But the remorse that rocks back and forth in the heart, until it complains, as the floorboards in Sintram's parlor complained under the rocker; but the doubt that rings in your eyes, the way the sleigh bells rang for Anna Stjärnhök in the desolate forest, when does that turn into lies and poetry?

Oh, if they only could!

CHAPTER 12

EBBA DOHNA'S STORY

You must be wary of entering the fair promontory on Löven's eastern shore, around which the inlets glide in with silky waves, the proud promontory where Borg's manor sits.

Löven was never more magnificent than when seen from this height.

No one can know how fair it is, this lake of my dreams, until he has seen the morning mists gliding away across the polished surface from Borg's point; before he has seen it reflect a pale red sunset from the windows in the little blue study, where so many memories reside.

But I say to you still: do not go there!

For perhaps you will be seized by a desire to remain in the old manor's sorrow-laden halls, perhaps make yourself owner of this fair soil, and if you are young, rich, and fortunate, you, like many another, make your home there with a young spouse.

No, it is better not to see the beautiful promontory, for no happiness can reside at Borg. Know that however rich, however fortunate you may be, once you move in, those old tear-drenched floors would soon be drinking your tears as well, and those walls, which could repeat so many sounds of sorrow, would collect your sighs too.

An unfavorable fate hangs over this lovely estate. It is as if misfortune were buried there, but, finding no peace in its grave, constantly rises up out of it to torment the living. If I were master at Borg, I would ransack the ground, both the bedrock of the stands of fir and the cellar floors of the houses and the fertile soil out on the fields, until I found the witch's worm-eaten corpse, and then I would give her a grave in hallowed ground at the Svartsjö churchyard. And at the burial I would not skimp on payment for the bell ringer; the bells would sound long and powerful over her, and I would send expensive gifts to the minister and organist, so that with doubled energy they might consecrate her to eternal rest with oratory and song.

Or if this did not help, one stormy night I would let the fire approach the buckling wooden walls and let it ravage everything, so that people might no longer be enticed to dwell in this home of misfortune. Then no one would be able to enter this doomed place, only the church steeple's black jackdaws would found a colony in the large chimney, rising, blackened and eerie, over the desolate ground.

Yet I would surely be anxious when I saw the flames intertwined over the roof, when thick smoke, reddened by the firelight and interspersed with sparks, poured forth out of the old count's estate. In the crackling and sighing I would think I heard the lament of homeless people; at the blue tips of the flames I would think I saw disturbed phantasms hovering. I would think about how sorrow beautifies, how misfortune adorns, and weep, as if a temple to old gods had been doomed to disintegration.

Yet, quiet now, you who are cawing about misfortunes! Borg still stands, shining at the height of the promontory, protected by its stand of massive fir trees, and the snow-covered fields below glisten in the March day's piercing sunlight; within its walls the merry laughter of the happy Countess Elisabet is still heard.

On Sundays she goes to Svartsjö church, which is close to Borg, and gathers together her little dinner party. The judge at Munkerud and his wife usually come and the captain from Borga and the assistant vicar and their wives and the malevolent Sintram. If Gösta Berling were to come to Svartsjö, wandering on the ice of Löven, she would invite him too. Why shouldn't she invite Gösta Berling?

She does not know, does she, that slander is starting to whisper that Gösta often comes over to the eastern shore to meet her. Perhaps he also comes to drink and play cards with Sintram, but that doesn't raise as many questions; everyone knows that his body is made of iron, but his heart is another matter. There is simply no one who believes that he can see a pair of glistening eyes and light hair, curling around a white forehead, without falling in love.

The young countess is good to him. There is nothing remarkable about that; she is good to everyone. She sets ragged beggar urchins on her lap, and when she rides past an old wretch on the highway, she lets the coachman stop to let the poor pedestrian into her sleigh.

Gösta usually sits in the little blue study, where there is a splendid view over the lake, and reads poetry to her. There cannot be anything wrong with that. He does not forget that she is a countess and he a homeless adventurer, and it is good for him to associate with someone who stands high and holy to him. He may just as well imagine falling in love with the Queen of Sheba, who adorns the panels on the balcony in Svartsjö church, as with her.

He desires simply to serve her, as a page serves his elevated mistress, to tie her skate, hold her skein of yarn, guide her sled. There can be no question of love between them, but he is the right man to find his happiness in a romantic, harmless infatuation.

The young count is silent and serious, and Gösta is exuberantly happy. He is the kind of companionship that the young countess wants. No one who sees her thinks she is harboring a forbidden love. She thinks about dance, about dance and merriment. She wishes that the earth were completely flat, without stones, without hills and lakes, so that you could go everywhere dancing. From cradle to grave she would dance in narrow, thin-soled silk shoes.

But rumors are not merciful to young women.

When these guests come to Borg and have dinner, after the meal the gentlemen usually go into the count's room to sleep and smoke, the old ladies usually sink down into the armchairs in the drawing room and lean their venerable heads against the high arms, but the countess and Anna Stjärnhök go into the blue study and exchange endless confidences.

The Sunday after the one when Anna Stjärnhök fetched Ulrika Dillner back to Berga, they are again sitting there.

No one on earth is unhappier than this young girl. All her merriment is gone, and gone is the happy defiance that she would set against everything and everyone who wanted to get too close to her.

Everything that happened to her on the way home has descended in her awareness into the twilight out of which it was enchanted: she has not a single clear impression left.

Well, one, that poisons her soul.

"What if it wasn't God who did it," she would whisper to herself, "what if it wasn't God who sent the wolves?"

She demands signs, she demands miracles. She gazes round heaven and earth. But she sees no finger extending out of the sky to point out her path. No columns of mist and light go before her.

As she is now sitting across from the countess in the little blue study, her gaze falls on a small bouquet of blue anemones that the countess is holding in her white hand. Like a thunderbolt it strikes her that she knows where those anemones have grown, that she knows who has picked them.

She does not need to ask. Where in the entire region do blue anemones grow already at the beginning of April except in the birch meadow that is on the lakeshore slope at Ekeby?

She stares and stares at the small blue stars, these fortunate ones who have everyone's heart, these small prophets, who, lovely themselves, are also irradiated by the luster of everything lovely, which they herald, of everything lovely that is to come. While she observes them, her soul begins to resound with wrath, rumbling like thunder, deafening like lightning. "By what right," she thinks, "does Countess Dohna carry this bouquet of blue anemones, picked on the shore path at Ekeby?"

They were all tempters: Sintram, the countess, they all wanted to lure Gösta Berling to that which was evil, but she would defend him. Even if it were to cost her heart's blood, she would do it.

She thinks that she must see those flowers torn from the countess's hand and thrown away, trampled, crushed, before she leaves the blue study.

She is thinking this, and she begins a struggle against the small blue stars. Out in the drawing room the old women lean their venerable heads against the chair arms and suspect nothing, the gentlemen puff on their pipes in calm and quiet in the count's room, all is peace; only in the little blue study is a desperate struggle raging.

They do well who keep their hands from the sword, they who understand to quietly bide their time, to set their hearts at peace and let God direct! The restless heart always goes astray. Evil always makes the evil worse.

But Anna Stjärnhök believes that she has now finally seen the finger in the sky.

"Anna," says the countess, "tell a story!"

"About what?"

"Oh," says the countess, stroking the bouquet with her white hand. "Do you know anything about love, anything about being in love?"

"No, I know nothing about love."

"The way you talk! Isn't there a place here called Ekeby, a place full of cavaliers?"

"Well," says Anna, "there is a place here called Ekeby, and there are men who suck the marrow of the land, who make us incapable of serious work, who destroy our maturing youth and lead our best minds astray. Do you want to hear about them, do you want to hear love stories about them?"

"I would. I like the cavaliers."

Then Anna Stjärnhök speaks, speaks in short stanzas, like an old hymnbook, for she is close to suffocating from tempestuous feelings. Concealed passion trembles under every word, and the countess must listen to her with both fear and interest.

"What is the love of a cavalier, what is the faith of a cavalier? One sweetheart today, one tomorrow, one in the east, one in the west. Nothing is too high for him, nothing too low; one day a count's daughter, another day a beggar lass. Nothing on the earth is so capacious as his heart. But poor, poor anyone who loves a cavalier! She has to seek him where he lies drunk on the roadside. She must silently look on as he fritters away her child's home at the gaming table. She has to put up with him swooning around strange women. Oh, Elisabet, if a cavalier asks an honorable woman for a dance, then she ought to deny him that; if he sends her a bouquet of flowers, then she ought to cast the flowers to the ground and trample on them; if she loves him, then she ought to die rather than marry him. Among the cavaliers there is one, who was a defrocked minister. He lost his minister's robe for drunkenness. He was drunk in the church. He drank up the communion wine. Have you heard tell of him?"

"No."

"Immediately after he was removed from his position, he wandered around the countryside as a beggar. He drank like a lunatic. He would steal to get liquor."

"What is his name?"

"He is no longer at Ekeby. The majoress at Ekeby took care of him, gave him clothes, and convinced your mother-in-law, the Countess Dohna, to make him a tutor for your husband, the young Count Henrik."

"A defrocked minister!"

"Oh, he was a young, powerful man, with good abilities. There was no problem with him, as long as he did not drink. The Countess Märta was not particular. It amused her to annoy the dean and the assistant vicar. She forbade, however, that anyone should mention his previous life to her children. Then her son would have lost respect for him, and her daughter would not have been able to tolerate him, for she was a saint.

"Then he came here to Borg. He stopped right inside the door, sat at the very edge of the chair, kept silent at the table, and fled out to the park when visitors came here.

"But out there he used to encounter the young Ebba Dohna on the deserted pathways. She was not one who loved the noisy parties that thundered through the halls of Borg since the countess had become a widow. She was not one who sent defiant glances out into the world. She was so gentle, so shy. She was still a gentle child when she had already reached the age of seventeen, but she was nonetheless very lovely with her brown eyes and the faint, fine redness of her cheeks. Her delicate, slender body leaned feebly forward. Her narrow hand sneaked its way into yours with a shy pressure. Her small mouth was the most silent of mouths and the most serious. Oh, her voice, her sweet little voice, which pronounced the words so slowly and well, but never ringing with youthful energy, youthful heat, but instead came dragging with muted intonation like a tired musician's final chord!

"She was not like others. Her foot walked the ground so lightly, so silently, as if she had only been a frightened refugee down here. She kept her eyes lowered so as not to be disturbed in observing the magnificence of her inner visions. Her soul had turned away from the earth, even when she was a small child.

"When she was small, her grandmother used to tell stories to her, and one evening the two of them were sitting by the fire, but the stories had come to an end. Carsus and Moderus and Lunkentus and the lovely Melusina had risen and lived. Like the flames of the fire they had tumbled about in life and luster, but now the heroes lay defeated, until the next fire awakened them again. But the little girl's hand was still on the old woman's skirt, and she slowly stroked the silk, that lusty fabric that peeped like a little bird. And this stroking was her prayer, for she was one of those children who never pray in words.

"Then very quietly the old woman started to tell her about a little child in the land of Judah, about a little child who was born to become a great king. The angels had filled the earth with songs of praise when he was born. The kings of the east had come, led by the star of the heavens, and offered him gold and incense, and old men and women prophesied his glory. This child grew up to greater beauty and wisdom than all other children. Even when he was twelve years old, his wisdom was greater than the high priests and the scholars.

"Then the old woman told her about the most beautiful thing the earth has seen, about the child's life while it existed among humankind, about the wicked people who did not want to acknowledge him as their king.

"She told her about how the child became a man, but miracles still radiated from him.

"Everything on the earth served him and loved him, except the people. The fishes let themselves be caught in his net, bread filled his baskets, water turned itself into wine, when he wished it.

"But the people did not give the great king a golden crown, a shining throne. He had no bowing courtiers around him. They let him go among them as a beggar.

"Yet he was so good to them, this great king. He healed their sick, gave the blind back their sight, and awakened the dead.

"'But,' said the old woman, 'the people would not have the good king as their lord.'

"They sent their soldiers against him and imprisoned him; in derision they dressed him in a crown and scepter and in a silk mantle and let him walk out to the execution site, carrying a heavy cross. Oh, my child, the good king loved the tall mountains. At night he would climb them to speak with the residents of heaven, and he liked to sit on the mountain slopes during the day and speak to listening people. But now they led him up onto a mountain in order to crucify him. They hammered nails through his hands and feet and hanged the good king on a cross, as if he had been a robber and evildoer.

"And the people mocked him. Only his mother and his friends wept, because he was going to die before he had time to become a king.

"Oh, how lifeless things grieved at his death!

"The sun lost its light, and the mountains shook, the veil in the temple was torn, and the graves opened for the dead, that they might go out and show their sorrow.

"Then the little girl lay with her head in her grandmother's lap and sobbed as if her heart would burst.

"'Don't cry, little one, the good king rose up from his grave and went up to his father in heaven.'

"'Grandmother,' sobbed the poor little thing, 'so he never got a kingdom?'

"'He is sitting at God's right hand in heaven.'

"But this did not console her. She wept as helplessly and un-restrained as a child can weep.

"'Why were they so mean to him? Why did they have to be so mean to him?'

"The old woman was almost afraid of this overwhelming sorrow.

"'Tell me, Grandmother, tell me that you haven't told the story right! Say that it didn't end like that! Say that they weren't so mean to the good king! Say that he got a kingdom on earth!'

"She wrapped her arms around the old woman and begged with tears still streaming.

"'Child, child,' her grandmother then said to console her, 'there are those who believe that he will come again. Then he will place the earth under his dominion and govern it. A magnificent kingdom will be made of the beautiful earth. It will stand for a thousand years. Then the bad animals will become good; little children will play in the viper's nest, and bears and cows will graze together. No one will harm or injure the other any longer; spears will be bent into scythes and swords hammered into plows. And everything will be play and happiness, for the good will possess the earth.'

"Then the little one's face lit up behind her tears.

"'Will the good king get a throne then, Grandmother?'

"'A throne of gold.'

"'And servants and courtiers and a golden crown?'

"'Yes, he will.'

"'Is he coming soon, Grandmother?'

"'No one knows when he is coming.'

"'May I sit on a stool at his feet then?'

"'Yes, you may!'

"'Grandmother, I am so happy,' said the little one.

"Evening after evening through many winters these two sat by the fire and talked about the good king and his realm. The little one dreamed about the thousand-year realm both night and day. She never tired of adorning it with every lovely thing she could think of.

"It is that way with many of the silent children who surround us, that they harbor a secret dream that they do not dare to mention. Strange thoughts dwell under many a soft head of hair, the brown, gentle eyes see strange things behind their closed eyes, many a lovely maiden has her bridegroom in heaven. Many a rosy cheek wants to rub the good king's feet with ointment and dry it with her hair.

"Ebba Dohna did not dare mention to anyone, but ever since that evening she lived only for the Lord's thousand-year kingdom and to await his arrival.

"When the red skies of evening opened the western gate, she wondered if he would not step out from it, radiant with gentle brilliance, followed by an army of millions of angels, and march past and allow her to touch the folds of his mantle.

"She also thought gladly about the pious women who had hung a veil over their heads and never raised their eyes from the earth, instead closing themselves within the peacefulness of gray cloisters, in the darkness of small cells, so as to always be able to see the radiant visions that appear out of the night of the soul.

"She had grown up that way, she was that way, when she and the new tutor met in the desolate pathways of the park.

"I do not wish to say more bad things about him than I have to. I want to believe that he loved this child, who soon chose him as a companion on lonely wanderings. I believe that his soul regained its wings as he walked at the side of this silent girl who had never confided in anyone else. I think that he himself felt like a child, good, pious, virtuous.

"But if he loved her, why did he not think about the fact that he could not give her a worse gift than his love? He, one of the castoffs of this world, what did he want, what was he thinking as he walked beside the count's daughter? What was the defrocked minister thinking about, as she confided her pious dreams to him? What did he want—he who had been a drinker and a brawler and would be so again, when the occasion arose—at the side of her, who dreamed of a bridegroom in heaven? Why did he not flee far, far away from her? Would it not have been better for him if he had wandered begging and thieving around the countryside than that he should be there in the silent lanes of conifers and again become good, pious, virtuous, when it still could not be lived over, that life that he had led, and when it could not be avoided that Ebba Dohna would love him?

"Do not believe that he looked like a drunken wretch with pale-gray cheeks and reddened eyes! He was still a stately man, handsome and unbroken in soul and body. He had a posture like a king and a body of iron, which was not ruined by the wildest living."

"Is he still alive?" asked the countess.

"Oh no, he must be dead by now. All of this was so long ago."

There is something within Anna Stjärnhök that begins to shudder at what she is doing. She starts to think that she must never tell the countess who the man is that she is talking about, that she must let her believe that he is dead.

"At that time he was still young." She begins her story anew. "The happiness of living was ignited again in him. His was the gift of beautiful words and the fiery, easily impassioned heart.

"There came an evening when he talked with Ebba Dohna about love. She did not reply, she said to him only what her grandmother had told her on the winter evening and described for him the land of her dreams. Then she took a promise from him. She let him swear that he would become a herald of God's word, one of those who would prepare the way of the Lord, so that his arrival would be hastened.

"What should he do? He was a defrocked minister, and no way was so barred for him as the one that she wanted him to embark on. But he dared not tell her the truth. He did not have the heart to distress this kindly child, whom he loved. He promised everything that she wanted.

"Then no further words were required between them. It was clear that she would one day become his wife. This was not a love with kisses and embraces. He hardly dared get close to her. She was as delicate as a fragile flower. But her brown eyes were lifted at times from the ground to seek his. On moonlit evenings as they sat on the veranda, she crept close to him, and then he kissed her hair, without her noticing it.

"But you realize that his sin was that he forgot both past and future. That he was poor and insignificant, he would of course prefer to forget, but he ought always to have known that a day must come when in her awareness love would rise up against love, earth against heaven, and when she would be forced to choose between him and the radiant lord of the thousand-year realm. And she was not one who could endure such a struggle.

"A summer passed, an autumn, a winter. When spring came and the ice melted, Ebba Dohna became ill. The ground was thawing in the valleys, the brooks were swelling, the lakes were unsafe, the roads impossible to travel either by sleigh or cart.

"Then Countess Dohna wanted to have the doctor fetched from Karlstad. There was no one closer. But she commanded in vain. She could not induce a servant to go, either with prayers or threats. She fell on her knees for the coachman, but he refused. She had cramps and convulsions from sorrow over her daughter. She is wild in sorrow as well as in happiness, Countess Märta.

"Ebba Dohna had pneumonia, and her life was in danger, but no doctor could be fetched.

"Then the tutor went to Karlstad. Making that journey with the roads in such a state was gambling with your life, but he did it. The journey went across buckling ice and breakneck swells; at times he had to cut stair steps for the horse in the ice, at times pull the horse out of the road's deep clay. It was said that the doctor refused to come with him, but that with pistol in hand he forced him to go along.

"When he came back, the countess was ready to throw herself at his feet. 'Take everything!' she said. 'Say what you want, what you desire, my daughter, my estate, my money!'

"'Your daughter,' replied the tutor."

Anna Stjärnhök suddenly falls silent.

"Well, what then, what happens next?" asks Countess Elisabet.

"That's enough for now," answers Anna, for she is one of those pitiful people who live under the anxiety and fear of doubt. For an entire week now she has been like that. She does not know what she wants. What seems right to her one moment becomes wrong the next. Now she wishes she had never started this story.

"I am starting to think that you want to make fun of me, Anna. Don't you understand that I *must* hear the end of this story?"

"There is not much left to tell. The hour of struggle had come for the young Ebba Dohna. Love raised up against love, earth against heaven.

"Countess Märta told her about the marvelous journey which the young man had made for her sake, and she told her that as a reward she had therefore granted him her hand.

"The young Miss Ebba was then so far advanced on the way to improvement that she was lying dressed on a sofa. She was weak and tired and even more silent than usual.

"When she heard these words, she raised her brown eyes reproachfully toward her mother and said to her, 'Mama, have you given me away to a defrocked minister, to one who has forfeited his right to be God's servant, to a man who has been a thief, a beggar?'

"'But, child, who told you this? I thought you didn't know anything.'

"'I found out. I heard your guests talking about him, the same day I got sick.'

"'But child, keep in mind that he saved your life!'

"'I am keeping in mind that he has deceived me. He should have told me who he was.'

"'He says that you love him.'

"'I did love him. I cannot love anyone who has deceived me.'

"'In what way has he deceived you?'

"'You will not understand, Mama.'

"She did not want to speak with her mother about the thousand-year realm of her dreams, which her beloved would have helped her to make a reality.

"'Ebba,' said the countess, 'if you love him, then you should not ask about what he has been, but rather marry him. The husband of a Countess Dohna will be rich and powerful enough, so that the sins of his youth will be excused.'

"'I do not care about the sins of his youth, Mama; it is because he can never become what I wanted him to become that I cannot marry him.'

"'Ebba, don't forget that I have given him my word!'

"The girl turned corpse white.

"'Mama, I am telling you that if you marry me to him, you are separating me from God.'

"'I have decided to make you happy,' says the countess. 'I am certain that you will be happy with this man. Haven't you already succeeded in making a saint out of him? I have decided to overlook the demands of ancestry and forget that he is poor and despised, to give you the opportunity to restore his reputation. I know that I am doing what is right. You know that I despise all ancient prejudices.'

"But she is saying all this simply because she does not tolerate anyone setting herself against her will. Perhaps also because she meant it, when she said it. Countess Märta is not easy to understand.

"The young woman remained lying on her sofa a long while after the countess had left her. She fought her battle. Earth rose up against heaven, love against love, but her childhood's beloved won the victory. Where she lay, right here on the sofa, she saw the western sky glowing with a magnificent sunset. She thought that this was a greeting from the good king, and as she would not have been able to remain faithful to him if she had lived, she decided to die. She could do nothing else, when her mother wanted her to belong to one who could not be the good king's servant.

"She went over to the window, opened it, and let the twilight's cold, damp air thoroughly chill her poor, weak body.

"It was an easy task for her to bring death on herself. It was certain, if the illness were to begin anew, and it did.

"There is no one other than myself who knows that she sought death out, Elisabet. I found her by the window. I heard her feverish fantasies. She liked having me by her side during her final days.

"It was I who saw her die, who saw how one evening hour she extended her arms toward the glowing west and died, smiling, as if she had seen someone appear from the brilliance of the sunset to meet her. I was also the one who had to convey her final greeting to the one whom she had loved. I was to ask him to forgive that she could not become his wife. The good king did not allow it.

"But I have not dared tell that man that he was her murderer. I have not dared set the weight of such agony on his shoulders. And yet, he, who lied his way to her love, was he not her murderer? Wasn't he, Elisabet?"

The Countess Dohna had long ceased stroking the blue flowers. Now she gets up, and the bouquet falls to the floor.

"Anna, you are still making fun of me. You say that the story is old, and that the man was dead a long time ago. But I know that it is scarcely five years since Ebba Dohna died, and you are telling about it as if you yourself have been part of the whole thing. You are not old. Tell me who the man is!"

Anna Stjärnhök started to laugh.

"You wanted a love story. Now you've got one, which has cost you both tears and worry."

"Do you mean that you have lied?"

"Nothing other than poetry and lies, the whole thing!"

"You are mean, Anna."

"That may be. I am not altogether happy either, I should say. But the wives are awake, and the gentlemen have come into the drawing room. Let us go out there!"

On the threshold she is stopped by Gösta Berling, who is coming to look for the young ladies.

"You must have patience with me," he says laughing. "I will only bother you for ten minutes, but you must hear some verse."

He tells them that last night he dreamed as vividly as seldom before, dreamed that he had written verse. He, whom people called "the poet," although up until now he had not deserved such a nickname, got up in the middle of the night and, half asleep, half awake, started to write. It was a complete poem that he found on his writing table in the morning. He would never have believed any such thing about himself. Now the ladies would hear it.

And he reads:

Now the moon came up, and with it came the sweetest hour of
the day.
From the clear, pale blue, high arch
he molded his shimmer onto vine-encircled terrace,
at whose foot trembled in its garden urn
a yellow-red lily, whose cup is edged by golden rays.
On the broad staircase's solid surface
we had all sat down, the old ones and the young ones,
silent at first to let our feelings sing
the heart's old ballads in the sweetest hour of day.

From the mignonette cluster its sweet aroma spread to us,
and from the dark thicket of the bushes
shadows stole across glistening, dew-drenched lawn.
Then from the darkness of the bodies
the spirit dances to the realm of light,
to the regions he can scarce perceive,
to the light, pale blue, high loft,
in whose clarity a star can almost be discerned.
Oh, who against the play of feelings can defend
the play of night shadows, with the sorrow-laden odor
of mignonette?

A French rose lets fall its final, pallid petal,
without the play of wind forcing its offering.
So, we thought, would we our own lives give,
vanish in space like the sound of notes,
like autumn's yellowed leaves without complaint becoming
nothing.
Oh, we extend the row of years,
disturb the peace of nature to enjoy the illusion
of living.
Death is life's reward. So we must leave it quietly,
as a French rose lets fall its final, pallid petal.

On its fluttering wing a bat flew past us,
flew and was seen again there, where'er the moon shone.
But then it rose up from distressed hearts,
the question, that no one had yet answered,
the question, like sorrow heavy, the question, old as pain:
"Oh, where are we going, what paths shall we wander, we,
when we no longer on earth's verdant meadows walk?"
If anyone can show the spirit's path to another,
he more easily shows the way to the animal that just
fluttered past us.

Then she leaned her head against my shoulder, her soft hair,
she, who loved me, and whispered quietly to me:

"Do not believe that souls fly off to distant realms of space,
   when I have died, do not believe that I am far away!
Into a beloved person's soul my homeless spirit will slip,
            and I will come and live in you."
   Oh, what anxiety! From sorrow my heart would burst.
   She would die then, die soon. Was this night her last?
   Did I give my last kiss to my beloved's billowing hair?

   Years have vanished since. Still I sit many a time
   at the old place, when the night is dark and silent.
But I shudder at the moon's sheen on vine-encircled terrace.
He who alone knows how often there my love I kissed,
he, who would blend his trembling light among the tears
            that fell down on my beloved's hair.
Woe to the torment of memory! Oh, this is the torment of my
                  poor, sinful spirit,
   that he is her home! What punishment can he expect to risk,
   who once bound himself to a soul, so pure, so sinless?

"Gösta," says Anna in a joking tone, while her voice is about
to be tied in knots by anxiety, "they say that you have experienced more poems than others, who have done nothing else their
whole lives, have written, but do you know, you do best composing in your own way. That poem should never see the light of day,
you know."

"You are not gentle."

"Coming and reading such things about death and misery!
Aren't you ashamed?"

Gösta is no longer listening to her. His eyes are directed at the
young countess. She is sitting completely rigid, immobile as a
statue. He thinks she is going to faint.

But with endless difficulty a word passes across her lips.

"Go!" she says.

"Who should go? Should I go?"

"The minister must go!" she stammers out.

"Elisabet, be quiet now!"

"The drunken minister must get out of my house!"

"Anna, Anna," asks Gösta, "what does she mean?"

"It's best that you go, Gösta."

"Why should I go? What does all this mean?"

"Anna," says the Countess Elisabet, "tell him, tell him. . . ."

The countess bites her teeth together and overcomes her agitation.

"Mr. Berling," she says, going over to him, "you have a remarkable ability to cause people to forget who you are. I have not known it before today. I have just heard the story about the death of Ebba Dohna, and that it was the information that she loved an unworthy man that killed her. Your poem has let me understand that this man is you. I cannot understand how anyone with the past you have lived can show himself in the company of an honorable woman. I cannot understand it, Mr. Berling. Am I clear enough now?"

"Yes, you are, countess. I only want to say a single word in defense. I was convinced, I have been convinced the entire time, that you have known everything about me. I have never tried to conceal anything, but it cannot of course be amusing to shout out the bitterest misfortunes of your life on the roads, least of all to do it yourself."

He leaves.

And at the same moment Countess Dohna sets her narrow foot on the little bouquet with the blue stars.

"You have now done what I have wanted," says Anna Stjärnhök harshly to the countess, "but now our friendship is also at an end. You must not think that I can forgive that you have been cruel to him. You have turned him away, mocked and wounded him, and I, I would follow him into prison, to the pillory, if such were the case. It is I who will guard him, preserve him. You have done what I wanted, but I will never forgive you."

"But Anna, Anna!"

"If I told you this, do you think I did it with a happy heart? Have I not been sitting here and, piece by piece, tearing the heart out of my chest?"

"So why did you do it?"

"Why? Because, you, I did not want—did not want him to become a married woman's lover. . . ."

CHAPTER 13

MAMSELL MARIE

Silence, by all means, silence!

There is a buzzing over my head. It must be a bumblebee flying around. No, just be quiet! Such an aroma! As sure as I'm alive, if it isn't southernwood and lavender and bird cherry and lilac and narcissus. It is a glory to sense this on a gray autumn evening in the heart of the city. Simply by setting out that blessed little patch of earth in my thoughts, right away there is buzzing and scents around me, and without noticing it I move into a small, square rosarium, filled with flowers and sheltered by a privet hedge. In the corners are lilac bowers with narrow wooden benches, and around the flower beds, shaped like hearts and stars, are narrow paths, strewn with white sand. The forest is on three sides of the rosarium. The rowan and bird cherry, which are half-domesticated and have beautiful blossoms, stand closest, blending their scents with the lilacs. Beyond them stand a few lines of birches, and then the spruce forest begins, the real forest, silent and dark, bearded and pungent.

And on the fourth side stands a little gray cottage.

Sixty years ago the rosarium I am thinking about was owned by old Mrs. Moreus in Svartsjö; she made a living by stitching quilts for the farmers and preparing food for their feasts.

Dear friends! Among all the good things I wish for you, I would first mention a quilting frame and a rosarium. I wish you a large, rickety, old-fashioned quilting frame with worn grooves and chipped spools, the kind at which five, six persons could work at one time, where you sew in teams and compete in making beautiful stitches on the reverse side, where you eat baked

apples and talk and "travel to Greenland" and "hide the thimble"
and laugh so that the squirrels off in the forest fall headlong to
the ground in fright. A quilting frame for winter, dear friends, and
a rosarium for summer! Not a garden, where you have to lay out
more money than the enjoyment is worth, no, a rosarium, as it
was called in former times! You should have such a thing, to care
for with your own hands. Small briar-rose bushes should sit atop
the small mounds of earth, and a wreath of forget-me-not wind
around its foot; there the big, flighty poppy, which seeds itself,
could come up everywhere, both on the grass strip and the sand
path, and there should be a dried-out turf bank in which there
should be columbines and crown imperials, both on the seat and
on the back support.

In her day old Mrs. Moreus was the owner of many things. She
had three happy and industrious daughters and a little cottage
by the roadside. She had a stash of coins at the bottom of a chest,
starched silk scarves, straight-backed armchairs, and knowledge
of many things that are useful to know by anyone who must earn
her bread herself.

But the best things she owned were the quilting frame, which
gave her work year-round, and the rosarium, which gave her joy
as long as summer lasted.

Now it should also be told that in Mrs. Moreus's little cottage
there was a lodger, a dry little *mamsell* about forty years old who
lived in a gable room in the attic. Mamsell Marie, as she was always called, had her own opinions on many things, such as someone is likely to have who is often alone and lets her own thoughts
revolve around what her own eyes have seen.

Mamsell Marie believed that love was the root and the cause
of all evil in this sorrow-filled world.

Every evening before she fell asleep, she would fold her hands
and say her evening prayers. After she had said the Lord's Prayer
and the benediction, she always concluded by praying to God to
preserve her from love.

"There would only be misery from it," she said. "I am old and
ugly and poor. No, may I only keep from falling in love!"

She sat day after day up in the attic room in Mrs. Moreus's
little cottage, sewing curtains and tablecloths with scalloped

edges. Then she sold all these to farmers and gentry. She was in the process of sewing together a cottage for herself.

For a little cottage on the hill with a view across from Svartsjö church was what she wanted, a cottage sitting high on a hill, so that from there you could see far and freely; that was her dream. But she would not hear a word about love.

When on a summer evening she heard the fiddle sounding from the crossroads, where the fiddler sat on the fence stile and the young people swung around in the *polska* dance so that the dust whirled, then she took a long detour through the forest to avoid hearing and seeing it.

On the day after Christmas, when the farm brides came five or six at a time to be dressed by Mrs. Moreus and her daughters, as they were adorned with wreaths of myrtle and high crowns of silk and glass beads, with showy silk sashes and corsages of homemade roses, and the skirt hemmed with garlands of taffeta flowers, then she stayed up in her room to avoid seeing how they were decked out in honor of love.

When the Moreus girls were sitting at the quilting frame on winter evenings and the large room on the left in the vestibule was radiant with coziness, when the white transparent apples were swinging and perspiring in the stove, hung before the blazing fire, when handsome Gösta Berling or kind Ferdinand, who had come on a visit, took the opportunity to pull the thread out of the needle for the girls or fooled them into sewing crooked stitches, and the room resounded with merriment and laughter and talking and flirtation and the pressure of hands met under the quilting frame, then in annoyance she rolled up her sewing and went her way, for she hated love and the ways of love.

But she knew the misdeeds of Love, and she knew how to tell about those. She marveled that it still dared to show its face on the earth, that it was not frightened away by the laments of the abandoned and curses from those whom it had turned into criminals, from the cries of woe of those whom it had cast into despicable chains. She marveled that its wings could carry it so free and light, that it did not sink into the nameless depths, weighed down by anguish and shame.

No, she must have been young at one time, like other people, but Love itself she had never loved. Never had she let herself be enticed into dancing and caresses. Her mother's guitar hung, dusty and without strings, in the attic. Never had she strummed it in a pallid love song.

Her mother's rosebush stood in her window. She gave it water sparingly. She did not love the flowers, those children of love. The leaves hung dustily. Spiders played between the branches, and the buds never opened.

And in Mrs. Moreus's rosarium, where butterflies fluttered and birds sang, where aromatic flowers sent love notes to hovering bees, where everything spoke of the hateful thing, she seldom set foot.

There came a time when Svartsjö parish was having an organ installed in the church. It was summer before the year when the cavaliers were in charge. A young organ builder came there. He too became a lodger with Mrs. Moreus and was housed, he too, in a small gable room in the attic.

Then he set up this organ, which has such strange tones, whose dreadful bassoon stop intermittently bursts forth in the middle of a peaceful hymn—no one knows why or how—and causes the children to cry in church on Christmas morning.

It may well be doubted whether this young organ builder was a master of his trade. But he was a merry fellow, with sunshine in his eyes. He had a friendly word for each and every one, for rich and poor, for old and young. He soon became good friends with his landlords, ah, more than a friend.

When he came home from work in the evening, he held Mrs. Moreus's skein of yarn and worked at the young girls' side in the rosarium. Then he declaimed "Axel" and sang "Fritjof." Then he picked up Mamsell Marie's ball of thread, however often she dropped it, and even started her wall clock.

He ended no ball before he had danced with all of them, from the oldest lady to the youngest lass, and if he suffered a setback, he sat down by the side of the first woman he encountered and made her his confidante. Yes, this was a man such as women create in their dreams! It should not be said of him that he spoke with anyone about love. But when he had been living in Mrs. Moreus's little gable room a few weeks, all the girls were in love with him, and poor Mamsell Marie knew, she too, that she had said her prayers in vain.

It was a time of sorrow and a time of joy. Tears fell upon the quilting frame and erased the chalk marks. In the evening a pale dreamer often sat in the lilac bower, and up in Mamsell Marie's little room the newly stringed guitar was strummed to pallid love ballads, which she had learned from her mother.

The young organ builder remained, however, just as carefree and happy, strewing out smiles and favors among these languishing women, who quarreled about him when he was away at work. And finally came the day when he must leave.

The carriage stood by the door. The portmanteau was bound fast at the back of the cart, and the young man said farewell. He kissed Mrs. Moreus on the hand and took the weeping girls in his arms and kissed them on the cheek. He himself wept at having to leave, for he had had a sunny summer in the little gray cottage. Finally he looked around for Mamsell Marie.

Then she came down the old attic stairs in her best finery. The guitar was hanging around her neck on a wide, green silk strap, and in her hand she held a bouquet of Chinese monthly roses, for this year her mother's rose tree had bloomed. She stopped before the young man, strummed the guitar and sang:

You're leaving us now. Welcome back soon again!
The voice of true friendship is speaking.
Be happy; forget not a kindhearted friend
In the forests and valleys of Värmland!

Then she placed the flowers in his buttonhole and kissed him right on the mouth. Yes, and then she vanished up the attic stairs again, the old apparition.

Love had avenged itself on her and made her into a laughingstock. But she never complained about it anymore. She never put away the guitar and never again forgot to tend her mother's rose tree.

She had learned to love Love with all its torment, its tears, its longing.

"Better mournful with him than happy without him," she said.

Time passed. The majoress at Ekeby was driven away, the cavaliers came to power, and it happened, as was just mentioned, that one Sunday evening Gösta Berling recited a poem for the countess at Borg and was then forbidden by her to show himself in her house.

It is said that when Gösta closed the front door behind him, he saw some sleighs driving up to Borg. He cast a glance at the little lady who sat in the lead sleigh. Dreary as the hour was for him, it became even drearier at that sight. He hurried away so as not to be recognized, but a sense of doom filled his mind. Had the conversation within called forth this woman? One misfortune always breeds another.

But servants hurried out, foot warmers were unbuttoned, fur rugs cast aside. Who had come? Who was the little lady who was riding in the sleigh? It was actually Märta Dohna, the notorious countess herself!

She was the most amusing and the most foolish of women. The world's delight had raised her up onto its throne and made her its queen. Games and amusements were her subjects. When the fortunes of life were distributed, play and dance and adventures fell to her share.

She was now not far from her fiftieth year, but she was one of the wise ones who do not count the number of years. "Anyone who cannot raise his foot in a dance or his mouth in a smile," she would say, "he is old. He feels the horrid burden of age, not me."

Delight had no unshaken faith in the days of her youth, but variety and uncertainty only increased the pleasure in her amusing existence. Her majesty with the butterfly wings held a coffee party one day in the court ladies' apartment at Stockholm's palace and the next day danced in evening dress and *knölpåk* in Paris itself. She visited Napoleon's encampments, she attended a congress in Vienna, she dared to go to Brussels to a ball the night before a famous battle.

And wherever Happiness was, there was Märta Dohna, his chosen queen. Dancing, playing, joking pursued Countess Märta the world around. What had she not seen, what had she not experienced? Thrones toppled in dance, *écarté* played for princedoms, devastating wars joked away! Her life had been merriment and madness and would always remain so. Her body was not too old for the dance nor her heart for love. When did she grow tired of masquerades and comedies, of merry stories and melancholy ballads?

When at times joy was homeless in a world transformed into a battlefield, she would drift up to the old count's estate on Löven's long lake for longer or shorter stays. She had likewise drifted up there when the princes and their courts had become too dreary for her in the time of the Holy Alliance. It was during such a visit that she had decided to make Gösta Berling her son's tutor. She felt quite at home up there. Joy had never had a more magnificent realm. There was song and play, adventure-loving men and lovely, happy women. There was no lack of dinner parties and balls, boat rides across moonlit lakes, sleigh rides through dark forests, no lack of heart-stirring events and the sorrow and pain of love either.

But when her daughter died, she stopped visiting Borg. She had not seen it in five years. Now she came to see how her daughter-in-law was enduring life among the spruce forests, bears, and snowdrifts. She considered it a duty to come and see whether stupid Henrik had tortured her to death with his tedium. Now she would be the gentle angel of domestic bliss. Sunshine and happiness were packed in her forty leather portmanteaus, Merriment was the name of her chambermaid, Joking her coachman, Play her lady's companion.

And as she sprang up the steps, she was met with open arms. Her old room on the bottom floor awaited her. Her servant, her lady's companion and chambermaid, her forty portmanteaus, her thirty hatboxes, her necessaries and shawls and furs, little by little all of it came into the house. There was noise and clamor everywhere. There were slamming doors and commotion on the stairs. It was noticeable that Countess Märta had arrived.

———

It was a spring evening, a really beautiful evening, although it was still only April and the ice had not broken up. Mamsell Marie had opened her window. She was sitting up in her room, strumming the guitar and singing.

She was so occupied with the guitar and her singing that she did not notice how a carriage came driving along the road and stopped at the cottage. In the carriage sat Countess Märta, and she enjoyed seeing Mamsell Marie, who sat in the window with her guitar around her neck and, with her eyes turned toward heaven, sang old, worn-out love songs.

At last the countess got out of the carriage and went into the cottage, where the kind girls were sitting around the quilting frame. She was never haughty: the wind of revolution had swept over her and blown fresh air into her lungs.

She could not help it that she was a countess, she always said; but in any event she wanted to live the sort of life that pleased her. She had just as much fun at a peasant wedding as at court balls. She played comedies for her maids when no other audience was at hand, and she brought delight to all gatherings where she appeared with her beautiful small face and her overflowing intrepidness.

She ordered quilts from Mrs. Moreus and praised the girls. She looked around in the rosarium and told about her adventures on her journey. She always had adventures, she did. And at last she ventured up the attic stairs, which were frighteningly steep and narrow, and visited Mamsell Marie in her gable room.

There she let her black eyes flash down over the lonely little person, and the melodic voice caress her ears.

She bought curtains from her. She could not live up there at Borg without having scalloped curtains on all her windows, and she wanted to have one of Mamsell Marie's tablecloths on all the tables.

Then she borrowed her guitar and sang for her a song of joy and love. And she told stories for her, so that Mamsell Marie found herself moved out into the amusing, bustling world. And the countess's laugh was such music that the frozen birds in the rosarium started to sing when they heard it, and her face, which was scarcely beautiful anymore, for her skin was ravaged by makeup and there were features of crude sensuality around her mouth, seemed so beautiful to Mamsell Marie that she marveled how the little mirror could let it go away, once it had captured it on its shiny surface.

When she left, she kissed Mamsell Marie and invited her to come up to Borg.

Mamsell Marie's heart was as empty as the little swallows' nest at yuletide. She was free, but she sighed for bonds like a slave freed in old age.

Now began again a time of joy and a time of sorrow for Mamsell Marie, but not for long, only eight short days.

The countess fetched her incessantly up to Borg. She played comedy for her and told her about her suitors, and Mamsell Marie laughed like she had never laughed before. They became the best of friends. The countess soon knew all about the young organ builder and about his departure. And in the twilight she let Mamsell Marie sit in the window seat in the little blue study. Then she hung the guitar strap around her neck and got her to sing love songs. Then the countess sat and watched how the old girl's dry, meager figure and ugly little head were outlined against the reddish evening light, and she said that the poor *mamsell* resembled a languishing castle maiden. But every song spoke of tender shepherds and cruel shepherdesses, and Mamsell Marie's voice was the very thinnest of voices, and one can easily understand that the countess would be delighted by such a comedy.

Then there was a dinner party at Borg, as was naturally the case when the count's mother had come home. And it was merry as usual. The company, however, was not large. Only parish residents were invited.

The dining room was on the main floor, and after supper it happened that the guests did not make their way up the stairs again, but instead took a seat in Countess Märta's rooms, which were adjacent. Then the countess took hold of Mamsell Marie's guitar and started to sing for the company. She was an amusing lady, Countess Märta, and she could imitate anyone. Now she got the idea of imitating Mamsell Marie. She turned her eyes toward heaven and sang in a thin, shrill child's voice.

"Oh no, oh no, countess!" pleaded Mamsell Marie.

But the countess was enjoying herself, and most of them could not keep from laughing, although they probably felt sorry for Mamsell Marie.

The countess took a handful of dry rose petals from a pot-pourri vase, went with tragic gestures over to Mamsell Marie, and sang with deep feeling:

> You're leaving us now. Welcome back soon again!
> The voice of true friendship is speaking.
> Be happy; forget not a kindhearted friend
> In the forests and valleys of Värmland!

Then she scattered rose petals over her head. People laughed, but Mamsell Marie became wild with rage. She looked as if she might tear the eyes out of the countess.

"You are a bad woman, Märta Dohna," she said. "No honorable woman ought to associate with you."

Countess Märta became angry too.

"Out with you, *mamsell*!" she said. "I have had enough of your follies."

"Yes, I will leave," said Mamsell Marie, "but first I want to be paid for my tablecloths and curtains that you have set up here."

"Those old rags!" cried the countess. "Do you want to be paid for those old rags! Take them with you! I never want to see them again! Take them with you at once!"

With that the countess threw the tablecloths at her and pulled down the curtains, for now she was in a complete frenzy.

The next day the young countess asked her mother-in-law to make amends with Mamsell Marie, but the countess did not want to. She was tired of her.

Countess Elisabet then left and bought the entire supply of curtains from Mamsell Marie and set them up in the entire upper story. In doing so she felt that Mamsell Marie's reputation was again restored.

Countess Märta made many jokes with her daughter-in-law about her love for scalloped curtains. She could also conceal her wrath, keeping it healthy and fresh for years. She was a richly talented being.

CHAPTER 14

COUSIN KRISTOFFER

They had an old bird of prey up in the cavaliers' wing. He always sat in the chimney corner, keeping watch so the fire did not go out. He was ruffled and gray. The little head with the great beak and the lifeless eyes leaned sorrowfully on the long, emaciated neck, sticking up from a bushy fur collar. For that bird of prey wore furs both winter and summer.

In times past he had been part of the swarm that swept across Europe in the wake of the great emperor, but nowadays no one dares say what name and title he bore. In Värmland it was only known that he had taken part in the great wars, that he wreaked dreadful havoc in thundering battles, and that after 1815 he had to take to his wings away from an ungrateful fatherland. He found refuge with the Swedish crown prince, who advised him to disappear in far-off Värmland. The times were such that he, whose name caused the world to tremble, must now be happy that no one knew his once feared name.

He had given the crown prince his word of honor not to leave Värmland and not to mention who he was unnecessarily. And so he was sent to Ekeby with a personal letter from the crown prince, who recommended him most highly. Then the cavaliers' wing opened its doors to him.

At first there was much speculation about who the notorious man hiding under an assumed name was. But by and by he was transformed into a cavalier and a Värmlander. Everyone called him cousin Kristoffer, without really knowing how he got that particular appellation.

But it is not good for a bird of prey to live in a cage. It is understandable that he is used to something other than jumping from perch to perch and taking food out of his caretaker's hand. In times past, the incitement of slaughter and mortal danger set his pulse aflame. The somnolence of peace revolts him.

It is also true that the other cavaliers were not mere domesticated birds either, but in none of them did the blood burn as hot as in cousin Kristoffer. A bear hunt was the only thing capable of enlivening his slackened lust for life, a bear hunt or a woman, a particular woman.

He livened up when, ten years earlier, he had seen Countess Märta, who by then was already a widow, for the first time. A woman changeable as war, exhilarating as danger, a sparkling, extravagant being. He loved her.

And now he sat there getting old and gray, not able to ask her to be his wife. Now he had not seen her for five years. Little by little he was withering and dying, as captive eagles do. With each year he got drier and colder. He had to creep farther down into the fur and closer to the fire.

So there he sits, freezing, ruffled and gray, the morning of the day on whose evening the Easter firecrackers would be shot off and the Easter witch would be burned. The cavaliers are all out, but he is sitting inside in the chimney corner.

Oh, cousin Kristoffer, cousin Kristoffer, do you not know?

Smiling he has arrived, the enticing spring.

Up leaps nature from indolent sleep, and in the blue sky butterfly-winged spirits tumble in boisterous play. Thick as roses on a wild bush their faces glitter up among the clouds.

The earth, the great mother, is coming alive. Giddy as a child she rises up from her bath in the spring flood, from the shower of spring rain. Stone and soil glisten with desire. "Into the circle of life!" rejoices the smallest of things. "We will journey as wings in clear air. We will shimmer in the blushing cheeks of young girls."

The lusty spring spirits swim on air and water into bodies, quiver like eels in the blood, set the heart swaying. It is the same sound everywhere. In hearts and flowers, in everything that can sway and tremble, the butterfly-winged ones cling tightly and ring it out as with a thousand tocsins: "Joy and delight, joy and delight! He has arrived, the smiling spring."

But cousin Kristoffer sits quietly, understanding nothing. He leans his head against his stiffened fingers and dreams of showers of bullets and of honor, grown on the fields of war. In his mind's eye he conjures laurels and roses that do not need the feeble beauty of spring to blossom.

It is too bad about him, though, the lonely old invader, sitting up there in the cavaliers' wing, without a people, without a country, he who never hears a word of the language of his homeland, he who will have an unmarked grave in the churchyard in Bro. Is it his fault that he is an eagle, born to pursue and kill?

Oh, cousin Kristoffer, you have sat dreaming in the cavaliers' wing long enough. Get up and drink the sparkling wine of life in the high castles! Know, cousin Kristoffer, that this day a letter has come to the major, a royal letter, stamped with the seal of the realm of Svea! It is addressed to the major, but its contents concern you. It will be marvelous to see you, as you read the letter, old bird of prey. Your eye will begin to shine and your head will be raised. You will see the door of your cage open and free space granted to your longing wings.

Cousin Kristoffer is digging deep down at the bottom of his clothes trunk. Then he anxiously pulls out the stored gold-laced uniform and puts it on. He presses the plume-adorned hat on his head, and soon he is fleeing Ekeby, riding on his splendid white saddle horse.

This, however, is something different than sitting frozen in the chimney corner. Now he too sees that spring has come.

He raises himself in the saddle and sets off at a gallop. His fur-lined dolman flutters. The plume of the hat sways. The man is rejuvenated like the earth itself. He has awakened from a long winter. Old gold can still gleam. The bold warrior's face under the three-cornered hat is a proud sight.

His ride is remarkable. From the ground brooks spurt and anemones spiral up where he rides along. The migrating birds shout and rejoice around the released prisoner. All of nature takes part in his delight.

Magnificent as a triumphator he comes. Spring itself rides ahead on a floating cloud. He is light and airy, a spirit of light. He has the krummhorn at his mouth and bubbles with happiness as he moves up and down in the saddle. And round about cousin Kristoffer a troop of old brothers in arms caracoles their horses: there is fortune, standing on tiptoe in the saddle, and honor on its stately courser, and love on its fiery Arabian. Remarkable is the ride, remarkable is the rider. The polyglot song thrush calls to him, "Cousin Kristoffer! Cousin Kristoffer! Where are you riding? Where are you riding?"

"To Borg to propose, to Borg to propose," answers cousin Kristoffer.

"Don't go to Borg, don't go to Borg! An unmarried man has no sorrow," shrieks the song thrush after him.

But he does not listen to the warning. Uphill and downhill he rides, until finally he arrives. He leaps out of the saddle and is led in to see the countess.

Everything goes well. The Countess Märta is gracious toward him. Cousin Kristoffer sees that she will not refuse to bear his glorious name or rule at his castle. He sits, delaying the moment of rapture when he will show her the royal letter. He enjoys this expectation.

She talks and entertains him with a thousand stories. He laughs at everything, admires everything. But as they are sitting in one of the rooms where the Countess Elisabet has hung up Mamsell Marie's curtains, the countess also starts to tell the story about them. And she makes it as amusing as she can.

"Look," she says at last, "see how wicked I am! These curtains are hanging here now so that I will think about my sin daily, hourly. It is a penance without equal. Oh, these horrible scalloped curtains!"

The great warrior cousin Kristoffer looks at her with burning glances.

"I am also old and poor," he says, "and I have sat in the chimney corner for ten years and longed for my beloved. Do you, gracious countess, laugh at that too?"

"That is another matter!" the countess exclaims.

"God has taken fortune and fatherland from me and forced me to eat another's bread," cousin Kristoffer says seriously. "I have had to learn to have respect for poverty, I have."

"You too!" cries the countess, holding up her hands. "How virtuous people are! Oh, how virtuous they have become!"

"Yes," says the man, "make note, countess, that if one day God were to give me back wealth and power, then I would make better use of them than to share them with the sort of worldly woman, the sort of made-up, heartless Jezebel, who makes a joke out of poverty."

"You are right about that, cousin Kristoffer."

And then cousin Kristoffer marches out of the room and rides home to Ekeby again. But the genies do not follow him, the song thrush does not call to him, and he can no longer see the smiling spring.

He comes to Ekeby as the Easter firecrackers are to be shot off and the Easter witch burned. The Easter witch is a large doll made of straw, with a face made of rags on which eyes, nose, and mouth are drawn with coal. She has on the pauper's discarded clothes. The long-shafted oven rake and broom are set beside her, and she has the butterhorn around her neck. She is ready for a witch's ride.

Major Fuchs loads his shotgun and fires it straight up in the air, time after time. A bonfire of dry sticks is lit; the witch is thrown on it and is soon burning lustily. No doubt the cavaliers are doing all they can to destroy the power of evil in an old, proven manner.

Cousin Kristoffer stands watching with a gloomy expression. Suddenly he pulls the great royal letter out of his sleeve and casts it on the fire. God alone knows what he was thinking. Perhaps he imagined that it was Countess Märta herself who was burning over there on the bonfire. Perhaps he thought that because this woman, when all was said and done, was only made of rags and straw, that there was nothing of value left on the earth.

He goes into the cavaliers' wing again, lights the fire, and hides his uniform. He sits down again in the chimney corner, and with each day he becomes more and more bushy and gray. He is dying little by little, as old eagles do in captivity.

He is not a prisoner anymore, but he does not care to make use of his freedom. Space stands open to him. Battlefields, honor, life await him. But he no longer has the strength to spread his wings in flight.

CHAPTER 15

THE PATHS OF LIFE

Toilsome are the pathways that people must wander on this earth.

Desert paths, marsh paths, mountain paths.

Why does so much sorrow go undisturbed, until it gets lost in the desert or sinks into the marsh or falls on the mountain? Where are the little flower gatherers, where are the little fairy-tale princesses, out of whose tracks roses grow, where are they who should strew flowers across the toilsome ways?

Now Gösta Berling, the poet, has decided to marry. He is only seeking a bride who is poor enough, lowly enough, rejected enough for an insane minister.

Beautiful and noble women have loved him, but they may not come forward to compete for his hand. The disowned one chooses among the disowned.

Who should he choose, who should he seek out?

Sometimes a poor girl comes to Ekeby from a deserted forest village far up in the hills and sells brooms. In this village, where constant poverty and great misery prevail, there are many who do not have full possession of their mental faculties, and the girl with the brooms is one of them.

But she is beautiful. Her ample black hair forms such thick braids that they scarcely fit on her head, her cheeks are finely rounded, her nose straight and properly proportioned, her eyes blue. She has a melancholy, Madonna-like type of beauty, such as you still find in beautiful girls on the shores of Löven's long lake.

Well, there of course Gösta has found his fiancée! A half-crazy broom girl will be a good wife for an insane minister. Nothing would be more suitable.

He only needs to travel to Karlstad for the rings, and then they may once again have a joyful day on the shore of Löven. They may laugh at Gösta Berling once again when he gets engaged to the broom girl, when he celebrates the wedding with her! Let them laugh! Has he ever come up with a more comical prank?

Must not the disowned go the way of the disowned, the way of wrath, the way of sorrow, the way of misfortune? What does it matter if he falls, if he is ruined? Is there anyone who cares to stop him? Is there anyone who extends him a supporting hand or a refreshing drink? Where are the little flower gatherers, where are the little fairy-tale princesses, where are they who should strew roses across toilsome ways?

No, no, the young, gentle countess at Borg must not disturb Gösta Berling in his plans. She must think about her reputation, she must think about her husband's anger and her mother-in-law's hatred, she must not do anything to hold him back.

During the long church service in Svartsjö church she will bow her head, clasp her hands, and pray for him. During sleepless nights she may weep and worry about him, but she has no flowers to strew on the path of the disowned, no drop of water to give him who thirsts. She does not reach out her hand to pull him back from the edge of the abyss.

Gösta Berling does not care to wrap his chosen one in silk and jewelry. He lets her go from farm to farm with brooms, as is her habit, but when he has gathered all the excellent men and women of the region at a great banquet at Ekeby, he will announce his engagement. Then he will call her in from the kitchen, as she has arrived from her long wanderings, with the dust and dirt of the road on her clothes, perhaps ragged, perhaps uncombed, with confused eyes, with a confused flow of words on her lips. And he will ask the guests if he hasn't chosen a suitable bride, if the insane minister shouldn't be proud of such a lovely fiancée, of this gentle Madonna face, of these blue, dreamy eyes.

It was his intention that no one should know anything ahead of time, but he did not succeed in keeping the secret, and one of those who found out was the young Countess Dohna.

But what could she do to hinder him? The engagement day is near, its late twilight hour has arrived. The countess stands at the window in the blue study and looks northward. She almost believes that she can see Ekeby, although tears and mist obscure it. She sees so well how the large three-story house radiates with three illuminated rows of windows, she imagines how the champagne is being poured into the glasses, how the toasts resound, and how Gösta Berling announces his engagement to the broom girl.

What if she were near him now and very slowly placed her hand on his arm or simply gave him a friendly glance, would he not then turn away from the wicked way of the disowned? If a word from her has driven him to such a desperate action, would not a word from her then stop him?

She shudders at the sin that he will commit against this poor, unfortunate child. She shudders at his sin against the poor being, who will now be enticed into loving him, perhaps simply for a one-day joke. Perhaps too—and then she shudders even more at the sin he commits against himself—in order to be chained fast to his life, like an oppressive burden, and for all time take from his spirit the power to reach the heights.

And ultimately the guilt was hers. She had thrown him out onto the wicked way with a word of condemnation. She, who had come to bless, to alleviate, why had she twisted yet another spike in the sinner's crown of thorns?

Yes, now she knows what she will do. She will have the black horses harnessed to the sleigh, hurry across Löven, storm into the Ekeby estate, place herself before Gösta Berling and tell him that she does not despise him, that she did not know what she was saying when she chased him away from her home. . . . No, she still could not do any such thing, she would be ashamed and dare not say a word. She, who was married, must be careful. There would be so much slander if she did such a thing. But if she did not do it, what would happen to him?

She had to go.

Then she thinks that such a journey is impossible. This year no more horses can travel across the ice of Löven. The ice is melting, it has already come apart from land. The ice lies loose, cracked, terrible to see. Water purls up and down through it; in some places it has collected in black pools, in other places the ice is blinding white. For the most part it is gray, however, dirty from melting snow, and the pathways go like long black strips across its surface.

How can she think about going? Old Countess Märta, her mother-in-law, would never allow such a thing. She had to sit next to her the whole evening in the drawing room and listen to those old court stories, which are the old woman's amusement.

Yet, the night is coming, and her husband is away, now she is free.

She cannot drive, she dares not call the servants, but her anxiety drives her out of her home. She can do nothing else.

Toilsome are the pathways people wander on the earth: desert paths, marsh paths, mountain paths.

But this nighttime pathway across melting ice, what should I compare it to? Is it not the pathway that the little flower gatherers themselves must go, an uncertain, tottering, slippery way, the way of those who wish to heal inflicted wounds, the way of those who wish to set things right, the way of the light foot, the quick eye, and the brave, loving heart?

It was past midnight when the countess reached the shore of Ekeby. She had fallen on the ice, she had jumped across wide fissures, she had hurried across places where her footsteps were filled with purling water, she had slipped, she had crawled.

It had been a toilsome journey. She had wept as she went. She was wet and tired, and out there on the ice the darkness, desolation, and emptiness had given rise to gruesome thoughts.

Now finally at Ekeby she had to wade in foot-deep water in order to reach land. And when she had come onto the shore, she had no courage for anything other than sitting down on a stone and weeping from fatigue and helplessness.

Toilsome ways walk the children of humankind, and the little flower gatherers collapse at times next to their baskets, just when they have caught up to the person's path they want to strew with flowers.

This young, noble lady was, however, a charming little heroine. She had not walked such pathways in her bright homeland. Well might she sit at the edge of this horrible, dreadful lake, wet, tired, unhappy as she is, and think about the gentle, flower-edged paths of her southern fatherland.

For her it is no longer a question of south and north. She stands in the midst of life. She is not crying from homesickness. She is crying, this little flower gatherer, this little heroine, because she is so tired that she will not catch up to the person's pathway that she wants to strew with flowers. She cries because she believes that she has come too late.

Then people come running along the shore. They hurry past her without seeing her, but she hears their words.

"If the dam collapses, then the smithy will go," says one. "And the mill and the workshops and the blacksmiths' houses," another fills in.

Then she gets new courage, gets up, and follows them.

Ekeby mill and smithy were on a narrow point, around which the Björksjö River roared. It came rushing down toward the point, whipped white in the massive falls above, and at that time a massive breakwater was in front of the point to protect the built-up ground from the water. But the dam had gotten old, and the cavaliers were in charge. In their time the dance went over the hills at the ironworks, but no one took the time to see how the current and cold and time were working on the old stone dam.

Then comes the spring flood, and the dam starts to give way.

The fall at Ekeby is a mighty granite stair, down which the waves of the Björksjö River come rushing. They become dizzy with the speed, tumbling end over end and spraying foam over one another, again tumbling down over a stone, over a log, and then up again to fall again, again and again, foaming, hissing, roaring.

And now these wild, inflamed waves, intoxicated by the spring air, dizzy with their newfound freedom, start to storm the old stone wall. They come hissing and tearing, storm high up on it and then pull back, as if they had struck their white-locked heads. This is a storming as good as any; they take great pieces of ice as shelter, they take logs as battering rams, they pry, break, roar against this poor wall, until suddenly it seems as if someone had called them to attention. Then they rush backward, and after them a large stone comes loose from the dam and sinks with a crash down into the stream.

It appears as if this surprised them; they stand still, they rejoice, they take counsel . . . and then set about anew! There they are again with ice chunks and logs, mischievous, unmerciful, wild, crazy with the lust to destroy.

"If only the dam were gone," say the waves, "if only the dam were gone, then it would be the smithy's turn and the mill's turn.

"Now is the day of freedom . . . away with people and the works of people! They have sooted us with coal, they have dusted us with flour, they have put yokes on us like oxen, driven us in a ring, closed us in, impeded us with locks, forced us to pull the heavy wheels, carry the ungainly logs. But now we will win our freedom.

"The day of freedom has come! Hear that, waves up in Björk Lake, hear that, brothers and sisters in bog and marsh, in mountain brook and forest stream! Come, come! Rush down to the Björksjö River, come with fresh forces, booming, hissing, ready to break the centuries-old oppression, come! The bulwark of tyranny must fall. Death to Ekeby!"

And they come—wave after wave rushes down the falls to drive its head against the dam wall, to lend its help to the great work. Intoxicated by spring's newfound freedom, numerous, united they come and loosen stone upon stone, tuft upon tuft from the tottering breakwater.

But why then do the people let the wild waves rage without putting up any resistance? Is Ekeby deserted?

No, there are people there, a confused, perplexed, helpless group of people. Dark is the night, they do not see one another, do not see their own way. High up the falls roar, the boom of breaking ice and crashing logs is dreadful, they do not hear their own voices. The wild dizziness that ensouls the roaring waves fills the brains of the people as well; they do not have a thought left, no reason.

The ironworks bell is clanging. "May anyone who has ears, hear! We down here at Ekeby smithy are about to disappear. The river is upon us. The dam is quaking, the smithy is in danger, the mill is in danger, and our own poor houses, beloved in their insignificance."

The waves may believe that the bell ringing is calling their friends, for no person appears. But off in forests and marshes there is urgency. "Send helpers, send helpers!" rings the bell. "After centuries-long slavery we have finally set ourselves free. Come, come!" roar the waves. The booming water mass and the clanging ironworks bell sing a death song over all the glory and luster of Ekeby.

And in time message after message goes up to the estate for the cavaliers.

Are they in a mood to think about smithy and mill? The hundred guests are gathered in the expansive halls of Ekeby. The broom girl is waiting out in the kitchen. The exciting moment of surprise has come. The champagne sparkles in the glasses, Julius rises to give the banquet speech. All the old adventurers at Ekeby are pleased by the petrifying astonishment that will settle over the assembly.

Out on the ice of Löven the young Countess Dohna walks a dreadful, dangerous path to whisper a word of warning to Gösta Berling. Down at the waterfall the waves are making an assault against all the glory and power of Ekeby, but in the expansive halls only joy and eager expectation prevail; the wax candles radiate and the wine is flowing. No one there is thinking about what is moving about in the dark, stormy spring night.

Just now the moment has arrived. Gösta gets up and goes out to bring in the fiancée. He has to go through the vestibule, and its great doors stand wide open. He stops, he looks out into the coal-black night . . . and he hears, he hears.

He hears the bell clang, the rapids roar. He hears the boom of breaking ice, the din of crashing logs, the roaring, mocking, victory-rejoicing freedom song of the rebellious waves.

Then he rushes out into the night, forgetting everything. Let them stand in there with raised glasses and wait until the world's final day; he no longer cares about them. The fiancée can wait, Squire Julius's speech can die on his lips. The rings will not be exchanged this night, the petrifying astonishment will not settle over the brilliant assembly.

Now woe to you, rebellious waves, now in truth this will be a fight for your freedom! Now Gösta Berling has come down to the falls, now the people have a commander, now courage is lit in terrified hearts, now the defenders climb up onto the walls, now a mighty battle begins.

Hear how he calls to the people! He gives orders, he puts everyone into action.

"We must have light, light above all, the miller's horn lantern won't suffice here. Look at those piles of twigs; carry them up on the slope and light them! That's a job for women and children. Just do it quickly, make a big, flaming bonfire and light it! It will light up our labor, it will be seen far and wide and summon helpers here. And never let it go out! Bring straw, bring twigs, let bright flames flare against the sky!

"Look, look, you grown-up men, here is work for you! Here is lumber, here are planks, put together an emergency dam that we can lower down in front of the failing wall. Hurry, hurry to work, do it solid and steady! Arrange stones and sandbags to lower down too! Quick, swing your axes, let the hammer strokes thunder, let the drill bite into the wood, the saw screech in the dry planks!

"And where are the boys? Onward, onward, you wild good-for-nothings! Get poles, get boat hooks and come here into the thick of battle! Out onto the dam with you, lads, in the midst of the waves that are foaming, hissing, and spraying over us with white foam! Fend off, weaken, repel these attacks that are cracking the walls! Push aside logs and chunks of ice, throw yourselves down, if nothing else helps, and hold tight to the loosening stones with your hands! Bite into them, hold on to them with claws of iron! Fight, boys, good-for-nothings, wild brains! Out onto the wall with you! We will fight for every inch of ground!"

Gösta himself takes his place at the farthest end of the dam and stands there sprayed with foam, the ground quaking beneath him, the waves thundering and raging, but his wild heart delights in the danger, the commotion, the battle. He laughs, he has merry quips for the boys on the dam around him; he was never part of a more amusing night.

The rescue work goes quickly ahead, the fires flare, the lumbermen's axes boom, and the dam stands.

The other cavaliers and the hundred guests have also come down to the waterfall. People come running from near and far, all are working: at the fires, at the emergency dam, with the sandbags, out on the failing, shaking stone dam.

So, now the carpenters have the emergency dam ready, now it will be lowered in front of the tottering breakwater. Keep stones and sandbags ready and boat hooks and rope, so that it isn't pulled away, so that the victory may be the people's and the suppressed waves go back to slave service!

Then it happens, right before the decisive moment, that Gösta catches sight of a woman sitting on a stone by the river shore. The flames from the bonfire illuminate her where she sits staring out into the waves. Of course he can not see her clearly through the smoke and foam, but his eyes are unceasingly drawn to her. He feels as if this woman had some business with him in particular.

Among all of these hundreds who are working and busy on the river's edge, she is the only one who is sitting still, and his glances turn to her incessantly, he sees no one other than her.

She is sitting so far out that the waves strike against her feet, the foam sprays over her. She must be dripping wet. She is dark-clothed, with a black shawl over her head; she is sitting hunched up, supporting her chin with her hands, and staring unceasingly at him out on the breakwater. He feels how these staring eyes draw and entice, although he cannot even make out her face; he thinks of nothing other than the woman who is sitting at the edge of the white waves.

"It is the sea witch from Löven, who has come up into the river to lure me to destruction," he thinks. "She is sitting there and luring and luring; I have to chase her away."

All these waves with their white heads appear to him like the armies of the black woman. She was the one who incited them, she who led them forth against him in attack.

"I truly must chase her away," he says.

He grasps a boat hook, leaps ashore, and hurries over to the woman.

He leaves his place on the breakwater's outermost tip in order to chase away the sea witch. In this moment of agitation, to him it is as if the evil forces of the deep are fighting with him. He does not know what he thinks, what he believes, but he must chase away the black woman from the stone at the river's edge.

Oh, Gösta, why does your place stand empty at the decisive moment? They are coming now with the emergency dam, a long row of fellows are lining up on the breakwater. They have rope and stones and sandbags ready to weigh it down and keep it in place, they stand ready, they wait, they listen. Where is the commander? Is the voice that will order and organize not heard?

No, Gösta Berling is chasing away the sea witch, his voice is not heard, his commands lead no one.

Then the emergency dam must be lowered without him. The waves step aside, it plunges down into the depths and after it stones and sandbags. But how is the work carried out without the leader? No caution, no orderliness. The waves rush forth anew, they break with renewed fury against these new obstacles, they start rolling aside the sandbags, tearing the ropes, loosening the stones. And they succeed, they succeed! Mocking, rejoicing, they lift the whole wall on strong shoulders, pull and tear at it, and then they have it in their power. Away with this miserable bulwark, down into Löven with it! And then onward again against the tottering, helpless stone dam.

But Gösta Berling is chasing after the sea witch. She sees him as he is coming toward her, swinging the boat hook. She becomes afraid. It appears as if she intends to rush out into the water, but she changes her mind and runs toward land.

"Sea witch!" calls Gösta, swinging the boat hook over her. She hurries in among the alder shrubs, gets entangled in the dense branches, and remains standing.

Then Gösta throws away the boat hook, goes over, and places his hand on her shoulder.

"You are out late tonight, Countess Elisabet," he says.

"Let me be, Mr. Berling, let me go home!"

He obeys at once and turns away from her.

But because she is not only a noble lady, but actually a kind little woman who cannot bear the thought that she has brought someone to despair, because she is a little flower gatherer, who always has roses enough in her basket to adorn the most desolate pathway, she regrets it at once, goes after him, and takes his hand.

"I came," she says, stammering, "I came because . . . Oh, Mr. Berling, you haven't done it, have you? Say that you haven't done it! . . . I was so afraid when you came running after me, but it was just you I wanted to see. I wanted to ask you, that you shouldn't think about what I last said, and that you could come home as usual."

"How did you get here, countess?"

She is laughing nervously. "I guess I knew that I would come too late, but I did not want to tell anyone that I had gone. And besides, you understand, you can't drive across the lake any longer."

"Have you walked across the lake, countess?"

"Yes, of course, but Mr. Berling, tell me now! Are you engaged? You understand: I wanted so badly that you weren't. It is so wrong, you see, and it felt as if I were guilty of the whole thing. You should not have paid so much attention to a word from me. I am a stranger who does not know the customs of this land. It is so empty at Borg since you don't come there anymore, Mr. Berling."

It seems to Gösta Berling, as he stands among the wet alder bushes on the marshy ground, as if someone is throwing an entire armful of roses over him. He is wading in roses all the way up to his knees, they shine before his eyes out of the darkness, he greedily drinks in their fragrance.

"Have you done it?" she repeats.

He has to resolve to answer her and put an end to her anxiety, although he feels such a great delight over it. No, he gets so warm inside, and so light, as he thinks about what a pathway she has wandered, how wet she is, how chilled, how anxious she must be, how cried-out her voice sounds!

"No," he says, "I am not engaged."

Then she once again seizes his hand and caresses it. "I am so happy, I am so happy," she says, and her breast, which has been constricted by anxiety, is shaking with sobs.

Then there are flowers enough on the poet's path. All that is dark, evil, and hateful melts away from his heart.

"How good you are, how good you are!" he says.

Immediately above them the waves are on the assault against all the glory and luster of Ekeby. Now the people no longer have a leader, no one infuses courage and hope into their hearts, now the breakwater collapses, the waves close up over it, and then they rush, certain of victory, toward the point, where mill and smithy stand. No longer is anyone working to stand against the waves, no longer is anyone thinking about anything other than saving life and possessions.

It is so natural for both of these young people that Gösta should follow the countess home. Of course he cannot leave her alone in the dark night, nor let her wander alone once again across the melting ice. They do not even think about the fact that he is needed up at the smithy, they are so happy about being friends again.

It is so easy to believe that these young people harbor a warm love for one another, but who can know that for sure? The shining adventures of their lives have come down to me in broken and scattered shards. I of course know nothing, as good as nothing, about what dwelled deep in their souls. What can I say about the motives for their actions? I simply know that that night a young, lovely woman risked her life, her honor, her reputation, her health to put a poor wretch back on the right pathway. I simply know that that night Gösta Berling let the beloved estate's power and luster fall in order to follow her, who for his sake had overcome the fear of death, the fear of shame, the fear of punishment.

I have often followed them in my thoughts across the ice that dreadful night, which for them, however, had such a good ending. I do not believe that in their souls there was anything concealed and forbidden that had to be suppressed and held down just then as they wander across the ice, merrily talking about everything that has happened during this time of discord.

He is once again her slave, her page, who lies at her feet, and she is his lady.

They are only happy, only fortunate. Neither of them speaks a word that could mean love.

Laughing they splash along through the shore water. They laugh when they find the way, when they lose it, when they slip, when they fall, when they get up again, always they laugh.

It is again an amusing game, this blessed life, and they are children who have been naughty and quarreled. Oh, how good it is to be reconciled and start the game again!

Rumors came and rumors went. In time the story of the countess's wandering made its way to Anna Stjärnhök.

"So I see," she said, "that God does not have only one string on his bow. I will put my heart at ease and stay where I am needed. He can make a man of Gösta Berling without me."

CHAPTER 16

PENANCE

Dear friends, if you should happen to meet a pitiful wretch on your way, a dear, distressed being who lets his hat hang on his back and holds his shoes in his hand so as not to have any protection against the fire of the sun and the stones of the road, a defenseless person who of his own free will summons all misfortune upon his head, well, then go past him with a silent shudder! It is the penitent, you see, the penitent, en route to the sacred graves.

The penitent must wear the rough cowl and live on plain water and dry bread, even if he were a king. He must walk, not ride. He must beg, not own. He must sleep among the thistles. He must wear down the hard grave slabs with genuflection. He must swing the thorny scourge across his back. He can experience no sweetness except in suffering, no delight except in sorrow.

At one time the young Countess Elisabet was one who wore the rough cowl and traversed the thorny paths. Her heart accused her of sin. It yearned for pain as if it were aching for a warm bath. She brought cruel misfortune upon herself, as rejoicing she descended into the night of suffering.

Her husband, the young count with the old man's head, came home to Borg the morning after the night when Ekeby mill and smithy were destroyed by the spring flood. He had scarcely arrived before Countess Märta summoned him and related strange things to him.

"Your wife was out last night, Henrik. She was away for many hours. She came home in the company of a man. I heard how he said good night to her. I know who he is too. I heard her when she left and when she came back, although that was probably not the idea. She is deceiving you, Henrik. She is deceiving you, that sanctimonious creature, hanging up scalloped curtains on all the windows just to make things unpleasant for me. She has never loved you, my poor boy. Her father only wanted her to marry well. She took you to be taken care of."

She argued her case so well that Count Henrik became furious. He wanted a divorce. He wanted to send his wife home to her father.

"No, my friend," said Countess Märta, "that way she would only be completely consigned to what is wicked. She is spoiled and poorly brought up. But let me take care of her, let me return her to the path of duty!"

And the count called in his countess to tell her that she would now be under his mother's command.

Oh, what a scene now ensued! A more pitiable scene has probably never been played out within this house dedicated to sorrow.

The young man let the young woman hear many angry words. He raised his hands to heaven and accused it because it had let his name be dragged in filth by a shameless woman. He shook his clenched fist before her face and asked her what punishment she thought great enough for a crime such as hers.

She was not at all afraid of the man. She still believed that she had acted rightly. She told him that she already had a dreadful cold, and that might be punishment enough.

"Elisabet," says Countess Märta, "these are not joking matters."

"The two of us," answers the young woman, "have never been able to agree on the right moment for levity and seriousness."

"But you still ought to realize, Elisabet, that no honorable woman leaves her home to wander around in the middle of the night with a known adventurer."

Then Elisabet Dohna saw that her mother-in-law had decreed her destruction. She saw that she would have to fight to the utmost to avoid a terrible misfortune.

"Henrik," she pleads, "do not let your mother set herself between us! Let me tell you what happened! You are just, you will not judge me unheard. Let me tell you everything, and you will see that I have only acted the way you have taught me."

The count nodded a mute accord, and Countess Elisabet now told how she had driven Gösta Berling onto wicked pathways. She spoke of everything that had gone on in the little blue study, and how she had felt driven by her conscience to go and rescue the one she had wronged. "Of course I had no right to judge him," she said, "and my husband himself has taught me that no sacrifice is too great if you want to make good a wrong. Is that not so, Henrik?"

The count turned to his mother.

"What do you say about that, Mother?" he asked. His little body was now completely rigid with dignity, and his high, narrow forehead was majestically furrowed.

"I say," answered the countess, "I say that Anna Stjärnhök is a wise girl, and she knew what she was doing when she told this story to Elisabet."

"Mother, you choose to misunderstand me," said the count. "I am asking, Mother, what you think about this story. Has the Countess Märta Dohna attempted to convince her daughter, my sister, to marry a defrocked minister?"

Countess Märta was silent for a moment. Oh, that Henrik, so stupid, so stupid! Now of course he was pursuing the wrong tracks. Her hunting dog was pursuing the hunter herself and letting the rabbit run. But if Märta Dohna was speechless for a moment, it was not for longer than that.

"Dear friend!" she said with a shrug of her shoulders. "There is a reason for letting all these old stories about that unfortunate man rest, the same reason that I now ask you to suppress all public scandal. It is highly probable that he passed away last night."

She spoke in a gentle, complaining tone, but there was not a word of truth in what she said.

"Elisabet has slept a long time today and therefore has not heard that people have already been sent out around the lake to inquire about Mr. Berling. He has not returned to Ekeby, and it is feared that he has drowned. The ice broke up this morning. See, the storm has split it into a thousand pieces."

Countess Elisabet looked out. The lake was almost clear.

Then she felt sorry for herself. She wanted to escape God's

justice. She had lied and been a hypocrite. She had thrown the white mantle of innocence around herself.

The desperate woman fell to her knees before her husband, and the confession rushed out across her lips.

"Judge me, reject me! I have loved him. Do not doubt that I have loved him! I tear my hair, I rip my clothes in sorrow. I do not care about anything now, when he is dead. I do not care about protecting myself. You will find out the whole truth. I have taken the love of my heart from my husband and given it to a stranger. Oh, I am rejected, I am one of those whom forbidden love has enticed!"

You young, desperate woman, lie there at the feet of your judges, and tell them everything! Welcome, martyrdom! Welcome, ignominy, welcome! Oh, how will you be able to force the lightning bolts of heaven to flash down on your young head!

Tell your spouse how appalled you were when passion came over you, powerful and irresistible, how you shuddered at the wretchedness of your heart! You would sooner have encountered the churchyard ghosts than the demons in your own soul.

Tell them how you, banished from the face of God, felt yourself unworthy to walk the surface of the earth! In prayers and tears you have struggled. "Oh God, save me! Oh son of God, expeller of demons, save me!" you have prayed.

Tell them how you felt it best to conceal everything! No one should find out about your wretchedness. You believed that it was pleasing to God to act in that way. You also believed that you were on the path of God when you wanted to rescue the man you loved. He knew nothing about your love. He would not be lost for your sake. Did you know what was right? Did you know what was not right? God alone knew it, and he judged you. He broke the idol of your heart. He led you onto the great, healing way of penance.

Tell them that you know there is no salvation in concealment! The demons love the darkness. May your judges' hands wrap themselves around the scourge! The punishment will fall like comforting balsam on the wounds of sin. Your heart longs for suffering.

Tell them all this, while you are on your knees on the floor, wringing your hands in violent sorrow, speaking in the wild tones of desperation, with shrill laughter welcoming the thought of punishment and dishonor, until your husband takes hold of you and jerks you up from the floor!

"Behave as befits a Countess Dohna, or I must ask my mother to punish you like a child!"

"Do with me as you wish!"

Then fell the count's judgment.

"My mother has prayed for you. Therefore you may remain living here in my home. But from here on out it is she who commands, and you who obey."

See the way of penance! The young countess has become the most insignificant of servants. For how long, oh, for how long?

How long is a proud heart able to submit? How long should impatient lips keep silent, how long an impatient hand be held back?

Sweet is the misery of degradation. While your back aches from heavy labor, the heart is quiet. To one who sleeps a few short hours on a hard bed of straw, sleep comes unbidden.

May the older woman be transformed into an evil spirit to be able to torment the young one sufficiently! She thanks her benefactress. The evil within her has not yet died. Rouse the sleep-deprived girl at four o'clock every morning! Set an unreasonable day's labor on the unpracticed drill weaver! That is good. Perhaps the penitent does not have strength enough herself to swing the scourge with sufficient force.

When it is time for the big spring washing, Countess Märta lets her stand at the tub in the laundry room. She comes personally to look at her work. "The water is too cold in your tub," she says and takes boiling water from a kettle and throws it over her bare arms.

Cold is the day when the washerwomen have to stand by the lake and rinse the clothes. Storm clouds rush forth and shower them with rain and sleet. The washerwomen's skirts become dripping wet and heavy as lead. Working with the clothes beaters is hard. Blood spurts forth under her fine nails.

But Countess Elisabet does not complain. Praised be the goodness of God! Where does the penitent have her sweetness, except in suffering? The thorny knots of the scourge fall softly, as if they were rose petals, on the penitent's back.

The young woman soon finds out that Gösta Berling is alive. The old woman simply wanted to trick her into a confession. Yes, so what? See God's path! See God's guidance! Thus has he lured the sinful woman onto the path of reconciliation.

There is only one thing she is anxious about. How will it go for her mother-in-law, whose heart God has hardened for her sake? Oh, he will judge her with mercy. She must be evil in order to help the sinful woman win back God's love.

She did not know how often a soul which has sampled all other sensual pleasures turns to seek its amusement in cruelty. When flattery and caresses and the whirl of the dance and the allurement of play are lacking in the impatient, darkened soul, it dives down into its murky depths and brings up cruelty. In tormenting animals and people there is still a source of enjoyment for enervated emotions.

The old woman is not aware of any wrong. She only believes herself to be rebuking a loose-living wife. So sometimes she lies awake at night, brooding over new means of torment.

One evening she goes through the apartment and lets the countess light her way with a candle. This she carries in her hand without a candlestick.

"The candle is used up," says the young woman.

"When the candle is done the candlestick should burn," answers Countess Märta.

And they go further, until the smoldering wick goes out on the scorched hand.

But this is childishness. There are torments for the soul that surpass all the sufferings of the body. Countess Märta invites guests and lets the housewife herself wait on them at her own table.

See, this is the penitent's great day. Outsiders will see her in her degradation. They will see that she is no longer worthy to sit at her husband's table. Oh, with what scorn their cold glances will rest on her!

Worse, it is three times worse. Not a glance meets hers. Everyone at the table sits silent and dejected, men and women equally subdued.

But she gathers all this up like glowing coals to set on her head. Is her sin so terrible then? Is it shameful to be near her?

Then comes the temptation: see, Anna Stjärnhök, who has been her friend, and the sheriff of Munkerud, their neighbor at the table, take hold of her as she arrives, tear the meat platter from her, push over a chair, and will not let her flee.

"Sit there, child, sit there!" says the sheriff. "You have done no wrong."

And with one voice all the dinner guests explain that if she does not remain sitting at the table, they must leave. They are not executioners' helpers. They are not running Märta Dohna's errands. They are not as easily duped as mutton-headed counts.

"Oh, you good gentlemen! Oh, beloved friends! Do not be so merciful! You force me to cry out my sin myself. There is someone whom I have held far too dear."

"Child, you don't know what sin is. You don't understand how innocent you are. Of course Gösta Berling didn't know that you liked him. Now take back your place in your home! You have done no wrong."

They hold her courage up for a while and are themselves suddenly as merry as children. Laughter and joking resound around the table.

These passionate, easily moved people, they are so good, but nonetheless they are sent by the tempter. They want her to believe that she is a martyr, and openly mock Countess Märta as if she were a witch. But they do not understand the matter. They do not know how the soul longs for purity, how the penitent is forced by her heart to subject herself to the stones of the road and the fire of the sun.

Sometimes Countess Märta forces her to sit quietly for long days at the quilting frame, and then she tells her endless stories about Gösta Berling, this minister and adventurer. If her memory is not sufficient, she makes things up, just so his name will sound throughout the day in the young woman's ear. It is this she fears the most. During such days she sees that her penance will never have an end. Her love will not die. She believes that she herself will die before it. Her physical strength is starting to fail her. She is often very sick.

"But where is your hero lingering?" the countess asks scornfully. "Day after day I have awaited him at the head of the cavaliers. Why doesn't he storm Borg, set you up on the throne, and throw me and your husband tied up into the tower? Are you already forgotten?"

She would almost like to defend him and say that she herself has forbidden him to give her any aid. But no, best to keep silent, keep silent and suffer.

Day by day she is consumed more and more by the fire of overexcitation. She has a constant fever and is so weak that she can scarcely hold herself up. She only wants to die. The strong forces of life are suppressed. Love and happiness dare not make a move. No longer does she harbor any fear of suffering.

It is as if her husband no longer knows that she exists. He sits enclosed in his room all day and studies hard-to-read manuscripts and theses in old, blurred script.

He reads charters of nobility on parchment, on which hang the seal of the Svea realm, large and impressive, formed in red wax and preserved in a lathed wooden box. He inspects old armorial bearings with lilies on white fields and griffins in blue. He understands such things, and he interprets such things with ease. And he reads over and over again old funeral orations and biographies of the noble counts Dohna, in which their exploits are compared with the heroes of Israel and the gods of Hellas.

See, these old things have always made him happy. But he does not care to think about his young wife any longer.

Countess Märta has said one word, which has killed all the love inside him: "She took you for your money's sake." No man can bear to hear such a thing. It stifles all love. Now it was of no importance to him what happened to the young woman. If his mother brought her back to the path of duty, that was fine. Count Henrik had great admiration for his mother.

This misery went on for a month's time. Yet this time was not as stormy and agitated as it might sound, when the events are compressed onto a few written pages. Countess Elisabet seems to have always been calm on the outside. Only once, when she found out that Gösta Berling might be dead, did she become overwhelmed by emotion. But so great was her anxiety over not being able to preserve her love for her husband that she would probably have allowed Countess Märta to torture her to death, if her old housekeeper had not spoken with her one evening.

"Countess, you should speak with the count," she said. "Lord God, countess, you are such a child. Perhaps you don't know what is going to happen, but I see well enough what's going on."

But it was just this that she could not say to her husband, while he harbored such a dark suspicion against her.

That night she got dressed silently and went out. She wore a common farm girl's dress and had a bundle in her hand. She intended to run away from her home and never turn back.

She was not leaving to avoid torments and suffering. But now she believed that God had given her a sign, that she had leave to go, that she must preserve her bodily health and strength.

She did not head westward across the lake, for there lived the one of whom she was very fond. Neither did she go northward, for there lived many of her friends, and not toward the south, for far, far southward was her father's home, and she did not want to take one step closer to it. But eastward she went, for there she knew that she had no home, no beloved friend, no familiar person, no help or consolation.

She did not walk with light steps, for she did not think she was reconciled with God. And yet she was happy that she would henceforth carry the burden of her sin among strangers. Their indifferent glances would rest on her, soothing as steel placed on a swollen limb.

She intended to wander until she found a poor cottage at the forest edge, where no one would know her. "You can see what has happened to me, and my parents have chased me away," she would say. "Let me get food and a roof over my head, until I can earn my bread myself! I am not without money."

Thus she went onward through the light June night, for the month of May had passed during her difficult suffering. Oh, month of May, that lovely time when the birches blend their light greenery into the dark of the spruce forests, and when the south wind comes again far from the south, saturated with heat!

I must seem more ungrateful than others who have enjoyed your gifts, you beautiful month. Not a word have I used to show your beauty.

Oh May, you dear, light month, have you ever observed a child sitting in its mother's lap, listening to stories? As long as the child hears tales of cruel giants and the bitter suffering of lovely princesses, it holds its head upright and its eyes open, but if the mother starts talking about happiness and sunshine, then it shuts its little eyes and falls asleep so quietly with its head on its mother's breast.

See, you beautiful month, I am also such a child. May others listen to talk of flowers and sunshine, but for myself I choose dark nights, full of visions and adventures, for me the hard fates, for me the sorrow-filled passions of wild hearts.

CHAPTER 17

IRON FROM EKEBY

It was spring, and iron from all the ironworks in Värmland was to be shipped to Gothenburg.

But at Ekeby they had no iron to ship. During the autumn there had been a periodic shortage of water; in the spring the cavaliers were in charge.

In their time strong, bitter beer foamed down the Björksjö falls' broad granite stairway, and Löven's long lake was not filled with water, but with liquor. In their time no pig iron was placed in the forge, but the smiths stood in shirts and wooden clogs before the hearths turning enormous steaks on long spits, while the smithy boys held fat capons over the coals with long tongs. In those days the dance proceeded over the hills of the ironworks. Then the planing bench was for sleeping on and the anvil was for playing cards. In those days no iron was being forged.

But spring came, and down at the trading office in Gothenburg they began to wait for iron from Ekeby. Contracts entered into with the major and the majoress, where deliveries of many hundredweights were mentioned, were examined.

But what did the cavaliers care about the majoress's contracts? They kept joy and fiddle playing and partying alive. They saw to it that the dance proceeded over the hills of the ironworks.

Iron came from Stömne, iron from Sölje. Iron from Kymsberg made its way through wilderness down to Lake Vänern. From Uddeholm it came and from Munkfors and from all of the many ironworks. But where was the iron from Ekeby?

Is Ekeby no longer the most prominent of the ironworks of Värmland? Does no one watch over the honor of the old estate?

Like ashes in the wind it is left in the hands of the careless cavaliers. They let the dance proceed over the hills of the ironworks.
What else do their miserable brains manage to look after?

But rapids and rivers, small cargo boats and barges, harbors
and locks marvel and ask, "Is no iron coming from Ekeby?"

And it is whispered and asked from forest to lake, from mountain to valley, "Is no iron coming from Ekeby? Will no iron ever
again come from Ekeby?"

And deep in the forest the charcoal pile begins to laugh and the
great hammerheads in the dark smithies seem to sneer, the mines
open wide their mouths and laugh, the desks at the trading office
where the majoress's contracts are filed writhe with laughter.
"Have you heard anything so amusing? They have no iron at
Ekeby, at the finest of Värmland's ironworks they have no iron!"

Up, you carefree ones, up, you homeless ones! Will you let such
ignominy befall Ekeby? Oh, as sure as you love the fairest place
on God's green earth, as sure as it is the object of your longing on
distant pathways, as sure as you cannot mention its name among
strangers without a tear coming to your eye, stand up, cavaliers,
save the honor of Ekeby!

Well, but if the hammers of Ekeby have rested, have they been
working at our six underlying works? There must be iron enough
and more than enough.

So Gösta Berling departs to speak with the managers of the
six ironworks.

Now to begin with it should be mentioned that he felt there
was no reason to go to Högfors, which is on the Björksjö River,
a short ways above Ekeby. It was much too close to Ekeby, it had
been as good as under the rule of the cavaliers.

But he traveled a dozen miles north, until he came to Lötafors.
It is a beautiful place, of that there is no doubt. Upper Löven wid-
ens out before it, and close behind it is Gurlita Bluff with steeply
rising top and a section of wildness and romance that well suits
an old mountain. But the smithy, of course, it is not the way it
should be: the flywheel is broken and has been like that the entire year.

"Well, why hasn't it been fixed?"

"The carpenter, my dear friend, the carpenter, who was the only one in the entire district who could fix it, has been occupied elsewhere. We have not been able to forge a single hundredweight."

"Well, why didn't you send for the carpenter?"

"Send for! As if we didn't send for him every day, but of course he hasn't been able to come. He has been busy building bowling alleys and garden pavilions at Ekeby."

Then Gösta suddenly realizes how this trip will turn out.

He travels on northward up to Björnidet. A beautiful and splendid place too, with a location fit for a palace. The large manor house dominates a semicircular valley, surrounded on three sides by massive heights and on the fourth by Löven, which has its endpoint there. And Gösta knows that there is no better place for moonlit promenades and swooning than the shoreline paths along the river, past the falls and down toward the smithy, which is housed in massive vaults blasted out of the mountain wall itself. But iron, is there any iron?

No, of course not. They did not have any charcoal, and they had not been able to get money from Ekeby to pay colliers and drivers. The entire ironworks operation had been suspended during the winter.

So Gösta turns southward again. He comes to Hån, on the eastern shore of Löven, and to Lövstafors, far into the forests, but it turns out no better for him there. Nowhere do they have iron, and everywhere it seems to be the cavaliers' own fault that such is the case.

Then Gösta turns home to Ekeby, and with gloomy expressions the cavaliers take the one hundred and fifty hundredweights or so, which are in the storehouse, into consideration, and their brows are weighed down by sorrow, for they hear how all of nature is sneering at Ekeby, and they feel that the ground is shaking with sobs, that the trees threaten them with angry gestures, and that grass and herbs lament that the honor of Ekeby is past.

But what is the use of so many words and so much wondering? Of course there is iron from Ekeby!

There it is, loaded on barges on the shore of the Klara River, ready to sail down the river, ready to be weighed on the iron scales in Karlstad, ready to be conveyed on Vänern by boat to Gothenburg. So it is rescued then, the honor of Ekeby.

But how is this possible? At Ekeby there is of course no more than one hundred and fifty hundredweights of iron; at the six other ironworks there is no iron. How is it possible that fully loaded barges will now convey such an enormous quantity of iron to the scales in Karlstad? Yes, one would have to ask the cavaliers about that.

The cavaliers are themselves on board the heavy, ugly vessels; they intend to accompany the iron from Ekeby to Gothenburg themselves. No ordinary barge hand, no ordinary mortal may accompany the iron. The cavaliers have come with bottles and food baskets, with horns and fiddles, with rifles and fishing lines and decks of cards. They will do everything for their dear iron and not abandon it before it is unloaded at the wharf in Gothenburg. They will themselves load and unload, mind the sail and the rudder. They are just the right ones for such a task. Can there be a sandbank in the Klara River or a reef in Vänern that they do not know? Don't the tiller and tackle lie equally easy in their hands as bow and rein!

If they love anything in the world, then it is the iron on these barges. They guard it like the finest glass; they drape tarpaulins over it. Not a patch of it may lie bare. It is these heavy, gray bars that will hold up the honor of Ekeby. No stranger may cast indifferent glances at them. Oh Ekeby, you our land of longing, may your honor shine!

None of the cavaliers has remained at home. Uncle Eberhard has left his writing desk, and cousin Kristoffer has emerged from the chimney corner. Even gentle Lövenborg is there. No one can stay away where the honor of Ekeby is concerned.

But for Lövenborg it is not beneficial to see the Klara River. He has not seen it in thirty-seven years; he has not been on a boat in an equally long time. He hates the blank surfaces of lakes and the gray rivers. He is reminded of overly gloomy things when he gets out on the water, and he usually avoids it, but today he has not been able to stay at home. Even he must go along to save the honor of Ekeby.

You see, it happened that thirty-seven years ago Lövenborg saw his fiancée drown in the Klara River, and since then his poor head has often been confused.

As he stands looking at the river, his old brain begins to be more and more disordered. The gray river, flowing along with many small glittering waves, is a large snake with silver scales, waiting in ambush. The high, yellow sand walls, through which the river has scoured its furrow, are the walls of a trap at whose bottom the snake is lurking, and the wide highway that makes a hole in the wall and wades down through deep sand to the ferry, next to which the barges are moored, is the very opening to the frightful hole of death.

And the little old man stands staring with his little blue eyes. His long, white hair is flying in all directions, and his cheeks, which most often blossom in a soft rose color, are completely pale from anxiety. He knows as surely as if someone has told him that someone will soon arrive on that road and fall down into the jaws of the lurking snake.

Now the cavaliers intend to cast off and take hold of the long poles to drive the barges out into the stream, but then Lövenborg calls out, "Stop, I'm telling you, stop, for God's sake!"

They understand that he is starting to get confused because he feels the barge swaying under him, but they immediately stop the raised poles.

And he, who sees that the river is lying in wait and that someone must arrive immediately to fall down into it, points with a warning gesture up toward the road, just as if he saw someone coming down it.

Each of them knows well enough that life gladly arranges such coincidences as the one that now ensued. Anyone who can still be astonished may well marvel at the fact that the cavaliers would be with their barges at the ferry station across the Klara River just that morning, after the night when Countess Elisabet embarked eastward on foot. But it would certainly have been more peculiar if the young woman had not found any help in her distress. It now happened that she, who had been walking the whole night, came along on the road that went down to the ferry just as the cavaliers intended to put out, and they remained standing and looked at her as she spoke with the ferryman and he unmoored the boat. She was dressed like a farm maid, and they did not suspect who she was. But they nonetheless stood staring at her, because there was something familiar about her. Now while she stood there talking with the ferryman, a cloud of dust was visible on the road, and from out of the cloud of dust a large, yellow calash emerged. She realized that it was from Borg, that they were out looking for her, and that she would now be discovered. She could no longer think about getting away in the ferryman's boat, and the only hiding place she saw was the cavaliers' barges. She rushed toward them without seeing what sort of people were on board. And it was well that she did not see that, for otherwise she would sooner have thrown herself under the horses' feet than taken refuge there.

When she had come on board, she simply shouted, "Hide me, hide me!" And then she stumbled and fell down on the load of iron. But the cavaliers bade her to be calm. They pushed quickly away from land, so that the barge came out in the stream and drifted down toward Karlstad just as the calash came up to the ferry station.

In the coach sat Count Henrik and Countess Märta. Now the count ran over to ask the ferryman if he had seen his countess. But as Count Henrik was a little embarrassed at having to ask about a runaway wife, he simply said, "There is something missing!"

"I see," said the ferryman.

"There is something missing. I am asking if you have seen something."

"What is it you're asking about?"

"Yes, that's all the same, but there is something missing. I am asking whether you have ferried something across the river today."

In that manner, however, he found out nothing, and Countess Märta had to speak with the fellow herself. She knew in a minute that the missing person was on board one of the barges gliding sluggishly away.

"What sort of people are on those barges?"

"It's the cavaliers, as we always say."

"Ah!" says the countess. "Yes, then your wife is in good hands, Henrik. We may as well return home at once."

Out on the barge no happiness prevailed as great as Countess Märta believed. As long as the yellow calash was visible, the frightened young woman sat curled up on the load without either moving or saying a word. She only stared at the shore.

It is probable that she recognized the cavaliers only when she had seen the yellow calash depart. She sprang up. It was as if she wanted to flee again, but she was stopped by the one standing closest, and then she again sank down with a drawn-out whimper onto the load.

And the cavaliers did not dare speak to her or ask her any questions. She looked as if she was on the verge of madness.

These carefree heads truly started to be weighed down with responsibility. This iron was already a heavy burden for unaccustomed shoulders, and now they would have to watch over a young, noble-born lady to boot, who had run away from her husband.

When they had encountered this young woman during the winter's parties, one or another of them had come to think of a little sister whom they had loved in the past. When he had played and wrestled with this sister, he had to be careful with her, and when he talked with her, he had to learn to keep an eye on himself and not say bad words. If a strange boy chased her too wildly in play or sang dirty songs to her, then he had thrown himself upon this boy with boundless fury and nearly pounded the life out of him, for his young sister should never hear anything bad or suffer any sorrow or ever be met by evil and hatred.

Countess Elisabet had been the happy sister of them all. When she had placed her small hands in their hard fists, it had been just as if she had said, "Feel how fragile I am! But you are big brother, you will protect me both against others and against yourself." And they had been courteous gentlemen, as long as they had seen her.

Now the cavaliers viewed her with dismay and did not really recognize her. She was haggard and emaciated, her throat had no roundness, her face transparent. She must have hurt herself during her nocturnal wandering, for now and then a drop of blood trickled out of a small wound on her temple, and the curly, light hair that hung down over her forehead was sticky with blood. Her dress was dirty after the long walk on roads damp with dew, and her shoes were badly battered. The cavaliers had the terrible feeling that this was a stranger. The Countess Elisabet they had known did not have such wild, glowing eyes. Their poor sister had been almost driven to madness. It was as if a soul come down from other dimensions was struggling with the right soul for dominion in this tormented body.

But they do not need to worry about what they should do with her. The old thoughts awaken within her. Temptation is again upon her there. God wants to test her again. See, she stands among friends! Does she intend to leave the way of penance?

She got up and cried that she must leave.

The cavaliers tried to calm her. They told her that she could feel secure. They would protect her against all persecution.

She asked only to be allowed to climb down into the little boat that followed the barge, and row to shore to continue her wandering alone.

But they could not just let her go. What would become of her? It was better that she stay with them. They were only poor old men, but they would certainly find some way to help her.

Then she wrung her hands and pleaded with them to let her go. But they were not able to grant her plea. They saw her so distressed and weak that they thought she would die on the road.

Gösta Berling stood a short distance away, looking down into the water. Perhaps the young woman would not gladly see him. He did not know it, but his thoughts were playing and smiling in any event. "Now no one knows where this young woman is," he thought, "now we could convey her at once to Ekeby. We would keep her hidden there, we cavaliers, and we would be good to her. She would be our queen, our sovereign, but no one else would know that she is there. We would guard her so well, so well. Perhaps she would be happy among us; she would be cherished like a daughter by all the old men."

He had never dared make it completely clear to himself that he loved her. He could not have her without sin, and he did not want to drag her down to anything low or base; that was what he knew. But to have her hidden at Ekeby and be able to be good to her after others had been cruel, and let her enjoy all the good things life possesses, oh, what dreams, what blessed dreams!

But he awakened from them, for the young countess was in complete despair, and her words had the cutting intonation of despair. She had thrown herself on her knees in the midst of the cavaliers and pleaded with them to be able to go.

"God has not yet forgiven me," she cried. "Let me go!"

Gösta saw that none of the others were capable of obeying her, and understood that he must do it. He, who loved her, must do it.

He found it difficult to walk, as if every limb in his body put up resistance to his will, but he dragged himself over to her and said that he would convey her to shore.

She got up at once. He lifted her down into the boat and rowed her to the eastern shore. He landed at a narrow gangway and helped her out of the boat.

"What will become of you now, countess?" he said.

She raised her finger seriously and pointed toward the sky.

"If you are in distress, countess . . ."

He could not speak, his voice betrayed him, but she understood him and replied, "I will send a message to you, when I need you."

"I would have liked to protect you against all evil," he said.

She extended her hand to him in farewell, and he was not capable of saying anything more. Her hand lay cold and limp in his.

The countess was not aware of anything other than inner voices, which compelled her to go away among strangers. Perhaps she scarcely knew that it was just the man she loved whom she now left.

So he let her go and rowed back to the cavaliers. When he came up onto the barge, he shook with fatigue and seemed worn-out and powerless. He had done the heaviest work of his life, it seemed to him.

For a few more days he kept up his courage, until the honor of Ekeby was saved. He conveyed the iron to the scales at Kanikenäset, then for a long time his energy and his intrepidness were at an end.

The cavaliers noticed no change in him, as long as they were on board. He tensed every nerve to keep up the merriment and levity, for it was through merriment and levity that the honor of Ekeby would be saved. How would this venture succeed if they tried it with worried faces and discouraged hearts?

If it is true, as rumor has it, that at that time the cavaliers had more sand than iron on the barges, if it is true that they carried the same rods incessantly up and down to the scale at Kanikenä-set, until the many hundredweights of iron were weighed, if it is true that all of this could go on because the weighing master and his people were so well regaled from the food baskets and can-teens brought along from Ekeby, then you must know that they had to be merry on the iron barges.

Who can know it now? But if it was that way, then it is certain that Gösta Berling could not have time to grieve. He knew noth-ing, however, of the delight of adventure and danger. As soon as he dared, he sank into desperation.

"Oh Ekeby, you land of my longing," he then called to him-self, "may your honor shine!"

As soon as the cavaliers had the weighing master's receipt, they loaded their iron onto a boat on Lake Vänern. It was otherwise customary that professional skippers took care of the transport down to Gothenburg, and generally the Värmland ironworks had no further concerns for their iron, once they had the weighing master's receipt that the delivery was complete. But the cavaliers did not want to do their business by half; they would accompany the iron all the way to Gothenburg.

On the way there they encountered misfortune. A storm broke out at night, the boat went adrift, ran against a reef, and sank with all of its valuable cargo. Then horns and card games and unemptied wine bottles went to the bottom. But if one were to view the matter correctly, what did it matter if the iron was lost? The honor of Ekeby was still saved. The iron had been weighed at the scales at Kanikenäset. And even if the major had to sit down and inform the commodities traders down there in the big

city in a gruff letter that he did not want their money because
they had not received his iron, then that didn't matter either.
Ekeby was very rich, and its honor was saved.

But if harbors and locks, if mines and charcoal stacks, if boats
and barges start to whisper strange things? If a muted sighing
passes through the forests, that the entire journey was a deception, if it is asserted all across Värmland that there was never
more than a meager one hundred and fifty hundredweights on
the barges, and that the shipwreck was arranged on purpose? A
bold deed had then been carried out, and a genuine cavalier trick
completed. Such things do not injure the honor of the old estate.

But that is long ago now. It is just possible that the cavaliers
had purchased iron from another place, or that they had found
it in some previously unknown warehouse. The truth in such a
matter will never be revealed. The weighing master at least would
never hear it said that a deception had been possible, and of
course he ought to know.

When the cavaliers came home, they received news. Count
Dohna's marriage was to be annulled. The count had sent his
steward down to Italy to gather evidence that the marriage had
not been legal. The steward also came back toward summer with
satisfying information. What this consisted of, well, that I do not
know for certain. You have to proceed carefully with the old
legends; they are like aged roses: they lose their petals easily if
you get too close to them. People say that the wedding in Italy
had not been performed by the proper priest. I know nothing
more myself, but it is nonetheless true that at the court in Bro the
marriage between Count Dohna and Elisabet von Thurn was declared never to have been a marriage.

Of this the young woman knew nothing. She was living among
peasants in distant regions, if she was even alive.

CHAPTER 18

LILLIECRONA'S HOME

Among the cavaliers there was one whom I have often mentioned as a great musician. He was a tall, coarse-limbed man with a large head and bushy, black hair. He was surely not much more than forty years old at this time, but he had an ugly, rough-hewn face and a leisurely manner. This meant that many people counted him as old. He was a good man, but gloomy.

One afternoon he took the fiddle under his arm and went away from Ekeby. He did not say good-bye to anyone, although he did not intend to ever return. He was disgusted with life there, ever since he had seen Countess Elisabet in her misfortune. He walked the whole evening and the whole night without pausing to rest, until at early sunrise he came to a small farm, called Lövdala, which belonged to him.

It was so early that no one was yet awake. Lilliecrona sat down on the green swing outside the manor house and looked at his property. Lord God! A more beautiful place did not exist. The lawn in front of the house was on a gentle rise, covered with fine, light green grass. There was no match to this lawn. The sheep could graze on it and the children romp there in their games, but still it remained equally dense and green. The scythe never passed over it, but at least once a week the mistress of the house had all the sticks and straw and dry leaves swept out of the fresh grass. He looked at the sand pathway in front of the house and suddenly pulled in his feet. Late in the evening the children had raked it in regular patterns, and his big feet had done terrible damage to their fine work. Just imagine how everything grew at this place! The six rowan trees that guarded the farmyard were as tall as beeches and broad as oaks. Have such trees ever been seen before? They were magnificent with their thick trunks clad with yellow lichens and with large, white sprays sticking out of the dark greenery. It made him think of the sky and its stars. One had to marvel at how the trees grew there in the yard. There was an old willow so thick that two men could not reach around it. It was rotten now and hollowed out, but it would not die. Every spring a bunch of fresh greenery came up out of the broken-off main trunk to show that it was alive. That hedge at the east gable had become a tree so large that it overshadowed the whole house. The whole sod roof was white with its fallen flower petals, for the hedge was already through blooming. And the birches that stood in small clumps here and there on the fields, they certainly had their own paradise on his estate. There they developed so many different ways of growing, as if they had devoted themselves to imitating all other trees. One was like a linden, dense and shady with a white arch over it; another stood even and pyramid-like as a poplar; and the branches of a third hung like a weeping willow. Not one was like the other, and altogether they were magnificent.

Then he got up and walked around the buildings. There was the orchard so wondrous fair that he had to stop and take a breath. The apple trees were blooming. Yes, he knew that of course. He had seen that at all the other farms too, but it was simply this: in no other place did they bloom the way they did at the farm where he had seen them bloom ever since he was a child. He walked with clasped hands and careful steps up and down the sand paths. The ground was white, and the trees were white, one or two with a tinge of pink. He had never seen anything so beautiful. He knew every tree the way you know your siblings and playmates. The astrakhan trees were completely white, as were the winter fruit trees. But the blossoms of the summer yellows were pink, and the paradise apple blossoms were downright red. The most beautiful was the old, ungrafted apple tree, whose small, bitter fruits no one could eat. It was not sparing with blossoms; it looked like a large snowdrift in the morning radiance.

For consider this as well, that this was early morning! The dew made all the petals glisten, all the dust was rinsed away. Behind the forest-clad hills, close under which the estate was located, the first rays of sun hurried forth. It was as if they had ignited the tops of the spruces. Over the young clover fields, over rye and barley fields and over the newly sprouted oat crop rested the very lightest mist, one of the sheerest beauty veils, and the shadows fell sharply as in moonlight.

Thus he stood quietly and looked at the great "herb beds" between the orchard pathways. He knows that his wife and her maids have been at work here. They have dug, raked, and fertilized, pulled up couch grass, and tended the earth until it has become fine and light. After they have made the bed even and the edges sharp, they have taken cord and marking sticks and drawn borders and squares. And the children have been there and been pure happiness and eagerness at getting to help out, although it has been heavy work for them to stand bent over and stretch their arms across the wide beds. And they have been unbelievably helpful, as anyone can understand.

Now what had been sown was starting to come up.

God bless them, so bravely they stood there, peas and beans with their two thick heart-shaped leaves! And so even and nice the carrots and turnips had come up! Funniest of all were the small curly parsley leaves, which lifted a little on the ground level above it, playing peekaboo with life for the time being.

And here was a small bed where the lines were not as even, and where the little squares seemed to be a test map of everything that might be planted and sown. It was the children's garden.

And Lilliecrona hastily brought his fiddle up to his chin and began to play. The birds began to sing in the large thicket that shielded the orchard from the north wind. There was no way for any being gifted with a voice to remain silent; the morning was that splendid. The strings moved all on their own.

Lilliecrona walked up and down the paths and played. "No," he thought, "a more beautiful place does not exist." What was Ekeby against Lövdala! His home was sod covered and just one story high. It was at the edge of the forest with the mountain above it and the long valley before it. There was nothing remarkable about it: there was no lake there, no waterfall, no shore meadows and parks, but it was beautiful all the same. It was beautiful because it was a good, peaceful home. Life was easy to live there. Everything, which at other places would have brought forth bitterness and hatred, was smoothed out there with gentleness. That is how it should be in a home.

Inside the house the wife lies sleeping in a room that faces toward the orchard. She awakens suddenly and listens, but she does not move. She lies smiling and listens. Then the music comes closer and closer, and finally it is as if the fiddler has stopped under her window. It is not the first time she has heard fiddle playing under her window. He usually comes like that, her husband, when they have been up to some unusually wild deed over there at Ekeby.

He stands there, confessing and asking for forgiveness. He describes for her the dark forces that lure him away from what he loves the most: from her and the children. But he loves them. Oh, certainly he loves them!

While he is playing, she gets up and puts her clothes on without really knowing what she is doing. She is so completely occupied by his playing.

"It is not luxury and good living that has lured me away," he plays, "not love for other women, not honor, but life's tempting multiplicity; I must feel its sweetness, its bitterness, its richness around me. But now I have had enough of that, now I am tired and satisfied. I will no longer leave my home. Forgive me, have mercy on me!"

Then she pulls the curtain aside and opens the window, and he sees her beautiful, good face.

She is good, and she is wise. Her glances fall like the sun's, bringing blessings on all they meet. She directs and she tends. Where she is, everything must grow and flourish. She bears happiness within her.

He swings himself up onto the windowsill by her and is happy as a young lover.

Then he lifts her out into the orchard and carries her down under the apple trees. There he explains to her how beautiful everything is and shows her the herb beds and the children's planting and the small, comical parsley leaves.

When the children wake up, there is rejoicing and rapture that Father has come. They commandeer him. He must see all the new and remarkable things: the small, water-driven nail hammer pounding over in the brook, the bird's nest in the willow, and the small carp fry in the pond, swimming at the water's edge by the thousands.

Then father, mother, and children take a long walk out on the fields. He has to see how thickly the rye stands, how the clover is growing, and how the potatoes are starting to poke up their wrinkled leaves.

He has to see the cows as they come in from the pasture, greet the newcomers in the calf pens and sheep barn, search for eggs, and give all the horses sugar.

The children hang at his heels the whole day. No lessons, no work, just roaming around with Father!

In the evening he plays *polskas* for them, and he has been such a good comrade and playmate to them the whole day that they fall asleep with a pious prayer that Father will always stay with them.

He stays a whole eight days too, and is happy as a boy the whole time. He is in love with everything there at home, with his wife and children, and never thinks about Ekeby.

But then comes a morning when he is gone. He couldn't hold out any longer, it was too much happiness for him. Ekeby was a thousand times worse, but Ekeby was in the midst of the whirl of events. Oh, how much there was to dream about and play about there! How could he live separated from the deeds of the cavaliers and from Löven's long lake, around which the wild pursuit of adventures surged forth?

On his property everything was calm as usual. Everything flourished and grew under the protection of the gentle mistress of the house. Everything moved in a quiet happiness there on the farm. Everything, which in other places would have brought forth discord and bitterness, passed there without complaint and pain. Everything was as it should be. And if the master of the house longed to live as a cavalier at Ekeby, what of it? Does it serve anything to complain about the sun in the heavens because every evening he disappears in the west and leaves the earth in darkness?

Who is unconquerable without submissiveness? Who is certain of victory without patience?

CHAPTER 19

THE WITCH OF DOVRE

Now the witch of Dovre is walking on the shore of Löven. She has been seen there, small and round backed, in a leather skirt and with a silver-mounted belt. How does she emerge from wolf dens to the world of people? What does the old woman from the mountains seek in the greenery of the valley?

She comes begging. She is stingy, greedy for gifts, rich as she is. In the mountain clefts the old woman conceals heavy ingots of white silver, and on succulent meadows deep among the mountains she pastures her large herds of black, yellow-horned cows. Nonetheless she wanders forth in birch-bark shoes and greasy leather garment, on which gaudy border seams can be glimpsed under centuries of dirt. She has moss in her pipe and begs from the poorest. Shame on such a one, who never says thank you, never gets enough!

She is old. When did the rosy luster of youth rest on the wide face with the brown skin, glistening with grease, over the flat nose and the narrow eyes, which gleam out of the dirt like fiery coals from gray ashes? When did she sit as a young lass on the mountain pasture and with birch-bark horn answer the shepherd boy's love songs? She has lived for several hundred years. The oldest people do not recall a time when she wasn't wandering through the countryside. Their parents saw her old, when they were young. Nor is she dead yet. I, who am writing this, have seen her myself.

She is powerful. She, daughter of Finns skilled in magic, submits to no one. Her wide feet set no timid tracks on the highway's gravel. She can call forth hail, she can control lightning. She can lead herds astray and send wolves onto the sheep. She

can work little good, but much evil. Best to be on good terms
with her. Even if she were to beg for the only goat and an entire
bale of wool, then give it to her! Otherwise the horse will fall
dead, otherwise the cottage will burn, otherwise the cow will be
ruined, otherwise the child will die, otherwise the frugal housewife will lose her mind.

She is never a welcome guest. Best, however, to meet her with
a smile. Who knows on whose account this bringer of misfortune
is roaming through the valley? She never comes simply for the
purpose of filling her beggar's pouch. Evil omens accompany her:
armyworms appear, fox and owl howl frightfully in the twilight,
red and black lizards that spit venom creep out of the forest all
the way to the threshold of the door.

She is proud. In her head the powerful wisdom of her ancestors is hidden. Such things elevate the mind. Priceless runes are
carved on her staff. She will not sell it for all the gold in the valley. She can sing troll songs, she can brew ancient magic, she has
plant knowledge, she can fire magic bullets across a water mirror, and she can tie storm knots.

If only I could interpret the strange thoughts of a centuries-old
brain! Coming from the dark of the forests and from the mighty
mountains, what does she think of the people in the valley? To
her, who believes in Thor, the killer of giants, and in powerful
Finnish gods, the Christians are like tame farm dogs before a gray
wolf. Untamed like the snowstorm, strong as the rapids, she can
never love the sons of the cultivated plain.

Yet still she comes back down from the mountains to see their
dwarfish ways. People shudder with terror when they see her, but
the strong daughter of the wilderness walks confidently among
them, protected by that fear. The deeds of her tribe are not forgotten, nor her own deeds either. As the cat believes in his claws,
she believes in the wisdom of her brain and in the power of di-
vinely granted troll song. No king is more certain of his dominion than she of the realm of terror that she rules.

Thus the witch of Dovre has roamed through many villages.
Now she has come to Borg and does not shrink from wandering
up to the count's estate. She seldom takes the kitchen entrance.
Right up on the stairs of the terrace she comes. She sets her broad

birch-bark shoes on flower-edged gravel paths, just as confident as if she walked on pasture paths.

It happens that Countess Märta has just then stepped out onto the stairs to observe the splendor of the June day. Down below on the sand path, two maids have stopped on their way to the larder. They have come from the sauna, where the ham is being smoked, and are carrying the freshly smoked hams on a pole between them. "Does our gracious countess wish to smell and feel them?" say the maids. "Is the ham smoked enough?"

Countess Märta, mistress of the household at Borg at that time, leans over the railing and looks at the ham, but at the same moment the old woman puts her hand on one of the hams.

Just look at this brown, shining bacon, this thick layer of fat! Smell the fresh aroma of juniper from the freshly smoked hams! Oh, food for the bygone gods! The witch wants all of it. She puts her hand on the ham.

Oh, the daughter of the mountains is not used to begging and pleading! Is it not from her mercy that flowers flourish and people live? The frost and the devastating storm and the water flood, all are in her power to send. Therefore, it does not become her to plead and beg. She puts her hand on what she wants, and it is hers.

Countess Märta, however, knows nothing about the old woman's power.

"Away with you, beggar hag!" she says.

"Give me the ham!" says the witch of Dovre, the horsewoman of wolves.

"She's crazy!" the countess cries out. And she orders the maids to go to the larder with their burden.

The centuries-old eyes flash with anger and desire.

"Give me the brown ham!" she repeats. "Otherwise it will go badly for you."

"I would rather give it to the magpies than to someone like you."

Then the old woman shakes under the storm of wrath. She extends her rune-inscribed staff toward the heights and swings it wildly. Her lips utter peculiar words. Her hair stands straight up, her eyes shine, her face is distorted.

"It is you that the magpies will eat!" she shrieks at last.

Then she leaves, muttering curses, swinging the staff wildly. She turns homeward. She walks no farther toward the south. Now the daughter of the wilderness has performed the errand for whose sake she has marched down from the mountains.

Countess Märta remains standing on the stairs and laughs at her unreasonable wrath. But soon the laughter will fall silent on her lips, for there they come! She cannot believe her eyes. She thinks she is dreaming, but there they come, the magpies that will eat her.

From park and orchard they swoop down toward her, dozens of magpies with claws extended and beaks stretched out to peck. They come with howling and laughter. Black and white wings shimmer before her eyes. As in delirium she sees behind this swarm all the magpies of the district approaching, the whole sky full of black and white wings. In the sharp sunlight of forenoon the metallic colors of their wings glisten. Their throats are ruffled up as on angry birds of prey. In tighter and tighter circles the animals fly around the countess, aiming with beaks and claws at her face and hands. Then she has to flee into the vestibule and close the door. She leans against it, panting with anxiety, while the laughing magpies circle outside.

With that she is also closed off from the sweetness and greenery of summer and from the joy of life. After this, for her there were only closed rooms and drawn curtains; for her, despair; for her, anxiety; for her, confusion bordering on madness.

This story may also well be seen as madness, yet it must be true. Hundreds of people will recognize it and testify that such is the old legend.

The birds settled down on the stair railing and the roof of the house. They sat as if they were simply waiting for the countess to show herself, to be able to throw themselves over her. They took up residence in the park, and there they stayed. It was impossible to chase them from the estate. It only got worse if you shot at them. For one that fell, ten new ones came flying. At times large groups had to leave to get food, but faithful sentries always remained. And if Countess Märta showed herself, if she looked out through a window or simply pulled back a curtain for a moment, if she tried to go out on the steps—they came at once. The entire terrible swarm rushed up toward the house with thundering wing strokes, and the countess fled into her inner-most room.

She lived in the bedroom within the red parlor. I have often heard the room described such as it was during that time of ter-ror, when Borg was besieged by magpies. Heavy blankets before the doors and windows, dense rugs on the floor, stealthy, whis-pering people.

In the countess's heart pale dismay resided. Her hair turned gray. Her skin became wrinkled. She became an old woman in a month. She could not steel her heart with doubts about hateful magic. She leaped up from the night's dreams with loud cries that the magpies were eating her. She wept throughout the day about this fate, which she could not avoid. Fleeing people, afraid that the swarm of birds would follow on the heels of anyone coming in, most often she sat silently with her hands before her face, rocking back and forth in her armchair, listless and dejected in the stifling air, at times leaping up with cries of complaint.

No one had a more bitter life. Can anyone keep from pity-ing her?

I do not have much more to tell about her now, and what I have told has not been good. It is as if my conscience struck me. Yet she was good-hearted and full of life when she was young, and many amusing stories about her have gladdened my heart, although here has not been the place to tell them.

But it is the case, although this poor wanderer did not know it, that the soul is the eternal hungerer. He cannot live on frivol-ity and play. If he does not get nourishment, like a wild animal he will first tear apart others and finally himself.

This is the meaning of the story.

CHAPTER 20

MIDSUMMER

It was midsummer then, as it is now as I am writing. The most magnificent time of the year had arrived.

That was the time of year when Sintram, the malevolent iron mill owner at Fors, grew anxious and sorrowful. He was annoyed by the victory march of light through the hours of the day, and by the defeat of darkness. He was angry at the leaf garb that enveloped the trees, and at the motley carpet that clad the ground.

Everything was enveloped in beauty. The road, gray and dusty as it was, even the road had its edge of flowers: yellow and violet midsummer blossoms, wild chervil, and babies'-slippers.

When the splendor of Midsummer Day was upon the hills and the sound of bells from Bro church was borne by the quivering air all the way up to Fors, when the inexpressible stillness of the holiday reigned over the countryside, then he rose up in anger. It seemed to him as if God and men dared forget that he existed, and he too decided to go to the church. Those who rejoiced at summer would see him, Sintram, lover of darkness without morning, of death without resurrection, of winter without spring.

He put on his wolf-skin fur and shaggy bellows gloves. He had the red horse harnessed to a racing sleigh and put sleigh bells in the shiny, scroll-adorned harness. Outfitted as though the temperature were twenty below zero, he drove to the church. He believed that the creaking under the runners came from the severe cold. He believed that the white foam on the horse's back was hoarfrost. He felt no heat. Cold radiated from him like heat from the sun.

He drove along across the broad plain north of Bro church. Large, wealthy villages were in his way and fields over which singing larks fluttered. Never have I heard larks sing as over these fields. I have often wondered if he was able to make himself deaf to these hundreds of singers.

There was much he had to travel past on the way, which would have annoyed him if he had granted it a glance. He would have seen two bowing birches at every cottage door, and through open windows he would see into rooms whose ceilings and walls were covered with flowers and green branches. The smallest beggar lass walked on the highway with a bunch of lilacs in her hand, and every farm wife had a little bunch of flowers stuck in her kerchief.

Maypoles with shriveled blossoms and drooping wreaths were raised on the farmyards. Around them the grass was trampled down, for the merry dance had gone on there in the summer night.

Down on Löven the log rafts crowded together. The small white sails were raised in honor of the day, although no wind filled them, and the top of every mast wore a green wreath.

On the many roads that lead to Bro the churchgoers came walking. The women were especially stately in their light, hand-woven summer dresses, which were made ready just for this day. Everyone was dressed for celebration.

And the people could not stop rejoicing at the holiday peace and rest from daily labor, at the sweet warmth, at the promising harvest, and at the wild strawberries that had started to ripen along the roadside. They took note of the stillness in the air, the cloudless sky, and the lark song and said, "It seems that this day belongs to our Lord."

Then Sintram came driving along. He swore, swinging the whip over the toiling horse. The sand creaked unpleasantly under the runners, the shrill clang of the sleigh bells deadened the sound of the church bells. His forehead was furrowed in anger under his fur cap.

Then the churchgoers shuddered and thought they had seen the evil one himself. Not even today, the festival of summer, could they forget evil and cold. Bitter is their lot, who wander on the earth.

The people, who were standing in the shadow of the church or sitting on the churchyard wall, waiting for the service to begin, looked at him with quiet wonder as he walked up toward the church door. A moment ago the magnificent day had filled their hearts with gladness that they could walk the paths of earth and enjoy the sweetness of existence. Now, when they saw Sintram, a sense of strange misfortune came over them.

Sintram entered the church and took his place in his seat, throwing the gloves onto the pew, so that the rattling of wolf claws sewn into the leather was heard throughout the church. And a few women, who had already taken a place in the front pews, fainted when they saw the furry figure and had to be carried out.

But no one dared drive out Sintram. He disturbed the people's devotions, but he was much too feared for anyone to dare order him to leave the church.

The old minister spoke in vain about the light festival of summer. No one was listening to him. The people were thinking only about evil and cold and about the strange misfortune that the malevolent mill owner portended for them.

When everything was done, the malevolent man was seen climbing out on the edge of the hill where Bro church sits. He looked down on Broby Sound and followed with his gaze past the parsonage and the triple promontories on the left bank out to Löven. And it was seen how he clenched his fist and shook it over the sound and its verdant shores. Then his gaze swept southward over lower Löven all the way to the blue-tinged promontories that seemed to close off the lake. And northward his gaze flew for miles past Gurlita Bluff up to Björnidet, where the lake ends. He looked west and east, where the long hills edge the lake, and he clenched his fist again. And everyone felt that if he had a bundle of lightning bolts in his hand he would have hurled them in wild delight out over the calm countryside and spread misery and death as far as he was able. For now he had so accustomed his heart to evil that he knew no joy other than in misery. Little by little he had learned to love everything ugly and base. He was crazier than the wildest lunatic, but no one realized this.

Then there was strange talk throughout the countryside. It was said that when the church sexton came to close the church, the bit of the key broke, because a tightly rolled-up piece of paper was inserted into the lock. This he gave to the minister. It was, as one might well understand, a writing intended for a being in the other world.

It was whispered about what was written there. The minister had burned up the paper, but the church sexton had watched while the diabolic thing burned. The letters had shown clear red on a black background. He had not been able to keep from reading. He read, it was said, that the malevolent one wanted to lay the land desolate as far as the steeple of Bro church was visible. He wanted to see the forest hide the church away. He wanted to see bear and fox in the dwelling places of people. He wanted the fields to lie uncultivated, and neither dog nor rooster should be heard in these parts. The malevolent one wanted to serve his master by being the cause of every man's misfortune. This was what he had promised.

And the people bided their time in silent desperation, for they knew that the malevolent one's power was great, that he hated all living things, that he wanted to see the wilderness force its way down over the valley, and that he would gladly take the plague or starvation or war into his service to drive away everyone who loved good, joy-bringing labor.

CHAPTER 21

LADY MUSICA

As nothing could make Gösta Berling happy since he had helped the young countess to flee, the cavaliers decided to seek help from the good Lady Musica, who is a powerful sylph and comforts many who are unhappy.

To that end, one evening in July they threw open the doors to the large drawing room at Ekeby and raised the window latches. The sun shone and air was let in; the large, red sun of late evening, the gentle, vaporous air of cool evening.

The striped covers were taken off the furniture, the piano was opened, and the gauze around the Venetian chandeliers was removed. The golden griffins under the white marble tabletops could again shine in the light. The white goddesses danced in the black field above the mirror. The silk damask's multiform flowers shimmered in the glow of evening. And roses were picked and brought in. The entire room was filled with their scent. There were marvelous roses with unfamiliar names, transported to Ekeby from foreign lands. There were yellow roses, in whose veins the blood shimmers red like in a person, and the cream-whites with ragged edges, and the pinks with large leaves, which become colorless at the very edge like water, and the dark reds with black shadows. They brought in all of Altringer's roses, which had come from foreign lands to delight the eyes of beautiful women.

Then sheet music and music stands and brass instruments and bows and fiddles of all sizes were brought in, for now it is the good Lady Musica who will rule at Ekeby and try to console Gösta Berling.

Lady Musica has selected the Oxford Symphony by the amiable Papa Haydn, and the cavaliers rehearse it. Squire Julius wields the baton, and each of the others tends to his own instrument. All of the cavaliers can play an instrument. Otherwise they would not be cavaliers.

When all is ready, word is sent to Gösta. He is still weak and disheartened, but he delights in the grand room and the beautiful music he will soon hear. For it is commonly known that the good Lady Musica is the best company for anyone who is suffering. She is merry and playful as a child. She is fiery and captivating as a young woman. She is good and wise as the elderly who have lived a good life.

And then the cavaliers play, so slowly, so gently murmuring.

Little Ruster takes the matter to heart. He reads the music with his glasses on his nose, kissing gentle tones from the flute and letting his fingers play around the keys and holes. Uncle Eberhard sits bent over the cello; his wig has slipped onto his ear, his lips tremble with emotion. Bergh proceeds proudly with his long bassoon. Sometimes he forgets himself and lets loose the full force of his lungs, but then Julius thumps him with the baton right on his thick skull.

It goes well, it goes brilliantly. From the lifeless sheet music they conjure up Lady Musica herself. Spread out your magic mantle, Lady Musica, and bring Gösta Berling to the land of delight, where he used to live!

Oh, to think that it is Gösta Berling who sits there pale and disheartened, and whom the old gentlemen now must amuse, as if he were a child! Now there is a shortage of joy in Värmland.

I understand why the old men loved him. I know how long the winter evenings can be and how gloom can steal its way into the mind on isolated, desolate farms. I well understand how it felt when he arrived.

Imagine a Sunday afternoon, when work was set aside and thoughts were sluggish! Imagine a stubborn north wind, whipping cold into the room, cold against which no fire could bring relief! Imagine a single tallow candle that must constantly be trimmed! Imagine the monotone singing of hymns coming from the kitchen.

Well, and then sleigh bells jingle, then rapid feet stomp off the snow out on the landing, then Gösta Berling enters the room.

He laughs and jokes. He is life, he is warmth. He opens the lid of the piano, and he plays so that the old strings astonish you. He can sing all songs, play all melodies. He makes all the inhabitants of the house happy. Never was he cold, never was he tired. The sorrowful person forgot his sorrows when he saw him. Oh, what a good heart he had! How compassionate he was to the weak and poor! And what a genius he was! Yes, you should have heard the old people talk about him.

But now, as they are playing, he bursts into tears. He thinks that life, all of life, is so miserable. He leans his head against his hands and weeps. The cavaliers are dismayed. These are not the gentle, healing tears that Lady Musica usually evokes. He is sobbing in despair. They set their instruments aside, completely at a loss.

The good Lady Musica, who is fond of Gösta Berling, is about to lose heart, but then she reminds herself that she still has a mighty champion among the cavaliers.

It is gentle Lövenborg, who lost his fiancée in the turbid river, and who is Gösta Berling's slave more than any of the others. Now he steals over to the piano. He walks around it, touching it carefully, caressing the keys with a soft hand.

Up in the cavaliers' wing Lövenborg has a large wooden table, on which he has painted a keyboard and set up a music holder. There he can sit for hours and let his fingers run across the black and white keys. There he practices scales and études, and there he plays his Beethoven. He never plays anything but Beethoven. Lady Musica has stood by him with particular favor, so that he has been able to transcribe many of the thirty-six sonatas.

But the old man never dares attempt any instrument other than the wooden table. He has a reverential terror of the piano. It entices him, but it frightens him even more. The blaring instrument, on which so many *polskas* have thundered forth, is his shrine. He has never dared touch it. Just imagine the marvelous thing with its many strings, which could give life to the great master's works! He only needs to set his ear next to it, and immediately he hears the *andantes* and *scherzos* murmuring within. Yes, the piano is just the right altar where Lady Musica should be worshipped. But he has never played on such a thing. Of course he has never been rich enough to buy one for himself, and he has never dared play this one. The majoress has not been willing to open it for him either.

He has no doubt heard how *polskas* and waltzes have been played and Bellman melodies clinked on it too. But during such unholy music the magnificent instrument could only blare and complain. No, if Beethoven were to come, then it would let its proper, pure tone be heard.

Now he thinks that the hour may have come for him and Beethoven. He will pluck up courage and touch the shrine and let his young master be gladdened by the slumbering euphony.

He sits down and begins to play. He is uncertain and agitated, but he stumbles his way through a few measures, seeking to find the right tone, wrinkles his brow, tries it over again, and then puts his hands to his face and cries.

Yes, dear Lady Musica, this is bitter for him. The shrine is of course no shrine. No clear, pure tones lie dreaming within, there is no muffled, powerful thunder, no powerfully roaring hurricane. None of the endless euphony that murmured through the air of paradise has been left behind here. This is an old, blaring piano and nothing else.

But then Lady Musica gives the cunning colonel a hint. He takes Ruster with him, and they go down in the cavaliers' wing and bring up Lövenborg's table, on which the keys are painted.

"Look here, Lövenborg," says Beerencreutz as they come back, "here's your piano! Play now for Gösta!"

Then Lövenborg stops crying and sits to play Beethoven for his distressed young friend. Now he will no doubt be happy again.

Inside the old man's head resound the most magnificent tones. He cannot help but think that Gösta hears how beautifully he is playing. Surely Gösta notices how well he is playing this evening. There are no more difficulties for him. He does his runs and trills quite effortlessly. He performs the most difficult reaches. He even wishes that the master himself could have heard him.

The longer he plays, the more transported he becomes. He hears every note with a supernatural force.

"Sorrow, sorrow," he plays, "why should I not love you? Because your lips are cold, your cheeks withered, because your embraces suffocate, your glances petrify?

"Sorrow, sorrow, you are one of those proud, lovely women whose love is hard to win, but which burns stronger than others. You repudiated woman, I set you to my heart and loved you. I caressed the cold from your limbs, and your love has filled me with blessedness.

"Oh, how I have suffered! Oh, how I have longed since I lost the one I first held dear! Dark night it was within me and without me. In prayer I was submerged, in heavy, unheard prayers. Heaven was closed to my long waiting. No sweet spirit came from the star-strewn sky to my consolation.

"But my longing tore asunder the concealing veil. You came, floating down to me on a bridge of moonbeams. You came in light, oh my beloved, and with lips smiling. Happy genies encircled you. They carried wreaths of roses. They played zither and flute. It was blessedness to see you.

"But you vanished, you vanished! And there was no bridge of moonbeams for me when I wanted to follow you. On earth I lay, wingless, bound to matter. My complaint was like the roaring of a wild animal, like the deafening thunder of the sky. I wanted to send lightning as a messenger to you. I cursed the green earth. Might fire incinerate the plants and plague strike humankind! I invoked death and the abyss. I thought that torment in eternal fire would be sweetness compared to my suffering.

"Sorrow, sorrow! It was then you became my friend. Why should I not love you, as one loves those proud, stern women whose love is hard to win but burns stronger than the others?"

That was how he played, the poor mystic. He sat there, radiating enthusiasm and emotion, hearing the most marvelous tones, certain that Gösta too must hear them and be consoled.

Gösta sat looking at him. At first he was bitter at this farce, but little by little he softened. He was irresistible, the old man, as he sat enjoying his Beethoven.

And Gösta started to think how this man too, who was now so gentle and carefree, had been submerged in suffering, how he too had lost his beloved. And now he sat there, radiantly happy at his wooden table. Was that all that was required for a person's happiness?

He felt humiliated. "What, Gösta," he said to himself, "can

you no longer endure and persevere? You, who have been tempered in poverty all of your life, you, who have heard every tree in the forest, every tuft of grass on the meadow preach self-denial and patience, you, who have been brought up in a land where winter is harsh and summer meager, have you forgotten the art of enduring?

"Oh, Gösta, a man must bear everything that life has to offer, with courage in his heart and a smile on his lips, otherwise he is no man. Feel loss as much as you want, if you have lost your beloved, let pangs of conscience tear and eat at your insides, but show yourself to be a man and a Värmlander! Let your gaze shine with joy and meet your friends with happy words!

"Life is stern, nature is stern. But both of them generate courage and joy as a counterweight against its hardness; otherwise no one could endure them.

"Courage and joy! It is as if these were life's first duties. You have never betrayed them before, nor will you do so now.

"Are you worse than Lövenborg, who sits there at his wooden piano, than all the other cavaliers, courageous, carefree, ever youthful? You know well enough that none of them has avoided suffering."

And then Gösta looks at them. Oh, such an entertainment! They sit there, all of them, deeply serious and listening to the music that no one can hear.

Suddenly Lövenborg is wrenched from his dreams by a hearty laugh. He lifts his hands from the keys and listens as if in ecstasy. It is Gösta Berling's old laughter, his good, amiable, contagious laughter. It is the sweetest music the old man has heard in his entire life.

"Didn't I know it, that Beethoven would help you, Gösta!" he exclaims. "Now you are well again." Thus it was that good Lady Musica cured Gösta Berling's melancholy.

CHAPTER 22

THE MINISTER OF BROBY

Eros, all-governing god, you must realize that it often seems as if a person must have been freed from your dominion. All the sweet feelings that unite humankind seem dead in their hearts. Madness extends its claws toward the unfortunate, but then you arrive in your omnipotence, you master guardian of life, and, like the staff of a powerful saint, the dried-out heart blossoms.

No one is stingier than the Broby minister, no one more isolated from people through meanness and mercilessness. His rooms are unheated in winter, he sits on an unpainted wooden bench, dresses in rags, lives on dry bread, and rages when a beggar steps inside his door. He lets the horse starve in the stable and sells the hay; his cows gnaw the dry grass by the roadside and the moss from the roof of the house. All the way up to the highway the bleating of the hungry sheep can be heard. The farmers throw gifts of food to him that their dogs will not eat, of clothes that their poor reject. His hand is extended in request, his back bowed in thanks. He begs from the rich, lends to the poor. If he sees a coin, his heart aches with anxiety until it finds itself in his pocket. Unhappy the man who is not ready for him the day payment is due!

He married late, but it would have been better if he never had. His wife died, tormented and overexerted. Now his daughter is a servant among strangers. He is getting old, but age brings him no relief in his striving. The madness of stinginess never leaves him.

But one fine day in the beginning of August a heavy coach arrives, pulled by four horses, up the hills of Broby. A fine old miss comes riding in great pomp, with a coachman and servant and chambermaid. She is coming to see the Broby minister. She was in love with him in the days of her youth.

When he served as a tutor on her father's estate, they loved each other, although the proud family separated them. And now she comes riding up the hills of Broby to see him before she dies. All that life has to offer her is to get to see the love of her youth again.

The fine little miss sits in the great coach, dreaming. She is not driving up the hills of Broby to a poor little rectory. She is on her way to the cool, dense arbor down in the park, where her beloved waits. She sees him, he is young, he can kiss, he can love. Now, when she knows that she will see him, his image rises up before her with unusual clarity. So handsome he is, so handsome! He can swoon, he can burn, he fills her being with the fire of rapture.

Now she is sallow, withered, and old. Perhaps he will not recognize her with her sixty years, but she is coming not to be seen, but to see, to see the beloved of her youth, who has avoided the onslaught of time unscathed, who is still young, lovely, warmhearted.

She comes from so far away that she has not heard a word about the Broby minister.

Then the coach rattles up the hills, and at the top the parsonage is visible.

"For the sake of God's mercy," whimpers a beggar at the roadside, "a coin for a poor man!"

The noble lady gives him a silver coin and asks if the Broby parsonage is in the vicinity.

The beggar directs a shrewd, sharp glance at her.

"The parsonage is over there," he says, "but the minister is not at home; no one is home at the parsonage."

The fine little miss appears to turn completely pale. The cool arbor disappears, the beloved is not there. How could she imagine, after forty years of waiting, finding him there again?

What business did the gracious miss have at the parsonage?

The gracious miss has come to see the rector. She knew him in days gone by.

Forty years and four hundred miles have separated them. And with the miles she has come closer, she has driven away the years with their burden of sorrows and memories, so that now when she has arrived at the rectory, she is again a twenty-year-old without sorrows, without memories.

The beggar stands looking at her, sees her transformed before his eyes from twenty to sixty, and again from sixty to twenty.

"The minister is coming home this afternoon," he says. The gracious miss would be wisest in going down to the Broby inn and coming again in the afternoon. This afternoon the beggar guarantees that the rector will be home.

The next moment the heavy coach with the little withered dame rolls down the hills to the inn, but the beggar stands trembling and watches her. He thinks he would like to fall down on his knees and kiss the wheel tracks.

Elegant, fresh shaven, and polished, in shoes with shiny buckles, in silk stockings, in ruffles and cuffs, the Broby minister stands that same day at dinner before the dean's wife in Bro.

"A fine miss," he says, "a count's daughter. Do you think that I, a poor man, can ask her to come in to visit me? My floors are grimy, my parlor has no furniture, the dining room ceiling is green with mold and damp. Help me! Bear in mind that she is a noble count's daughter!"

"Say that he has gone away!"

"Dear woman, she has traveled four hundred miles to see me, a poor man. She does not know my situation. I have no bed to offer her. I have no bed for her servants."

"Well, then, let her go back!"

"For pity's sake, woman! Don't you understand what I mean? I would rather give everything I own, everything I have acquired with diligence and effort, than that she should leave without my having received her under my roof. She was twenty years old when I last saw her, and that is now forty years ago; think about that! Help me, so that I may see her in my home! Here is money, if money can help, but more than money is needed here."

Oh Eros! Women love you. They would rather take a hundred steps for you than one for other gods.

At the deanery in Bro the rooms are emptied, the kitchen is emptied, the pantry is emptied. At the deanery in Bro the wagons are filled and driven up to the rectory. When the dean comes home from communion, he will enter empty rooms, crack open the kitchen door and ask about his dinner and find no one there. No dinner, no wife, no maid! Who can help it? Eros has so desired, Eros, all-governing.

A little later in the afternoon the heavy coach comes rattling up the hills of Broby. And the little miss sits wondering whether a new mishap would not occur, if it really was true that she is now on her way to meet the one joy of her life.

Then the coach turns into the parsonage, but it stops in the archway. The large coach is too wide, the archway too narrow. The coachman cracks his whip, the horses rear back, the servant swears, but the back wheels of the coach are helplessly stuck. The count's daughter cannot come into the beloved's yard.

But someone is coming, there he comes! He lifts her out of the coach, he carries her in his arms, whose strength is unbroken, she is pressed in an embrace as warm as before, forty years ago. She looks into eyes that radiate as they did when they had only seen five-and-twenty springs.

Then a storm of emotions comes over her, warmer than ever. She recalls that he once carried her up the stairs to the terrace. She, who believed that her love had lived all these years, she had nonetheless forgotten what it was like to be enclosed in strong arms, to look into young, radiant eyes.

She does not see that he is old. She only sees his eyes, his eyes.

She does not see the grimy floors, the ceiling green with damp, she sees only his radiant eyes. The Broby minister is a stately fellow, a handsome gentleman at that moment. He becomes handsome simply by looking at her.

She hears his voice, his clear, strong voice; caressingly it sounds. Then he speaks only to her. To what end did he need furniture from the deanery for his empty rooms, to what end food, to what end servants? The old woman would hardly have missed any such things. She hears his voice and sees his eyes.

Never, never before has she been so happy!

How elegantly he bows, elegant and proud, as if she were a princess and he the favored one! He uses the many phrases of the old when he speaks to her. She simply smiles and is happy.

Toward evening he offers her his arm, and they walk in his old, decrepit orchard. She sees nothing ugly and neglected. Overgrown bushes become clipped hedges, the weeds arrange themselves into even, glistening lawns, long lanes shadow her, and in niches of dark greenery glisten white statues of youth, of faithfulness, of hope, of love.

She knows that he has been married, but she does not recall that. How could she recall something like that? She is twenty years old, after all, he twenty-five. He is of course only twenty-five, young, with ample powers. Is he the one who will become the stingy Broby minister, he, this smiling youth? At times forebodings of dark destinies brush past his ear. But the laments of the poor, the curses of the swindled, the jibes of contempt, the satirical songs, the mockery, none of this exists yet for him. His heart is burning simply with a pure and innocent love. Will the proud youth not one day love gold so that he would creep in the lowest filth, beg it from the wayfarer, suffer humiliation, suffer disgrace, suffer cold, suffer hunger in order to get it? Would he not starve his child, torment his wife for this same, miserable gold? It is impossible. He cannot be like that. He is a good person like everyone else. He is not a monster.

The beloved of his youth does not walk at the side of a despised wretch, unworthy of the position he has dared accept! This she does not do.

Oh Eros, all-governing god, not this evening! This evening he is not the Broby minister, nor the next day, nor the day after that.

The following day she leaves. The archway is widened. The coach rolls down the hills of Broby as rapidly as the rested horses can run.

Such a dream, such a magnificent dream! For these three days, not a cloud.

Smiling she rides home to her palace and her memories. She never heard his name mentioned again, she never asked any questions about him. She would dream about this dream as long as she lived.

The Broby minister sat in his desolate home and wept in desperation. She had made him young. Would he now get old? Would the evil spirit come back, and would he become despicable, as despicable as he had been?

CHAPTER 23

SQUIRE JULIUS

Squire Julius carried his red-painted wooden trunk down from the cavaliers' wing. He filled a small green keg that had accompanied him on many journeys with aromatic bitter-orange liquor, and in the large, carved food box he put butter, bread, and old cheese, sweetly alternating green and brown, fat ham and pancakes swimming in raspberry jam.

Then Squire Julius departed and with tears in his eyes said farewell to all the magnificence of Ekeby. He caressed the worn bowling pins for the last time and the round-cheeked children at the ironworks. He went around to the arbors in the orchard and the grottoes in the park. He was in the stable and barn, stroking the horses across the hindquarters, tugging at the horn of the fierce bull, and letting the calves lick his bare hands. Finally he went with crying eyes up to the manor house, where the farewell breakfast awaited him.

Woe to existence! How can it possess so much darkness? It was poison in the food, gall in the wine. The cavaliers' throats were just as choked with emotion as his own. The fog of tears clouded their eyes. The farewell speeches were interrupted by sobbing. Woe to existence! His life would henceforth be one extended longing. Never would he draw his lips into a smile; the songs would die away from his memory, as flowers die from an autumnal earth. He would fade away, fall off, wither like a frostbitten rose, like a thirsting lily. Never again would the cavaliers see poor Julius. Heavy premonitions passed over his soul, as shadows of storm-chased clouds pass over freshly cultivated fields. He was going home to die.

Blooming with health and well-being, he stood now before them. Never again would they see him like that. Never again would they jokingly ask him when he last saw the tips of his toes, never again would they wish his cheeks into bowling balls. The evil was already ensconced in his liver and lungs. It gnawed and consumed. He had sensed it for a long time. His days were numbered.

Oh, that the cavaliers of Ekeby would yet preserve the dead man in faithful memory! Oh, that they might not forget him!

Duty called him. There at home sat his mother, waiting for him. For seventeen years she had awaited his arrival home from Ekeby. Now she had written a letter of summons, and he would obey. He knew that this would be his death, but he would obey like a good son.

Oh, those heavenly banquets! Oh, the sweet shore meadows, the proud rapids! Oh, the exultant adventures, the white, smooth dance floors, the beloved cavaliers' wing! Oh, fiddles and horns, oh, life of happiness and joy! It was death to be separated from all this.

Then Squire Julius went out into the kitchen and said farewell to the household help. Each and every one, from the housekeeper to the almswoman, embraced and kissed him with overflowing emotion. The maids wept and lamented at his fate. That such a good, amusing gentleman would die, that they would never get to see him again!

Squire Julius gave the order that his chaise should be pulled out of the wagon shed and his horse taken from the stable.

His voice almost betrayed Squire Julius as he gave this order. So the chaise would not get to molder in peace at Ekeby, old Kajsa would be separated from the familiar manger! He did not want to say anything bad about his mother, but she ought to have thought about the chaise and about Kajsa, if she didn't think about him. How would they endure the long journey?

Most bitter of all, however, was the parting from the cavaliers.

Round little Squire Julius, built more for rolling than for walking, felt tragic all the way to his fingertips. He remembered the great Athenian who calmly emptied the beaker of poison in the circle of weeping disciples. He remembered old King Gösta who prophesied to the people of Sweden that one day they would pull him up out of the ground.

Finally he sang his best song for them. He thought about the swan who dies in song. He wanted them to remember him like that: a kingly spirit who does not lower himself to complaint, but instead goes forth, borne by euphony.

At last the final beaker was emptied, the final song sung, the final embrace doled out. He put on his coat and held the whip in his hand. No eye was dry around him; his own were so filled with the rising mist of sorrow that he saw nothing.

Then the cavaliers seized him and raised him up. Cheers thundered around him. They set him down somewhere, he did not see where. A whip cracked, the carriage moved beneath him. He was carried away. When he regained the use of his eyes, he was out on the highway.

The cavaliers had indeed wept and been touched by deep loss, yet sorrow had not stifled all the happy emotions of the heart. One of them—was it Gösta Berling, the poet, or Beerencreutz, the *kille*-playing old warrior, or the world-weary cousin Kristoffer?—had arranged it so that old Kajsa did not need to be taken out of her stable, nor the moldering chaise out of its shed. But a large, rose white ox had been harnessed to a hayrack, and after the red trunk, the green keg, and the carved food box had been set there, Squire Julius himself, whose eyes were dim with tears, was lowered, not on the food box or the trunk, but on the back of the rose white ox.

See, such is humankind! Too weak to meet sorrow in all its bitterness! The cavaliers grieved for this friend who was going off to die, this withering lily, this mortally wounded swan of song. Yet the heaviness of their hearts was lightened when they saw him go away riding on the back of the great ox, while his fat body was shaken by sobbing, his arms, extended in a final embrace, sinking down in despair, and his eyes sought justice in an unpropitious heaven.

Out there on the highway the mists began to disperse for Squire Julius, and he noticed that he was sitting on an animal's swaying back. And then it is said that he began brooding about all that can happen during seventeen long years. Old Kajsa was visibly transformed. Could the oats and clover pastures at Ekeby have caused such a thing? And he shouted—I do not know if the stones on the highway or the birds in the thicket heard it— but it is true that he shouted. "Let the devil martyr me if I don't believe you've got horns, Kajsa!"

After yet another period of brooding he let himself glide slowly from the ox's back, climbed up into the hayrack, sat down on the food box and drove on, deep in thought.

In a while, as he came up toward Broby, he could hear measured song:

> One and two,
> six and seven.
> the hussars of Värmland are on their way.

So it rang to meet him, but it was not a troop of hussars, but rather the happy misses from Berga and a couple of the judge in Munkerud's beautiful daughters who came wandering along the road. They had set their small food bundles on long poles, which rested on their shoulders like rifles, and they marched courageously forth in the summer heat, singing in good measure, "One and two, six and seven . . ."

"Where to, Squire Julius?" they cried as they met him, without taking notice of the cloud of sorrow that covered his brow.

"I'm going away from the house of sin and futility," replied Squire Julius. "I no longer wish to dwell among lazybones and miscreants. I am going home to my mother."

"Oh," they cried, "that isn't true! Squire Julius doesn't want to leave Ekeby!"

"Yes," he said, striking his fist on the clothes trunk. "As Lot fled from Sodom and Gomorrah, so I flee from Ekeby. There is not a just man there now. But when the earth falls apart beneath them and the rain of sulfur clatters down from the sky, then will I rejoice at God's righteous judgments. *Adieu*, girls, and watch out for Ekeby!"

With that he wanted to travel on, but this was by no means the happy girls' intention. Their intention was to hike up to

Dunderklätten to climb the hill, but the road was long, and they had a good mind to ride all the way to the foot of the mountain in Julius's hayrack.

Fortunate are they who can rejoice at the sunshine of life and do not need a gourd to shield their head! Within two minutes the girls had their way. Squire Julius turned around and headed up toward Dunderklätten. Smiling he sat on the food box, while the hayrack was full of girls. Along the road daisies and chamomile and bitter vetch were growing. The ox had to rest awhile. Then the girls got off and picked flowers. Soon showy wreaths were hanging around Julius's head and the horns of the ox.

Farther along they encountered light young birches and dark alder bushes. Then they got out and broke off branches to decorate the hayrack. Before long it was like looking at a traveling grove. It was fun and games the whole day.

Squire Julius became more and more gentle and light, the longer the day went on. He doled out his food supply among the girls and sang songs for them. When they stood at the top of Dunderklätten, with the wide landscape lying below so proud and lovely that they got tears in their eyes from its beauty, then Julius felt his heart beat powerfully, the words stormed forth across his lips, and he spoke about his beloved province.

"Ah, Värmland," he said, "lovely, magnificent! Often when I have seen you before me on a map, I have wondered what you might depict, but now I understand what you are. You are an old, pious hermit, who sits quietly and dreams, with legs crossed and hands resting in your lap. You have a pointed cap pulled down over your half-closed eyes. You are a brooder, a holy dreamer, and you are very lovely. Wide forests are your garments. Long ribbons of blue water and evenly running rows of blue hills border it. You are so simple that the stranger does not see how lovely you are. You are poor, as the pious wish to be. You sit quietly while the waves of Vänern rinse your feet and your crossed legs. To the left you have your ore fields and mines. There is your beating heart. To the north you have dark, lovely regions of desolation, of secrecy. There is your dreaming head.

"As I see you, giantlike, serious, my eye must be filled with tears. You are stern in your loveliness, you are meditation, poverty, privation, and yet I see in the midst of your sternness the sweet features of gentleness. I see you and worship. If I simply look into the wide forest, if I simply touch a corner of your garment, my spirit is healed. Hour after hour, year after year I have looked into your holy face. What secrets do you conceal under lowered lids, you deity of privation? Have you solved the mystery of life and death, or do you still brood, holy, giantlike? For me you are the guardian of great, serious thoughts. But I see people crawl upon you and around you, beings who never seem to notice the majesty of seriousness on your brow. They simply see the beauty of your face and limbs and are so enchanted by it that they forget everything.

"Woe to me, woe to us all, children of Värmland! Beauty, beauty and nothing else do we demand of life. We, children of privation, of seriousness, of poverty, raise our hands in a single long prayer and desire only this one good thing: beauty. May life be like a rosebush, bloom with love, wine, and amusements, and may its roses be available to every man! See, this we want, and our land wears the features of sternness, seriousness, privation. Our land is the eternal symbol of brooding, but we have no thoughts.

"Oh, Värmland, lovely, magnificent!"

Thus he spoke with tears in his eyes and a voice trembling with inspiration. The girls heard him with admiration and not without feeling. They scarcely sensed the depth of the emotions that were hidden under this glittering surface of jokes and smiles.

As evening approached and they got into the hayrack again, the girls hardly knew where Squire Julius was driving them until they stopped before the stairs to Ekeby.

"Now we will go in here and have a dance, girls," said Squire Julius.

What did the cavaliers say when they saw Squire Julius arrive with a withered wreath around his hat and the hayrack full of girls?

"We were sure the girls had gone off with him," they said, "otherwise he would have been back here a few hours earlier." For the cavaliers remembered that this was only the seventeenth time Squire Julius had tried to leave Ekeby, once each passing year. Now Squire Julius had already forgotten both this attempt and all the others. Once again his conscience slept its year-long sleep.

He was a funny man, Squire Julius. He was light in the dance, keen at the gaming table. Pen, brush, and bow sat equally well in his hand. He had an easily moved heart, lovely words on his tongue, a throat full of songs. But of what use would all this be to him if he had not possessed a conscience that let itself be felt only once a year, like those mayflies who free themselves from the gloomy depths and take wing, simply to love for a few hours in daylight and sun-shimmer?

CHAPTER 24

THE CLAY SAINTS

Svartsjö church is white both outside and inside: the walls are white, the pulpit, the pews, the balcony, the ceiling, the window frames, the altar cloth, all are white. There are no ornaments in Svartsjö church, no images, no coats of arms. Only a wooden cross with a white linen cloth stands over the altar. It was not like that before. Then the ceiling was full of paintings, and varied, gaudy images of stone and clay were found in this house of God.

Once, a very long time ago, an artist in Svartsjö stood observing the sky on a summer day and noticed the flight of the clouds toward the sun. He had seen the white, shining clouds, which sit low on the horizon in the morning, pile up higher and higher, seen all the expectant colossi expand and rise to storm the heights. They set up sails like sailing ships. They raised banners like warriors. They went to invade whole heavens. Face to face with the sun, the ruler of space, these growing marvels play-acted, taking on a harmless appearance. There was a ravenous lion; it turned into a powdered lady. There was a giant with stifling arms. He lay down like a dreaming sphinx. Some adorned their white nakedness with gold-trimmed mantles. Others splashed rouge over cheeks of snow. There were plains. There were forests. There were walled fortresses with high towers. The white clouds became masters of the summer sky. They filled the blue arch entirely. They reached the sun and covered her.

"Oh, how lovely," the pious artist then thought, "if the yearning spirits could rise up on these towering mountains and be carried by them as on a swaying ship, ever higher and higher upward!"

And suddenly he realized that the white clouds of the summer day were the sailing ships on which the souls of the departed travel.

He saw them there. There they stood on the gliding masses with lilies in their hands and gold crowns on their heads. Space resounded with their song. Angels swooped down on broad, strong wings to meet them. Oh, what a throng of the departed! As the clouds expanded, more and more of them became visible. They rested on cloud beds like water lilies on a lake. They adorned them, as the lilies adorn the meadow. What an exultant ascent! Cloud rolled up behind cloud. And they were all filled by the heavenly hosts in armor of silver, of immortal singers in purple-edged mantles.

This artist had then painted the ceiling in Svartsjö church. There he tried to reproduce the ascending clouds of the summer day, which transported the departed into the magnificence of heaven. The hand wielding the brush had been powerful, but also somewhat stiff, so the clouds ended up looking more like the curly locks of a full-bottomed wig than growing mountains of soft mist. And the artist had not been able to reproduce the holy ones as they had taken form in his imagination either; instead he had clothed them, modeled on the human race, in long, red cowls and stiff bishop's caps or in black caftans with rigid, fluted ruffs. He had given them large heads and small bodies, and he had supplied them with kerchiefs and prayer books. Latin maxims flew from their mouths, and for those whom he believed to be the best, he placed sturdy wooden chairs on the backs of the clouds, so that, sitting comfortably, they could travel into eternity.

But everyone knew that spirits and angels had never appeared to the poor artist, and so it was no great surprise that he had not been able to make them supernaturally lovely. The good master's pious painting no doubt seemed exceedingly delightful to many a person, and it had aroused much holy emotion. It might well have been worthy of being seen by our eyes too.

But during the cavaliers' year Count Dohna had the whole church painted white. Then the ceiling painting was destroyed. Likewise all the clay saints were annihilated.

Ah, those clay saints!

It would be better for me if human distress could cause me as much sorrow as I have felt over their destruction, if human cruelty to other human beings could fill me with such bitterness as I have felt for their sake.

But just think: there was a Saint Olaf with a crown on the helmet, ax in hand, and a kneeling giant under his feet; on the pulpit there was a Judith in red shirt and blue skirt, with a sword in one hand and an hourglass in the other, instead of the Assyrian general's head; there was a mysterious Queen of Sheba in blue shirt and red skirt, with a goose foot on one leg and a hand full of sibylline books; there was a gray Saint George, lying alone on a pew in the choir, for both horse and dragon had been broken; there was Saint Christopher with the blossoming staff, and Saint Erik with scepter and broadax, clad in ankle-length, gold-flowered cowl.

I have sat there in Svartsjö church on many a Sunday and grieved that the images were gone, yearning for them. I would not have looked too closely to see if there was a nose or foot missing, if the gilding had faded and the paint peeled off. I would have seen them irradiated by the glow of legends.

It seems always to have been that way for these saints, that they lost their scepters or ears or hands and had to be repaired and cleaned up. The congregation grew tired of that and longed to be rid of them. But the farmers would probably not have done the saints any damage if Count Henrik Dohna had not existed. It was he who had them taken away.

I have hated him for that, as only a child can hate. I have hated him, as the starving beggar hates the stingy housewife who denies him bread. I have hated him, as a poor fisherman hates a mischievous boy who has ruined his nets and cut holes in his boat. Was I not hungry and thirsty during those long church services? And he had taken away bread on which my soul could have lived. Did I not yearn out into infinity, up to heaven? And he had ruined my craft and torn the net with which I could have captured sacred visions.

There is no room in the world of grown-ups for a proper hatred. Nowadays how would I be able to hate such a deplorable

being as this Count Dohna or a crazed person such as Sintram
or an enervated woman of the world such as Countess Märta?
But when I was a child! It was their good fortune that they were
dead so long ago.

Perhaps the minister stood up there in the pulpit and spoke
of peace and reconciliation, but his words could never be heard
at our place in the church. Oh, if I had had them there, those old
clay saints! They would probably have preached to me, so that
I could have both heard and understood.

But most often I sat thinking about how it was that they were
stolen away and destroyed.

When Count Dohna had his marriage annulled instead of seeking out his wife and having it legalized, this had aroused the indignation of everyone, for they knew that his wife had left his
home simply not to be tormented to death. It now seemed as if
he wanted to win back God's grace and people's respect through
a good work, and so he had Svartsjö church repaired. He had the
entire church painted white and the ceiling painting torn down.
He and his assistants carried the images down in a boat and sank
them into the depths of Löven.

Yet how could he dare lay his hand on these, the Lord's
mighty ones?

Oh, that the outrage was allowed to happen! The hand that
cut off Holofernes' head, did it not still wield a sword? Had the
Queen of Sheba forgotten all secret knowledge, which wounds
more dangerously than a poisoned arrow? Saint Olaf, Saint Olaf,
old Viking, Saint George, Saint George, old dragon-slayer, so the
thunder of your exploits is dead, the halo of miracles put out! But
it was just as well that the holy ones would not use force against
the destroyers. Because the Svartsjö farmers no longer wanted to
pay for paint for their coats and gilding for their crowns, they
allowed Count Dohna to carry them out and sink them in the
bottomless depths of Löven. They no longer wanted to stand
there and disfigure the house of God. Oh, those helpless ones,
did they remember the time when prayers and genuflection were
brought to them?

I thought about this boat with its cargo of saints, gliding across
the surface of Löven one quiet summer evening. The fellow who

was rowing made slow strokes of the oar and cast shy glances at the unusual passengers who were lying at the prow and stern, but Count Dohna, who was also there, was not afraid. He took them one by one with upraised hands and threw them into the water. His forehead was clear, and he breathed deeply. He felt like a champion of the pure evangelical doctrine. And no miracle occurred for the glory of the old saints. Silent and dispirited, they sank down into annihilation.

But next Sunday morning Svartsjö church was shining white. No longer did images disturb the peace of inner reflection. Only with the eyes of the soul would the pious observe the magnificence of heaven and the faces of the holy. People's prayers would reach the Almighty on their own strong wings. No longer would they cling tightly to the hems of the saints' garments.

Oh, green is the earth, beloved dwelling place of humankind, blue is the sky, goal of her yearning. The world radiates colors. Why is the church white? White as winter, naked as poverty, pale as anxiety! It does not glisten from hoarfrost like a wintry forest. It does not radiate in pearls and lace like a bride dressed in white. The church is in white, cold whitewash, without an image, without a painting.

That Sunday Count Dohna sat in a flower-bedecked armchair in the choir so as to be seen and praised by every person. Now he would be honored, he who had the old pews repaired, had the disfiguring images destroyed, had new glass installed in all the broken windows, and had the entire church coated with whitewash. He was of course free to do that sort of thing. If he wanted to appease the wrath of the Almighty, then it was good that he adorned His temple to the best of his understanding. But why then did he accept praise for it?

He, who came with unreconciled severity on his conscience, he might have gotten down on his knees down by the pillory and begged his brothers and sisters in the church to call upon God, that He might tolerate him in His sanctuary. It would have been better for him if he had stood there like a poor miscreant, than to sit honored and blessed up in the choir and accept praise, because he had wanted to become reconciled with his God.

Oh, count, of course He had expected you at the pillory. He could not let himself be mocked, just because the people had not dared accuse you. He is still the zealous God, who lets stones speak when people remain silent.

When the service was over and the final hymn sung, no one left the church; instead the minister went up to the pulpit to say a word of thanks to the count. But it did not get that far.

For the doors were thrown open, and there came the old saints into the church again, dripping with the water of Löven, soiled with green mud and brown muck. They must have sensed that here the praises would be spoken of him who had cast them into annihilation, who drove them out of God's sacred house and lowered them into the cold, dissolving waves. The old saints wished to have a word too in the matter.

They do not love the monotonous lapping of the waves. They are used to hymn singing and prayers. They kept silent and let everything happen, as long as they believed that it would redound to the glory of God. But this was not the case. Here sits Count Dohna in honor and glory up in the choir and wants to be adored and praised in the house of God. They could not tolerate that sort of thing. So they have risen up from their wet grave and marched into the church, recognizable to all the people. There goes Saint Olaf with the crown on his hat, and Saint Erik with the golden flowers on his cowl, and the gray Saint George and Saint Christopher, no others: the Queen of Sheba and Judith had not come.

But when the people have managed to recover from their astonishment, an audible whisper goes through the church: "The cavaliers!"

Yes, of course it is the cavaliers. And they go right up to the count without saying a word and lift up his chair on their shoulders and carry him out of the church and set him down on the church green.

They say nothing and look neither to the right nor to the left. They simply carry Count Dohna out of the house of God, and once this is done, they go away again, taking the nearest route down to the lake.

They were not accosted, nor did they waste much time in explaining their intention. It was clear enough: "We, cavaliers of Ekeby, have our own opinion. Count Dohna is not worthy of being praised in the house of God. Therefore we are carrying him out. May anyone who wishes cart him back in again."

But he was not carried in. The minister's word of thanks was never said. The people streamed out of the church. There was no one who did not believe that the cavaliers had acted rightly.

They remembered the light, young countess, who had been so cruelly tormented there at Borg. They remembered her, who had been so good to poor people, who had been so sweet to look at that it had been a consolation for them to look at her.

It was a sin to come to church with wild pranks, but both the minister and the congregation felt that they themselves had been on the verge of making a greater mockery of the Omniscient. And they stood ashamed before the wild old lunatics.

"When the people are silent, stones must speak," they said.

But after that day Count Henrik could not be happy at Borg. One dark night at the beginning of August a covered coach drove right up to the large staircase. All the servants positioned themselves around it, and Countess Märta came out, concealed in shawls, with a thick veil before her face. The count led her, but she trembled and shook. It was with the utmost difficulty that they were able to get her to cross the vestibule and staircase.

When she was in the coach, the count leaped up after her, the doors slammed shut, and the coachman let the horses set off as if out of control. When the magpies awoke the next morning, she was gone.

The count later lived a long time in the south. Borg was sold and has changed owners many times. Everyone has to love it; there must be but few who have owned it in happiness.

CHAPTER 25

GOD'S PILGRIM

God's pilgrim, Captain Lennart, came wandering one afternoon in August up to the Broby inn and went into the kitchen there. He was on his way to his home, Helgesäter, which is a mile or so northwest of Broby, close by the edge of the forest.

Captain Lennart did not yet know that he would become one of God's pilgrims on this earth. His heart was filled with anticipation and happiness at getting to see his home again. He had experienced a dark fate, but now he was home, and now everything would be fine. He did not know that he would become one of those who are not allowed to rest under their own roof, not warm themselves at their own stove.

God's pilgrim, Captain Lennart, had a cheerful disposition. Not finding anyone in the kitchen, he rearranged things in there as if he had been a giddy lad. In haste he disturbed the selvage in the weaving and upset the thread of the spinning wheel. He tossed the cat down on the dog's head and laughed so it sounded around the house, as the two comrades let the heat of the moment breach longtime friendship and attacked each other with claws extended, savage eyes, and bristling fur.

Then the proprietress came in, attracted by the din. She remained standing on the threshold watching the man, who was laughing at the struggling animals. She knew him well, but when she last saw him, he had been sitting on the prisoners' cart in handcuffs. She remembered it well. Five and a half years ago, thieves had stolen the governor's wife's jewelry during the winter market in Karlstad. Many rings, bracelets, and clasps, valued highly by the noble lady, for most of them were legacies and gifts, had then been lost. They were never recovered. But a rumor soon ran around the countryside that Captain Lennart at Helgesäter might be the thief.

The woman had never been able to understand how such a rumor could have arisen. Was he not a good and honorable man, this Captain Lennart? He lived happily with his wife, whom he had only brought home a few years ago, for he was older before he had the means to get married. Did he not have a good livelihood nowadays from his salary and the little farm? What could entice such a man to steal old bracelets and rings? And it seemed even stranger to her that such a rumor could be so believed, so fully substantiated, that Captain Lennart was fired, lost his military position, and was sentenced to five years hard labor.

He said himself that he had been at the market, but left before he heard talk of the theft. On the highway he found an ugly old clasp, which he had taken home with him and given to the children. This clasp, however, was gold, and was one of the stolen items. It became the cause of his misfortune. But it had really all been Sintram's fault. The malevolent mill owner had played informer and given the damning testimony. It seemed as though he needed to be rid of Captain Lennart, for shortly thereafter a case was opened against Sintram, that he had sold powder to the Norwegians during the war of 1814. People thought that he had been afraid of the testimony Captain Lennart might have given against him. Now he was set free due to lack of evidence.

The innkeeper could not get her fill of looking at him. He had acquired gray hair and a stooped back; he had no doubt had a difficult time. But he still had his amiable face and his cheerful temperament. He was still the same Captain Lennart who had led her up to the altar when she was a bride, and danced at her wedding. He would surely still stand and talk to every person he encountered on the road and toss a coin to every child. He would still say to every wrinkled old lady that she got younger and more beautiful day by day, and he would once again get up on a barrel and play fiddle for those who were dancing around the maypole. Oh, good Lord, yes!

"Well, mother Karin," he began, "don't you dare to look at me?"

He had actually come there to hear how things were going in his home and if they expected him. They might know, of course, that he had served his sentence by this time.

The innkeeper gave him nothing but good news. His wife had been as capable as a man. She had rented the cottage and farm from the new officer, and everything had gone well for her. The children were healthy, and it was a joy to see them. And of course they expected him. The captain's wife was a stern woman who never said what she was thinking, but the innkeeper knew that no one had been allowed to eat with Captain Lennart's spoon or sit in his chair while he was away. Now in spring not a day had gone by without her going up to the stone on top of the Broby hills to look down toward the road to see if he wasn't coming. And she had arranged new clothes for him, homespun clothes, on which she herself had done most of the work. See, by such things it could be known that he was expected, even if she said nothing.

"They don't believe it then?" said Captain Lennart.

"No, captain," answered the farm woman. "No one believes it."

Then Captain Lennart did not stay inside the kitchen any longer, as he wanted to go home.

It happened that he met dear old friends just outside. The cavaliers at Ekeby had just arrived at the inn. Sintram had invited them there to celebrate his birthday. And the cavaliers did not hesitate a moment to shake the prisoner's hand and welcome him home. Sintram did so too.

"Dear Lennart," he said, "be sure that God had some meaning with this!"

"Watch it, scoundrel," shouted Captain Lennart. "Don't you think I know that it wasn't our Lord who saved you from the scaffold?"

The others laughed. But Sintram did not become the least bit angry. He had nothing at all against someone alluding to his pact with the devil.

Yes, so then they took Captain Lennart in with them again to empty a welcome glass with him. Then he could go right on. But then things went badly for him. He had not drunk such treacherous things in five years. He had perhaps not eaten the entire day, and he was worn out by his long wandering. Consequently his head got dizzy from a few glasses.

When the cavaliers got him to the point that he no longer knew what he was doing, they forced glass after glass into him, and they meant nothing bad by it; they had purely good intentions toward him, who had not tasted anything good for five years.

Otherwise he was the most sober of men. He probably did not intend to become intoxicated either; after all, he was going home to his wife and children. But instead he remained lying on the bench in the inn and fell asleep there.

As he was lying there, temptingly unconscious, Gösta took a piece of coal and a little lingonberry juice and painted him. He gave him a true criminal physiognomy; he thought that well suited someone who came directly from prison. He gave him a black eye, drew a red scar across his nose, brushed his hair down onto his forehead in tangled tufts, and blackened his whole face.

They laughed at that awhile, and then Gösta wanted to wash it off.

"Let it be," said Sintram, "so that he gets to see it when he wakes up! It will amuse him."

So it stayed the way it was, and the cavaliers thought no more about the captain. The banquet lasted the whole night. The party broke up at daybreak. Then there was more wine than sense in their brains.

The question now was what they would do with Captain Lennart. "We should drive him home," said Sintram. "Think how happy his wife will be! It will be a joy to see her delight. I'm moved when I think about it. Let us drive home with him!"

They were moved, all of them, by the thought. Lord God, how she would be happy, the stern wife up at Helgesäter!

They shook life into Captain Lennart and lifted him up into one of the carriages, which the sleepy stable hands had driven up long ago. And then the entire troupe drove up to Helgesäter. Some were half asleep and about to fall out of the carriage, others sang to keep themselves awake. Altogether they looked no better than a band of vagabonds, sluggish and with swollen faces.

In the meantime they arrived, left the horses at the back, and marched up to the staircase with a certain solemnity. Beerencreutz and Julius led Captain Lennart between them.

"Pull yourself together, Lennart," they said to him, "you're home now. Don't you see that you're home?"

He raised his eyes and became almost sober. He was moved that they had accompanied him home.

"Friends," he said, stopping to speak to them all, "I have asked God, friends, why so much evil has been allowed to befall me."

"Oh, hush, Lennart, don't preach!" roars Beerencreutz.

"Let him go on!" says Sintram. "He speaks well."

"Have asked him and not understood, you see. He wanted to show me what kind of friends I had. Friends, who follow me home to see my happiness, and my wife's. For my wife is expecting me. What are five years of misery compared to this?"

Now hard fists pounded against the door. The cavaliers did not have time to hear more.

There was movement inside. The maids awoke and looked out. They threw on clothes, but dared not open for this band of men. Finally the bolt was pulled aside. The captain's wife herself emerged.

"What do you want?" she asked.

It was Beerencreutz who replied.

"We are here with your husband."

They pushed Captain Lennart forward, and she saw him stagger toward her, drunk, with the face of a criminal.

She took a step back; he followed with open arms. "You left as a thief," she exclaimed, "and come home like a vagabond!" With that she intended to go inside.

He did not understand. He wanted to follow her, but then she gave him a shove on the chest.

"Do you think that I intend to take in someone like you as master of my house and my children?"

The door slammed shut, and the bolt came down into the lock.

Captain Lennart rushed toward the door and began to shake it.

Then the cavaliers could not help it; they began to laugh. He had been so sure of that wife of his, and now she did not want to hear about him. It was ridiculous, they thought.

When Captain Lennart heard they were laughing, he rushed at them and wanted to strike them. They ran away and jumped up into the carriages. He followed, but in his eagerness he tripped over a stone and fell flat. He got up again, but made no further pursuit. One thought struck him in his confusion. In this world nothing happens without God's will, nothing.

"Where will you lead me?" he said. "I am a feather, driven by the exhalation of your breath. I am your toy ball. Where will you lead me? Why do you close the gates of my home to me?"

He wandered away from his home, believing that this was the will of God.

As the sun came up, he was standing at the height of the Broby hills looking out over the valley. Oh, did the poor folk of the valley not know that their savior was approaching! No poor or distressed person had bound wreaths of withered lingonberry branches to hang above their cabin door. No leaves of scented lavender and flowers from the headland were placed on the thresholds he would soon cross. Mothers did not lift their children on their arms so they could see him as he came. The interiors of the cabins were not polished and fine, with the blackened hearth concealed by scented juniper. The men were not working with eager diligence in the fields, so that his glances might delight in tended fields and well-dug ditches.

Ah, where he stood his anxious gaze saw how drought had ravaged, how the harvests were burned up, and how the people hardly seemed to care about preparing the earth for the coming year's harvest. He looked up toward the blue hills, and the sharp sun of morning showed him the areas burned brown, across which the forest fires had ravaged. He saw the roadside birches almost destroyed by drought. He understood by many small signs, by the odor of mash as he passed by a farm, by the tumble-down fences, by the pitiful quantity of timber brought home and chopped, that the people were not taking care of themselves, that distress had come, and that the people sought consolation in indifference and liquor.

But perhaps it was just as well for him that he saw what he saw. It was not granted to him to see verdant harvests sprout forth on his own fields, to watch the glowing coals die down on his own hearth, to feel his children's soft hands resting in his, to have a pious wife as his support. Perhaps it was just as well for him, whose mind was weighed down by heavy sorrow, that others existed to whom he might give consolation in their poverty. Perhaps it was just as well for him that this was such a bitter time, when the barrenness of nature came to visit the poorer people with want, and when many whose lot had been more fortunate did their part to ruin it.

Captain Lennart stood there on the Broby hills and started to think that perhaps God needed him.

It should be noted that later the cavaliers could not understand at all what culpability they had in the hardness of the captain's wife. Sintram kept silent. Much censorious talk went around the region about this wife, who had been too proud to take in such a good husband. It was said that anyone who tried to talk with her about her husband was immediately interrupted. She could not bear to hear his name mentioned. Captain Lennart did nothing to change her mind.

It is one day later.

An old farmer is lying on his deathbed in Högberg village. He has taken the sacrament, and his life's energies are exhausted; he must die.

Restless as one who will begin a long journey, he has his bed moved from the kitchen to the main room and from the main room to the kitchen. By this it is understood, more than by heavy wheezing and failing gaze, that his hour has come.

Around him stand his wife, his children, and servants. He has been fortunate, wealthy, respected. His deathbed is not abandoned. Impatient strangers do not surround him in his final hour. The old man speaks of himself as if he were standing before the face of God, and with frequent sighs and affirmative words those standing around him bear witness that what he says is true.

"I have been a diligent worker and a good husband," he says. "I have held my wife as dear as my right hand. I have not let my children grow up without discipline and care. I have not drunk. I have not moved boundary marks. I have not pressed the horse going uphill. I have not let the cows starve in winter. I have not let the sheep be tormented in their wool in summer."

And around him the weeping servants repeat like an echo: "He has been a good husband. Oh, Lord God! He has not pressed the horse on the hills, not let the sheep sweat in their wool in summer."

But through the door, completely unnoticed, a poor man has come in to ask for a meal. He too hears the dying man's words, where he stands silently by the door.

And the sick man continues: "I have cleared forest, I have drained meadows. I drove the plow in straight furrows. I built the barn three times larger for a harvest three times larger than in my father's time. From shiny *daler* coins I had three new silver beakers made. My father made only one."

The words of the dying man reach the listener at the door. He hears him testify about himself as if he were standing before the throne of God. He hears the servants and children repeat in affirmation, "He drove the plow in straight furrows, yes, he did."

"God will grant me a good room in his heaven," says the old man.

"Our Lord will receive the husband well," say the servants.

The man at the door hears these words, and he is filled with horror, he who for five long years has been God's plaything, a feather driven by the exhalation of his breath. He goes up to the sick man and takes his hand.

"Friend, friend!" he says, his voice trembling with fear. "Have you considered who that Lord is, before whose face you will soon appear? He is a great God, a terrible God. Planets are his fields. The storm his horse. Broad skies quake under the weight of his foot. And you place yourself before him and say, 'I have driven straight furrows, I have sown rye, I have chopped down forest.' Do you want to praise yourself before him and compare yourself to him? You do not know how powerful the Lord is, to whose kingdom you will travel!"

The old man's eyes widen, his mouth twitches in horror, the rattling of his breath becomes heavier.

"Do not step before your God with big talk!" the pilgrim continues. "The mighty on earth are like threshed straw in his barn. His day labor is building suns. He has dug the seas and raised the mountains. He has dressed the earth with herbs. He is a worker without equal; you must not compare yourself with him. Bow before him, you fugitive human soul! Lie deep in the dust before your Lord, your God! God's storm rages over you. God's wrath is upon you like a ravaging thunderbolt. Bow down! Take hold of the hem of his mantle like a child and pray for protection! Lie deep in the dust and beg for mercy! Humble yourself, human soul, before your creator!"

The sick man's mouth is wide open, his hands are folded, but his face lights up and the rattling ceases.

"Human soul, fleeting human soul," the man cries out. "As certain as you in your final hour have now placed yourself in humility before God, as certain he must set you on his arm like a child and carry you into the magnificence of heaven!"

The old man lets out a final sigh, and all is over. Captain Lennart lowers his head and prays. Everyone in the room prays, with heavy sighing.

When they look up, the old peasant is lying in quiet peace. His eyes still seem to glisten with the reflection of magnificent visions, his mouth is smiling, his face is lovely. He has seen God.

"Oh, you great, lovely human soul!" they who see him think, "thus have you broken the bonds of matter! In your final hour you raised yourself to your creator. You humbled yourself before him, and he lifted you like a child on his arm."

"He has seen God," the son says and closes the dead man's eyes. "He saw heaven open," sob children and servants.

The old wife places her trembling hand in Captain Lennart's. "You helped him over the worst, captain."

He stands mute. The gift of powerful words and great actions has been given to him. He does not know how. He quivers like a butterfly on the edge of the pupa, while his wings expand out into the sunshine, they too glistening like sunshine.

It was that hour that drove Captain Lennart out among the people. Otherwise he might well have gone home and let his wife see his proper face, but from that moment on he believed that God needed him. Then he became God's pilgrim, who came with help to the poor. The need at that time was great, and there was much misery, which wisdom and goodness could help better than gold and power would have.

One day Captain Lennart came up to the poor farmers who lived in the vicinity of Gurlita Bluff. Among them need was great: the potatoes were gone, and the rye sowing, which should be done where the cleared forest debris had been burned, could not be accomplished, for there was no seed.

Then Captain Lennart took a small rowboat and rowed directly across the lake to Fors and asked Sintram to donate rye and potatoes to the people. Sintram received him well: he brought him up to large, well-stocked grain bins and down into cellars where potatoes from last year's harvest still remained, and let him fill all the sacks and bags he had with him.

But when Sintram caught sight of the little rowboat, he found that it was too small for so large a load. The malevolent man had the sacks carried down to one of his large boats and had his farmhand, strong Måns, row it across the lake. Captain Lennart only had to tend to the empty rowboat.

He fell behind strong Måns, however, for he was a master of rowing and tremendously strong. Captain Lennart sits too and dreams, and he is thinking about the strange fate of the little seeds of grain. Now they would be thrown out on the black, ash-enriched soil in the midst of stones and stumps, but they will probably grow and take root in the wilderness. He thinks about the tender, clear-green straws that will clothe the earth, and in his thoughts he bends over and caresses the tender tops. And then he imagines how autumn and winter will proceed over these weak little wretches and how they will still be healthy and brave when spring arrives and they can start growing in earnest. Then his old soldier's heart is gladdened at the thought of the rigid straws that will stand straight and several ells high with pointed ears at the tops. The pistils' small plumes will tremble, the powder of the stamens will whirl all the way up to the treetops, and then amid visible strife and anxiety the ears will be filled with a soft, sweet kernel. And then, when the scythe goes forth and the straws fall and the flail starts to thunder over them, when the mill grinds the kernels into flour and the flour is baked into bread, ah, won't there be a lot of hunger stilled by the seed grain in the boat before him!

Sintram's farmhand tied up at the Gurlita people's boat dock, and many hungry people came down to the boat. Then the fellow said, as his master had commanded him, "The mill owner is sending you malt and grain here, farmers. He has heard that you have no liquor."

Then the people became as if crazy. They rushed down to the boat and sprang out into the water to snatch bags and sacks, but such had not been Captain Lennart's intention. Now he was there too, and he became angry when he saw the people's behavior. He had never thought of asking for malt.

He shouted to the people to let the sacks be, but they did not obey.

"May the rye become sand in your mouths and the potatoes stones in your throat!" he called then, for he was extremely embittered that they snatched the seed for themselves.

At the same moment it appeared as if Captain Lennart might have performed a miracle. Two women who were fighting over a bag tore a hole in it and found only sand. The men who had lifted up the potato sacks felt how they weighed as if they were filled with stone.

It was sand and stone, all of it, only sand and stone.

The people stood in silent horror at the miracle man of God who had come to them. Captain Lennart himself stood for a moment, struck with amazement. Only strong Måns was laughing.

"Get home now, fellow," said Captain Lennart, "before the farmers realize that there was never anything other than sand in those sacks! Otherwise I am afraid they will sink your boat."

"I'm not afraid," said the fellow.

"Go anyway!" said Captain Lennart in such an authoritative voice that he left.

Then Captain Lennart let the people know that Sintram had

fooled them, but however it was, they did not want to believe anything other than that a miracle had occurred.

The rumor soon spread, and as the people's love for the miraculous is great, it was generally believed that Captain Lennart could perform miracles. In that way he gained great power among the peasants, and they called him God's pilgrim.

CHAPTER 26

THE CEMETERY

It was a lovely evening in August. Löven was mirror bright, sun-smoke veiled the hills, the cool of evening had come.

Then Beerencreutz, the colonel with the white mustaches, short of stature, strong as a giant, and with a pack of *kille* cards in his back pocket, came ambling down to the lakeshore and took a seat in a flat-bottomed rowboat. Accompanying him was Major Anders Fuchs, his old comrade in arms, and little Ruster, the flute player, who had been a drummer with Värmland's hussars and for many years had followed the colonel as his friend and servant.

On the other side of the lake is the cemetery, the untended cemetery of Svartsjö parish, sparsely set with crooked, rattling iron crosses, mossy as a never-plowed meadow, overgrown with sedge and striped reed canary grass, which has been sown there as a reminder that no person's life is like any other's; they change like leaves of grass. There are no graveled pathways, no shadowing trees except the great linden tree on an old rector's forgotten grave. A stone wall, steep and high, surrounds the poor field. Poor and inconsolable is the cemetery, ugly as a miser's face withered by the woeful cries of those whose fortune he has stolen. And yet they who rest within are blessed, they who have been lowered into consecrated earth to the sound of hymns and prayers. Acquilon, the card player, who died at Ekeby the year before, had to be buried outside the wall. This man, who once was so proud and so gallant, the courageous warrior, the cunning hunter, the card player who held good luck captive, had ended up ruining his children's inheritance, everything he himself had acquired,

everything his wife had tended. He had abandoned wife and children many years ago to lead a cavalier's life at Ekeby. One evening last summer he gambled away the estate that gave them
their livelihood. Rather than pay off his debt, he shot himself.
But the corpses of suicides were buried outside the poor cemetery's moss-covered wall.

After he died, there had been only twelve cavaliers; after he
died, no one had come to occupy the thirteenth place, no one
other than the black one who came creeping out of the smelting
furnace on Christmas Eve.

The cavaliers found his fate more bitter than that of his predecessors. Of course they knew that one of them must die every
year. What was wrong with that? Cavaliers may not get old. If
their clouded eyes cannot make out the cards, their trembling
hands not raise the glass, then what is life to them, and what are
they to life? But to lie like a dog at the cemetery wall, where the
sheltering turf may not rest in peace, but instead is trampled by
grazing sheep, wounded by spade and plow, where the wanderer
passes without slowing his pace, and where children play without dampening their laughter and jokes, to rest there where the
stone wall blocks the sound when the angel awakens the dead
within on judgment day with his bassoon—oh, to rest there!

Now Beerencreutz rows his boat across Löven. He travels at
evening across the lake of my dreams, around whose shores I
have seen gods wander, and from whose depths my magic castle
rises. He travels past the lagoons of Lagön, where the spruce trees
rise right up out of the water, growing on low, circular sand reefs,
and where the remnants of the fallen pirate fortress still remain
at the steep top of the island. He travels along under the spruce
grove on the promontory at Borg, where the old pine tree still
hangs out over the cliff on thick roots, where a massive bear has
been captured, and where old cairns and burial mounds bear witness to the age of the place.

He rows around the promontory, gets out below the cemetery,
and then walks across mown fields that belong to the count at
Borg, up to Acquilon's grave.

Once there, he bends down and pats the turf, the way one
lightly caresses the blanket under which a sick friend is resting.

Then he takes out a pack of *kille* cards and sits down beside the grave.

"It's so lonely for him out here, Johan Fredrik. Probably longs for a game."

"It's a crying shame that such a man should be buried out here," says the great bear hunter Anders Fuchs, sitting down by his side.

But little Ruster, the flute player, speaks in an agitated voice, while tears drip steadily down from his small, red eyes.

"Next to you, colonel, next to you he was the finest man I've ever known."

These three worthy men are now sitting around the grave, earnestly and fervently dealing out the cards.

I look out over the world, I see many graves. There rests the mighty, weighed down by marble. The funeral march thunders over him. Banners are lowered over the grave. I see the graves of those whom many have loved. Flowers, wet with tears, caressed by kisses, rest lightly on their green grass. I see forgotten graves, presumptuous graves, mendacious resting places, and others that say nothing, but never before did I see the black-and-white-checked Harlequin and the Mask with the bells in his cap offered for the delight of a grave's guest.

"Johan Fredrik has won," says the colonel proudly. "Didn't I know it! I taught him to play. Yes, now we are dead, the three of us, and he is alone in life."

With that he gathers up the cards, gets up, and, followed by the others, retreats to Ekeby.

Now the dead man must know and feel that not everyone has forgotten him or his abandoned grave. Wild hearts bring strange tribute to those they love, but the one who lies outside the wall, he whose dead body cannot find peace in consecrated earth, he may still be glad that not everyone has rejected him.

Friends, children of mankind, when I die, I will surely rest in the midst of the cemetery, in the grave of my ancestors. Surely I have not stolen my family's livelihood, not raised my hand against my own life, but I have certainly not won such a love; surely no one will do as much for me as the cavaliers for this miscreant. Certainly no one will come in the evening, as the sun goes away and the courts of the dead become solitary and mournful, to set the motley cards between my bony fingers.

Nor will anyone come—which I would prefer, for cards hardly tempt me—with fiddle and bow to the grave, so that my spirit, hovering around the decaying matter, might rock in the stream of notes like a swan in glistening waves.

CHAPTER 27

OLD BALLADS

Marianne Sinclaire sat in her room one quiet afternoon at the end of August, organizing her letters and other papers.

Around her was disorder. Large leather knapsacks and trunks with iron fittings had been dragged into the room. Her clothes covered chairs and benches. Everything was pulled out of attics and cupboards and from the drawers of the stained chest, silk and linen glistened, the jewelry was set out to be cleaned, shawls and furs would be inspected and chosen.

Marianne was preparing for a long journey. She was unsure whether she would ever again return home. She stood at a turning point in her life, and therefore she was burning a pile of old letters and diaries. She did not want to be weighed down by memories of the past.

As she was sitting there, she found a bundle of old verses in her hands. They were transcriptions of old ballads that her mother used to sing for her when she was little. She untied the ribbon that held them together and began to read.

She smiled in melancholy, when she had read awhile. The old ballads proclaimed strange wisdom to her:

Believe not in fortune, believe not in the signs of fortune, believe not in roses and comely leaves!

Believe not in laughter! they said. See, the lovely maiden Valborg rides in a golden carriage, and her lips smile, but she is so sorrowful, as if hooves and wheels should pass over her life's good fortune.

Believe not in the dance! they said. Many a foot swings lightly over a polished floorboard, while the heart is heavy as lead. Lusty and giddy was little Kerstin in the dance, while she danced away her young life.

Believe not in jests! Many go to table with a joke on her lips, while she wants to die from sorrow. There sits young Adeline and lets Count Fröjdenborg offer her his heart in jest, certain that is the sight she needs to have the strength to die.

Oh, you old ballads, in what should one believe, in tears and sorrow?

The grieving mouth is easily forced to smile, but someone who is happy cannot weep. The old ballads believe in tears and sighs, in sorrow alone and the signs of sorrow. Sorrow is real, is lasting, it is the firm bedrock under loose sand. In sorrow one can believe and in the signs of sorrow.

But happiness is only sorrow that is playacting. There is really nothing on the earth but sorrow.

"Oh, inconsolable ones," said Marianne, "your ancient wisdom falls short before the fullness of life!"

She went over to the window and looked out into the garden, where her parents were taking a walk. They were walking up and down the broad pathways and talking about everything that met their eyes, about the grass of the ground and the birds of the sky.

"Look," said Marianne, "there goes a heart now, sighing with sorrow, while it has never been so happy before!"

And she suddenly thought that in the end perhaps everything was in the individual person, that sorrow and happiness only depended on her various ways of looking at things. She asked herself whether it was good fortune or misfortune that had passed over her this year. She herself hardly knew.

She had lived through bitter times. Her soul had been sick. She had been bent to the earth under her deep humiliation. For when she had come back to her home, she had said to herself: "I do not want to remember anything bad about my father." But that was not what her heart said. "He has done me mortal sorrow," it said, "he has separated me from the one I loved, he has brought me to despair when he struck Mother. I wish him no ill, but I am afraid of him." And so she noticed how she had to force herself to sit quietly when her father sat down beside her. She only wanted to flee from him. She tried to summon her courage, she spoke with him as usual and was almost constantly in his company. She could control herself, but she suffered unspeakably. She ended by loathing everything about him: his rough, strong voice, his heavy gait, his large hands, the entire form of the enormous giant. She wished him no ill, she did not wish to hurt him, but she could no longer approach him without experiencing a sense of terror and loathing. Her suppressed heart took revenge. "You did not let me love," it said, "but I am still your master; you will end up by hating."

Accustomed as she was to take note of everything that moved within her, she noticed how this loathing became deeper and deeper, how it grew with every passing day. At the same time it was as if she would be bound to her home for all time. She understood that it would be best if she traveled out among people, but she could not bring herself to it now after her illness. No relief would ever come in all this. She would only be more and more tormented, and one day her self-control would give way, and she would burst out against her father and show him the bitterness of her heart, and then there would be strife and unhappiness.

In this way spring and early summer had passed. In July she became engaged to Baron Adrian to have a home of her own.

One lovely forenoon Baron Adrian had burst into the yard, riding a splendid horse. His hussar's jacket shone in the sun, his spurs and saber and sword belt glittered and gleamed, not to mention his own fresh face and smiling eyes. Melchior Sinclaire himself stood on the stairway and received him when he arrived. Marianne had been sitting at the window, sewing. She had seen him come and now heard every word that he spoke with her father.

"Good day, knight Sunshine!" the mill owner called to him. "Heavens, so fine looking you are! You wouldn't be out courting, would you?"

"Well now, uncle, that is just what I'm doing," he answered, laughing.

"Do you have no shame, lad? What do you have to feed a wife with?"

"Nothing, uncle. If I had anything, do you think I would marry?"

"So you say, so you say, knight Sunshine. But that fine-looking jacket there, you've still had the means to acquire that."

"On credit, uncle."

"And the horse you're riding, that's worth a lot of money, I can tell you that, dear squire. Where did you get that from?"

"The horse isn't mine, uncle."

This was more than the great mill owner could resist. "God be with you, lad!" he said. "You surely need a wife who has something. If you can get Marianne, then take her!"

In that way it was all cleared up between them, before Baron Adrian had even got off the horse. But Melchior Sinclaire knew what he was doing, for Baron Adrian was a good fellow.

Then the suitor had come in to Marianne and stormed forth at once with his business.

"Oh, Marianne, dear Marianne! I have already spoken with your father. I would like so much to have you as my wife. Say that you will, Marianne!"

She had charmed the truth out of him. The old baron, his father, had been away and let himself be tricked into buying some empty mines again. The old baron had been buying mines his whole life, and there had never been anything in them. His mother was worried, he himself had gone into debt, and now he was courting her to rescue his ancestral home and his hussar jacket.

His home was Hedeby Manor, which was on the other side of the lake, almost directly across from Björne. She knew him well; they were the same age and childhood playmates.

"You may as well marry me, Marianne. I lead such a miserable life. I have to ride on borrowed horses and can't pay my tailoring bills. In the long run this just can't go on. I'll be forced to leave, and then I'll shoot myself."

"But, Adrian, what kind of marriage would this be? We're not even a tiny bit in love with one another."

"Yes, as far as love is concerned, I don't care a bit about that," he then explained. "I like riding a good horse and hunting, but I'm no cavalier, yes, I'm a worker. If I could just get money, so that I could take over the estate at home and get some days of peace for Mama, then I would be content. I would both plow and sow, for I like work."

Then he had looked at her with his honorable eyes, and she knew that he spoke the truth, and that he was a man to rely on. She became engaged to him, mostly to get away from home, but also because she had always thought well of him.

But she would never forget the month that followed that August evening when her engagement was announced, all that time of madness.

With each day Baron Adrian became more sorrowful and silent. He did come to Björne very often, sometimes several times a day, but she could not help noticing how subdued he was. Together with others he could still joke, but in her company he became impossible; he was nothing but silence and boredom. She understood how it was with him. It was not as easy as he believed to marry an ugly woman. Now he had developed distaste for her. No one knew better than she did how ugly she was. She had shown him that she did not want any caresses or tokens of affection, yet still he was tormented by thinking of her as his wife, and it got worse for him day by day. Why then did he go on suffering? Why didn't he break off the engagement? She had given him hints that were clear enough. She herself could do nothing. Her father had simply told her that her reputation would not tolerate any more adventurousness in the way of engagement. Then she despised them both just as deeply, and to her any way out seemed good enough to get away from these, her masters.

So, only a few days after the great engagement party, the change had come suddenly and strangely.

In the sand path right in front of the staircase at Björne was a large stone, which was the cause of much inconvenience and annoyance. Vehicles ran into it, horses and people stumbled over it, maids coming with heavy milk tubs bumped into it and spilled the milk, but the stone was still there, because it had already been there for so many years. It had been there in the time of the mill owner's parents, long before anyone had thought of building the Björne estate. Iron mill owner Sinclaire did not understand why he should take it out of the ground.

But one of the last days in August it happened that two maids, who were carrying a heavy tub, stumbled over the stone. They fell, hurting themselves badly, and their resentment toward the stone was great.

It was still only breakfast time. The mill owner was out for his morning walk, but as the household help was home at the estate between eight and nine, Mrs. Gustava ordered some men to come and dig up the large stone.

They came then with iron rods and spades, digging and prying and finally getting the old disturber of the peace out of his hole. Then they carried him away to the backyard. It was labor enough for six men.

The stone had just been removed when the mill owner came home and immediately had his eyes on the misery. You may believe that he became angry. It wasn't the same yard anymore, he thought. Who had dared to move the stone? Well, Mrs. Gustava had given the order. Yes, these womenfolk did not have a heart in their bodies. Did that wife of his not know that he loved that stone?

And then he went right to the stone, lifted it with manly force, and carried it across the backyard and the yard all the way up to the place where it had been, and there he threw it down. And this was a stone that six men had barely been able to lift. That deed was greatly admired across all of Värmland.

While he was carrying the stone across the yard, Marianne had been standing at the window in the dining room, watching him. She had never seen him so terrible. He was her master, this frightful man with his boundless strength, an unreasonable, capricious master, who never asked about anything other than his own pleasure.

They were in the midst of eating breakfast, and she stood with a table knife in her hand. Uncontrollably she raised the knife.

Mrs. Gustava took hold of her wrist.

"Marianne!"

"What's going on, Mother?"

"Oh, Marianne, you looked so strange. I was afraid."

Marianne observed her for a long time. She was a small, dry person, already gray haired and wrinkled at the age of fifty. She loved like a dog, she did, without counting the blows. Most often she was in good spirits, and yet she made a mournful impression. She was like a storm-lashed tree on the seashore; she had never had peace to grow. She had learned to do things in a round-about way, lied when necessary, and made herself out to be stupider than she was in order to avoid reproaches. In everything she was the creation of this man.

"Would you grieve much, Mother, if Father were to die?" asked Marianne.

"Marianne, you are angry at Father. You are always angry at him. Why can't everything be fine now, now that you have a new fiancé?"

"Oh, Mother! I can't help it. Can I help that I shudder at him? Don't you see how he is, Mother? Why should I like him? He is impetuous, he is ill-mannered, he has tortured you so that you've become old before your time. Why should he be our master? He carries on like a lunatic. Why should I honor and respect him? He is not good, he is not compassionate. I know that he is strong. He can throw us out of the house if he wants. Is that why I should love him?"

But then Mrs. Gustava had not at all been the same as before. She found force and courage and spoke authoritative words.

"You should watch yourself, Marianne. It almost seems to me as if your father was right when he locked you outside last winter. You must see that you will be punished for this. You must learn to tolerate without hating, Marianne, to suffer without taking revenge."

"Oh, Mother, I am so unhappy."

Right after that came the decisive moment. From the vestibule they heard the thunder of a heavy fall.

They never found out whether Melchior Sinclaire had been standing on the stairs listening to Marianne's words through the open dining room door, or whether it was simply the physical exertions that caused the stroke. When they came out, he was lying unconscious. Later they never dared ask him about it. He himself never let on that he had heard anything. Marianne never dared complete the thought that she had involuntarily avenged herself. But the sight of her father, lying there on this same staircase where she had learned to hate him, took the bitterness from her heart at once.

He soon regained consciousness, and when he had kept quiet for a few days, he was himself again—and yet not at all himself.

Marianne saw her parents strolling together through the garden. It was always like that now. He never went out alone, never went off anywhere, grumbling about visitors and about anything that separated him from his wife. Age had caught up with him. He could not bring himself to write a letter. His wife had to do it. He never decided anything on his own, instead asking her about everything and letting it be as she decided. And he was always gentle and amiable. He himself noticed the change that had come over him, and how happy his wife was. "Things are good for her now," he said one day to Marianne and pointed at Mrs. Gustava.

"Oh, dear Melchior," she exclaimed then, "you know that I would rather that you were healthy again."

And she probably did wish that. It was her joy to talk about the great mill owner, the way he was in his prime. She told how he had withstood storm and strife as well as any of the Ekeby cavaliers, how he made business deals and earned lots of money, just when she thought that in his wildness he would force them from house and estate. But Marianne knew that she was happy despite all her complaining. To be everything for that man, that was enough for her. They both looked old, prematurely broken. Marianne thought that she could see their approaching lives. He would gradually get weaker and weaker, more strokes making him more and more helpless, and she would tend him until death did them part. But of course the end might be far off. Mrs. Gustava would have her happiness in peace awhile yet. So it must be, thought Marianne. Life was in debt to her.

For her as well things had gotten better. No anxious despair compelled her to marry to get another master. Her wounded heart had found peace. Hatred had flared up there as well as love, but she no longer thought about the suffering this had cost her. She had to admit that she was a truer, richer, greater person than before. What then would she wish undone of what had happened? Was it the case that all suffering was a good

thing? Could everything be turned to happiness? She had begun to regard everything as good which might contribute to
developing her to a higher level of humanity. The old ballads
were not right. Sorrow was not the only lasting thing. Now she
would travel and look around to find some place where she
was needed. If her father had been in his old temperament, he
would never have allowed her to break off the engagement.
Now Mrs. Gustava had mediated the matter. Marianne had
even gotten the right to leave Baron Adrian the financial assis-
tance he needed.

She could also think about him with joy. Now she would be
free from him. In his cheekiness and lust for life he had always
reminded her of Gösta; now she would see him happy again.
He would again become this knight of sunshine, who had come
in his brilliance to her father's estate. She would get him earth
that he could plow and dig as much as his heart desired, and
she would see him lead a beautiful bride to the altar.

With such thoughts she sits down and writes to give him back
his freedom. She writes tender, inspiring words, good sense
wrapped up in humor, and yet in such a way that he must understand the seriousness of her intent.

While she is writing, horse hooves are heard striking against
the road.

"My dear knight Sunshine," she thinks, "this is the last time."

Right after that Baron Adrian comes directly into her room.

"No, Adrian, are you coming in here?" and she looks with
dismay at all the packing things.

At once he becomes shy and stammers out an excuse.

"I'm just writing to you," she says. "Look here, you might
just as well read it at once."

He takes the letter, and she sits observing him as he reads.
She longs to be able to see his face light up with happiness.

But he has not read far before his face turns fiery red and he
throws the letter on the floor, stomps on it, and swears, a genuine storm oath.

Then a slow tremor passes through Marianne. She is no be-
ginner in the study of love, yet she has not understood this in-
experienced boy, this large child.

"Adrian, dear Adrian!" she says. "What kind of comedy are you playing for me? Come and tell me the truth!"

He was about to downright smother her with caresses. Poor lad, he had been in such agony and longing!

After a while she looked out. There Mrs. Gustava was still walking and talking with the great mill owner about flowers and birds, and here she sat babbling about love. "Life has taught us both to feel its hard seriousness," she thought, smiling mournfully. "It will console us, we have each gotten our own big child to play with."

Yet it was good that she could be loved. It was sweet to hear him whisper about the enchantment that emanated from her, and how he had been ashamed of what he had said during their first conversation. He had not known then what power she had. Oh, no man could get close to her without loving her, but she had frightened him; he had felt so strangely subdued.

It was not happiness, not unhappiness, but she would try to live with that man.

She started to understand herself and thought about the old ballads' words about the turtledove, that bird of longing. She never drinks clear water, but instead first she muddies it with her foot, so that it might better suit her sorrowful sensibility. Neither would she go forth to the well of life and drink clear, unmixed happiness. Life, muddied by melancholy, pleased her best.

CHAPTER 28

DEATH THE LIBERATOR

My pale friend, Death the liberator, came in August, when the nights were bleached by moonlight, to the home of Captain Uggla. But he dared not go directly into the hospitable home, for there are few who love him.

My pale friend, Death the liberator, has a brave heart. He delights in riding through the air, borne by glowing cannonballs. He takes the hissing grenade on the neck and laughs as it bursts and the shrapnel flies. He swings around in a ghost dance in the cemeteries and does not shun the plague wards of the hospital, but he trembles at the threshold of the right-minded, at the gate of the good. For he does not want to be greeted by weeping, but rather by quiet happiness, he who frees the spirits from the bonds of pain, he who frees the spirits from burdensome matter and lets them try the free, splendid life in space.

Into the old grove behind the residence—where even today slender, white-trunked birch trees crowd to win the sky's light for the sparse bunches of leaves at their tops—Death slipped in. In the grove, which was young then and full of concealing greenery, my pale friend hid while day prevailed, but at night he stood at the forest edge, white and pale, with his scythe flashing in the moonlight.

Oh Eros! You were the god who most often owned the grove. The old ones can tell about how in bygone days loving couples sought its peace. And even today, when I travel past Berga farm, grumbling about the steep hills and the suffocating dust, I delight in seeing the grove with its thinned-out white trunks, which shine in the memory of the love of beautiful young people.

But then Death was standing there, and the animals of the night saw him. Evening after evening people at Berga farm heard how the fox howled to announce his arrival. The grass snake wriggled up the sand path to the residence. He could not speak, but they still understood that he came as a harbinger of the mighty one. And in the apple tree outside the captain's wife's window the owl let out its shriek. For all of nature knows Death, and trembles.

It so happened that the Munkerud judge and his wife, who had been at a banquet at Bro parsonage, came riding past Berga farm about two o'clock in the morning and saw a light burning in the window of the guest room. They saw the yellow flame and the white light clearly, and later they told about this surprising light that had burned in the summer night.

Then the happy girls at Berga laughed and said that the judge and his wife had been seeing things, for they had run out of tallow candles at their house; they were already used up in March. Then the captain swore that no one had stayed in the guest room for days and weeks. But the captain's wife kept quiet and turned pale, for this white light with the clear flame used to show itself when someone in her family would be delivered by Death, Death the liberator.

Shortly thereafter, one day in radiant August, Ferdinand came home from the surveying service in the northern forests. He arrived pale and sick with an incurable ache lodged in his lungs, and as soon as the captain's wife saw him, she knew that her son must die.

So he would pass away, this good son who had never given his parents any sorrow. The young man would leave the sweetness and joy of the earth and the beautiful, beloved bride who awaited him, and the rich estates, the thundering hammers, which would have been his.

Finally, when my pale friend had waited one lunar cycle, he plucked up courage and approached the house one night. He thought about how hunger and need had been met there by happy faces; why shouldn't he too be received with joy?

He came slowly up the sand path, casting a dark shadow across the lawn, where the dewdrops shone in the moonbeams. He did not come as a happy harvester with flowers in his hat and his arm around a girl's waist. He walked hunched over like a worn-out invalid and held the scythe concealed in the folds of his cloak, while owls and bats fluttered around him.

In the night the captain's wife, who was awake, heard knocking at the windowsill, and she sat up in bed and asked, "Who is knocking?"

And the old ones tell that Death answered her, "It is Death who is knocking."

Then she got up, opened her window, and saw bats and owls fluttering in the moonlight, but Death she did not see.

"Come," she said in a half whisper, "friend and liberator! Why have you waited so long? I have waited, I have called. Come and deliver my son!"

Then Death slipped into the house, happy as a poor deposed monarch who in the decrepitude of old age gets back his crown, happy as a child when it is called to play.

The next day the captain's wife was sitting by her son's sick-bed and spoke with him about the blessedness of emancipated spirits and their splendid lives.

"They labor," she said, "they work. What artists, my son, what artists! When you are among them, tell me, what will you become then? One of those sculptors without a chisel, who creates roses and lilies, one of the masters of sunset glow. And when the sun goes down at its fairest, I will sit and think: Ferdinand has done this.

"My dear boy, just think, so much to see, so much to do! Think about all the seeds that will be awakened to life in spring, the storms that will be guided, the dreams that will be sent! And think about those long journeys through space from world to world!

"Remember me, boy of mine, when you get to see so much that is lovely. Your poor mother has never seen anything other than Värmland.

"But one day you will stand before our Lord and ask him to let you have one of the small worlds that roll around in space, and he will give it to you. When you get it, it is cold and dark, full of chasms and cliffs, and there are neither flowers nor animals.

But you work on that star, which God has given you. You bring light and heat and air there, you bring herbs and nightingales and clear-eyed gazelles there, you let rapids rush down into the chasms, you raise up mountains and sow the plains with the reddest roses. And when I die, Ferdinand, when my soul trembles before the long journey and fears being separated from known regions, then you sit waiting outside the window in a carriage harnessed with birds of paradise, in a glistening golden coach, my Ferdinand.

"And my poor, worried soul will be taken up in your carriage and be placed by your side, honored like a queen. Then we drive through space past the shimmering worlds, and when we come close to these heavenly estates and they become more and more splendid, then I, who don't know any better, ask, 'Shouldn't we stay here, or here?'

"But you laugh silently to yourself and urge on the team of birds. At last we come to the smallest of the worlds, but the loveliest of all I have seen, and there we stop outside a golden palace, and you let me enter into the eternal home of delight.

"There the storehouses are filled, and the bookcases. The spruce forest does not stand there, like here at Berga, covering up the lovely world; instead I look out over wide seas and sunny plains, and a thousand years are like a day."

Then Ferdinand died, charmed by sweet visions, smiling at the magnificence to come.

My pale friend, Death the liberator, had never been involved in anything so sweet. For of course there were those who wept at Ferdinand Uggla's deathbed, but the sick man himself smiled at the man with the scythe when he took his place at the bedside, and his mother listened for the death rattles as if for sweet music. She trembled that Death might not be able to complete his task, and when all was over, tears came from her eyes, but they were tears of joy that fell on her son's rigid face.

Never had my pale friend been so celebrated as at Ferdinand Uggla's burial. If he had dared to show himself, he would have come in a feather-adorned beret and gold-stitched robe and danced ahead of the funeral procession up the cemetery path, but now he sat, old and lonely, curled up on the cemetery wall with his old, black coat on and watched the procession arrive.

Oh, that was a curious funeral! Sun and light clouds made the day happy, long rows of rye shocks adorned the fields, the astrakhans in the parsonage orchard shone transparent and clear, and in the rosarium outside the parish clerk's residence were showy dahlias and carnations.

It was a curious funeral procession that advanced between the lindens. Ahead of the flower-bedecked casket walked beautiful children, strewing flowers. No mourning clothes were to be seen, no crepe, no white wing collars with broad hems, for she, the captain's wife, did not want someone who had died happy to be conveyed into the good sanctuary by a gloomy funeral procession, but instead by a glittering wedding procession.

Next after the casket came Anna Stjärnhök, the dead man's lovely, radiant bride. She had placed the bridal crown on her head, hung the bridal veil over her, and dressed in a trailing bridal gown of white, rustling silk. Thus adorned, she went to be wed at the grave to a decaying bridegroom.

After her they came two by two, tall old ladies and stately men. The splendid, shining ladies came with dazzling clasps and brooches, with milk white pearl necklaces and gold bracelets. The plumes in their turbans were raised high over the cannon curls with silk and lace, and from their shoulders floated the thin, silk-woven shawls, which they had once received as a wedding gift, down over dresses of gaudy silk. And the men came in their best finery, with swelling ruffles, in high-collared tailcoats with gilded buttons and in vests of stiff brocade or richly embroidered velvet. This was a wedding procession; thus had the captain's wife wanted it.

She herself came next after Anna Stjärnhök, led by her husband. If she had owned a dress of shining brocade, she would have worn it; if she had owned jewelry and a shining turban, she would also have worn them to honor her son on his festival day. But she only owned this black taffeta gown and its yellowed lace, which had seen so many parties, and she wore them to this one too.

Although the funeral guests came with pomp and splendor, there was likewise not a dry eye as they proceeded up to the grave while the bells rang quietly. Men and women wept, not so much for the dead man but for themselves. See, there went the bride, there the bridegroom was carried, there they themselves walked, dressed up for a banquet, and yet—is there anyone who tramps the verdant paths of earth and does not know that he is destined for grief, for sorrow, for misfortune, for death? They walked and wept at the thought that no earthly thing would be able to protect them.

The captain's wife did not weep, but she was the only one whose eyes were dry.

When the prayers had been said and the grave filled in, they all went from there to the carriages. Only the captain's wife and Anna Stjärnhök lingered at the grave to offer the dead man a final farewell. The old woman sat down on the grave mound, and Anna took a seat by her side.

"Look," said the captain's wife, "I have said to God: 'Let Death the liberator come and take away my son, let him take away the one I love the most to the peace of the quiet places, and no tears other than those of joy will come from my eyes. I want to accompany him with wedding pomp to his grave, and I will move my red rosebush, rich with blossoms, which stands outside my bedroom window, out to him at the churchyard.' And now it is so: my son is dead. I have greeted Death as a friend, called him by the sweetest names, I have wept tears of joy over my son's rigid face, and in autumn, when the leaves have fallen, I will move my red rosebush here. But do you, who are sitting here by my side, know why I have sent such prayers to God?"

She looked questioningly at Anna Stjärnhök, but the girl sat silent and pale beside her. Perhaps she struggled to deaden inner voices that already began whispering to her, there by the dead man's grave mound, that now she was finally free.

"The fault is yours," said the captain's wife.

Then the girl collapsed as though struck by a club. She did not answer a word.

"Anna Stjärnhök, you were once proud and self-willed. Then

you played with my son, took him, and rejected him. What was there to do? He had to accept it, as others did. Perhaps also because he and all of us loved your money as much as you. But you came back, you came with blessing to our home, you were gentle and meek, strong and good when you came back. You cherished us with love, you made us so happy, Anna Stjärnhök, and we poor people were lying at your feet.

"And yet, yet I wished that you had not come. Then I would not have had to pray to God to shorten my son's life. Last Christmas he could have endured losing you, but since he came to know you, the way you are now, he did not have the strength for it.

"Know this, Anna Stjärnhök, who today have put on your bridal gown to accompany my son, that if he had lived, then you would never have been allowed to follow him in that garb to Bro church, because you did not love him.

"I saw it: you came only out of compassion, because you wanted to ease our hard lot. You didn't love him. Don't you think I know love, that I see it wherever it is, and understand when it is lacking? Then I thought: may God take my son's life, before he has his eyes opened!

"Oh, if only you had loved him! Oh, if only you had never come to us and sweetened our life, when you didn't love him! I knew my duty. If he had not died, I would have had to say to him that you didn't love him, that you wanted to marry him because you were compassion itself. I would have had to force him to set you free, and then his life's happiness would have been wasted. Do you see, that is why I prayed to God that he would get to die, so that I would not need to disturb the calm of his heart. And I have been happy about his sunken cheeks, delighted in his rattling breath, trembled that Death might not complete his task."

She fell silent and wanted for a reply, but Anna Stjärnhök could not yet speak; she was still listening to the many voices in the depths of her soul.

Then the captain's wife burst out in despair, "Oh, how fortunate they are, who can mourn their dead, those who are able to weep rivers of tears! I must stand with dry eyes at my son's grave, I must be happy about his death. How unfortunate I am!"

Then Anna Stjärnhök pressed her hands hard against her breast. She recalled the winter night when she had sworn by her young love to be the support and consolation of these poor people, and she trembled. Had all that been in vain then, was her sacrifice not one of those that God accepts? Would it all be turned into a curse?

But if she sacrificed everything, would not God then give his blessing to the work and let her become a bringer of happiness, a support, a help to people?

"What is required for you to grieve for your son?" she asked.

"What is required is that I should no longer believe the evidence of my old eyes. If I thought you loved my son, then I would grieve over his death."

Then the girl got up with eyes burning with rapture. She tore off the bridal veil and spread it out over the grave; she tore off the wreath and crown and set them alongside.

"See now how I love him!" she called out. "I give him my crown and veil. I am wed to him. Never will I belong to another."

Then the captain's wife also got up. She stood silently awhile, all of her body shaking, and her face twisted, but finally came the tears, the tears of sorrow.

But my pale friend, Death the liberator, shuddered when he saw those tears. So he had not really been greeted with happiness, not even here had they rejoiced in their hearts over him.

He pulled the cowl far down over his face, slipped slowly down from the churchyard wall, and vanished between the rye shocks of the fields.

CHAPTER 29

DROUGHT

If dead things love, if earth and water divide friends from enemies, I would gladly own their love. I would like the green earth not to feel my steps as a heavy burden. I wish that she would gladly forgive that for my sake she was wounded with plow and harrow, and that she would willingly open herself for my dead body. And I would like the wave, whose bright mirror is shattered by my oars, to have the same patience with me that a mother has with an eager child, when it climbs up on her lap without paying heed to the unwrinkled silk of the special-occasion dress. I would be friends with the clear air that quivers over the blue hills and with the glistening sun and the beautiful stars. For it often seems to me as if dead things feel and suffer with the living. The barrier between them and us is not as great as people think. What part of the earth's matter is there that has not been part of the cycle of life? Hasn't the drifting dust of the road been caressed as soft hair, loved as good, benevolent hands? Hasn't the water in the waterwheel flowed in bygone days as blood through beating hearts?

The spirit of life still lives in dead things. What does he sense, where he slumbers in dreamless sleep? The voice of God he hears. Does he also take note of the human?

Oh, latter-day children, haven't you seen it? When discord and hatred fill the earth, then dead things too must suffer greatly. Then the wave becomes wild and rapacious as a robber, then the field becomes barren as a miser. But woe to anyone for whose sake the forest sighs and the hills weep!

That year, when the cavaliers ruled, was peculiar. It seemed to me as if the people's anxiety must have disturbed the peace of dead things. How should I depict the contagion that then spread across the land? Should we not believe that the cavaliers were the parish gods, and that everything was animated by their spirit? The spirit of adventure, carefreeness, wildness.

If everything that went on among the people on Löven's shore that year could be told, then a world would be astonished. For then old love awakened, then new love was ignited. Then old hatred flared up, and long-nurtured revenge seized its prey. Then everyone rose up in desire for the sweetness of life: they grasped at dance and games, play and drink. Then all that was most inwardly concealed in their souls was revealed.

This contagion of anxiety emanated from Ekeby. It first spread to the ironworks and the estates and drove people to misfortune and sin. We have been able to follow it thus far to some degree, because the old people preserved memories of the events at some of the large estates, but we know little of how it spread further among the people. No one should doubt, however, that the anxiety of the age passed from village to village, from hut to hut. Where a vice was concealed, it had its eruption; where there was a fissure between woman and man, it turned into a chasm; where a great virtue or strong will was concealed, it too must emerge. For not all that occurred was bad, though the times were such that the good was often as ruinous as the bad. It was as with great windfalls deep in the forest, where tree falls over tree, pine draws pine with it, and even the undergrowth is torn apart by falling giants.

Do not doubt that madness spread among farmers and servants! Everywhere hearts became wild and brains confused. Never was the dance so merry at the crossroads, never was the beer keg emptied so quickly, never was so much grain thrown into the distilling kettle. Never were the banquets so many, never was there a shorter path between the angry word and the sting of the knife.

But anxiety did not stop among people. It spread to all living things. Never had wolf and bear ravaged more severely, never had fox and owl howled more gruesomely, never did the sheep go astray more often in the forest, never did so much illness rage among the costly livestock.

Anyone who wishes to see the context of things must go away from cities and live in a solitary hut at the forest edge. If he must guard the charcoal pile night after night or live out on the long lakes day and night during a light summer month, while the log raft makes its slow journey to Vänern, then he must learn to pay heed to all the signs in nature and understand how dead things depend on the living. He must see that when there is anxiety on the earth, the peace of the dead things is disturbed. The people know that. It is in such times that the wood nymph puts out the charcoal pile, the sea witch breaks apart the boat, the water sprite sends sickness, the gnome starves the cow. And so it was this year. Never had the spring floods ravaged so severely. Ekeby mill and smithy were not their only victims. Small rivers, which in bygone days, when spring had given them strength, at the most would have been able to carry off an empty barn, now went on the attack against entire farms and washed them away. Never had the thunder been heard to do so much damage even before midsummer—after midsummer she was no longer heard. Then came the drought.

During the long days of summer, no rain came. From the middle of June to the beginning of September the Lövsjö district was bathed in uninterrupted sunshine.

The rain refused to fall, the earth to nourish, the winds to blow. Sunshine alone streamed down over the earth. Oh, that beautiful sunshine, that life-granting sunshine, how can I tell of its evil deeds? Sunshine is like love: who doesn't know the outrages he has committed, and who can keep from forgiving him? Sunshine is like Gösta Berling: it gives delight to everyone, because everyone keeps quiet about the bad things it has caused.

Such a drought after midsummer would probably not be as calamitous in other regions as in Värmland. But spring had come late there. The grass was not far along and would never grow out. The rye remained without nourishment, just when it needed to gather food in its ears. The spring grain, from which most bread was baked at that time, bore thin, small clusters on straws a quarter of an ell high. The late-sown turnips could never grow; not even the potatoes were able to suck nourishment from this petrified earth.

During such years they start to worry off in the forest cabins, and from the hills fear creeps down to the calmer folk on the cultivated plain.

"The hand of God is seeking someone," the people say.

And everyone beats their chests and says, "Is it me? Oh, Mother, oh, Nature, is it me? Is it out of fear for me that the stern earth is dried and hardened? And this endless sunshine, does it stream in its gentleness every day from a cloud-free sky to heap glowing coals on my head? Or if it isn't me, who is it the hand of God is seeking?"

While the rye withers in its small ears, while the potato cannot gather nourishment from the earth, while the livestock, red eyed and panting from the heat, huddle together around the dried-up springs, while worry about the future squeezes the heart, strange talk goes through the area.

"This kind of affliction doesn't happen without a reason," the people say. "Who is it the hand of God is seeking?"

It was a Sunday in August. The church service was over. The people wandered along in flocks on the blazing hot roads. Round about them they saw scorched forests and ruined harvests. The rye was set in shocks, but it stood sparsely with thin sheaves. Those who had debris to burn had good and easy labor that year, but then many a time it also happened that they set fire to the dry forest. And what the forest fire spared, the insects had taken: the pine forest had shed its leaves and stood bare as a deciduous forest in autumn; the leaves of the birches hung split apart with bare veins and ruined blades.

The gloomy flocks did not lack topics for conversation. There were many who could tell about how hard it had been during the famine years of 1808 and '09 and during the cold winter of 1812, when the sparrows froze to death. Starvation was not foreign to them; they had encountered his stern countenance before. They knew how to prepare bark for bread and how the cows could be accustomed to eating moss.

There was a woman who had made attempts with a new type of bread from lingonberry and barley meal. She had samples of it with her and let people have a taste. She was proud of her invention.

But the same question hovered over them all; it stared out of all their eyes, was whispered on all their lips.

"Who is it, O Lord, your hand is seeking?"

"You God of severity, who has denied you offerings of prayers and good deeds, because you take from us our poor bread?"

One man in these somber flocks, who had gone westward across the sound bridge and struggled up the Broby hills, stopped a moment before the road that led up to the residence of the stingy Broby minister. He picked up a dry stick from the ground and threw it onto the rectory lane.

"Dry as that stick have those prayers been, which he has given our Lord," said the man.

The one who was walking closest to him stopped too. He picked up a dry twig and threw it where the stick had fallen.

"This is the right offering for that minister," he said.

The third in the flock followed the given pattern. "He has been like a drought. Sticks and straw are all that he has let us keep."

The fourth said, "We are giving him back what he has given us."

And the fifth: "For eternal shame I throw this to him. May he dry up and wither, like this twig has dried up!"

"Dry fodder for the drought minister," said the sixth.

People who are behind them see what they are doing and hear what they are saying. Now they get many answers to their long questioning.

"Give him what is due to him! He has brought the drought upon us," it was said among the crowd.

And each one of them stops, each one of them has his say and throws his branch, before he goes on.

In the corner between the roads there was soon a pile of sticks and straws: a pile of shame for the Broby minister.

This was the people's entire revenge. No one raised his hand against the minister or said an unkind word to him personally. Desperate hearts unloaded part of their burden by throwing a dry twig on this pile. They did not take revenge themselves. They simply pointed out the guilty one before the god of retribution.

"If we have not worshipped you rightly, see, it's that man's fault. Be merciful, Lord, and let him suffer alone! We mark him with shame and dishonor. We are not one with him."

Very quickly it became the custom that everyone who went past the rectory threw a dry twig on the pile of shame. "May God and man see it!" thought each passerby. "I too despise him, who has brought the wrath of God upon us."

The old miser soon noticed the pile at the roadside. He had it taken away. Some said that he fired his kitchen stove with it. The next day at the same place a new pile had been gathered, and as soon as he had this one taken away, a new one was thrown up.

The dry twigs lay there saying, "Shame, shame on the Broby minister!"

These were hot, dry dog days. Heavy with smoke, saturated with fumes, the air settled over the area, oppressive as despair to breathe in. Thoughts became dizzy in overheated brains. The minister in Broby had become the demon of drought. To the farmers it seemed as if the old miser sat guarding the wellsprings of heaven.

Soon the people's opinion became clear to the Broby minister. He realized that they singled him out as the origin of the misfortune. It was in wrath at him that God let the earth languish. Sailors who suffered distress on the boundless sea cast lots. He was the man who was to go overboard. He tried to laugh at them and their twigs, but when this had gone on a week, he was no longer laughing. Oh, such childishness! How could these dry twigs injure him? He understood that years-long hatred was seeking an opportunity to vent itself. What of it! He was not used to love.

He did not become gentler from such things. Perhaps he had wished to better himself, ever since the old miss had visited him. Now he could not. He would not be forced into improvement.

But by and by that pile became too much for him. He had to think about it constantly, and the opinion that everyone felt took root in him too. It was the most appalling testimony, this throwing of dry twigs. He took notice of this pile, counted the branches that had been added each day. The thought of it spread out and encroached on all other thoughts. The pile was destroying him.

With each day he had to agree with the people more and more. He declined and grew old in a few weeks. He had pangs of conscience and cramps. But it was as if everything would latch onto this pile. It was as if the pangs of conscience would have been silenced and the weight of age again fall away from him, if only the pile had stopped growing.

Finally he sat there for whole days and watched. But the people were merciless; at night too new twigs were thrown there.

One day Gösta Berling came traveling along the road. The Broby minister was sitting by the roadside, old and decrepit. He sat, picking at the dry sticks and placing them together in rows and heaps, playing with them as if he had become a child again. Gösta became distressed at his misery.

"What are you doing, pastor?" he says, jumping quickly out of the carriage.

"Oh, I'm sitting here gathering. I'm not really doing anything."

"Pastor, you should go home and not sit here in the dust of the road."

"It's probably best that I sit here in any case."

Then Gösta Berling sits down beside him.

"It's not so good being a minister," he says after a while.

"It seems to work out down here, where there are people," answers the minister. "It's worse up there."

Gösta understands what he is saying. He knows about those parishes in northern Värmland, where sometimes there isn't a house for the minister; the large forest parishes, where the Finns live in smoke lodges; the poor areas with a few people per square mile, where the minister is the parish's only gentleman. The Broby minister had been in such a parish for over twenty years.

"That's where we're sent when we're young," says Gösta. "It's impossible to endure life there. And then you're ruined forever. There are many who have gone under up there."

"Yes, there are," says the Broby minister. "Loneliness destroys you."

"You arrive," says Gösta, "eager and passionate, you talk and admonish, and you think that everything will be fine, that the people will soon follow better paths."

"Yes, that's right."

"But soon you notice that words don't help. Poverty stands in the way. Poverty hinders all improvement."

"Poverty," repeats the minister. "Poverty has destroyed my life."

"The young minister comes up there," explains Gösta, "poor like everyone else. He says to the drinker: 'Lay off drinking!'"

"Then the drinker replies," the minister puts in: "'Then give me something better than liquor! Liquor is a fur in the winter, coolness in summer. Liquor is a warm cabin and a soft bed. Give me that, and I won't drink anymore!'"

"And then," Gösta resumes, "the minister says to the thief: 'Thou shalt not steal,' and to the mean-spirited: 'Thou shalt not strike thy wife,' and to the superstitious: 'Thou shalt believe in God and not in the devil and trolls.' But then the thief replies: 'Give me bread!' and the mean-spirited says: 'Make us rich, and we won't argue!' and the superstitious: 'Teach me better!' But who can help them without money?"

"It's true, every word is true!" exclaims the old man. "They believe in God, even more in the devil, but mostly in the trolls in the hills and the gnome in the barn. All the crops were destroyed in the liquor kettle. No one could see any end to the misery. In most of the gray cabins hunger prevailed. Hidden sorrow made the women's tongues bitter. Tension at home drove the men out to drink. They could not tend the fields and livestock. They feared the gentry and made a fool of the minister. What could you do with them? What I told them from the pulpit, they didn't understand. What I wanted to teach them, they didn't believe. And no one to take counsel with, no one who could help me keep my courage up!"

"There are those who have endured," says Gösta. "God's mercy has been so great over some that they haven't returned

from such a life as broken men. Their strength has been sufficient; they have endured loneliness, poverty, hopelessness. They
have done the little good they could and not despaired. There
have always been such men, and there still are. I want to hail
them as heroes. I want to honor them, as long as I live. I would
not have been able to endure."

"I couldn't," adds the minister.

"The minister up there thinks," says Gösta thoughtfully, "that
he will become a rich man, an exceedingly wealthy man. No poor
person can fight against evil. And then he starts to hoard."

"If he didn't hoard, he would drink," answers the old man,
"he sees so much misery."

"Or become sluggish and lazy and lose all energy. Going up
there is dangerous for anyone who isn't born there."

"He has to harden himself in order to hoard. He pretends at
first, then it becomes a habit."

"He must be hard both to himself and to others," Gösta
continues. "Hoarding is difficult. He must put up with hatred
and contempt, he has to freeze and starve and harden his heart:
it is almost as if he forgot why he started hoarding."

The Broby minister looked at him shyly. He wondered whether
Gösta was making fun of him. But Gösta was all eagerness and
gravity. It was as if he were talking about his own case.

"That's how it's been for me," says the old man quietly.

"But God protects him," Gösta puts in. "He awakens in him
the thoughts of his youth, when he has hoarded enough. He gives
the minister a sign when the people of God need him."

"But what if the minister doesn't obey the sign, Gösta
Berling?"

"He cannot resist it," says Gösta, smiling happily. "He is enticed so sweetly by the thought of the warm huts that he can
help the poor to build."

The minister looks down at the small buildings he has erected
with the sticks from the pile of shame. The longer he talks with
Gösta, the more convinced he becomes that Gösta is right. He
has always had this idea of doing good, once he has acquired
enough. He clings to this: of course he had this idea.

"So why hasn't he ever built those huts?" he asks shyly.

"He's ashamed. Many might think that out of fear of the people he was doing what he had always meant to do."

"He doesn't tolerate being forced, that's how it is."

"Yet he could help in secret. Much help is needed this year. He can find someone who can dole out his gifts. I understand the meaning of it all!" exclaims Gösta, and his eyes are radiant. "This year thousands will receive their bread from the one whom they shower with curses."

"So it will be, Gösta."

A feeling of intoxication came over these two, who had been so little able to fulfill the calling they had chosen. The desire of their youth to serve God and people was upon them. They reveled in the good deeds they would perform. Gösta would be the minister's helper.

"Now we must get bread to start with," says the minister.

"We must get schoolteachers. We must get surveyors here, to distribute the land. Then the people will learn to tend the fields and care for the livestock."

"We must build roads and break new ground."

"We should build canals down at Berg rapids, so that there is an open passage between Löven and Vänern."

"All the wealth that is in the forest will be a double blessing when the passage to the sea is opened."

"Your head will be weighed down with blessings!" exclaims Gösta.

The minister looks up. They read in each other's eyes the same, flaming rapture.

But at the same moment both of their gazes are drawn to the pile of shame.

"Gösta," says the old man, "all this would require a healthy man's energies, but I am about to die. You see what is killing me."

"Take it away!"

"How, Gösta Berling?"

Gösta moves close to him and looks him sharply in the eyes. "Pray to God for rain!" he says. "You will preach next Sunday, pastor. Pray to God then for rain!"

The old minister collapses in dismay.

"If this is serious, pastor, if you are not the one who has brought drought upon the land, if you have wanted to serve the Most High with his hardness, then pray to God for rain! That will be the sign. By that we will know whether God wants what we want."

When Gösta again traveled down the hills of Broby, he was astonished at himself and the rapture that had seized him. But this could yet become a fine life. Yes, but not for him. Up there they didn't want to hear of his services.

In Broby church the sermon was just concluded, and the usual prayers were read. The minister was just about to step down from the pulpit. But he hesitated. Finally he fell to his knees up there and prayed for rain.

He prayed as a desperate person prays, with few words without real coherence.

"If it is my sin that has called forth your wrath, punish only me! If there is compassion with you, you God of mercy, let it rain! Take the shame from me! Let it rain on my prayer! Let rain fall on the fields of the poor! Give your people bread!"

The day was hot; it was insufferably muggy. The congregation sat as if in a stupor, but at these broken words, this hoarse desperation, everyone woke up.

"If there is still a path to rehabilitation for me, grant rain . . ."

He fell silent. The doors stood open. Now a powerful gust of wind came rushing. It moved along the ground, whirling up toward the church and sending a cloud of dust within, full of sticks and straw. The minister could not go on. He staggered down from the pulpit.

The people shuddered. Could this be an answer?

But the gust of wind was only the precursor to the thunderstorm. It was coming at a velocity without equal. When the hymn was sung and the minister was standing at the altar, the lightning was already flashing and the thunder broke out, covering up the sound of his words. As the organist played the recessional hymn, the first drops of rain were already pattering against the green windowpanes, and the people all stormed out to look at the rain. But they were not content to look: some wept, others laughed, all while they let the torrential rain stream down over them. Oh, how great their need had been! How unfortunate they had been! But God is good. God lets the rain fall. What happiness, what happiness!

The Broby minister was the only one who did not come out into the rain. He was on his knees at the altar and did not get up. The happiness was too powerful for him. He died of joy.

CHAPTER 30

THE CHILD'S MOTHER

The child was born in a peasant cottage east of the Klara River. The child's mother had come there looking for a position one day at the beginning of June. Things had gone badly for her, she said to the farm folk, and her mother had treated her so harshly that she had to run away from home. She called herself Elisabet Karlsdotter, but she would not say where she was from, for then perhaps they would tell her parents that she was there, and if they found her, she would be tortured to death, she knew it. She asked for no pay, only food and a roof over her head. She could work: weave or spin or tend the cows, whatever they wanted. If they wished, she could also pay for herself.

She had been shrewd enough to come to the farm barefoot, with her shoes under her arms; she had rough hands, she spoke the dialect of the province, and she wore the clothes of a farm woman. She was believed.

The farmer thought she looked frail, and didn't count much on her capacity for work. But the poor thing had to be somewhere. And so she was allowed to stay.

There was something about her that made everyone on the farm be friendly to her. She had come to a good place. The people were serious and taciturn. The farmwife liked her, once she discovered that she could do drill weaving. They borrowed a drill loom from the parsonage, and the child's mother sat at the loom the whole summer.

It occurred to no one that she needed to be spared. She had to work like a farmwife the whole time. She herself also liked working the best. Life among the peasants pleased her, although she had to do without all accustomed comforts. But everything was taken simply and calmly there. Everyone's thoughts revolved around work, and the days passed so evenly and uniformly that you lost track of the days and thought it was the middle of the week when Sunday came.

One day at the end of August there had been some urgency with the rye harvest, and the child's mother had gone out with them to bind on the field. Then she had overexerted herself, and the child had been born, but too early. She had expected it in October.

Now the farmwife was standing with the child in the main room to warm it by the fire, for the poor thing was shivering in the midst of the August heat. The child's mother was lying in the bedroom within, listening to what was being said about the little boy. She could imagine how farmhands and maids stepped forward and observed him.

"Such a poor little thing!" they would always say, and then it came, consistently and unmistakably: "Poor baby, who has no father!"

They were not exactly complaining about the child's wailing. In a certain respect they were convinced that children must wail, and, all things considered, the child was sturdy for its age. If it had only had a father, all would have been good and well, it seemed.

Lying in bed, the mother listened, and wondered. The matter suddenly seemed unbelievably important to her. How would he get through life, the poor little thing?

She had drawn up her plans before. She would stay at the farm the first year. Then she would rent a room and earn her bread at the loom. She intended to earn enough herself to feed and clothe the child. Her husband might continue to believe that she was unworthy of him. She had thought that perhaps the child might become a better person by being brought up by her alone than if a stupid, conceited father were to guide it.

But now, since the child was born, she could not see things that way. Now she thought that she had been selfish. "The child must have a father," she said to herself.

If the little boy had not been such a deplorable thing, if he had been able to eat and sleep like other children, if its head had not constantly hung down on one shoulder, and if he had not been so close to dying that the spasms came, the question would not have had such an immense weight.

It was not so easy to make a decision, and she must make a decision at once. The child was three days old, and the peasants in Värmland seldom wait longer than that to take their children to baptism.

Under what name would the little boy now be entered into the church register, and what would the minister want to know about the child's mother? It would be an injustice to the child to have it registered as fatherless. If this child were to turn out to be a weak and sickly man, how then could she answer for having deprived it of the advantages of lineage and wealth?

The child's mother had probably noticed that there is usually great happiness and excitement when a child comes into the world. Now it seemed to her that living must be a burden for the little boy whom everyone pitied. She wanted to see him sleep on silk and lace, as befits a count's son. She wanted to see him surrounded by happiness and pride.

The child's mother also began to think that she had committed a great injustice against its father. Did she have the right to keep it for herself alone? She could not have that right. Such a precious little thing, whose value is not in the power of man to assess—should she take it for herself? That would not have been a just action.

But she would prefer not to go back to her husband. She feared that would be her demise. But the little boy was in greater peril than she. He might die at any moment, and he was not baptized.

What had driven her away from home, the difficult sin that had dwelled in her heart, was gone. Now surely she had no love for anyone other than the little boy. It was not too heavy a duty to try to get him his rightful place in life.

The child's mother summoned the farmer and his wife and told them everything. The man traveled to Borg to tell Count Dohna that his countess lived, and that there was a child.

The farmer came home late in the evening. He had not seen the count, for he was away, but he had been with the minister in Svartsjö and spoken with him about the matter.

So the countess found out that her marriage had been declared unlawful, and that she no longer had a husband.

The minister wrote a friendly letter to her and offered her a home in his house.

A letter from her own father to Count Henrik, which must have arrived at Borg a few days after her flight, was also sent to her. It was probably this very letter, in which the old man had asked the count to hasten the legalization, which had shown the count the easiest way to be rid of his wife.

One might imagine that the child's mother was seized with rage, even more than with sorrow, when she heard the farmer's story.

The whole night sleep stayed away from her bed. "The child must have a father!" she thought, over and over again.

The next morning the farmer had to travel to Ekeby on her behalf and fetch Gösta Berling.

Gösta placed many questions to the taciturn man, but found out nothing. Yes, the countess had been in his house the whole summer. She had been healthy and worked. Now a child was born. The child was frail, but the mother would soon be healthy again.

Gösta asked if the countess knew that the marriage had been annulled.

Yes, she knew that now. She had found out yesterday.

And as long as the journey lasted, Gösta alternated between fever and chills.

What did she want from him? Why had she sent for him?

He thought about summer life up there on the shores of Löven. With joking and play and parties they had let the days go by, and during that time she had worked and suffered.

Never had he imagined the possibility of getting to see her again. Oh, if he still had dared to hope! Then he could have appeared before her as a better man. What did he have to look back on now other than the usual follies?

At about eight in the evening he was there and was brought at once to the child's mother. It was murky in the room. He could hardly see her, where she was lying. The farmwife and farmer also came in.

Now it should be known that she, whose white face shone toward him from the twilight, was still the highest and purest he knew, the loveliest soul who had taken on earthly form. When he again felt the blessing of her presence, he wanted to get down on his knees and thank her for revealing herself to him anew, but he was so overwhelmed with happiness that he could say or do nothing.

"Dear Countess Elisabet!" he simply exclaimed.

"Good evening, Gösta!"

She extended her hand to him, which again seemed to have become soft and transparent. She was lying quietly, while he struggled with his emotions.

The child's mother was not shaken by any powerful, surging feelings when she saw Gösta. It simply astonished her that he seemed to attach most importance to her, when he really ought to comprehend that it now only concerned the child.

"Gösta," she said gently, "now you must help me, as you once promised. You know that my husband has abandoned me, so that my child does not have a father."

"Yes, countess, but this must of course be changed. Now that there is a child, the count can certainly be forced to legalize the marriage. Be assured that I will help you, countess!"

The countess smiled. "Do you think that I want to force myself on Count Dohna?"

The blood rushed to Gösta's head. What did she want from him then? What was she asking of him?

"Come here, Gösta," she said, again extending her hand. "You must not get angry at me for what I am saying now, but I was thinking that you, who are, who are . . ."

"A defrocked minister, a drinker, a cavalier, Ebba Dohna's murderer, I know the whole litany. . . ."

"Are you already angry, Gösta?"

"I would prefer that you did not say anything more, countess."

But the child's mother continued.

"There are many, Gösta, who would have wanted to be your wife for the sake of love, but that is not the case with me. If I loved you, I would not dare speak the way I am now speaking.

For my own sake I would not ask for such a thing, Gösta, but, you see, for the child's sake I can do it. You surely understand already what I intend to ask you. It is no doubt a great humiliation for you, because I am an unmarried woman who has a child. I was not thinking that you would want to do it because you are worse than others, although yes! I was also thinking of that. But mostly I was thinking that you might want to do it because you are good, Gösta, because you are a hero and can sacrifice yourself. But perhaps that is too much to ask. Such a thing is perhaps impossible for a man. If you despise me too much, if it is too repulsive to you to be named as father of another's child, then just say so! I will not be angry. I understand well enough that this is too much to ask, but the child is so sick, Gösta. It is so cruel not to be able to mention the name of his mother's husband at his baptism."

He who was listening to her had the same feeling as on that spring day when he had to take her ashore and abandon her to her fate. Now he must help her destroy her future, her whole future. He, who loved her, must do this.

"I will do everything you want, countess," he said.

The next day he spoke with the dean in Bro, for Bro is the mother parish to Svartsjö, and the banns must be read there.

The old, good dean was moved by his story and promised to take on all the responsibility of arranging for a guardian and the like.

"Yes," he said, "you must help her, Gösta, you must. Otherwise she might go crazy. She thinks she has harmed the child by depriving it of its station in life. She has an extremely sensitive conscience, that woman."

"But I know that I will make her unhappy," Gösta exclaimed.

"You will certainly do no such thing, Gösta. You will become a levelheaded man now, with a wife and child to care for."

In the meantime the dean would go down to Svartsjö and speak with both the minister and the judge. The result of it all was that the next Sunday, the first of September, banns were read in Svartsjö between Gösta Berling and Elisabet von Thurn.

So the child's mother was conveyed with the greatest care to Ekeby, and there the child was baptized.

The dean spoke with her then and told her that she could still retract her decision to marry such a man as Gösta Berling. She ought to write to her father first.

"I cannot change my mind," she said. "Think if my child were to die, before it has gotten a father!"

When the third day for reading the banns came, the child's mother had already been healthy and out of bed for several days. In the afternoon the dean came to Ekeby and wed her to Gösta Berling. But there was no one who thought of this as a wedding. No guests were invited. The child was simply getting a father, nothing else.

The child's mother radiated a quiet happiness, as if she had reached a great goal in life. The bridegroom was distressed. He thought about how she was throwing away her future in a marriage with him. He noticed with dismay how he actually scarcely existed for her. All her thoughts were with the child.

A few days afterward the father and mother were bereaved. The child had died during a spasm.

It seemed to many as if the child's mother did not grieve as powerfully and as deeply as might have been expected. There was a shimmer of triumph over her. It was as if she rejoiced that she had been able to throw away her entire future for the child's sake. When the little boy came up to the angels, he would remember, however, that on earth he had a mother who had loved him.

Everything happened quietly and unnoticed. When the banns were read for Gösta Berling and Elisabet von Thurn down in Svartsjö, most people did not even know who the bride was. The ministers and gentry, who did know about the matter, spoke little about it. It was as if they feared that someone who had lost faith in the power of conscience would interpret the young woman's course of action badly. They were so afraid, so afraid that someone might come and say, "Look here, it was still the case that she couldn't overcome her love for Gösta! Now she has married him under a fraudulent pretext." Oh, the old people were still so careful about the young woman. They could never tolerate it if anyone said anything bad about her. They hardly wanted to admit that she had sinned. They did not want to see that any guilt stained this soul, which was so afraid of evil.

Another great event occurred just then, which also meant that Gösta's marriage was little discussed.

It happened that Major Samzelius met with an accident. He had become more and more strange and shy of people. He mostly associated with animals and had gathered an entire little zoo down at Sjö.

He was also dangerous, because he always had his loaded shotgun with him and fired it again and again without paying any particular heed to where he was aiming. One day he was bitten by a tame bear, which he had shot unintentionally. The wounded animal pounced on him, where he was standing close by the grating, and managed to give him a massive bite on the arm. The animal then broke out and ran off into the forest.

The major was confined to bed and died from this wound, but not until right before Christmas. If the majoress had known he was sick, she could have retaken dominion over Ekeby. But the cavaliers realized that she would not come until their year was out.

CHAPTER 31

AMOR VINCIT OMNIA

Under the balcony staircase in Svartsjö church is a rubbish room, filled with the gravediggers' worn-out spades, with broken church pews, with discarded tin nameplates and other rubbish.

Inside there, where the dust lies thick and conceals it, as it were, from every human eye, is a chest, inset with mother-of-pearl in an elaborate mosaic. If you scrape the dust from it, it seems to shine and glitter like a mountain wall in a fairy tale. The chest is locked, and the key is in safekeeping; it may not be used. No mortal may take a look in the chest. No one knows what is in it. Only when the nineteenth century has reached its end may the key be set in the lock, the lid raised, and the treasures it has guarded be viewed by people.

It has been decreed so by the man who owned the chest.

On the brass plate on the lid is an inscription: *Labor vincit omnia*. But a different inscription would have been more suitable. It ought to read, *Amor vincit omnia*. Even the old chest in the rubbish room under the balcony staircase is testimony of the omnipotence of love.

Oh Eros, all-governing god!

You, oh love, are the assuredly eternal. Old is humankind upon the earth, but you have followed them through the ages.

Where are the gods of the east, the strong heroes who carried lightning as a weapon, those who on the shores of sacred rivers took offerings of honey and milk? They are dead. Dead is Bel, the strong warrior, and Thot, the hawk-headed champion. Dead are the magnificents who rested on the cloud beds of Olympus, as are the adventurers who lived in walled Valhalla. All the gods of the ancients are dead except Eros, Eros the all-governing.

His work is everything that you see. He upholds the races. Make note of him everywhere! Where can you go, where you do not find the track of his naked foot? What has your ear perceived, where the rushing of his wings has not been the keynote? He lives in people's hearts and in the slumbering seed of grain. Make note, with trembling, of his presence in dead things!

What exists that does not long and is not enticed? What is there that escapes his dominion? All the gods of vengeance will fall, all the powers of strength and violence. You, oh love, are the assuredly eternal.

Old uncle Eberhard sits at his writing desk, a magnificent piece of furniture with a hundred drawers, marble top, and darkened brass fittings. He works with eagerness and diligence, alone up in the cavaliers' wing.

Oh, Eberhard, why do you not swarm around forest and field during the vanishing last days of summer like the other cavaliers? No one, you know, worships the goddess of wisdom unpunished. Your back is bent at sixty and some-odd years, the hair covering your skull is not your own, wrinkles crowd your forehead, which arches over sunken eye sockets, and the decline of age is indicated in the thousand creases around your empty mouth.

Oh, Eberhard, why do you not swarm around forest and field? Death will separate you even sooner from your writing desk, because you did not let life beckon you away from it.

Uncle Eberhard draws a thick ink stroke under his final line. From the writing desk's innumerable drawers he takes out yellowed, fully scribbled-on bundles, all the various parts of his great work, the work that will carry the name of Eberhard Berggren through the ages. But just as he has piled bundle upon bundle and is gazing at them in silent enjoyment, the door opens, and in comes the young countess.

There she is, the young conqueror of the old gentlemen! She, whom they serve and adore more than grandparents serve and adore the first grandson. There she is, whom they found in poverty and illness and now have granted all the splendor of the world, like the king in the fairy tale did with the poor lovely he found in the forest. It is for her that horns and fiddles now sound at Ekeby. It is for her that everything moves, breathes, labors at the great estate.

She is healthy now, even if still very weak. The solitude in the great house seemed long to her, and as she knows that the cavaliers are away, she wants to see how it looks up in the cavaliers' wing, this renowned room.

So she comes slowly in and glances up at the plastered walls and the yellow-checked bedcovers, but she becomes embarrassed when she notices that the room is not empty.

Uncle Eberhard walks solemnly toward her and leads her over to the large pile of written paper.

"Look, countess!" he says. "Now my work is finished. Now what I have written will go out into the world. Now great things will happen."

"What is it that will happen, uncle Eberhard?"

"Oh, countess, it will come down like a bolt of lightning, a bolt of lightning that will illuminate and kill. Ever since Moses drew him out of the cloud of thunder on Sinai and set him on the mercy seat in the innermost part of the tabernacle, ever since then he has sat securely, old Jehovah, but now the people will see what he is: imagination, emptiness, smoke and mirrors, the stillborn fetus of our own minds. He will sink into nothing," said the old man, setting his wrinkled hand on the pile of papers. "Here it is, and when people read it, they will have to believe. They will rise up and see their own stupidity, they will use crosses for firewood, churches for grain bins, and ministers will plow the earth."

"Oh, uncle Eberhard," the countess says with a slight shudder, "are you such a frightful person? Are there such frightful things there?"

"Frightful!" repeats the old man. "It's just the truth. But we are like children who hide their faces in a woman's skirts as soon as they meet a stranger. We have gotten used to hiding from the truth, from the eternally strange. But now she will come and live among us, now she will be known by everyone."

"By everyone?"

"Not only by the philosophers, but by everyone, you see, countess, by everyone."

"And so Jehovah will die?"

"He and all the angels, all the saints, all the devils, all the lies."

"Who will guide the world then?"

"Do you think, countess, that anyone has guided it before? Do you believe in that providence that took note of sparrows and hairs? No one has guided it, no one will guide it."

"But we, we people, what will become of us then?"

"The same as we have been—dust. Anyone who is burned up cannot burn more, he is dead. We are wood, which is flickered around by the flames of life. The spark of life flies from one to another. You are ignited, flare up, and go out. That is life."

"Oh, uncle Eberhard, is there no spirit life then?"

"Nothing."

"Nothing on the other side of the grave?"

"Nothing."

"No good, no evil, no goal, no hope?"

"Nothing."

The young woman goes over to the window. She looks out over autumn's yellowing leaves, over dahlias and asters, which with heavy heads hang on stalks broken by the autumn wind. She sees the black waves of Löven, the dark storm sky of autumn, and for a moment she surrenders to denial.

"Uncle Eberhard," she says, "how gray and ugly the world is, how useless everything is! I want to lie down and die."

But then she hears as it were a groaning in her soul. The strong forces of life and seething emotions cry out loudly for the good fortune to live.

"Is there nothing then," she exclaims, "that can give life beauty, since you have taken God and immortality away from me?"

"Work," answers the old man.

But she looks out again, and a feeling of contempt for this pitiful wisdom rises up before her, she feels the spirit dwelling in everything, she senses the power that lies bound in apparently dead matter, but which can develop into a thousandfold varied lives. With a dizzying thought she searches for names for the presence of the spirit of God in nature.

"Oh, uncle Eberhard," she says, "what is work? Is it a god? Does it have a goal in itself? Name another!"

"I know no other," answers the old man.

Then she has found the name she was searching for, a pitiful, often sullied name.

"Uncle Eberhard, why do you not mention love?"

Then a smile slips across the empty mouth, where the thousand wrinkles crisscross.

"Here," says the philosopher, striking the heavy packet with clenched fists, "here all gods are murdered, and I have not forgotten Eros. What is love other than a yearning of the flesh? Why does he stand higher than other physical demands? Make hunger into a god! Make tiredness into a god! They are just as worthy. May there be an end to follies! May the truth live!"

Then the young countess lowers her head. It is not so, this is not true, but she cannot struggle.

"Your words have wounded my soul," she says, "but still I do not believe you. You may be able to kill the gods of vengeance and violence, but no more."

But the old man takes her hand, sets it on the book, and answers in the fanaticism of disbelief.

"When you have read this, you must believe."

"May it never come before my eyes then!" she says. "For if I believe this, I cannot live."

And submerged in sorrow, she leaves the philosopher. But he sits for a long time, brooding, when she has gone.

These old bundles, scribbled full of heretical writing, have not yet been tested before the world. Uncle Eberhard's name has not yet reached the pinnacles of fame.

His great work lies hidden in a chest in the rubbish room under the balcony staircase in Svartsjö church. Only at the end of the century will it see the light of day.

But why has he done this? Did he fear that he had not proven his case? Was he afraid of persecution? Little do you know uncle Eberhard.

Now understand: he loved the truth, not personal glory. So he sacrificed the latter, not the former, so that a child, loved in a fatherly way, could die believing that which she held dear.

Oh love, you are the assuredly eternal!

CHAPTER 32

THE GIRL FROM NYGÅRD

No one knows the place under the hill where the spruce trees are densest and deep layers of soft moss cover the ground. How could anyone know it? Never before has it been trampled by a human foot, no human tongue has given it a name. No path leads to this hidden place. Boulders tower round about it, entangling junipers guard it, windfalls close it in, the shepherd does not find it, the fox despises it. It is the most desolate part of the forest, and now thousands of people are searching for it.

What an endless procession of searchers! They would fill Bro church, not only Bro, but Lövvik and Svartsjö. No, what an endless procession of searchers!

Children of the gentry, not allowed to follow the parade, stand by the roadside or hang on the gates as the great procession passes by. The little ones did not think this world held such a crowd of people, such an innumerable quantity. When they grow up, they will recall this long, billowing river of people. Their eyes will fill with tears at the very memory of how overwhelming it was to see this endless procession pass by on roads where only a few lonely wanderers, a few bands of beggars, or a farmer's cart might be seen for whole days.

Everyone who lives by the road rushes up and asks, "Has misfortune come upon the land? Is the enemy upon us? Where are you going, wanderers? Where to?"

"We are searching," they answer. "We have searched for two days. We will search today too, then we won't be able to go on. We will search through Björne forest and the pine-clad heights west of Ekeby."

The procession first departed from Nygård, a poor area over in the eastern hills. The beautiful girl with heavy, black hair and red cheeks has been missing for eight days. The broom girl, whom Gösta Berling wanted to be his intended, has gone astray in the great forests. For eight days no one has seen her.

So the people from Nygård went out to search through the forest. And every person they met followed along to search. From every cottage people came to join the procession.

Often too it happens that a new arrival asks, "You men from Nygård, how did all this come about? Why do you let that beautiful girl walk alone on strange paths? The forest is deep, and God has taken her reason."

"No one harms her," they answer then, "she harms no one. She goes as securely as a child. Who goes more safely than someone whom God himself must care for? She has always come back before."

So the procession of searchers has proceeded across the eastern forests that separate Nygård from the plain. Now on the third day it is moving past Bro church up toward the forests west of Ekeby.

But where the procession proceeds, a storm of wonder is also brewing. A man from the crowd must constantly stop to answer questions. "What do you want? What are you searching for?"

"We are searching for the blue-eyed, dark-haired girl. She has gone out to die in the forest. She has been gone for eight days."

"Why has she gone out to die in the forest? Was she hungry? Was she unhappy?"

"She has not gone hungry, but she met with misfortune last spring. She has seen the mad minister, Gösta Berling, and loved him for several years. She didn't know any better. God has taken her reason."

"God has truly taken her reason from her, you men of Nygård."

"The misfortune came last spring. Before that he had never looked at her. Then he said to her that she should become his intended. It was only in jest, he let her go again, but she could not be consoled. She kept coming back to Ekeby. She hung on his tracks, wherever he went. He grew tired of her. When she was there last, they set the dogs on her. Since then no one has seen her."

Out of the house, out of the house! This is a matter of life and death. Someone has gone out to die in the forest. Perhaps she is already dead! Perhaps she is still wandering there without finding the right path! The forest is large and her reason is with God.

Follow the procession, follow it! Let the oats hang on the shocks, until the thin kernel falls from the husk, let the potatoes rot in the ground, let the horses loose so that they may not die of thirst in the stable, leave the sheep pen door open so that the cows may go under a roof at night, let the children come along, for children belong to God! God is with the little ones, he guides their steps. They will help, where the wisdom of men is baffled.

Come all, men and women and children! Who can dare stay home? Who knows whether or not God intends to use him in particular? Come all who need compassion, that your soul may not one day wander helplessly around dry places, seeking rest and finding none! Come! God has taken her reason, and the forest is large.

Who finds their way to the place where the spruce trees are densest and the moss is softest? Is there something dark in there close under the rock wall? Only the brown ants' mound of needles. Praised be the one who guides the way of fools, nothing else!

Oh, what a procession! Not a procession adorned for a holiday that greets the victor, that strews flowers in his path and fills his ears with shouts of jubilation, not the march of the pilgrims to hymn singing and swishing strokes of the scourge en route to the sacred tombs, not the train of emigrants on creaking wagons, who seek new homes for those in distress, not an army with drums and rifles, only farmers in homespun work clothes with worn leather aprons, only their wives with knitting in hand and children on their backs or dragging along at their skirts.

A great thing it is to see people united in great goals. May they go out to greet their benefactors, to praise their God, to seek earth, to defend their land, may they go! But it is not hunger, not fear of God, not war that has driven these people out. Their efforts are useless, their striving without benefit. They go simply to find a madwoman. However many drops of sweat, however many steps, however much anxiety, however many prayers it costs, yet it will not be rewarded with anything other than finding a poor stray again, whose reason is with God.

Oh, don't you love these people! Wouldn't anyone who has stood at the roadside and seen them pass by get tears in his eyes when he sees them again in his thoughts, men with coarse features and hard hands, women with brows furrowed early, and the tired children, whom God would lead to the right place?

It fills the highway, this procession of distressed searchers. They measure the forest with serious glances, gloomily they go forth, for they know that they are more likely searching for a dead person than a living one.

That black thing under the rock wall, is that nonetheless not the ants' needle stack, but a downed tree? Praised be heaven, only a downed tree! But it is difficult to see clearly, as the spruce trees stand so close together.

The procession is so long that those in front, the strong men, are up at the forest west of Björne, when the last, the cripples, the work-broken old men, and the women carrying their small children, have scarcely made it past Broby church.

And then the whole winding procession disappears into the dark forest. The morning sun shines in under the spruce trees—the sinking sun of evening will meet the bands as they are coming out of the forest.

It is the third day of their search: they are used to this labor. They search under the steep rock wall, on which a foot can slide; under the windfalls, where arms and legs can easily be broken; under the dense branches of the spruce trees, which, trailing down over soft moss, invite to rest.

The bear's lair, the fox's den, the badger's deep nest, the black base of the charcoal stack, the red lingonberry patch, the spruce with its white needles, the hill that the forest fire ravaged a month earlier, the stone that the giant threw: all this they have found, but not the place under the rock wall where the black thing lies. No one has been there to see if it is an anthill or a tree trunk or a person. Oh, it is probably a person, but no one has been there to see her.

The evening sun sees them on the other side of the forest, but the young woman, whose reason God has taken, has not been found. What will they do now? Will they search through the forest one more time? The forest is dangerous in the darkness: there are bottomless marshes and steep cliffs. And what could they, who found nothing when the sun was shining, find when the sun has vanished?

"Let us go to Ekeby!" someone in the crowd cries out.

"Let us go to Ekeby!" they all cry out together. "Let us go to Ekeby!"

"Let us ask these cavaliers why they let the dogs loose on someone whose reason God has taken, why they incited a madwoman to despair! Our poor, hungry children are crying, our clothes are torn, the grain is hanging on the shocks until the kernel falls from its husk, the potatoes are rotting in the ground, our horses are running around wild, our cows are not tended, we ourselves are close to collapsing from fatigue, and all this is their fault. Let us go to Ekeby and call them to account! Let us go to Ekeby!

"During this cursed year everything bad happens to us farmers. God's hand rests heavily over us, the winter will offer us starvation. Who is it that God's hand is seeking? It wasn't the Broby minister. His prayers could still reach God's ear. Who then, if not these cavaliers? Let us go to Ekeby!

"They have destroyed the estate, they have driven the majoress begging out onto the highway. It is their fault that we must go without work. It is their fault that we must go hungry. This distress is their doing. Let us go to Ekeby!"

So dark, embittered men jostle down toward Ekeby's great estate; hungry women with crying children on their arms follow them; and last come the cripples and the work-broken elderly. And the bitterness flows like a growing stream through the ranks, from the old to the women, from the women to the strong men at the head of the procession.

It is the autumn flood that is coming. Cavaliers, do you recall the spring flood? Now new waves come streaming down from the hills, now a new devastation befalls the glory and power of Ekeby.

A crofter who is plowing a pasture at the forest edge hears the raging cry of the people. He unharnesses one horse, gets up on it, and hurries off down to Ekeby. "Misfortune is coming!" he shouts, "the bears are coming, the wolves are coming, the trolls are coming to take Ekeby!"

He rides around the whole estate, wild with terror. "All the trolls in the forest are loose!" he shouts. "The trolls are coming to take Ekeby! Save yourselves, those who can! The trolls are coming to set fire to the estate and kill the cavaliers!"

And behind him is heard the thunder and howling of the surging crowd of people. The autumn flood is rushing down toward Ekeby.

Does it know what it wants, this storming stream of resentment? Does it want fire, does it want murder, does it want plunder?

It is not people who are coming: it is the trolls of the forest, the wild animals of the wilderness. We, dark powers who must keep hidden under the earth, we are free for a single blessed moment. Revenge has released us.

It is the hill spirits who have mined ore, it is the forest spirits who have felled trees and guarded charcoal piles, it is the field spirits who have let the bread grow: they are free, they turn to destruction. Death to Ekeby, death to the cavaliers!

It is here that liquor flows in currents. It is here that gold lies heaped in the cellar vaults. It is here that the storehouses are filled with grain and meat. Why should the children of righteousness starve and malefactors have enough?

But now their time has run out; the cup is full to the brim, cavaliers. You lilies, who have never spun, you birds, who have never gathered, the cup is full. In the forest lies the one who judges you: we are her emissaries. It is not judge and sheriff who pronounce your sentence. The one who lies in the forest has convicted you.

The cavaliers are standing up in the main building and see the people coming. They already know why they are accused. For once they are innocent. If the poor girl has gone out to die in the forest, then it is not because they incited the dogs on her—

they never did that—but rather because eight days ago, Gösta Berling married the Countess Elisabet.

But what good does it do to talk with these raging people? They are tired, they are hungry; revenge incites them, rapacity entices them. They come rushing with wild shouts, and ahead of them rides the crofter, whom terror has made crazy.

"The bears are coming, the wolves are coming, the trolls are coming to take Ekeby!"

The cavaliers have hidden the young countess in the innermost room. Lövenborg and uncle Eberhard will sit there and watch over her; the rest go out toward the people. They stand on the stairway before the main building, unarmed, smiling, when the first clamorous band arrives there.

And the people stop before this little band of calm men. There are those who in fiery resentment wanted to throw them down on the ground and trample them under their iron-shod heels, as the people at Sund's ironworks did with stewards and inspectors fifty years before. But they had expected closed doors, resolutely raised weapons, they expected resistance and struggle.

"Dear friends," say the cavaliers, "dear friends, you are tired and hungry, let us give you some food, and first taste a dram of Ekeby's own home-brewed liquor!"

The people do not want to hear such talk; they howl and threaten. But the cavaliers do not lose patience.

"Just wait," they say, "just wait a moment! See, Ekeby stands open. The cellar door stands open, the storehouse stands open, the dairy stands open. Your women are dropping from fatigue, your children are crying. Let us first get them food! Then you can kill us. We will not run away. But the attic is full of apples. Let us go after apples for the children!"

An hour later the party is in full swing at Ekeby. The greatest party the great estate has ever seen is celebrated there in the autumn night, under the great shining full moon.

Stacks of wood have been toppled and set afire; across the entire yard, bonfire flames by bonfire. The people sit there in groups, enjoying the heat and rest, while all the good gifts of the earth are strewn upon them.

Resolute men have gone into the barn and taken what might be needed. Calves and sheep have been killed and even one or two of the large animals. The animals have been butchered and roasted in the blink of an eye. These hundreds of hungry people gobble up the food. Animal after animal is led out and killed. It looks as though the entire barn will be emptied in one night.

There has been fall baking at Ekeby just at that time. Since the young Countess Elisabet had arrived, there had once again been energy in domestic activities. It was as if the young woman did not remind them for a moment that she was Gösta Berling's wife. Neither he nor she made any pretense about it, but on the contrary she made herself into the wife at Ekeby. Like a good, capable woman must always do, she sought with consuming fervor to remedy the extravagance and carelessness that prevailed at the estate. And she was obeyed. The people experienced a certain well-being from once again having a mistress of the house over them.

But what did it help now that she had the kitchen ceiling filled with bread, that curdling and churning and brewing had been done during the month of September that she had been there? What did it help?

Out to the people with everything there was, so that they won't burn Ekeby and kill the cavaliers! Out with bread, butter, cheese! Out with the barrels and beer kegs, out with the hams from the storehouse, out with the casks of liquor, out with the apples!

How can all the wealth of Ekeby suffice to soften the wrath of the people? If we get them away from here without any black deed having been done, then we ought to be happy.

Everything that happens is, however, ultimately for her sake, she who is now the housewife at Ekeby. The cavaliers are courageous men, skilled with weapons; they would have defended themselves if they had followed their own inclinations. They would rather have driven away these greedy mobs with their sharp shooting, if it had not been for her sake, who is gentle and tender and prays for the people.

As the night goes on, the groups become gentler. The heat and rest and food and liquor assuage their terrifying agitation. They start to joke and laugh. They are at the Nygård girl's funeral feast. "Shame on anyone, who fails at drinking and joking at a funeral feast! That is where it's needed."

The children throw themselves on the masses of fruit that are brought to them. Poor croft children, who think of cranberries and lingonberries as delicacies, throw themselves over clear astrakhan apples that melt in their mouths, oblong, sweet paradise apples, yellow-white citron apples, pears with red cheeks, and plums of all types, yellow, red, and blue. Oh, nothing is good enough for the people, when it pleases them to show their power.

As it approaches midnight, it appears as if the groups are preparing to break camp. The cavaliers stop bringing food and wine, pulling out corks, and tapping beer kegs. They heave a sigh of relief, sensing that the danger is passed.

But just then a light is seen in one of the windows of the main building. All who see it let out a shriek. It is a young woman who carries the candle.

It was just for a moment. The sight disappears, but the people think they have recognized the woman.

"She had long, black hair and red cheeks," they shout. "She is here. They have her hidden here."

"Oh, cavaliers, do you have her here? Do you have our child, whose reason God has taken, here at Ekeby? Godless men, what are you doing with her? Here you let us worry about her the whole week, search for her for a whole three days! Away with wine and food! Woe on us, that we have taken anything from your hands! First, out with her now, then we will know what we need to do with you."

The tamed wild animal roars and bellows. With a few wild leaps it rushes up toward Ekeby.

The people are quick, quicker than the cavaliers are. They rush up and bar the door. But what can they accomplish against this surging mob? Door after door is thrown open. The cavaliers are cast aside; they have no weapons. They are crowded in among the dense mob so that they cannot move. The people want in, to find the girl from Nygård.

In the innermost room they find her. No one has time to look to see if she is light or dark. They lift her up and carry her out.

She should not be afraid, they say. It is only the cavaliers they are after. They are here to rescue her.

But they who now stream out of the building are met by another procession.

No longer resting in the most desolate place in the forest is the body of a woman who has fallen from the high precipice above and died in the fall. A child has found her. Searchers who were left behind in the forest lifted her up on their shoulders. There they come. She is lovelier in death than in life. Fair she lies with her long, dark hair. Splendid is her face, since eternal peace rests over it.

Raised high on the men's shoulders, she is borne along through the crowd of people. They become silent as she passes. With bowed heads all hail the majesty of death.

"She is recently dead," whisper the men. "She has probably been walking in the forest until today. We think she wanted to flee from us, who have been searching for her, and so she fell down the precipice."

But if this is the girl from Nygård, who then is she who has been carried out from Ekeby?

The procession from the forest meets the procession from the building. The bonfires flame around the whole yard. The people can see both women and know them. The other one is of course the young countess at Borg.

"Oh, what does this mean? Is this a new outrage that we have stumbled upon? Why have we been told that she was far away or even dead? In the name of holy righteousness, should we not now throw ourselves upon the cavaliers and trample them to dust under iron-shod heels!"

Then a far-resounding voice is heard. Gösta Berling has climbed up on the railing of the stairway and speaks from there.

"Hear me, you monsters, you devils! Do you not think that there are rifles and powder at Ekeby, you lunatics? Do you not believe that I have had the desire to shoot all of you down like mad dogs? But she prayed for you. Oh, if I had known that you would have touched her, not one of you would have been alive!

"What is it you are hissing about tonight, coming upon us like robbers and threatening us with murder and arson? What do I have to do with your crazy girls? Do I know where they run off to? I have been too good to her, that is the matter. I should have set the dogs on her—it would have been better for us both—but I haven't done that. Nor have I promised her that I would marry her, that I have never done. Remember that!

"But now I say to you, that you will release her whom you have dragged out of the house here. Release her, I say, and may those fists that have touched her ache in eternal fire! Don't you understand that she is as much above you as the sky is above the earth, she is just as fine as you are rough, just as good as you are wicked?

"Now I will tell you who she is. First, she is an angel from heaven; second, it is she who has been married to the count at Borg. But her mother-in-law tormented her both night and day. She had to stand by the lake and wash clothes like an ordinary maid, she was beaten and tortured so that none of you women can have it worse. Yes, she almost threw herself into the river, because the life was being tortured out of her. I wonder just which one of you, you rascals, would have been on hand to save her life then. None of you were there, but we cavaliers, we did it. Yes, we did it.

"And then she gave birth to a child away on a farm and the count sent her greetings to say: 'We were married in a foreign country, we did not follow law and ordinance. You are not my wife, I am not your husband. I do not care about your child,' yes, when it was like that and she did not want the child to be recorded as fatherless in the church register, then you would probably have been haughty, if she had said to any of you, 'Come and marry me! I must have a father for the child.' But she chose none of you. She took Gösta Berling, the poor minister who may never again speak God's word. Yes, I say to you, farmers, that I have never done a more difficult thing, for I was so unworthy of her that I did not dare look her in the eyes, but I dared not say no either, for she was in great distress.

"And now you may think what evil you want to about us cavaliers, but toward her we have done what good we could. And it is due to her that we haven't shot all of you dead tonight. But now I say to you: let her go and go your way, otherwise I think the earth will open up and swallow you! And when you leave here, then pray to God to forgive you, that you have frightened and grieved one who is so good and innocent! And now away with you! We have had enough of you!"

Long before he had finished speaking, those who had carried out the countess had set her down on one of the stone stair steps, and now a big farmer came over to her quite deliberately and extended his large hand to her.

"Thanks and good night!" he said. "We wish you no harm, countess."

After him came another and gave her a careful handshake. "Thanks and good night! You must not be annoyed with us!"

Gösta jumped down and placed himself at her side. They took him by the hand too.

So they now came up slowly and leisurely, one by one, to say good night to them before they left. They were subdued again, again they were human, as they were when in the morning they left their homes, before hunger and revenge had turned them into wild animals.

They looked the countess right in the eyes, and Gösta noticed how the sight of the innocence and piety they saw there brought tears to many eyes. There was in all of them a silent adoration of the noblest thing they had seen. These were people who were happy that one of them had such a great love for the good.

Of course they could not all shake hands with her. There were so terribly many, and the young woman was tired and weak. But they all wanted to go up and see her, and then they could take Gösta by the hand; his arms could no doubt handle the shaking.

Gösta stood as if in a dream. In his heart this evening a new love rose up.

"Oh, my people," he thought, "Oh, my people, how I love you!" He felt how he loved this entire crowd, which wandered off in the night darkness with the dead girl at the head of the procession, all of these in rough clothes and foul-smelling footwear, all of these who lived in the gray cabins by the forest edge, all of these who could not wield a pen and often could not read either, all of these who did not know the fullness and richness of life, only the striving for daily bread.

He loved them with a painful, ardent tenderness, which brought tears to his eyes. He did not know what he wanted to do for them, but he loved them, each and every one, with faults and vices and infirmities. Oh, Lord God, if the day might come when he was also loved by them!

He awakened from his dream: his wife laid her hand on his arm. The people were gone. They were alone on the stairway.

"Oh, Gösta, Gösta, how could you?"

She put her hands before her face and wept.

"It is true what I said," he exclaimed. "I never promised the girl from Nygård that I would marry her. 'Come here next Friday, then you'll see something funny!' was all that I said to her. I can't help it if she liked me."

"Oh, it wasn't that, but how could you say to the people that I was good and pure? Gösta, Gösta, don't you know that I loved you when I didn't yet have leave to do so? I was ashamed before the people, Gösta. I wanted to die of shame."

And she was shaking with sobs.

He stood, looking at her.

"Oh, my friend, my beloved!" he said quietly. "How fortunate you are, who is so good! How fortunate you are, who has such a lovely soul within you!"

CHAPTER 33

KEVENHÜLLER

In the 1770s the subsequently learned and versatile Kevenhüller was born in Germany. He was the son of a burgrave and could have lived in tall castles and ridden at the emperor's side if he had had the desire, but he did not.

He would have liked to attach windmill sails to the castle's highest tower, turn the ceremonial hall into a blacksmith shop and the ladies' quarters into a clockmaker's workshop. He would have liked to fill the castle with whirring wheels and working levers. But as such things could not be done, he left it all and entered the clockmaker's trade. There he learned everything there was to be learned about gears, springs, and pendulums. He learned to make sundials and sidereal clocks, ornamental clocks with chirping canaries and horn-blowing gentlemen, carillons that filled an entire church steeple with their marvelous machinery, and clockworks so small that they could be contained in a medallion.

When he had become a master of his trade, he put a knapsack on his back, took his knobbed stick in hand, and wandered from place to place to study everything that worked with cylinders and wheels. Kevenhüller was no ordinary clockmaker; he wanted to become a great inventor and reformer.

When he had wandered through many lands, he also made his way to Värmland to study mill wheels and the mining arts. One beautiful summer morning he happened to be walking across the square in Karlstad. But at that same beautiful morning moment, the wood nymph found it pleasing to extend her wanderings all the way into the city. The high lady was also walking across the

square, but from the opposite direction, and thus she encountered Kevenhüller.

What an encounter for a journeyman clockmaker! She had
shining, green eyes and flowing, light hair that almost reached
the ground, and she was dressed in green, rustling silk. Troll and
heathen that she was, she was lovelier than all the Christian
women Kevenhüller had ever seen. He stood looking at her as
if thunderstruck as she came toward him.

She came straight from the thickets in the innermost part of
the forest, where the ferns are high as trees, where the gigantic
pines shut out the sunlight so that it only falls as golden splashes
on the yellow moss, and where the twinflower creeps across
lichen-clad stones.

I would dearly like to have been in Kevenhüller's place, to see
her as she came with fern leaves and spruce needles entangled in
her flowing hair and a little black viper around her neck. Imagine her, lithe of gait as a wild animal and conveying a fresh scent
of resin and wild strawberry, of twinflower and moss!

And how people must have stared at her as she strolled across
the square in Karlstad! Horses bolted in fright at her long hair,
which flew before the summer wind. Street urchins ran after her.
Men let go of scale and meat cleaver to gape at her. Women ran
screaming for the bishop and church council to drive the witch
out of the city.

She herself walked calmly and majestically, simply smiling at
the excitement with which Kevenhüller watched her small, pointed
predator's teeth shine behind her red lips.

She had hung a cloak across her back so that no one would
notice who she was, but as bad luck would have it, she had forgotten to cover her tail. Now it was dragging along the cobble-
stones.

Kevenhüller saw the tail too, but it hurt him that a highborn
lady should expose herself to the ridicule of city dwellers. Therefore he bowed to the lovely and said in a courtly manner, "Does
it not please your grace to elevate her train?"

The wood nymph was moved, as much by his goodwill as by
his courtesy. She stopped right in front of him and looked at him,
so that he thought that flashing sparks darted from her eyes into

his heart. "Mark this, Kevenhüller," she said, "hereafter shall you with your two hands be able to execute whatever work of art you wish, but only one of each type."

Thus she spoke, and she could keep her word. For who does not know that the green-clad woman from the forest thickets has the power to grant genius and marvelous powers to those who win her favor?

Kevenhüller stayed in Karlstad and rented a workshop there. He hammered and worked night and day. In eight days he had made a marvel. It was a wagon that moved by itself. It went uphill and downhill, went fast and slow, could be steered and turned, stopped and put into motion, exactly as you wished. A splendid wagon it was.

Now Kevenhüller became a renowned man and made friends in the whole city. He was so proud of his wagon that he drove up to Stockholm to show it to the king. He did not need to wait for stagecoaches or quarrel with stage drivers. He did not need to shake on a gig or sleep on the wooden bench at the way station. He drove proudly in his own wagon and was there in a few hours.

He drove right up to the palace, and the king came out with the court ladies and gentlemen and watched him ride. They could not praise him enough.

Then the king said, "You can surely give me the wagon, Kevenhüller." And although he answered no, the king was stubborn and wanted to have the wagon.

Then Kevenhüller saw that in the king's retinue stood a lady-in-waiting with light hair and green dress. He thought he recognized her, and he realized that it was she who had advised the king to ask him for his wagon. But he did not despair. He could not tolerate that someone else would own his wagon, but neither did he dare say no in the long run to the king. So he drove it with such speed against the palace wall that it burst into a thousand pieces.

When he came back home to Karlstad, he tried to make a new wagon. But he could not. Then he became dismayed at the gift the wood nymph had given him. He had left a life of indolence at his father's castle to become a benefactor for many, not to manufacture marvels that only one person could use. What good was it to him if he were to become a great master, yes, the greatest of all masters, if he could not multiply his marvels, so that they were of use for the thousands?

And the learned, versatile man longed so for calm, collected labor that he became a stonecutter and mason. It was then he built the great stone tower down by the West Bridge based on the plan of the castle keep in his father's knight's castle, and his intention was no doubt to also build covered sheds, portals, courtyards, ramparts, and oriels, so that an entire knight's castle would arise by the shores of the Klara River.

And within it he would realize his childhood dream. Everything that went by the name of industry and workmanship would have its home in the halls of the castle. White-dusted miller's hands and black-coated smiths, clockmakers with green shades before their strained eyes, dyers with dark hands, weavers, turners, filers, all would have their workshops in his castle.

And all went well. From the stones he crushed himself he built his tower with his own hands. He set up mill sails on it—for the tower was to be a mill—and now he wanted to get to work on the smithy.

So he stood one day observing how the light, strong sails turned before the wind. Then his old affliction came over him.

To him it was as though the green-clad woman was looking at him again with her shining eyes, until his brain caught fire again. He closed himself up in his workshop, tasted no food, enjoyed no rest, and worked without ceasing. Thus in eight days he made a new marvel.

One day he climbed up onto the roof of his tower and began to strap wings onto his shoulders.

Two street urchins and a student, who were sitting on the caisson fishing for bleak, caught sight of him, and they let out a scream that was heard through the whole city. They took off, they ran panting up and down the street, knocking on every door and shouting as they ran, "Kevenhüller is going to fly! Kevenhüller is going to fly!"

He stood calmly on the top of the tower, strapping on wings, and during that time groups of people came swarming forth from the narrow streets in old Karlstad.

The maids left the boiling kettle and the rising dough. The old women let go of their knitting, put their eyeglasses on, and darted along the street. The councilors and mayor rose up from the magistrate's table. The rector tossed his grammar book into the corner, the schoolboys swept out of their classes without asking permission. The whole city was on the run toward West Bridge.

Soon the bridge was thick with people. The salt market was packed, and the entire riverbank all the way up to the bishop's residence was teeming with people. There was a greater crowd than at the Feast of Saints Peter and Paul, there were more eager observers there than when King Gustav III came driving through the city, drawn by eight horses and at such a wild speed that the coach stood on two wheels on the turns.

Kevenhüller finally got the wings on and set off. He took a few flaps with them, and then he was out in the open air. He was swimming in the sea of air, high above the earth.

He breathed in air in full drafts; it was strong and pure. His chest expanded, and the old knightly blood began to seethe within him. He tumbled like a dove, he floated like a hawk, his wings were quick as the swallow's, he steered his way as surely as the falcon. And he looked down at the whole earthbound crowd, which was peering up at him, who was swimming in the air. If he had only been able to produce a pair of similar wings for each and every one of them! If he had only been able to give each of them the power to rise up into this fresh air! Think what people they would become! The memory of his life's misery did not leave him even in the moment of triumph. He could not enjoy simply for his own sake. That wood nymph, if only he could see her!

Then he saw with eyes almost blinded by the sharp sunlight and the shimmering air, how someone came flying right toward him. He saw great wings moving, just like his own, and between the wings a human body was swimming. Yellow hair fluttered, green silk billowed, wild eyes shone. There she was, there she was!

Kevenhüller did not hesitate. At a wild speed he hurled himself at the monster, to kiss her or strike her—he did not really know which—but in any case to force her to lift the curse from his existence. At this wild speed his senses deserted him. He did not see where he was heading, he noticed only the flying hair and the wild eyes. He came right up to her and stretched out his arms to grasp her. Then his wings got caught in hers, and hers were stronger. His wings tore and were destroyed; he was swung around and plummeted down, he knew not where.

When he regained his senses, he was lying on the roof of his own tower with the crushed flying machine at his side. He had flown right into his own windmill: the sails had seized him, swung him around a few turns, and thereupon hurled him down onto the tower roof.

That was how that game ended.

Kevenhüller was once again a desperate man. Honorable work bored him, and he dared not use his miracle arts. If he nonetheless did make a marvel and came to destroy it, then his heart would burst from sorrow. And if he did not destroy it, he would go mad at the thought that it could be of no use to others.

He dug out his journeyman's knapsack and knobbed stick, let the mill stand where it was, and decided to go out in search of the wood nymph.

He acquired a horse and carriage, for he was no longer young and light on his feet. And it is told that when he came to a forest, he got out of the carriage and went in there and called to the green-clad woman in the thicket.

"Wood nymph, wood nymph, it is I, Kevenhüller, Kevenhüller! Come, come!" But she did not come.

On these journeys he came to Ekeby, a few years before the majoress was driven away. There he was well received, and there he stayed. And the band in the cavaliers' wing was augmented by one tall, strong knightly character, a bold gentleman, who could hold his own at a beer tankard and in a hunting party. His childhood memories returned: he allowed them to call him "count," and he acquired more and more the appearance of an old German robber baron, with his large aquiline nose, his stern eyebrows, and his full beard, which was pointed under his chin and pluckily curled up above his lips.

He then became a cavalier among the cavaliers and was no better than any other in that crowd, which people believed that the majoress made ready for the foul fiend. His hair turned gray, and his brain slumbered. He was so old that he could no longer believe in the exploits of his youth. He was not the man with the miraculous powers. It was not he who had made the self-propelled wagon and the flying machine. Oh, no, tales, tales!

But then it happened that the majoress was driven out of Ekeby, and the cavaliers became masters at the great estate. Then a way of life began there, which had never been worse. A storm passed over the land: all old folly broke out in the delirium of youth, all that was evil started moving, all good trembled, the people fought on the earth and the spirits in the heavens. Wolves came from Dovre with troll hags on their backs, natural forces were set free, and the wood nymph came to Ekeby.

The cavaliers did not know her. They thought she was a poor, distressed woman, whom a cruel mother-in-law had pursued into despair. So they gave her shelter, revered her like a queen, and loved her like a child.

Kevenhüller alone saw who she was. To begin with he was probably blinded like all the others. But one day she wore a dress of green, rustling silk, and when she had it on, Kevenhüller recognized her.

There she sat, bedded on silk, on the best sofa at Ekeby, and all the old men made fools of themselves to serve her. One was a cook and another a chamberlain, one a reader, one a court musician, one a shoemaker: they had each taken a task.

She was supposedly sick, that evil troll, but Kevenhüller knew how things were with that sick person. She was making fools of them, all of them, she was.

He warned the cavaliers about her. "Look at those little sharp teeth," he said, "and the wild shining eyes! She is the wood nymph, all evil is on the move in this terrible time. I say to you, she is the wood nymph, come here to our ruin. I have seen her before."

But as soon as Kevenhüller had seen the wood nymph and recognized her, the desire to work came over him. His brain started to burn and seethe, his fingers ached with the desire to curl themselves around hammer and file, he could not fight with himself. With a bitter heart he put on his work coat and shut himself up in an old blacksmith shop, which would be his workshop.

Then a cry went out from Ekeby across all of Värmland: "Kevenhüller has started to work!"

And they listened breathlessly for hammer strokes from the closed workshop, for the rasping of files and the moaning of bellows.

A new marvel would see the light of day. What might it be? Would he now teach us to walk on water or raise a ladder up to the Seven Sisters?

Nothing is impossible for such a man. With our own eyes we have seen him carried through the air on wings. We have seen his wagon careen through the streets. He has the wood nymph's gift: nothing is impossible for him.

One night, the first or second of October, he had the marvel ready. He came out of the workshop and had it in his hand. It was a wheel that would go round without stopping. As it turned, the spokes shone like fire, and heat and light came out of it. Kevenhüller had made a sun. When he came out of the workshop with it, the night became so light that sparrows started chirping and the clouds started to burn in morning redness.

It was the most magnificent invention. On earth there would no longer be darkness or cold. His head became dizzy when that thought came to him. The sun of the day would continue to go up and down, but when it vanished, thousands and again thousands of his fire wheels would flame across the countryside, and the air would quiver with heat as if on the hottest summer day. Then ripe harvests could be brought in under the starry midwinter sky, wild strawberries and lingonberries would adorn the forest hills year-round, ice would never bind the water.

Now that the invention was finished, it would create a new earth. His fire wheel would be a fur coat for the poor and the mine worker's sun. It would be propulsion for the factories, life to nature, a new, rich and happy existence for humankind. But at the same moment he knew well that these were all dreams, and that the wood nymph would never allow him to multiply his fire wheel. And in his wrath and desire for revenge, he thought he wanted to kill her, and then he hardly knew what he was doing anymore.

He went up to the manor house, and in the vestibule right under the staircase he set down the fire wheel. It was his intention that the house would catch fire and the troll burn inside.

Then he went back into his workshop and sat there silently, listening.

There was shouting and screaming in the yard. Now it began to be noticed that a great deed had been done.

Yes, run, scream, climb! Now she is burning inside anyway, the wood nymph, whom you bedded on silk!

Is she writhing in torment, is she fleeing the flames from room to room? Ah, how that green silk will catch fire, and how the flames will play in the flowing hair! Cheer up, flames, cheer up, catch her, set fire to her! Witches burn! Fear not her magic words, flames! Let her burn! There is someone who for her sake has had to burn throughout his life.

Bells rang, wagons rattled, hoses were dragged out, water passed from hand to hand up from the lake, and people stormed in from all the villages. There were screams and wailing and orders, there were roofs caving in, there was a terrible crackling and thunder of conflagration. But nothing disturbed Kevenhüller. He sat on the chopping block, wringing his hands.

Then he heard a crash as if the sky fallen in, and he rose up in jubilation. "Now it is done!" he exclaimed. "Now she cannot escape, now she is crushed under the beams or burned by the flames. Now it is done!"

And he thought about the glory and power of Ekeby, which must be sacrificed in order to get her out of the world. The magnificent halls, where so much joy had dwelled, the rooms that had resounded with the delight of memories, the tables that had groaned under delicious dishes, the valuable old furniture, silver, and porcelain, which could not be replaced . . .

And then he leaped up with a shriek. His fire wheel, his sun, the model on which everything depended, had he not placed it under the stairway in order to cause the conflagration?

Kevenhüller looked down at himself, petrified with horror.

"Am I crazy?" he said. "How could I do such a thing?"

At the same moment the well-closed door of the workshop was opened, and the green-clad woman stepped in.

The wood nymph stood there on the threshold, smiling and fair. Her green dress had no blemish or stain, no smoke was clinging to her flowing hair. She was the way he had seen her on the square in Karlstad in his youth, the wild animal tail trailing between her feet, and she had all the wildness and aroma of the forest with her.

"Now Ekeby is burning!" she said, laughing.

Kevenhüller lifted the sledge and intended to cast it onto her head, but then he saw that she was carrying his fire wheel in her hand.

"Look what I've rescued for you!" she said.

Kevenhüller threw himself on his knees before her. "You have wrecked my wagon, you have crushed my wings, and you have destroyed my life. Have mercy, have pity on me!"

She climbed up on the planing bench and sat there, still as young and mischievous as when he saw her for the first time on the square in Karlstad.

"I see that you know who I am," she said.

"I know you, and I have always known you," said the poor man. "You are genius. But let me free now! Take my gift from me! Take the miracle gifts from me! Let me be an ordinary person! Why do you persecute me? Why do you persecute me?"

"Madman!" said the wood nymph. "I have never wished you any ill. I gave you a great reward, but I can also take it from you, if it does not please you. But consider well! You are going to regret it."

"No, no," he exclaimed, "take the miracle powers from me!"

"First you have to destroy this," she said, throwing the fire wheel before him on the floor.

He did not hesitate. He swung the sledge over the glittering fire sun, which was only a wicked piece of wizardry, as it could not be used for the benefit of the many. The sparks flew around the room, shards and flames danced around him, and then his final marvel too was lying in splinters.

"Yes, now I take my gift from you," said the wood nymph.

As she stood in the door to leave and the glow of the conflagration outside streamed over her, he looked after her for the last time.

Lovelier than ever she seemed to him, and no longer malicious, only stern and proud.

"Madman!" she said. "Did I ever forbid you to let others emulate your work? What did I want, other than to protect the man of genius from the work of the craftsman?"

With that she left. Kevenhüller was insane for a few days. After that he became an ordinary person again.

But during his madness he had burned down Ekeby. No one was harmed, however. Nonetheless it was a great sorrow for the cavaliers, that the hospitable home where they had enjoyed so much good, should suffer so much damage during their time.

Ah, latter-day children, if it had been you or I who had met the wood nymph on the square in Karlstad! Don't you think that I would have gone into the forest and cried, "Wood nymph, wood nymph, it is I, Kevenhüller, Kevenhüller!" But who sees her nowadays? Who complains, in our time, about having received too much of her gifts?

CHAPTER 34

BROBY MARKET

On the first Friday in October begins the great Broby market, which lasts for eight days. It is autumn's great festival. It is preceded by butchering and baking in every cottage, the new winter clothes are ready to be worn for the first time, the holiday dishes, such as *klengås* and *ostkaka*, are on the table all day long, the liquor rations are doubled, work is set aside. It is a festival at every farm. Servants and laborers are given their wages then and hold long deliberations over what they should buy at the market. People from far away come wandering along the road in small flocks with knapsacks on their backs and staff in hand. Many drive their livestock to market. Small, stubborn young bulls and goats, standing still with forelegs firmly set in the ground, create a great nuisance for the owner and much delight for the observer. The guest rooms at the estates are filled with dear guests: news is exchanged, and prices of cattle and goods are discussed. The children dream about market gifts and market coins.

And on the first market day—what a throng is moving then up the Broby hills and across the wide market field! Stands are erected where merchants from the cities have spread out their wares, while Dalecarlians and *västgötar*, visitors from the neighboring provinces of Dalarna and Västergötland, have piled up their goods on endless rows of "counters" over which white cloth canopies flutter. There are plenty of tightrope walkers, barrel organs, and blind fiddle players there, likewise fortune-tellers, sweets sellers, and makeshift taverns. Beyond the stands, wooden and stone containers are lined up. Onions and horseradish, apples and pears are offered by gardeners from the large farms. Extensive squares of ground are taken up by brick red copper containers with shiny tin plating.

It is quite noticeable in the market activity, however, that distress prevails in Svartsjö and Bro and Lövvik and the other Lövsjö parishes: trade is poor at the stands and counters. Most activity is at the large livestock market, for many a person must sell both cow and horse to survive through the winter. There the wild, exciting horse trading is also going on.

The Broby market is a merry place. If only you have money for a few drams, then you can keep your courage up. And it is liquor alone that produces delight: when people from the desolate forest homes come down to the market field in billowing masses and hear the roar of the whole shrieking, laughing crowd, they become as if dizzy with happiness, made wild by the bustling life of the market.

Of course there is much trade among so many people, but that, however, is hardly the main thing. The most important is to bring a group of relatives and friends with you to the carts and treat them to mutton sausage, *klengås*, and liquor or convince the lass to take a hymnbook and silk cloth or go looking for market gifts for the little ones back home.

Everyone who did not have to stay at home to look after the house and livestock has come to this Broby market. There are cavaliers from Ekeby and forest farmers from Nygård, horse traders from Norway, Finns from the northern forests, drifters from the highway.

Sometimes the whole bustling sea gathers in a whirlpool that swings in dizzy rings around a central point. No one knows what is in the middle until a few policemen force their way through the crowd to put an end to a fistfight or raise up an overturned cart. And at the next moment there is a new throng of people around a merchant who is bickering with a quick-witted woman.

Along toward midday the great fistfight begins. The farmers have gotten the idea that the *västgötar* are using too short an ellmeasure, and noisy quarreling erupts around their counters, which then turns into violence. Everyone knows that for many, who in these times saw nothing but want and misery ahead of them, it was a joy to be able to strike out, indifferent to who or what was hit. And as soon as the strong and pugnacious see that a fistfight is under way, they rush in from all directions. The cavaliers intend to simply force their way in to make peace in their own way, and the Dalecarlians hurry in to help the *västgötar*.

Strong Måns from Fors is the one who is most eagerly involved in the game. He is drunk, and he is angry. Now he has pulled down a *västgöte* and started thrashing him, but at the man's cry for help his countrymen hurry over and try to force strong Måns to let go of their comrade. Then strong Måns rolls the bundles of cloth down from one of the counters and seizes the counter itself, which is an ell wide and eight ells long as well as joined together with thick planks, and starts swinging it as his weapon.

He is a dreadful man, strong Måns. He kicked out a wall in the jail in Filipstad, he could lift a boat out of the lake and carry it on his shoulders. Now you can believe that when he starts striking around him with the heavy counter, the whole crowd of people flee and the *västgötar* with them. But strong Måns is after them, striking around him with the heavy counter. For him it is no longer a question of friends or enemies: now he only wants someone to hit, since he has a weapon.

The people flee from him in desperation. Men and women scream and run. But how is flight possible for the women, several of whom have their children by the hand? Stands and carts are in their way, oxen and cows, becoming wild from the clamor, keep them from getting away.

A group of women has been squeezed into a corner between the stands, and toward them storms the giant. He thinks he sees a *västgöte* in the midst of the group! He raises the counter and lets it fall. In pallid, terrified anxiety the women receive the attack, huddling together under the killing blow.

But as the counter falls headlong down over them, its force is broken by the outstretched arms of a man. One man has not curled up, but instead risen above the mass, one man has of his own free will taken the blow to rescue the many. Women and children stand unharmed. One man has broken the violence of the blow, but now he too lies unconscious on the ground.

Strong Måns does not lift up his counter to storm farther. He has met the man's gaze, just as the counter crashed down on his head, and this has paralyzed him. He lets himself be bound and taken away without resistance.

But at a rapid pace the rumor runs around the market that strong Måns has killed Captain Lennart. It is said that he, who has been the friend of the people, has died to rescue women and defenseless children.

And it gets quiet over the wild fields where life has just been bustling at its wildest tempo: trade tapers off, fistfights cease, the banquets at the food bundles come to an end, the tightrope walker entices spectators in vain.

The people's friend is dead; the people are in mourning. In a silent throng they all stream toward the place where he has fallen. He lies outstretched on the ground, completely unconscious; no wound is apparent, but the skull itself seems to be flattened.

Some men move him carefully up onto the counter that the giant has dropped. They think they notice that he is still alive.

"Where should we carry him?" they ask one another.

"Home!" answers a gruff voice from the crowd.

Oh yes, you good men, carry him home! Lift him up on your shoulders and carry him home! He has been God's plaything, he has been driven like a feather before the breath of his spirit. Carry him home now!

The wounded head has rested on the hard cot in the prison, on the straw bale in the barn. Let it now come home and rest on a stuffed pillow! He has suffered undeserved shame and torment, he has been driven from his own door. He has been a wandering refugee, wandering God's ways wherever he found them, but the land he longed for was this home, whose entryway God has closed to him. Perhaps his home stands open for one who has died to rescue women and children.

Now he is not coming home as a convict, led by staggering drinking companions: he is escorted by a sorrowing people in whose huts he has stayed while he has helped their suffering. Carry him home now!

And they do so. Six men lift the counter upon which he is lying onto their shoulders and carry him away from the market field. Where they proceed the people move aside and stand quietly: the men bare their heads, the women curtsy, like they do in church when the name of God is mentioned. Many weep and dry their eyes, others begin to talk about what a man he has been, so good, so merry, so resourceful, and so God-fearing. It is also remarkable to see how as soon as one of the bearers gets tired, another quite slowly comes and brings his shoulder in under the counter.

So Captain Lennart also comes past the place where the cavaliers are standing.

"May as well go along and see to it that he makes it home properly," says Beerencreutz, leaving his place at the roadside to go along up to Helgesäter. His example is followed by many.

The market field becomes as if deserted: the people wander with Captain Lennart up to Helgesäter. Of course they have to see to it that he makes it home. All the necessities that should be bought can wait; as it is, the market presents for the little ones back home are forgotten, the purchase of a hymnbook is never completed, the silk cloth which has shone in the girl's eyes remains lying on the counter. Everyone must go and see to it that Captain Lennart comes home.

As the procession comes up to Helgesäter, it is silent and deserted there. Again the colonel's fists pound against the closed entrance door. All the servants are at the market, the captain's wife is home alone guarding the house. Now too it is she who opens.

And she asks, as she asked once before, "What do you want?"

Whereupon the colonel replies, as he has replied once before, "We are here with your husband."

She looks at him, as he stands stiff and secure as always. She looks at the bearers behind him, who are weeping, and at the whole mass of people behind them. She stands there on the staircase and looks into hundreds of crying eyes who anxiously stare up at her. Finally she looks at the man lying outstretched on the stretcher and presses her hand to her heart.

"This is his right face," she murmurs.

Without asking more she leans down, drawing aside a bolt, opens wide the door, and then goes ahead of the others into the bedroom.

The colonel and the captain's wife help draw out the double bed and shake out the bolster, and then Captain Lennart is again bedded on soft down and white linen.

"Is he alive?" she asks.

"Yes," replies the colonel.

"Is there hope?"

"No. There is nothing to be done."

It is silent a moment, then a sudden thought comes over her.

"Are they weeping for his sake, all of these people?"

"Yes."

"What has he done then?"

"The last thing he did was to let strong Måns kill him to rescue women and children from death."

She again sits silently a moment, thinking.

"What kind of face did he have, colonel, when he came home two months ago?"

The colonel gives a start. Now he understands, only now does he understand.

"Gösta had painted him of course!"

"So it was for the sake of a cavalier joke that I shut him out of his home. How will you answer for such a thing, colonel?"

Beerencreutz raised his broad shoulders.

"I have much to answer for."

"But I mean, this might be the worst thing all of you have done."

"And I have never walked a heavier path than the one today up here to Helgesäter. Besides, there are two others who are guilty in this."

"Who then?"

"Sintram is the one, the other is you yourself, cousin. You are a stern woman, cousin. I know that many have tried to talk with you about your husband."

"It is true," she replies.

Then she asks him to tell about the drinking party in Broby.

He tells all, as well as he can recall, and she listens silently. Captain Lennart is still lying unconscious on the bed. The room is full of weeping people; no one thinks about keeping this grieving group out. All doors stand open, all rooms, stairs, and vestibules are filled with silent, anxious people, far out in the yard they stand in dense flocks.

When the colonel has finished, the captain's wife raises her voice and says, "If there are any cavaliers in here, then I ask them to go away from here. It is difficult for me to see them, as I sit by my husband's deathbed."

Without another word the colonel then gets up and leaves. So do Gösta Berling and a few of the other cavaliers who have accompanied Captain Lennart. The people shyly make way for the small band of humiliated men.

When they are gone, the captain's wife says, "Do any of those who have seen my husband during this time want to tell me where he has stayed and what he has been doing?"

Then those inside begin to bear witness about Captain Lennart for his wife, who has misjudged him and in severity hardened her heart to him. Now the language of the old hymns sounds again. Men speak who have never read any book other than the Bible. In imagery from the Book of Job, with turns of phrase from the days of the patriarchs, they speak of God's pilgrim, who went around helping the people.

It goes on a long time before they have had their say. While the twilight comes and evening, they remain standing and speak: one after the other steps forth and tells about him for his wife, who has not wanted to hear his name mentioned.

There are those who could speak about how he found them on the sickbed and healed them. There are wild fighters that he has tamed. There are grieving people whom he has raised up, drunks he has forced into sobriety. Each and every one who has been in a state of unbearable distress had sent word to God's pilgrim, and he had been able to help, at least he had been able to awaken hope and faith.

The language of hymns resounds the whole evening in the sickroom.

Out in the yard stand the compact groups, waiting for the end. They know what is going on inside. What is being said out loud by the deathbed is whispered from man to man out there. Anyone who has something to say slowly forces his way forward. "This is someone who can testify," someone says, leaving him room. And they step forth from the darkness, give their testimony, and again sink down into the darkness.

"What is she saying now?" those standing outside ask when someone comes out. "What is she saying, the stern wife at Helgesäter?"

"She is radiant as a queen. She smiles like a bride. She has moved his armchair up to the bed and set the clothes on it that she herself has woven for him."

But then there is silence among all the people. No one says it, everyone knows it at once: "He is dying."

Captain Lennart opens his eyes, sees, and sees enough.

He sees his home, the people, his wife, the children, the clothes, and he smiles. But he has only woken up in order to die. He draws a rattling breath and gives up the ghost.

Then the stories are silenced, but a voice takes up a death hymn. Everyone joins in, and borne by hundreds of strong voices the song rises to the heights.

It is the earth's farewell to the fleeing soul.

CHAPTER 35

THE FOREST CROFT

It was many years before the year when the cavaliers ruled Ekeby.

The herd boy and herd girl played together in the forest, building houses from flat stones, picking cloudberries, and making alderwood horns. Both were born in the forest. The forest was their home and pasture. They lived there in peace with everything, as one lives in peace with servants and livestock.

The little ones counted lynx and fox as their farm dogs, the weasel was their cat, hare and squirrel were their large livestock, owls and grouse were in their birdcage, the spruce trees were their servants, and the young birches the guests at their banquets. They knew the hole where the viper lay coiled during its winter sleep, and when they bathed, they had seen the grass snake come swimming through the clear water, but they feared neither snake nor forest witch; that sort of thing was part of the forest, and it was their home. Nothing could frighten them there.

Deep in the forest was the croft where the boy lived. A hilly forest path led there, hills stood around it and hid the sun, bottomless marsh was nearby, emitting ice-cold fog year-round. Such a residence was hardly enticing for the plains people.

The herd boy and herd girl would one day become a couple, live together in the forest croft, and survive by the labor of their hands. But before they were married, the misfortune of war passed over the land, and the boy enlisted. He came home without wounds or injured limb, but he had been marked for life by that journey. He had observed far too much of the world's evil and the cruel treatment of people by other people. He was no longer in a position to see what was good.

At first no one saw a change in him. He went to the minister with his childhood sweetheart and had the banns published. The forest croft above Ekeby became their home, as they had agreed long ago, but in that home no harmony prevailed.

The wife saw the husband as a stranger. Ever since he had come back from the war, she could not recognize him. He laughed bitterly and spoke little. She was afraid of him.

He caused no harm or damage, and he was a diligent worker. Yet he was not well liked, for he believed the worst about everyone. He himself felt like a despised stranger. Now the animals of the forest were his enemies. The hill that concealed the sun and the marsh that emitted fog were his adversaries. The forest is a horrid residence for anyone who bears evil thoughts.

Anyone who wishes to live in the wilderness should acquire sweet memories! Otherwise he will see only murder and oppression among plants and animals, as he had previously seen among people. He expects the worst from everything he encounters.

Jan Hök, the soldier, could not himself interpret what had broken within him, but he noticed that nothing went well for him. Home offered little peace. His sons, who were growing up there, became strong, but wild. They were hardened and courageous men, but they also lived in conflict with everyone.

In her sorrow his wife was drawn to exploring the secrets of the wilderness. In marsh and thicket she sought health-giving herbs. She pondered over beings of the underworld, and she knew what offerings pleased them. She could cure sickness and give good advice to those who had afflictions from lovemaking. She won a reputation as skilled in magic and was shunned, although she was very useful to people.

One time the wife decided to speak with the man about his worries.

"Ever since you went to war," she said, "you have been a different person. What did they do to you there?"

Then he leaped up and was close to striking her, and the same thing happened every time she talked about the war. He went into an insane rage then. He could not bear to hear the word "war" spoken by anyone, and soon it became known that he could not bear talk of it. So people were on their guard about that topic of conversation.

But none of his war comrades could say that he had done more evil than others. He had fought like a good soldier. It was simply all the terrible things he had seen that frightened him so that later he could see nothing but the bad. He attributed all his grief to the war. He thought that all of nature hated him because he had taken part in such things. Those who know better might console themselves with the fact that they fought for fatherland and glory. What did he know of such things? He knew only that everything hated him because he had shed blood and caused harm.

By that time, when the majoress was driven from Ekeby, he was living alone in his cabin. His wife was dead, and his sons were gone. At market times, however, the forest croft was full of guests. The black-haired, dark-skinned gypsies stayed there. They feel most at home with someone most people avoid. Small, long-haired horses then climbed up the forest path, pulling carts loaded with tin-plating tools, with children and bundles of rags. Women, prematurely aged, with features swollen from smoking and drinking, and men with pallid, sharp faces and sinewy bodies followed the carts. When the gypsies came to the forest croft, things got lively there. They brought liquor and card playing and noisy laughing and talking with them. They could tell stories about thefts and horse trading and bloody fistfights.

On Friday Broby market began, and then Captain Lennart was killed. Strong Måns, who gave the deathblow, was the son of the old man in the forest croft. Therefore, when on Sunday afternoon the gypsies sat together up there, they handed the flask of liquor to old Jan Hök more often than usual and spoke with him about prison life and prisoners' fare and trials, for they had often tried such things.

The old man sat on the chopping block in the chimney corner, hardly speaking. His large, lackluster eyes stared out over the wild band that filled the room. Twilight had come, but the wood fire gave light. It illuminated rags, misery, and bitter distress.

Then the door opened very slowly, and in came two women. It was young Countess Elisabet, followed by the Broby minister's daughter. She seemed strange to the old man when, charming and radiant in gentle beauty, she entered the fire's circle of light. She told those within that Gösta Berling had not been seen at Ekeby since Captain Lennart died. She and her servant had been in the forest looking for him the whole afternoon. Now she saw that there were men in here who were well traveled and knew all paths. Had they seen him? She had come in to rest and ask whether they had seen him.

It was a useless question. None of them had seen him.

They set out a chair for her. She sank down in it and sat quietly awhile. The clamor in the cabin had been muted. Everyone looked at her and wondered about her. Then she became frightened by the silence, sat up, and sought an indifferent matter to talk about.

She turned to the old man in the corner. "I seem to have heard that you have been a soldier, old father," she said. "Tell about something from the war!"

The silence became even more paralyzing. The old man sat as if he hadn't heard.

"It would amuse me greatly to hear a story about the war from someone who has been there himself," the countess continued, but she stopped speaking abruptly, for the Broby minister's daughter was shaking her head at her. She must have said something inappropriate. All of the assembled people were looking at her, as if she had violated the simplest rule of appropriateness. Suddenly a gypsy wife raised her sharp voice and asked, "She must be the one who has been a countess at Borg."

"That's the one."

"That's a different thing than running around the forest after the crazy minister. Ugh, what a trade!"

The countess got up and said farewell. She had rested enough. The woman who had spoken followed her out through the door.

"You understand, countess," she said, "I had to say something, for you just can't talk with the old man about the war. He can't stand to hear the word. I meant well, I did."

Countess Elisabet hurried away, but she soon stopped. She saw the threatening forest, the concealing hill, and the steaming bog. It must have been horrid living here for someone whose mind was filled with bad memories. She felt compassion for the old man sitting in there with the dark gypsies as company.

"Miss Anna Lisa," she said, "let us turn around! They were good to us in there, but I behaved badly. I want to talk with the old man about happier things."

And happy at having found someone to console, she went back into the cabin.

"It is the case," she said, "that I think that Gösta Berling is here in the forest, considering taking his own life. So it is important that he is found soon and kept from doing that. I and Miss Anna Lisa thought we saw him at times, but then he disappeared from us. He is keeping in the area of the hill where the Nygård girl was killed. I just happened to think that I don't need to go all the way down to Ekeby to get help. Here are many strong men who could easily capture him."

"Get on your way, fellows!" exclaimed the gypsy woman. "When the countess doesn't think she's too good to ask forest people for a favor, you must go at once."

The men got up at once and went to search.

Old Jan Hök sat quietly, staring ahead of him with a lackluster gaze. Terrifyingly gloomy and hard he sat there. The young woman did not find a word to say to him. Then she saw that a child was lying sick on a sheaf of straw, and that a woman had a sore hand. At once she started to see to the sick. She was soon good friends with the chattering woman and had the smallest children shown to her.

In an hour the men came back. They led Gösta Berling, bound, into the cabin. They set him down on the floor in front of the fireplace. His clothes were torn and dirty, facial features emaciated, and his eyes wild. His journey had been terrible during those days: he had lain on the damp ground, he had dug his hands and face into the mossy earth, dragged himself over flat rock, squeezed through the densest thickets. He had not gone with the men voluntarily, but they overpowered and bound him.

When his wife saw him like that, she became angry. She did not release his bound limbs, but left him lying on the floor. She turned from him with contempt.

"The way you look!"

"I had not intended to come before your eyes again," he replied.

"Am I not your wife then? Is it not my right to expect that you come to me with your sorrows? For these two days I have waited for you in bitter anxiety."

"I caused Captain Lennart's misfortune. How could I dare show myself to you? How could I?"

"You were seldom afraid, Gösta."

"The only favor I can do you, Elisabet, is to free you from me."

Inexpressible contempt flared under her knitted eyebrows down to him.

"You would make me into the wife of a suicide!"

His facial features were contorted.

"Elisabet, let us go out in the silent forest and talk together!"

"Why shouldn't these people hear us?" she exclaimed, speaking in shrill tones. "Are we better than any of them? Have any of them caused more sorrow and damage than we have? They are children of the forest and the highway, they are hated by everyone. Let them hear how sin and sorrow also follow the master of Ekeby, Gösta Berling, beloved by all! Do you think your wife thinks you are better than any of them—or do you?"

He rose courageously on his elbow and looked at her with heated defiance. "I am not as wretched as you think."

Then she heard the story of those two days. The first day Gösta Berling wandered around in the forest, pursued by pangs of conscience. He could not endure meeting the gaze of a person. But he was not thinking about dying. He intended to leave for a distant land. On Sunday, however, he came down from the heights and went up to Bro church. Once again he wanted to see the people: the poor, hungry people of the Lövsjö district, whom he had dreamed of serving when he was sitting by the Broby minister's pile of shame, and whom he had come to love when he had seen them wander forth in the night with the dead Nygård girl.

The service had begun, as he arrived at the church. He crept up into the balcony and looked down at the people. Cruel torment seized him then. He wanted to speak to them, console them in their poverty and hopelessness. If he had simply been able to speak in God's house, as hopeless as he was, he would have had words of hope and salvation for all.

Then he left the church, went into the sacristy, and wrote the proclamation, about which his wife already knew. He had promised that work would be resumed at Ekeby and seed grain distributed there to those most in need. He hoped that his wife and the cavaliers would fulfill his promises when he was gone.

As he came out, he saw a casket standing before the parish hall. It was rough, hewn in haste, but adorned with black crepe and wreaths of lingonberry branches. He realized that it was Captain Lennart's. The people must have asked the captain's wife to hasten the burial, so that the large number of market visitors could attend the burial.

He was looking at the casket when a heavy hand was placed on his shoulder. Sintram had come over to him.

"Gösta," he said, "if you want to play a real prank on someone, then lie down and die! There is nothing shrewder than dying, nothing that so fools an honorable man who suspects nothing bad. Lie down and die, I say!"

Appalled, Gösta listened to what the malevolent one was saying. He was complaining about the foiling of well-laid plans. He wanted to see deserted settlements by the shore of Löven. Therefore he had made the cavaliers the masters of the area, therefore he had let the Broby minister impoverish the people, therefore he had called forth drought and starvation. The decisive blow was to have been made at Broby market. Incited by misfortunes, the people would abandon themselves to murder and theft. Then legal proceedings would have impoverished them. Starvation, disorder, and all types of misfortune would have raged. Finally the countryside would have become so wicked and hateful that no one could live there, and all this would have been the work of Sintram. This would have been his pride and joy, for he was evil. He loved desolate regions and unbroken ground. But this man, who had the wit to die at the right moment, had ruined everything for him.

Then Gösta asked him to what end all this would have served.

"It would have pleased me, Gösta, for I am evil. I am the killer bear on the fell, I am the snowstorm on the plain, I like to murder and persecute. Away, I say, away with humankind and the works of humankind! I don't like them. I may let them run between my claws and caper about—that might be amusing too for a while—but now I am satiated with play, Gösta, now I want to strike out, now I want to kill and destroy."

He was insane, completely insane. A long time ago he had started with these hellish tricks, and now evil had the upper hand, now he believed himself to be a spirit from the abyss. Now he had nurtured and tended the evil within himself so that it had taken dominion over his soul. So can malevolence make people crazy, just like love and brooding.

He was raging, the malevolent mill owner, and in his wrath he started to tug at the wreaths and crepe on the casket, but then Gösta Berling shouted, "Don't touch the casket!"

"See, see, see, mustn't I touch it? Yes, I will throw my friend Lennart on the ground and trample his wreaths. Don't you see what he's done to me? Don't you see in what a fine, gray calash I come riding?"

And Gösta Berling then saw that a pair of prisoners' carts with sheriff and district officials stood waiting outside the churchyard wall.

"See, see, see, shouldn't I send the captain's wife at Helgesäter a thank-you, because yesterday she sat down to read old papers to find evidence against me in that gunpowder case, you know? Shouldn't I let her know that it would be better for her to keep busy with brewing and baking than to send the sheriff and district officials after me? Shouldn't I have something for the tears I've cried to persuade Scharling to let me come here and say a prayer by my good friend's casket?"

And he again started tugging on the crepe.

Then Gösta Berling stood close beside him and seized his arms.

"I would give anything to keep you from touching the casket!" he said.

"Do what you want!" said the lunatic. "Shout if you want! I'll still manage something before the sheriff comes. Fight with me, if that's what you want! That will be a happy sight here on the church green. Let's fight among wreaths and shrouds!"

"I will purchase peace for the dead man at whatever price, Sintram. Take my life, take everything!"

"You promise a lot, my boy!"

"You can test me."

"Well, so kill yourself then!"

"That I can do, but first the casket must be securely underground."

So it was. Sintram took an oath from Gösta that he would not be alive twelve hours after Captain Lennart had been buried. "So I know that you can never become a good man," he said.

This was easy to promise for Gösta Berling. He was happy to be able to give his wife freedom. Pangs of conscience had driven him dead tired. The only thing that appalled him was that he had promised the majoress not to die as long as the Broby minister's daughter was a servant at Ekeby. But Sintram said that she could not be counted as a servant now, since she had inherited her father's riches. Gösta objected that the Broby minister had hidden his goods so well that no one had been able to find his treasures. Then Sintram smiled and said that they were hidden among the dove nests in Broby church steeple. With that he left. After that Gösta went up to the forest again. It seemed best to him to die at the place where the Nygård girl had been killed. Up there he had wandered the whole afternoon. He had seen his wife in the forest, which was why he had not been able to kill himself at once.

This he told his wife, as he lay bound on the floor in the forest croft.

"Oh," she said mournfully, when he had finished, "how well I recognize this! Heroic gestures, heroic ostentation! Always ready to stick your hands in the fire, Gösta, always ready to throw yourself away! How great such things once seemed to me! How I now prize calm and self-control! What good did you do the dead man with such a promise? What of it if Sintram had been able to turn over the casket and tear off the crepe! It would have been raised up again, there would have been new crepe, new wreaths. If you had placed your hand on the good man's cas-

ket, there before Sintram's eyes, and sworn to live to help these
poor people whom he wanted to destroy, now that I would have
prized. If you had thought, when you saw the people in the church,
'I want to help them, I myself will use all my powers to help
them,' and not placed this burden on your weak wife and on old
men with failing powers, then I would have prized that too."

Gösta Berling remained silent awhile.

"We cavaliers are not free men," he said finally. "We have
promised one another to live for happiness and only for happiness. Woe to us all, if one of us fails!"

"Woe to you," said the countess with indignation, "that you
should be the most cowardly among the cavaliers and last in improvement of any of them! Yesterday afternoon they sat, all eleven
of them, in the cavaliers' wing, and they were gloomy. You were
gone, Captain Lennart was gone, the luster and honor of Ekeby
was gone. They left the toddy tray untouched, they would not
show themselves to me. Then Miss Anna Lisa, who is standing
here, went up to them. You know that she is a zealous little
woman, who has fought for years to the point of desperation
against negligence and waste.

"'Today I have once again been at home and sought dear Father's money,' she said to the cavaliers, 'but I have not found a
thing. All promissory notes are crossed out, and drawers and
cupboards are empty.'

"'It's too bad for you, Miss Anna Lisa,' thought Beerencreutz.

"'When the majoress left Ekeby,' continued the Broby minister's daughter, 'she asked me to look after her house. And if I
had found dear Father's money now, then I would have built up
Ekeby. But as I haven't found anything there at home, I took Father's pile of shame with me, for great shame awaits me when
my mistress comes back and asks me what I've done with Ekeby.'

"'Don't take it so hard, Miss Anna Lisa, this is not your fault!'
Beerencreutz said again.

"'But I have not brought the pile of shame for me alone,' said
the Broby minister's daughter. 'I also brought it on account of
the cavaliers. Welcome, dear gentlemen! Dear Father is probably not the only one who has caused shame and harm in this
world.'

"And she went from one to the other of them and set down some of the dry sticks for each of them. Some swore, but most of them let her have her way. Finally Beerencreutz said with the calm of a lofty gentleman, 'This is good. We should thank the young lady. The young lady may go now.'

"When she was gone, he slammed his clenched fist on the table so that the glasses jumped.

"'From this hour,' he said, 'absolutely sober! Liquor will not bring such a thing upon me again!' With that he got up and went out.

"By and by they followed him, all of the others. Do you know where they went, Gösta? Yes, down to the river, to the point where Ekeby mill and smithy stood, and there they started to work. They started to move logs and stones and clear the area. The old men have had a difficult time. Several of them are in mourning. Now they can no longer endure the dishonor of having destroyed Ekeby. I know that you cavaliers are ashamed to work, but now the others have taken this shame upon themselves. Even more, Gösta, they intend to send Miss Anna Lisa up to the majoress to fetch her. But you, what are you doing?"

He still found something to answer her.

"What do you demand of me, a defrocked minister? Rejected am I of humankind, hateful to God."

"I too have been in Broby church today, Gösta. I have a greeting to you from two women. 'Tell Gösta,' said Marianne Sinclaire, 'that a woman does not want to be ashamed of the one she has loved!' 'Tell Gösta,' said Anna Stjärnhök, 'that I'm doing well now! I govern my estates myself. People say of me that I am becoming another majoress. I don't think about love, only about work. At Berga too they have overcome the initial bitterness of sorrow. But we all grieve over Gösta. We believe in him and pray to God for him—but when, when will he become a man?'"

"Do you see then, are you rejected by people?" continued the countess. "You have received too much love, that is your misfortune. Women and men have loved you. If only you joked and laughed, if only you sang and played, they have forgiven you everything. What it has pleased you to do has been fine with them. And you dare call yourself a reject! Or are you hateful to God? Why didn't you stay and see Captain Lennart's burial?

"As he died on a market day, his reputation was spread far around. After the church service thousands of people came up to the church. The entire churchyard and wall and the fields around them were covered with people. The funeral procession lined up in front of the parish hall. They were only waiting for the old dean. He was sick and did not preach. But he promised to come to Captain Lennart's burial. And then he came, walking with lowered head and dreaming his own dreams, as he does now in his old age, and placed himself at the end of the procession. He noticed nothing unusual. The old man had walked in many funeral processions. He walked forth on the familiar road and did not look up. He read the prayers and threw earth on the casket and still noticed nothing. But then the organist started a hymn. I did not dare believe that his rough voice, which otherwise always used to sing alone, could waken the dean out of his dreams.

"But the organist did not sing alone. Hundreds of voices and hundreds more joined in. Men, women, and children sang. Then the dean awoke from his dreams. He passed his hands over his eyes and stepped up onto the pile of earth to see. Never had he seen such a crowd of mourners. The men had on their old, worn-out funeral hats. The women had the white aprons with the broad hems. All were singing, all had tears in their eyes—all were in mourning.

"Then the old dean started to tremble and become anxious. What should he say to these people, who were in mourning? It was necessary that he say a word of consolation for them.

"When the song was over, he stretched his arms out over the people.

"'I see that the people are in mourning,' he said, 'and sorrow is heavier to bear for anyone who will walk the paths of earth a long time, than for me who will soon depart this life.'

"He fell silent, dismayed. His voice was too weak, and he hesitated in his choice of words.

"But soon he began anew. His voice had regained the force of youth, and his eyes radiated.

"He gave a magnificent talk for us, Gösta. First he told as much as he knew about God's pilgrim. Then he reminded us that no exterior luster or great ability had made this man as honored as he now was, but simply the fact that he had always gone the ways of God. And now he asked us, for the sake of God and Christ, to do likewise. Each one should love the other and be his help. Each one should believe good about the other. Each one should act like this good Captain Lennart, for to do so no great gifts are required, simply a pious heart. And he explained to us everything that had happened this year. He said that it was a preparation for the time of love and happiness that was now sure to come. This year he had often seen human goodness burst forth in scattered rays. Now it would emerge as a whole, shining sun.

"And to all of us, it was as if we had heard a prophet speak. All wanted to love one another, all wanted to be good.

"He raised his eyes and hands and pronounced peace upon the region. 'In God's name,' he said, 'may worry cease! May peace dwell in your hearts and in all of nature! May the dead things and the animals and the plants feel calm and cease doing harm!'

"And it was as if a sacred peace settled over the area. It was as if the heights beamed and the valleys smiled and the autumn mists were clad in rose hue.

"Then he called on a helper for the people. 'Someone will come,' he said. 'It is not God's will that you should disappear. God will awaken someone who will feed the hungry and lead you on His paths.'

"Then we all thought of you, Gösta. We knew that the dean was talking about you. The people who had heard your announcement went home, talking about you. And you were here in the forest and wanted to die! The people expect you, Gösta. Round about in the huts they are saying that as the mad minister at Ekeby will help them now, then everything will be fine. You are their hero, Gösta. You are a hero to all of them.

"Yes, Gösta, it is certain that the old man was talking about you, and this should entice you to live. But I, Gösta, who am your wife, I say to you that you should simply go and do your duty. You must not dream of being sent by God. Each one should be that, you know. You must work without heroic deeds, you must not shine and astonish, you must arrange that your name does not sound too often on people's lips. Consider well, however, before you take back your word to Sintram! You have now acquired a kind of right to die for yourself, and life ought not to offer much delight from here on out. For a time it was my wish to go home to the south, Gösta. To me, debt laden, it seemed too much happiness to be your wife and accompany you through life. But now I will stay here. If you dare to live, I will stay. But do not expect any happiness from it! I will force you to wander the way of heavy duties. Never expect a word of happiness and hope from me! All the sorrow and misfortune that we both have caused, I will place as a watchman at our hearth. Can a heart that has suffered so like mine love anymore? Tearless and joyless I will wander beside you. Consider well, Gösta, before you choose to live! It is the way of penance we must wander."

She did not expect a reply. She waved to the Broby minister's daughter and left. When she came into the forest, she began to weep bitterly and wept until she reached Ekeby. Once there, she remembered that she had forgotten to talk about happier things than war with Jan Hök, the soldier.

In the forest croft all was quiet, when she was gone.

"Praise and glory be to the Lord God!" the old soldier suddenly said.

They looked at him. He had stood up and was looking around himself eagerly.

"Evil, all has been evil," he said. "All I have seen, since I had my eyes opened, has been evil. Evil men, evil women! Hate and anger in forest and field! But she is good. A good human being has stood in my home. When I am sitting here alone, I will remember her. She will be with me on the forest path."

He leaned down over Gösta, loosened his bonds, and helped him up. Then he solemnly took his hand.

"Hateful to God," he said and nodded, "that's just the matter. But now you are no longer like that, and neither am I, since she has been in my home. She is good."

The next day old Jan Hök came to Sheriff Scharling. "I want to bear my cross," he said. "I have been a bad man, therefore I got bad sons." And he asked to go to jail instead of his son, but of course that could not happen.

The choicest of old stories is the one about how he followed his son, walking alongside the prisoners' cart, how he slept outside his prison, how he did not abandon him, until he had suffered his punishment. That story will no doubt also find its teller.

CHAPTER 36

MARGARETA CELSING

A few days before Christmas the majoress traveled down to the Lövsjö district, but she did not come to Ekeby until Christmas Eve. She was sick during the entire journey. She had pneumonia and high fever, yet no one had ever seen her happier or heard more kindhearted words from her.

The Broby minister's daughter, who had been with her at the ironworks in the Älvdal forests ever since the month of October, sat by her side in the sleigh, hoping to hasten the journey, but she could not keep the old woman from stopping the horses and calling every traveler up to the sleigh to ask for news.

"How are things going for you down here in Lövsjö?" asked the majoress.

"It's going well for us," she would then get in reply. "Better times are coming. The mad minister down there at Ekeby and his wife are helping all of us."

"Good times have come," replied another. "Sintram is gone. The Ekeby cavaliers are working. The Broby minister's money was found in Bro church steeple. There's so much money that the honor and power of Ekeby can be restored with them. There's also enough to get bread for the hungry."

"Our old dean has awakened to new life and new energy," said a third. "Every Sunday he talks with us about the coming of the kingdom of God. Who would want to sin anymore? The reign of goodness is approaching."

And the majoress rode slowly along, asking whomever she encountered, "How are things going for you? Aren't you suffering want here?"

And the heat of fever and the jabbing pain in her chest were quieted when they answered her, "There are two good, rich women here, Marianne Sinclaire and Anna Stjärnhök. They help Gösta Berling by going from house to house and seeing to it that no one needs to starve. And nowadays no grain is being thrown into the distilling kettle."

It was as if the majoress had been sitting there in the sleigh, holding a long church service. She had come to a holy land. She saw old, furrowed faces brighten as they spoke about the times that had arrived. The sick forgot their pains in order to praise the day of happiness.

"We all want to be like good Captain Lennart," they said. "We all want to be good. We want to believe good of everyone. We do not want to harm anyone. This kind of thing will hasten the coming of the kingdom of God."

She found them all seized by the same spirit. At the manor houses free feedings were held for those most in need. Anyone who had a job to perform was now having it done, and operations were in full swing at all of the majoress's ironworks.

She had never felt healthier than when she sat there, letting the cold air stream into her aching chest. She could not pass by any farm without stopping and asking.

"Now all is well," said the farm folk. "There was great distress here, but the good gentlemen from Ekeby are helping us. The majoress will marvel at everything that has been done there. Now the mill is almost finished, and the smithy is in operation, and the burned house is framed to the roof ridge."

It was distress and the heart-stirring events that had transformed them all. Ah, it would only last a short time! But it was still good to return to a land where the one served the other, and where everyone wanted to do good. The majoress felt that she could forgive the cavaliers, and for that she thanked God.

"Anna Lisa," she said, "I, an old person, sit here thinking that I am already traveling into the heaven of the blessed."

When she finally came up to Ekeby and the cavaliers hurried to help her out of the sleigh, they could scarcely recognize her, for she was just as good and gentle as their own young countess. The older ones, who had seen her when she was young, whispered to each other, "It's not the majoress at Ekeby, it is Margareta Celsing who is coming back."

Great was the joy of the cavaliers at seeing her arrive so good and so free from all thoughts of revenge, but soon this changed to sorrow when they found how ill she was. She must be carried at once into the guest room in the office wing and be put to bed. But on the threshold she turned and spoke to them.

"It has been God's storm," she said, "God's storm. I know now that everything has been for the best."

With that the door to the sickroom was closed, and they were not allowed to see her anymore.

Yet there is so much to say to anyone who is about to die. The words crowd the tongue, when you know that in the next room there is someone whose ear will soon be closed for all time. "Ah, my friend, my friend," you want to say, "can you forgive? Can you believe that I have loved you, despite everything? Yet how could it be that I should cause so much sorrow while we wandered here together? Ah, my friend, thanks for all the joy you have granted me!"

This is what you want to say, and so much, much more.

But the majoress had a burning fever, and the voice of the cavaliers could not reach her. Would she never find out how they had labored, how they had taken up her work, how they had saved the honor and brilliance of Ekeby? Would she never find out?

Shortly thereafter the cavaliers went down to the smithy. There all work had stopped, but they were throwing fresh charcoal and new pig iron into the furnace and preparing to smelt. They did not call the smiths, who had gone home to celebrate Christmas, but instead worked at the hearth themselves. If only the majoress could live until the hammer started working, then they would state their case to her.

It became evening, and it became night during the work. Several of them thought how peculiar it was that they had now come to celebrate Christmas night in the smithy.

The versatile Kevenhüller, who had been the master builder for the smithy and mill during this busy time, and Kristian Bergh, the strong captain, stood at the hearth and tended the smelting. Gösta and Julius carried coal. Of the others, several sat at the anvil under the upraised hammer, and others were sitting on coal carts and piles of pig iron. Lövenborg, the old mystic, was speaking with uncle Eberhard, the philosopher, who sat next to him on the anvil.

"Tonight Sintram will die," he said.

"Why just tonight?" asked Eberhard.

"Brother, you know perfectly well that last year we made a bet. Now we have done nothing that has not been like a cavalier, and therefore he has lost."

"If you believe in such things, brother, then you also know full well that we have done many things that have not been like cavaliers. For one thing, we did not help the majoress, for another we started working, for a third it was not really right that Gösta Berling didn't kill himself when he had promised to do it."

"I've thought about that too," Lövenborg stated, "but I think, brother, that you do not understand the matter correctly. It was forbidden to us to act with the thought of personal, narrow-minded advantage, but not to act such as love or honor or our eternal salvation would require. I believe that Sintram has lost."

"You may be right, brother."

"I tell you, brother, I know it. I have heard his sleigh bells the entire evening, but these are not real sleigh bells. Soon he'll be here."

And the little old man sat staring ahead toward the smithy door, which stood open, and toward the patch of blue sky set with sparse stars that was visible through it.

After a while he got up.

"Do you see him, brother?" he whispered. "There he comes now, stealing in. Don't you see him in the door opening, brother?"

"I see nothing," replied uncle Eberhard. "You're sleepy, brother, that's the whole thing."

"I saw him so clearly against the light sky. He had his long wolf-skin fur and fur cap on. Now he's inside the darkness there, and I can't see him. Look, now he's over by the furnace! He's standing close beside Kristian Bergh, but Kristian of course doesn't see him. Now he's leaning forward and throwing something into the fire. Oh, how evil he looks! Watch out, friends, watch out!"

As he said this, a puff of flame shot out of the furnace, covering the smiths and their assistants with cinders and sparks. There was no damage, however.

"He wants vengeance," whispered Lövenborg.

"You're crazy, brother!" exclaimed Eberhard. "You ought to have had enough of such things."

"One may well think and wish such things, but it hardly helps. Don't you see, brother, how he is standing there at the post, leering at us? But truly, I believe he's loosening the hammer!"

He leaped up, pulling Eberhard with him. The very next moment the hammer struck thundering against the anvil. It was only a clamp that had come loose, but Eberhard and Lövenborg had narrowly escaped death.

"Look, brother, he has no power over us!" said Lövenborg triumphantly. "But it appears that he wants revenge."

And he called Gösta Berling to him.

"Go up to the women, Gösta! Perhaps he is showing himself to them too. They are not as accustomed as I am to seeing such things. They might be afraid. And be on your guard, Gösta, for he has much rancor toward you, and perhaps he has power over you because of that promise. Perhaps he does."

Later it was heard that Lövenborg was right, and that Sintram had died on Christmas night. Some said that he hanged himself in the prison. Others believed that the servants of justice had him killed in secret, for the trial seemed to be going well for him, and of course it would not do to let him loose on the people in Lövsjö again. There were still others who believed that a dark gentleman had come riding in a black wagon, pulled by black horses, and taken him away from the prison. And Lövenborg was not the only one who saw him during Christmas night. He was seen at Fors too and in Ulrika Dillner's dreams. Many told about how he had shown himself to them, until Ulrika Dillner moved his corpse to Bro cemetery. She also had the wicked servants from Fors driven away and established a good regime there. After that there was no more haunting.

It is said that before Gösta Berling made it up to the manor house, a stranger came to the office wing and there delivered a letter to the majoress. No one knew the courier, but the letter was brought in and set on the table beside the sick woman. Immediately thereafter she unexpectedly got better: the fever was stilled, the pains receded, and she was in a condition to read the document.

The old people readily believed that this improvement was due to the influence of dark powers. Sintram and his friends might profit from the majoress having read this letter.

It was a document written in blood on black paper. The cavaliers would no doubt have recognized it. It was authored the previous Christmas night in the smithy at Ekeby.

And the majoress was lying there now, reading that because she had been a witch and sent cavalier souls to hell, she was sentenced to lose Ekeby. She read this and other, similar folly. She inspected the date and signatures and found the following notation alongside Gösta's name: "Because the majoress has made use of my weakness to lure me away from honorable labor and retain me as a cavalier at Ekeby, because she has made me Ebba Dohna's murderer by revealing to her that I was a defrocked minister, I am signing this."

The majoress slowly folded up the paper and placed it in its cover. Then she quietly pondered what she had found out. She realized with bitter pain that this was how people thought of her. She was a witch and a sorceress to all those she had served, to whom she had given labor and bread. This was her reward, such would be her obituary. They could not believe better of an adulteress.

But what did she care about these ignorant people? In any event, they had not been close to her. But these poor cavaliers, who had lived off her grace and knew her well, even they believed it, or pretended to believe it to have a pretext to seize Ekeby. Her thoughts were racing. Wild wrath and thirst for revenge flared in her fever-hot brain. She had the Broby minister's daughter, who along with Countess Elisabet was watching over her, send word to Högfors for the manager and the inspector. She wanted to make her will.

Again she lay thinking. Her eyebrows were knitted together, her facial features were gruesomely contorted in pain.

"You are very sick, majoress," the countess said slowly.

"That I am, sicker than ever before."

There was silence again, but then the majoress spoke in a hard, gruff voice.

"It is strange to think that you too, countess, whom everyone loves, should be an adulteress."

The young woman gave a start.

"Yes, if not in action, then still in thought and desire, and that makes no difference."

"I know that, majoress."

"And yet you are happy now, countess. You can have your beloved without sin. The dark ghost will not stand between you, when you meet. You can belong to one another before the world, love one another in the light of day, go side by side through life."

"Oh, majoress, majoress!"

"How can you dare stay with him, countess?" the old woman cried out with increasing intensity. "Do penance, do penance in time! Go home to your father and mother, before they come and curse you! Do you dare count Gösta Berling as your spouse? Leave him! I will give him Ekeby. I will give him power and splendor. Do you dare share it with him? Do you dare receive happiness and honor? I dared it. Do you recall what happened to me? Do you remember the Christmas dinner at Ekeby? Do you remember the jail at the sheriff's?"

"Oh, majoress, we debtors go here side by side without happiness. I am here to keep watch so that no happiness will reside at our hearth. Don't you think I long for home, majoress? Oh, bitterly I long for the protection and support of home, but I will never again enjoy it. Here I will live in fear and trembling, knowing that everything I do leads to sin and sorrow, knowing that if I help one, I overturn another. Too weak and foolish for life here, and yet forced to live it, bound by an eternal penance."

"We fool our hearts with such thoughts!" exclaimed the majoress. "But this is weakness. You don't want to leave him, that is the only reason."

Before the countess had time to answer, Gösta Berling came into the room.

"Come here, Gösta!" the majoress said at once, and her voice became even sharper and harder. "Come here, you whom everyone in Lövsjö is praising! Come, you, who will be known to posterity as the rescuer of the people! You shall now hear how things have gone for your old majoress, whom you let go around the countryside despised and abandoned.

"First I will tell you what happened last spring, when I came home to my mother, for you ought to know the end of that story.

"In the month of March I came wandering up to the ironworks in the Älvdal forests, Gösta. I looked not much better than a beggar hag then. I was told when I arrived that my mother was in the dairy room. Then I went in there and stood silently by the door a long time. Round about the room were long shelves, and on them were shiny copper pans filled with milk. And my mother, who was over ninety years of age, took down pan after pan and skimmed off the cream. She was healthy enough, the old woman, but I noticed how much effort it took for her to reach the pans. I did not know if she had seen me, but in a while she spoke to me in a peculiar, shrill voice.

"'So things have gone for you just as I knew they would!' she said. I wanted to speak and ask her to forgive me, but it was not worth the effort. She did not hear a word of it: she was stone-deaf. But after a while she spoke again. 'You can come and help me,' she said.

"Then I went over and skimmed the milk. I took down the pans in the right order and put everything in its place and dipped just right with the ladle, and she was satisfied. She had not been able to entrust the milk skimming to any servant, but I knew from long before how she wanted it done.

"'Now you must take on this work,' she said. And with that I knew that she had forgiven me.

"And then it was suddenly as if she wasn't able to work anymore. She sat quietly in an armchair and mostly slept the entire day. Then she died a few weeks before Christmas. I would have preferred to have come before, Gösta, but I could not leave the old woman."

The majoress stopped talking. She started to have difficulty breathing again, but she summoned her courage and spoke further.

"It is true, Gösta, that I wanted to have you here with me at Ekeby. It is the case with you that everyone is happy to be in your company. If you had wanted to be a settled man, I would have given you much power. My hope was always that you would find a good wife. First I believed that it would be Marianne Sinclaire, for I saw that she loved you, even when you were living as a woodcutter in the forest. Then I thought that it would be Ebba Dohna, and one day I went over to Borg and told her that if she were to take you as a husband, I would let you inherit Ekeby. If I acted badly in that, you must forgive me for it."

Gösta was on his knees by the bed with his forehead against the edge of the bed. He let out a heavy moan.

"Tell me now, Gösta, how you mean to live! How will you support your wife? Tell me that! You do know that I have always wanted the best for you." And Gösta answered her with a smile, while his heart wanted to burst with sorrow.

"In bygone days, when I tried to become a laborer here at Ekeby, the majoress gave me my own croft to live in, and it is still mine. This autumn I have put everything in order there. Lövenborg has helped me, and we have whitewashed the ceiling and covered the walls with paper and painted them. The small, inside room Lövenborg calls the countess's cabinet, and he has searched in all the farms hereabouts for furniture that has come from manor auctions. These he has purchased so that now there are high-backed armchairs and chests of drawers with gleaming fittings in there. But in the outer, large room is the young woman's loom and my lathe, household utensils, and all kinds of things are there, and Lövenborg and I have already sat there many evenings talking about what it would be like for the young countess and me in the crofter's cottage. But my wife is only just now finding this out, majoress. We wanted to tell her this when we had to leave Ekeby."

"Go on, Gösta!"

"Lövenborg always talked about how much a maid would

be needed in the house. 'In summer it's blessedly beautiful here on the birch point,' he would always say, 'but in the winter it's too isolated for your young wife. You will have to have a maid, Gösta.'

"And I agreed with him, but I didn't know how I would have the means to keep one. Then one day he came carrying his music and his table with the painted keyboard and placed it in the cottage. 'It looks like it's you, Lövenborg, who will be the maid,' I said to him then. He replied that he would no doubt come if needed. Did I think the young countess would prepare food and carry wood and water? No, I hadn't thought that she would do anything at all, as long as I had a pair of arms to work with. But he still thought that it would be best that there were two of us, so that she could sit day after day in her corner, sewing tambour stitching. I could never know how much attending to such a little lady might need, he said."

"Go on!" said the majoress. "This relieves my pains. Did you think that your young countess would want to live in a crofter's cottage?"

He wondered at her mocking tone, but continued.

"Oh, majoress, I didn't dare believe it, but it would have been so splendid, if she had wanted to. Here it is thirty miles to any doctor. She, who has a light hand and a tender heart, would have work enough tending wounds and lowering fever. And I thought that all distressed people would find their way to the fine lady in the crofter's cottage. There is so much sorrow among the poor, which good words and a friendly heart can help."

"But you yourself, Gösta Berling!"

"I will have my work at the planing bench and the lathe, majoress. From here on out I will live my own life. If my wife will not follow me, then so shall it be. If I were now to be offered all the riches of the world, they would not entice me. I want to live my own life. Now I will be and remain a poor man among farmers and help them with what I can. They need someone who plays a *polska* for them at weddings and yuletide feasts, they need someone to write letters to their far-off sons, and that may as well be me. But poor I must be, majoress."

"It will be a gloomy life for you, Gösta."

"Oh no, majoress, it won't be if only there were two of us who stayed together. The rich and the happy would no doubt come to us as well as the poor. We would have a good enough time in our cottage. The guests would not be concerned that the food was prepared right before their eyes, or take offense at having to share the same plate."

"And what use would you make of all this, Gösta? What praise would you win?"

"My fame would be great, majoress, if the poor were to remember me a few years after my death. I would have been useful enough if I had planted a few apple trees by the houses, if I had taught the peasant fiddlers a few melodies of the old masters, and if the herding children could learn a few good songs to sing on the forest path.

"The majoress may believe me, I am the same crazy Gösta Berling as I was before. A peasant fiddler is all I can become, but that is enough. I have much sin to make good. Weeping and regret are not for me. I must give the poor happiness, that is my penance."

"Gösta," said the majoress, "this is too insignificant a life for a man with your energies. I want to give you Ekeby."

"Oh, majoress," he exclaimed in terror, "don't make me rich! Don't put such obligations on me! Don't divide me from the poor!"

"I want to give Ekeby to you and the cavaliers," the majoress repeated. "You are a virtuous man, Gösta, whom the people bless. I say like my mother: 'You must take on this work.'"

"No, majoress, we cannot accept such a thing. We, who have misjudged you and caused you so much sorrow!"

"Do you hear, I want to give Ekeby to you all."

She spoke gruffly and hard, without any friendliness. He was seized with anxiety.

"Don't set forth such a temptation to the old men, majoress! This would turn them back into idlers and drunkards! God in heaven, rich cavaliers! What would become of us?"

"I want to give you Ekeby, Gösta, but then you must promise to give your wife her freedom. You see, such a fine little woman is not for you. She has had to suffer too much here in bear country. She is longing again for her bright homeland. You must let her go. That is why I am giving you Ekeby."

But now Countess Elisabet came over to the majoress and knelt by the bed.

"I long no more, majoress. The man who is my husband has solved the riddle and found the life that I can live. No longer do I need to go stern and cold beside him and remind him of regret and penitence. Poverty and distress and hard labor will fulfill that mission. I can walk the roads that lead to the poor and the sick without sin. I no longer fear life up here in the north. But do not make him rich, majoress! Then I dare not remain."

The majoress raised herself in the bed.

"You require all happiness for yourselves," she shouted, threatening them with clenched fists, "all happiness and blessings! No, may Ekeby become the cavaliers', so that they may be ruined! May man and wife be separated, so that they may be ruined! A witch I am, an enchantress I am, I will incite you all to evil. As my reputation is, so must I myself be."

She grasped the letter and threw it in Gösta's face. The black paper fluttered out and sank to the floor. Gösta recognized it well enough.

"You have sinned against me, Gösta. You have misjudged the one who has been a second mother to you. Do you dare refuse to take your punishment from me? You will accept Ekeby, and this will destroy you, for you are weak. You will send your wife home, so that no one will be able to save you. You will die with a name just as hated as mine. Margareta Celsing's obituary is that of a witch. Yours will be that of a spendthrift and tormentor of farmers."

She sank down again onto the pillows, and all was silent. Then through this silence sounded a muffled thud, then another and yet another. The till hammer had begun its far-thundering action.

"Hear!" Gösta Berling said then. "So sounds Margareta Celsing's obituary! This is not the crazy prank of drunken cavaliers. This is the victory hymn of labor, sounded in honor of a good old worker. Do you hear what the hammer is saying, majoress? 'Thanks,' it is saying, 'thanks for good labor, thanks for the bread that you have given to the poor, thanks for the roads that you have cleared, for ground that you have broken! Thanks for the joy that has prevailed in your halls!'—'Thanks,' it is saying, 'and rest in peace! Your works will live and persist. Your estate will always be a sanctuary for work that brings happiness.'—'Thanks,' it is saying, 'and do not judge us who have gone astray! You, who are now embarking on the journey to the climes of peace, think gentle thoughts of us who are still alive!'"

Gösta fell silent, but the till hammer continued to speak. All the voices that had spoken well and amiably to the majoress were blended with the till hammer's. Gradually the tension disappeared from her features. They became slack, and it was as if the shadow of death had fallen over her.

The Broby minister's daughter came in and informed them that the gentlemen from Högfors had arrived. The majoress let them go. She did not want to make a will.

"Oh, Gösta Berling, man of many deeds," she said, "so you have won yet again! Bow down and let me bless you!"

The fever came back now with doubled strength. The death rattles began. Her body was dragged along through heavy suffering, but her soul soon knew nothing of it. It began to peer into the heavens that were opening for the dying woman.

An hour passed in that way, and the brief death struggle was over. Then she was lying there so peaceful and lovely that those standing around were deeply moved.

"My dear old majoress," Gösta said then, "I saw you like this once before! Now Margareta Celsing has come back to life. Now she will never again step aside for the majoress at Ekeby."

When the cavaliers came in from the smithy, they were met by the news of the majoress's death.

"Did she hear the hammer?" they asked.

She had, and they had to be content with that.

They found out later that she had intended to grant Ekeby to them, but that the will had never been made. This they took as a great honor and then praised themselves for it as long as they lived. But no one ever heard them complain about the riches they had lost.

It is also said that this Christmas night Gösta Berling stood by his young spouse's side and held his final talk to the cavaliers. He was distressed at their fate, when all of them would now have to depart from Ekeby. The pains of old age awaited them. The old and sullen encounter a cold welcome with the accustomed host. The poor cavalier, who has been forced to take lodgings at the farms, has no happy days; separated from friends and adventures, the lonely man withers.

And so he spoke to them, the carefree ones, hardened against all the vicissitudes of fortune. Once again he called them old gods and knights, who had appeared to bring delight into the land of iron and the age of iron. Yet he complained now that the paradise where butterfly-winged delight swarms is filled up with destructive larvae and its fruits are stunted.

Well he knew that delight was a good thing for the children of earth, and that it must be found. But like a difficult riddle, the question of how a man could be both happy and good still hung over the world. This he called the easiest and yet the most difficult question. Until now they had not been able to solve the riddle. Now he wanted to believe that they had learned it, that all of them had learned it during this year of happiness and distress and good fortune and grief.

Ah, you good gentlemen cavaliers, for me as well the bitterness of parting hangs over this moment! This is the last night we will have watched through together. I will no longer hear the hearty laughter and merry songs. I will now be separated from you and all the happy people on the shores of Löven.

You dear old men! In bygone ages you would have given me good gifts. To one living in great desolation you brought the first message of the rich variety of life. I saw you battle mighty Ragnarök battles round the lake of my childhood dreams. But what have I given you?

Perhaps, however, it would please you that your names resound again in connection with the beloved estates. May all the brilliance that was part of your lives again fall upon the region where you lived! Borg still stands, Björne still stands, Ekeby is still by Löven, splendidly wreathed by rapids and lake, by grove and smiling forest meadows, and as you stand on the broad terraces, the legends swarm around you like the bees of summer.

But speaking of bees, let me tell yet another old story! Little Ruster, who marched at the head of the Swedish army as a drummer when in 1813 it advanced into Germany, never tired of telling stories about the wonderful land in the south. The people there were tall as church steeples, the swallows as large as eagles, the bees like geese.

"Well, but what about the beehives?"

"The beehives were like our ordinary beehives."

"Then how did the bees get into them?"

"Yes, they had to keep their eyes open," said little Ruster.

Dear reader, must I not say the same? Here the giant bees of imagination have swarmed around us during years and days, but to get into the beehive of reality, they will truly have to keep their eyes open.

THE STORY OF PENGUIN CLASSICS

Before 1946 . . . "Classics" are mainly the domain of academics and students; readable editions for everyone else are almost unheard of. This all changes when a little-known classicist, E. V. Rieu, presents Penguin founder Allen Lane with the translation of Homer's *Odyssey* that he has been working on in his spare time.

1946 Penguin Classics debuts with *The Odyssey*, which promptly sells three million copies. Suddenly, classics are no longer for the privileged few.

1950s Rieu, now series editor, turns to professional writers for the best modern, readable translations, including Dorothy L. Sayers's *Inferno* and Robert Graves's unexpurgated *Twelve Caesars*.

1960s The Classics are given the distinctive black covers that have remained a constant throughout the life of the series. Rieu retires in 1964, hailing the Penguin Classics list as "the greatest educative force of the twentieth century."

1970s A new generation of translators swells the Penguin Classics ranks, introducing readers of English to classics of world literature from more than twenty languages. The list grows to encompass more history, philosophy, science, religion, and politics.

1980s The Penguin American Library launches with titles such as *Uncle Tom's Cabin* and joins forces with Penguin Classics to provide the most comprehensive library of world literature available from any paperback publisher.

1990s The launch of Penguin Audiobooks brings the classics to a listening audience for the first time, and in 1999 the worldwide launch of the Penguin Classics Web site extends their reach to the global online community.

The 21st Century Penguin Classics are completely redesigned for the first time in nearly twenty years. This world-famous series now consists of more than 1,300 titles, making the widest range of the best books ever written available to millions—and constantly redefining what makes a "classic."

The Odyssey continues . . .

The best books ever written

PENGUIN CLASSICS

SINCE 1946

Find out more at www.penguinclassics.com

Visit www.vpbookclub.com